SAVE THE KINGDOM

The shouts and hoofbeats were still behind them.

"We'll keep going south until we're in the clear. Then we'll circle around them and head back to the castle," Maddie told her horse. Bumper grunted, concentrating on following the narrow game trail.

They would launch their attack on the castle the following day. It was imperative that she get back there tonight, so she could warn her mother.

She was in a part of the fief she hadn't seen before, and realized that the ground beneath her was rising gradually. The trees were becoming more widely spaced as well, and she was conscious of low hills rising on either side of her as she rode on. They became progressively steeper and higher, and she realized that she was riding up a valley—wide at first but becoming narrower the farther she went, as the steep hills on either side closed in.

Then Bumper came to an abrupt stop and she looked up. A sheer rock wall barred the way in front of them. She swung Bumper to the right and cantered along it, seeking a way around. But there was none. The rock wall facing her abutted the steep side of the valley, leaving no way out. Desperately, she cantered back the other way, but found the same situation on the left side. The sides of the valley formed a solid U shape, too steep to climb.

With a sinking heart, she realized she was in a blind valley, with no way out other than the way she had come.

She turned Bumper's head back downhill, but as she did so, she saw the flare of torches among the trees below her. The men were at the wide end of the valley.

She was trapped.

RANGER'S APPRENTICE
SERIES

THE ROYAL RANGER

THE EARLY YEARS

BROTHERBAND CHRONICLES

THE ROYAL RANGER

BOOK 2

THE RED FOX CLAN

JOHN FLANAGAN

PUFFIN BOOKS

PUFFIN BOOKS
An imprint of Penguin Random House LLC, New York

First published in the United States of America by Philomel Books,
an imprint of Penguin Random House LLC, 2018
Published in Australia by Penguin Random House Australia in 2018.
Published by Puffin Books, an imprint of Penguin Random House LLC, 2019

THE LIBRARY OF CONGRESS HAS CATALOGED THE PHILOMEL BOOKS EDITION AS FOLLOWS:
Names: Flanagan, John (John Anthony), author.
Title: The Red Fox Clan / John Flanagan.
Description: U.S. edition. | New York, NY : Philomel Books, 2018. | Series: Ranger's apprentice:
the royal ranger ; 2 Summary: "The mysterious Red Fox Clan, a group of anarchists all donning fox masks,
have threatened Castle Araluen and question Princess Cassandra and Madelyn's succession
to the throne. Will they succeed in unseating Cassandra and Madelyn and take the throne for
themselves?"—Provided by publisher. Identifiers: LCCN 2018011891 | ISBN 9781524741389
(hardback) | ISBN 9781524741396 (ebook) Subjects: | CYAC: Apprentices—Fiction. |
Fantasy. | BISAC: JUVENILE FICTION / Action & Adventure / Survival Stories. | JUVENILE
FICTION / Legends, Myths, Fables / Arthurian. | JUVENILE FICTION / Fantasy & Magic.
Classification: LCC PZ7.F598284 Red 2018 | DDC [Fic]—dc23
LC record available at https://lccn.loc.gov/2018011891

Puffin Books ISBN 9781524741402

Printed in the United States of America

U.S. edition edited by Michael Green.   U.S. edition designed by Jennifer Chung.
Text set in Adobe Jenson Pro.

7 9 10 8 6

To Rick Raftos, Agent Extraordinaire

PROLOGUE

He stood in the shadows to one side, letting the rage build within him. He needed the rage. He fed off it. It inflamed the passion and fire that went into his words and his delivery.

Audiences felt it and reacted to it. He had the ability to arouse the same rage in them. His audiences were, for the most part, unsophisticated country folk and villagers, and he used all the tricks of the rabble-rouser's trade to play upon their prejudices and intolerance—to make them raise their fists to the heavens and cry for justice.

The basis for his own rage was simple. In his mind, he had been cheated out of his birthright, his right of inheritance. And it had been done at the whim of a monarch who sought to cement his own family's succession to the throne. At the stroke of a pen, he had changed a centuries-old law of the land and decreed that, in Araluen, a female heir could succeed to the throne.

Most Araluens accepted the new law without thinking. But a small number of fanatics and conservatives resented it. They formed the Red Fox Clan, a subversive group with the avowed aim of bringing back the old ways—the law of male succession.

The Red Fox Clan had been few in number when he had

first discovered them several years ago, with perhaps fewer than fifty members. But he had seen them as the key to attaining his destiny—the throne of Araluen. He had recognized that this movement, weak and unorganized as it was, could become the base from which he could launch his campaign.

Accordingly, he had joined them, bringing his undoubted talent for organization and leadership to their movement.

He had traveled from village to village, from town to town, preaching his message of prejudice in clandestine meetings, biding his time and watching the number of Clan members grow. That initial group of fewer than fifty now numbered in the hundreds. They were a powerful and well-financed movement. And he had gradually risen to the position of *Vulpus Rutilus*—the Red Fox, leader of the Clan.

He was a skilled and convincing orator, but that was only one aspect of his complex character. He could be hard and ruthless when he needed to be, and on more than one occasion he brutally crushed people who defied him or tried to impede his way to the top.

But, just as important, he had learned at an early age that a more effective way to achieve his ends was by charm and apparent friendliness. His mother had told him as a boy, when she dinned into his brain the injustice that had been done to him— "You catch more flies with honey than vinegar"—and he had applied that lesson well as he grew in years and maturity.

He had cultivated the ability to make others like him, to convince them he was their friend. A consummate actor, he had learned to hide animosity behind an outer show of warmth and geniality—and a winning smile. Even now, there were half a dozen people in the upper ranks of the Red Fox Clan whom he hated. Yet not one of them was aware of the fact, and all of them regarded him as a friend, a warm and generous ally.

And there were others—those outside the cult, people he viewed as his most bitter adversaries—who had no idea of the depths of hatred that simmered below his outer layer of easygoing cordiality.

Now the time was approaching when he could cast that pretense aside and reveal his true feelings, and he felt a deep sense of satisfaction at the thought of it.

The meeting was being held in a large clearing in the woods, between three large villages where he had recruited members to the Clan. He scanned them now. Only Clan members had been invited, and a screen of guards armed with clubs and swords were in place to make sure that no outsider would witness the meeting. There were nearly a hundred people present—an excellent turnout. In the beginning, he had spoken to audiences of fewer than a dozen people—people who were only half interested in what he had to say but were looking for some diversion from their drab, humdrum lives. The movement had gathered its own momentum and energy. There was an expectant buzz among the crowd as they waited for him to speak.

He judged that it was time to do so. The past few years had seen him develop a sense of timing when dealing with crowds. He had the ability to know when he should appear—and then to wait those vital few minutes longer until expectancy had turned into eagerness and enthusiasm for the cause.

There was a raised speaking platform to his left, lit by flaring torches and with a backdrop bearing the face of a red fox.

He donned his mask now—a stylized fox face that covered his eyes, nose and cheeks. He pulled the fur-trimmed scarlet cloak tighter around his body and mounted the three low steps at the back of the stage, pushing through the backdrop to appear, almost magically, in the flaring torchlight.

There was a moment's silence as he appeared, then shattering applause as he threw his arms wide, with the scarlet cloak spread behind him.

"My friends!" he shouted, having waited just the right amount of time so that the applause was beginning to ebb but was not yet completely silent.

Now it died away as they waited for his words. He spoke, his voice ringing out, reaching to those at the very back.

"For thousands of years, our country was guided by a law that said only a male heir could succeed to the throne. It was a good law. It was a just law. And it was a law that respected the will of the gods."

A rumble of approval ran through the crowd. He wondered briefly why they accepted so readily the concept that this was a law approved by the gods. But they did. They always did. It was part of that big lie that he had created—the lie that, told often enough, became truth in the minds of those listening.

"Then, some years ago, a king decided, without any consultation or discussion, that he could change this law. With the stroke of a pen, he changed it. Arbitrarily and arrogantly."

He stepped forward to the front of the stage and leaned toward his audience, his voice rising in pitch and volume. "Did we *want* this law changed?"

He paused, and the expected result came. "No!" roared the crowd. If they hadn't responded, he had people planted through their ranks who would have led the cry of protest.

"Did we *ask* for this law to be changed?"

"No!" The response echoed around the clearing.

"So why did he do it?" This time, he continued immediately. "To secure the succession of his own family. To ensure that his granddaughter would inherit the throne. And her daughter." When the King had changed the law, his granddaughter was yet to be born. But people were willing to overlook hard facts in the height of their passion.

"Was he right to do it?"

"NO-O-O!"

"Was it just?"

"NO-O-O!"

"Or was it an act of selfish arrogance—and total disregard for the people of this kingdom?"

"YE-E-S!"

He paused, letting their fervor die down a little, then resumed in a lower, more reasonable tone.

"Can a woman lead this country in time of war?" He shook his head. "No, she cannot. A woman isn't strong enough to stand up to our enemies. What does a woman know about war and military matters and holding our borders secure?"

This time he held out his hands, prompting an answer, and got it.

"NOTHING! NOTHING!"

"Then, my friends, the time has come for us to act upon what is right! To change this unjust, this unasked-for, this godless law back to the old law of this land. Are you with me?"

"YES!" they shouted.

But it wasn't enough for him. "Are you ALL with me? Will we go back to the old way? The right way? The way of the gods?"

"YESSSS!"

Their roar of agreement was so deafening that they woke the starlings roosting in the trees around the clearing. *Vulpus Rutilus* turned away to hide his smile of triumph. When he had his features under control, he turned back, speaking now in a low voice that had them craning forward to listen.

"Well, my friends, now is the time for the Red Fox Clan to rise up. In two months' time, we will gather at Araluen Fief, and then I will give you your orders."

1

THEY WERE COMING CLOSER TO MADDIE'S HIDING PLACE.

There were a dozen of them, spread out in a long cordon, five meters apart and covering sixty meters of territory. Each one carried a flaming torch, holding it high to dispel the gathering gloom of twilight. She was approaching the line of searchers head-on. If she could break through the line, or simply remain unseen while they passed her, she would be free and clear.

Actually, "hiding place" was something of an overstatement for Maddie's position. She was simply lying prone, covered from head to toe by her cloak, among knee-high, dried stalks of grass.

In the fields on either side of the one she had selected to hide in, the grass grew waist high, waving gently in the early evening breeze. It would have provided better concealment from the dozen men searching for her. But she had chosen the shorter grass for a reason.

They would expect a fugitive to seek concealment in the longer grass, so they would look more carefully there. The short stubble where she lay provided only scant cover, and the searchers would study the ground with less attention to detail, assuming they would easily spot someone trying to stay concealed there.

At least, that was what she hoped when she had selected her current path through the search line. In addition, the fields on either side were narrower, so the searchers would be closer together. Since they'd expect her to be hiding there, they would pay greater attention to the ground and any abnormalities they might see there.

Like a huddled shape under a gray-green Ranger cloak.

The uncertain light also gave her an advantage. The sun had sunk below the horizon, and only a reflection of its light remained in the western sky. It cast long shadows and pools of darkness across the rough surface of the field. And instead of aiding the searchers, the light from the pitch-fed torches was flickering and uneven, making their task even more difficult as it shifted and wavered.

She could sense the yellow glow of one of the torches now, as a searcher came closer. She resisted the unbearable temptation to look up and see where he was. Her face was darkened by the mud and grime she had smeared on it before setting out to break through the cordon. But even so, it would shine as a pale oval in the dusk. And the movement would be even more noticeable. She lay, facedown, her eyes fixed on the stalks of dry grass a few centimeters from her face, seeing the yellow torchlight creeping over them, casting shadows that gradually shortened as the source of light grew closer and closer.

Her heart pounded in her chest as she heard the rustle of boots. She could hear the blood pulsing in her ears like a drumbeat.

Trust the cloak. The old mantra, drummed into her brain over and over by her mentor, repeated itself now. The searcher couldn't hear her heartbeat. That was a fanciful notion, she knew. And if she stayed still as a corpse, he wouldn't see her either. The cloak would protect her. It always had in the past, and it would do so now.

"All right! I see you. Stand up and surrender."

The voice was very close. It couldn't have been more than three meters away. And there was a confident tone to it. For a second, she nearly gave in to the urge to stand. But then she remembered Will's words when he had been instructing her in the art of remaining unseen by searchers.

They may try to trick you into showing yourself. They might call out that they can see you and tell you to stand up. Don't fall for it.

So she lay motionless. The voice came again. "Come on! I said I can see you!"

But the voice wasn't as confident as it had been. There was a distinct uncertainty to it, as if the searcher realized the ruse had been unsuccessful—or that there was nobody near him concealed in the rough grass. After a few more seconds, he muttered a soft curse and began to move again. His boots crunched in the stubble, and she sensed he had passed her by—which meant he was casting his gaze ahead of him and away from her. She watched the tiny shadows thrown by the grass stalks elongate and angle to the left. He was moving to the right, then.

She realized she had been holding her breath and silently released it, feeling the tension in her body ease. Her heart rate slowed from its wild gallop to a more controlled canter.

In a few minutes, he'd be clear of her and unable to hear any slight noise she might make moving. She waited, counting slowly to 120, listening as the rustle of his boots moved away until she could no longer hear them. She tensed her muscles. When she had gone to ground, her left arm had been thrown out ahead of her. Her right was doubled underneath her body, and she would use that to help her rise from the ground a few centimeters and begin to creep slowly away from her hiding spot.

She began to apply pressure to her right hand, feeling the sharp grass stalks digging painfully into it. It would have been so natural to move her hand slightly to a more comfortable position. But again she resisted temptation.

Unnecessary movement might give her away. Better to put up with the discomfort. Of course, she'd *have* to move her arm to propel herself along the ground in a belly crawl. But that was a necessary movement. Otherwise, she'd be here all night. So she began to set her muscles once more.

Then stopped.

There had been a sound—faint and unrecognizable—from the grass in front of her. And as she registered it, she remembered another piece of advice that Will had given her.

Sometimes, there'll be a sweeper, she could hear his calm voice saying in her brain. *Another searcher who follows the line, ten or twelve meters behind it, looking to catch someone who's evaded the first line and is beginning to move again. It's an old trick, but you'd be surprised how many have been caught by it.*

She relaxed again and waited, head close to the ground, facedown. Now she heard the sound again, and this time she recognized it. Whoever was coming was lifting his feet high out of the grass, then setting them down evenly and squarely on the ground, testing each step so it didn't shuffle or create extra noise. It was the way she had been taught to step when she wanted to keep noise to a minimum, and she realized that this new arrival was well skilled in the art of silent movement.

She strained her ears, listening for any trace, any sound that would tell her how close he was and which direction he was coming from. He seemed to be slightly to her right and moving diagonally, so that he would cross close by her position. And so far, she could see no sign of light from a torch. She bit her lip with frustration. A torch would have given him uncertain, uneven light, which would actually help conceal her. Plus the brightness of the flame close to his face would reduce his night vision considerably. Now that it was nearly full dark, a torch was almost more hindrance than help.

He was close. Even with the care he was taking to keep noise to a minimum, she could hear the faint sounds that he made. His stepping smoothly and rhythmically helped her keep track of him. Once she figured out his timing, she knew when to listen for the next, almost silent, footstep.

Now he was very close. But he was moving across her front, angling to pass down her left side, and she knew she had eluded him. She felt a surge of triumph as he took another pace, taking him fractionally away from her. Three more steps in that direction and she'd be in the clear.

Then, inexplicably, he angled back again, changing direction to move parallel to where she lay. Her heart rate soared again as she realized how close he was to finding her.

She felt a searing pain in her left hand as he placed his foot squarely on it, bearing down with all his weight as he raised his other foot for another step.

"Ow!" she cried, before she could stop herself.

At the same time, she inadvertently flinched with the pain, just as he recoiled a pace, sensing a foreign object underfoot. It was only a small movement on her part, but it was enough. The sweeper gave a cry of triumph, and she felt an iron grip on the back of her cloak, just below the cowl, hauling her to her feet.

"Got you!" he said, the satisfaction obvious in his voice. He turned her to face him, at the same time that he called to the search line. "Back here! I've got him!"

He pushed her hood back and studied her face more closely.

"But you're not a him, are you?" he said. "You're Will Treaty's apprentice. Well, you *are* a catch, and no mistake."

She struggled in his grip, hoping to break free, even though the exercise was now well and truly over. The rest of the searchers, hearing his shout, hurried back and gathered round them, the torchlight showing their grinning faces all too clearly.

"Bad luck," said one, a handsome fourth-year apprentice. "You nearly made it."

He jerked his head to the edge of the field, and she twisted in her captor's grip to look. The little hut she had been tasked to reach was barely fifty meters away. If it hadn't been for this clod-hopping sweeper with his clumsy great feet, she would have made it.

And that would have given her a perfect score for her end-of-year assessment.

On a low hilltop a hundred meters away, Will Treaty and Gilan watched the events in the stubble field as the search line gathered around Maddie and her captor. Even at this distance, and in the gathering dark, the torchlight gave sufficient illumination for Will to see Maddie's dejected, frustrated reaction.

"That was bad luck," Gilan said. "She nearly made it. And she did everything right."

"Right up until the moment she went *Ow! You trod on me!*" Will grinned.

Gilan looked sidelong at his old friend. "As I said, that was bad luck."

"Halt always said a Ranger makes his own luck," Will replied.

"If I didn't know better, I'd think you were pleased she was caught," Gilan said.

Will shrugged. "I'm not too *dis*pleased," he admitted. "She was set for a perfect score, and I'm not sure I wanted that. It wouldn't have been good for her ego." He paused slightly. "Or my patience."

"I take it you speak from experience?" Gilan asked.

Will nodded. "She got a perfect score at the end of second year," he said. "And I heard about it for the next three months—anytime I tried to correct her or suggest that she might be going about a task the wrong way. She does tend to be a little headstrong."

Gilan nodded. "True. But she is very good, you have to admit."

"I admit it. But she's also her mother's daughter. Can you imagine how Evanlyn would have been in her place?"

This time, Gilan grinned at the thought. "You're referring to Her Highness Princess Cassandra in that derogatory tone, are you?" He was mildly amused by the fact that Will continued to refer to the princess by the name she had assumed when he first met her.

Will shook his head ruefully. "I am indeed," he replied. "The more I see of Maddie, the more I see her mother in her."

"Which possibly explains why she is such a high achiever," Gilan suggested, and Will had to agree.

"True." He stood up from where he had been sitting, leaning

against the bole of a tree. The search party and their quarry were heading back to the Gathering Ground, the line of torches twinkling in the darkness. "Let's get back to camp and sit in on the debrief," he said.

2

THE ANALYSIS OF MADDIE'S PERFORMANCE WAS HELD IN ONE of the large central command tents. The three senior assessors sat behind a trestle table, in comfortable canvas folding chairs, studying reports from the assessors who had examined her skills and abilities over the course of the Gathering.

Maddie stood before them, with her captor a half pace behind her. The assessors glanced up as Will and Gilan entered the tent, lifting the canvas flaps to the side. Harlon, the most senior, nodded permission for them to come in. Will was Maddie's mentor, of course, so he had every right to be here and listen as they passed judgment on her performance. And Gilan, as Commandant of the Ranger Corps, was entitled to go anywhere he pleased.

In the time it had taken for the two to reach the tent, the panel had listened to the report from Maddie's captor. Now Harlon spoke.

"Unfortunately, we can't give you a pass on your unseen-movement exercise," he said. His voice was not unkind. He was impressed with the overall level of Maddie's performance, as accounted in the written reports of those who had tested her. He glanced down at the reports fanned out in front of him.

Shooting—excellent, he read. And he noted an addendum to the report. Unlike the other apprentices, Maddie had been assessed for her skill with the sling as well as the bow, and he raised his eyebrows as he saw that her scores over half a dozen tests averaged 95 percent. She was even better with the sling than with the bow, where she had scored an impressive 92 percent. Knife throwing—excellent. Unarmed combat—very good. Mapmaking—another excellent result. Navigation skills—above average. And since "average" in the Ranger Corps meant excellent, that was saying something. Tactical planning—excellent.

He leafed through the papers, seeing more excellent and above-average ratings. He was impressed, and he knew his colleagues were as well. Third-year assessments were tough. It was the time when the examiners really began to bear down on the apprentices. They were more than halfway through their training, and they were expected to keep a high standard. He glanced up and caught Will Treaty's eye as the gray-bearded Ranger stood just inside the entrance to the tent. It wasn't surprising that she had performed so well, he thought. Will Treaty was one of the most accomplished members of the Ranger Corps. And he'd been trained by Halt, a legend among the green-and-gray-cloaked community.

Harlon switched his gaze now to the slightly built figure before him. Maddie had tossed back her cowl, and her short hair was tousled. There were even one or two wisps of dead grass caught in it. She stood erect, facing him with a look of determination, even defiance, on her face. She was slightly flushed, he noticed—angry at being caught so close to her objective, he assumed correctly.

"Overall, you've done well, Madelyn," he said. "Aside from

the unseen-movement exercise, you've pretty well topped the course." He indicated the report sheets in front of him. His two companions, with copies of their own, grunted their agreement.

"Your results are more than good enough for you to advance to fourth-year training," he said, and he saw a slight relaxation of her shoulders as she heard that piece of news. Then, after a second or two, she stiffened once more and her jaw set in a stubborn line.

He gathered the reports together, tapping them on the table to align them, and continued. "You'll take a makeup assessment for unseen movement in three months or so," he told her. "I'm sure you'll have no trouble passing it."

"It's not fair!" Maddie blurted the words out, unable to contain herself any longer. Harlon set the rearranged reports down on the table and raised an eyebrow at the angry face before him.

"Not fair? How is it not fair? You were caught fifty meters from your objective."

"But it's a test of unseen movement," she protested. "And he never saw me! He trod on my hand!"

"Are you saying you weren't apprehended?" Harlon asked quietly.

Maddie, now committed to her protest, went on. "I'm saying I wasn't *seen*!" She swung round and gestured to her captor. "The very fact that he stood on my hand proves it. He had no idea I was there. It was a test of unseen movement and he never saw me!"

"Until you cried out and moved," Harlon said. "*Then* he saw you."

She shook her head in defiance. "It wasn't a test of being

trodden on," she said, aware that the words sounded ridiculous, but unable to think of another way to frame them.

"It was a test of your ability to remain concealed," Harlon pointed out. "Have you considered what might have happened if you hadn't reacted? If you hadn't cried out?"

"Well, of course I cried out," Maddie blustered. "This great oaf stood on my hand! You'd have cried out too!"

The great oaf in question—who was, like most Rangers, slim in build and below-average height—couldn't help smiling at her description of him. He liked Maddie. He had watched her going through her assessments and admired her. He knew that she had to perform at a higher level than the other apprentices because she was a girl—the first to be accepted for Ranger training. There were too many people who were ready to dismiss her because of that fact. She couldn't just do as well as the boys in her year. She had to do better.

"Mertin," said the assessor on the right, "what would have happened had Madelyn remained silent?"

Maddie's captor shrugged. "In all likelihood, I would have continued on. Initially, I thought I'd trodden on a tree root or a fallen branch." He smiled. "But then the branch called out *Ow!* and I knew I was mistaken."

Maddie's scowl deepened. Harlon looked from Mertin to her once more.

"Did you think of not reacting?" he asked her.

She flushed angrily. "I didn't think. He trod on my hand with his great clumsy boot." She paused, then added defiantly, "Because he hadn't seen me!"

"Hmm," said Harlon thoughtfully.

Gudris, the Ranger seated to his right, leaned forward. "Tell me, Maddie," he said, "what made you choose that field to try to break through the line? After all, the grass in the adjacent fields was much longer."

She paused, swallowing her anger for a moment, then answered. "I figured they'd assume that I'd go through the longer grass," she explained. "So the searchers in the low grass wouldn't be as attentive as they might be. Plus they'd tend to spread out farther."

The three assessors exchanged a glance. Will and Gilan, at the back of the tent, did likewise. Gilan pursed his lips in an appreciative expression.

"That's good thinking," said Downey, the third assessor. The others grunted assent. Maddie's marks for tactical planning bore out the choice.

"Except," Harlon said, deciding that too much praise was not a good thing for this young woman, "she was caught."

"Only because he stood on me!" Maddie flared.

Behind her, Will raised an eyebrow at Gilan as if to say, *See what I mean?* Gilan shrugged.

"We've established that that was unfortunate," Harlon said, a trifle briskly, "but it doesn't alter the result."

Maddie heard the change of tone, from evenhanded and slightly sympathetic to decisive and final. She realized any further argument could well be counterproductive for her. She had opened her mouth to protest further. Now she shut it firmly.

Harlon noticed her capitulation and nodded approval. Then he continued, in a more conciliatory tone. "In any event, Maddie, your performance at this Gathering has been exceptional, and I'd like to congratulate you on passing your third-year assessment."

"Hear, hear," murmured Downey and Gudris. Maddie allowed herself the ghost of a smile, even though her flushed features indicated that she was still annoyed about failing her test by sheer accident.

Harlon looked up at the two senior Rangers behind the girl and singled out Will. "Congratulations to you too, Will Treaty," he said. "Her performance reflects well on your training and guidance."

Will shrugged. "I merely show the way, Harlon," he said. "Maddie follows it. Any success is due to her efforts."

"Quite so," said Harlon, smiling inwardly at the other man's humility. He looked back to Maddie and took her bronze oakleaf from the tabletop, where she had placed it when the hearing began. He handed it back to her now.

"Here, Maddie. I'm delighted to tell you that you are to advance to your fourth year of training with Ranger Will."

Maddie took the oakleaf and dropped the chain over her head, arranging the small bronze symbol at her throat. Had she failed the year's assessment, the oakleaf would have been marked by a small hole hammered through the brass. If she accumulated three of those throughout her training period, she would be politely asked to leave the Corps. She was proud that her oakleaf, symbol of her rank as an apprentice Ranger, was unmarked.

Harlon pushed back his chair now and stood, reaching across the table to shake her hand. Gudris and Downey did the same. Maddie shook hands and bowed her head as they congratulated her. She turned to go and found herself facing Mertin, the young Ranger who had caught her. He too offered his hand.

"Congratulations, Maddie," he said.

She hesitated. She was still angry about the way he had found her. But his smile was genuine and his manner was friendly. She shook hands with him.

"Thanks," she said briefly, and then she gave him a reluctant smile. It was impossible to stay angry with someone as cheerful as he was.

"You should be proud of yourself," he said to her. "One in four apprentices doesn't make it this far—not without having to repeat a year at least once."

She was too surprised to say anything. She hadn't realized that the failure rate was so high. Will certainly hadn't told her. He hadn't wanted to worry her about the possibility of failure— not that it was something Maddie ever considered. She relinquished Mertin's hand, mumbled a thank-you, and turned away to where Will and Gilan were waiting for her. Her mentor drew the tent flap aside and motioned her through ahead of him. He and Gilan followed, and the three of them strode in line abreast through the Gathering Ground toward the spot where they had pitched their simple one-person tents.

They walked in silence for several minutes. Then Maddie couldn't restrain herself any longer.

"I still say it's not fair," she said quietly.

Will glanced sidelong at her. "And I imagine you will keep saying so until you do your makeup assessment in three months," he said. There was a note of finality in his tone that warned her not to continue with the matter.

Gilan, however, had something to add. "Maddie, if you really think you've been badly treated, I am obliged to look into the matter. I am the Commandant, after all. Are you making an official complaint here?"

Maddie was aghast at the thought that she might be seen to be invoking the authority of the Corps Commandant.

"Good lord, no, Gilan!" she said quickly. "I don't think of you as the Commandant!"

"Well, thank you *very* much," Gilan said. "I'm glad my authority is so negligible."

She hastened to qualify her statement. "I mean, I know you're the Commandant, of course! And I respect you for it. But I think of you more as a friend."

"Well then," he replied, "as a friend, let me advise you. Accept the judgment and let this matter drop. In fact, keep it in mind for the future. You may well be the most accomplished person at unseen movement—"

"Am I?" said Maddie, brightening, but he simply looked at her for several seconds before replying.

"I'm saying that as a hypothetical," he said, and she subsided, her balloon of pride well and truly pricked. "But even if you were," he went on, "the fact is that accidents and bad luck happen. A little mistake, a little unexpected event, can give you away. Don't forget it."

She thought about his words, then nodded. "You're right, Gilan. I'm sorry." She turned to Will. "And I won't go on and on about this when we're home," she said.

Will snorted. "That'll be the day."

Before she could reply, Gilan drew their attention to a figure seated comfortably by the fire in front of their three tents.

"And unless my eyes deceive me, that would seem to be Halt waiting for us," he said.

"Wonder what he wants," Will mused.

"I'm sure he'll tell us," Maddie said in a self-satisfied voice. It was the kind of answer Will would give to her if she ever voiced a rhetorical question like that, and she was pleased to have an opportunity to say it to him.

"I think I preferred it when you were whining about being trodden on," Will said.

3

〰〰〰〰〰〰〰〰〰〰〰〰〰〰

HALT LOOKED UP AS WILL, MADDIE, AND GILAN APPROACHED the fire. He had just dropped a handful of coffee beans into a pot of water boiling over the coals and was stirring it with a thin stick.

"Good evening," he said. "I trust you've had a successful day?"

"Yes indeed. Maddie has passed her assessment and will advance to fourth-year training," Will said.

Halt inclined his head toward her. "Well, I can't say that was unexpected," he said. "In spite of the ham-fisted mentor you're stuck with." He smiled as he said the last words.

Will chose to ignore them.

"Another perfect score?" Halt asked, and Maddie scowled.

"Oh no," Will muttered. "Did you have to ask that?"

Halt's gaze shifted between them, and he raised an interrogative eyebrow. "Was there a problem?"

"They failed me on unseen movement," Maddie said, the anger returning.

Now both Halt's eyebrows shot up. "How did that happen? I've seen you, or rather, I *haven't* seen you, practicing unseen movement. You're an expert. You're nearly as good as Gilan." He smiled at his former apprentice.

"Well, technically, I'd passed all right. Nobody saw me. They'd all gone past me when a sweeper trod on my hand."

If she was expecting sympathy from the older Ranger, she was disappointed. He emitted a short bark of decidedly unsympathetic laughter.

"Ah well, these things do happen," he said. "You can't allow for bad luck."

Maddie drew breath to reply, but Will laid a restraining hand on her forearm.

"Don't say *It's not fair* again," he cautioned her. "Life isn't always fair, and you have to live with that fact."

His apprentice's protest died stillborn on her lips. She mumbled something under her breath, and he deemed it wiser to pretend he hadn't heard it. Halt busied himself pouring a mug of coffee, then looked around for the honey jar he knew would be somewhere close to hand.

"It's hanging from that tree branch," Gilan said, pointing to an overhanging limb that stretched out from the massive oak under which they had pitched their tents. "You didn't expect us to leave it by the fire where the ants could get at it, did you?"

Maddie reached up and passed the honey to Halt. He spooned a liberal amount into his cup and drank, letting out an "Aaaaah!" of quiet satisfaction when he had done so.

While Will poured coffee for himself and Gilan, Halt studied Maddie with an amused expression on his face.

He's mellowed, Gilan thought. Time was, Halt would go for a month on end without letting a smile show on his face. Must be Pauline's influence.

"You know," Halt said, leaning back against the log beside the fire and stretching his legs out, "a similar thing happened to me years ago."

"During your assessment?" Maddie asked.

The old Ranger shook his head. "I didn't have an assessment as such," he said. "Crowley just decided my skills were up to scratch and declared I was a Ranger." There was a wistful note in his voice as he mentioned the late Commandant. He missed Crowley, who had been his first true friend. Then he resumed his anecdote. "No. This happened when I was being chased by a band of Temujai."

"Was that when you stole their horse herd?" Will asked.

Halt regarded him with a small frown. Will grinned to himself. Halt didn't like to be reminded that he had stolen a herd of twenty horses from the Temujai, to add their bloodline to the Ranger horse-breeding program.

"Let's say I *acquired* them," Halt said. "I left a hundred and fifty silver pieces for them—far more than the horses were worth."

"But you didn't actually ask the Temujai if they were willing to sell the horses to you, did you?" Gilan put in. Like Will, he knew Halt's ticklish attitude about the way he had "acquired" the herd.

"Well, that would have been pointless," Halt admitted. "They never sold their horses."

"So, in fact, you did steal them," Will said, and Halt glared at him.

"Stealing is when you take something without payment," he said. "Something that doesn't belong to you."

"Whether you left money for them or not, you've admitted

that the Temujai weren't willing to sell, so in effect, you stole them," Gilan resumed, barely managing to hide a smile. Halt's eyebrows lowered as he looked from one former apprentice to another.

"I preferred you two when you showed a little respect for your elders," he said.

Will shrugged. "Well, we used to respect you. But then we found out you'd stolen a herd of horses, and it was hard to keep looking up to you after that."

Maddie took pity on the white-haired Ranger. She liked Halt. He was always a friend to her, and she'd only recently learned that it was he who had been instrumental in changing Ranger policy and having a girl admitted to the training program.

"You said something similar happened to you," she reminded him. "Did one of the Temujai tread on you?"

He nodded gratefully to her, glad the subject had been changed. He took a sip of his coffee and resumed his story.

"No. I'd concealed the horses—the ones I'd bought and paid for," he added, with a baleful glance at Gilan, "in a copse of trees. I was going to fetch water from a nearby stream when two Temujai appeared, driving half a dozen goats to the water. They were mounted, of course."

"So, one of their horses trod on you?" Maddie asked.

"Which one of us is telling this story?" Halt asked her, and she made an apologetic gesture, encouraging him to go ahead. He paused, making sure she wasn't about to interrupt again, then continued.

"So there I was, lying in the long grass, covered by my cloak—"

"Just like me," Maddie put in, then, seeing his exasperated expression, hastily added, "Sorry! Sorry! Please continue!"

"You're sure?" Halt asked, and she nodded repeatedly, lips pressed tightly together. "So there I was, lying on the ground, totally concealed from the Temujai, when a nanny goat started to chew my hair."

Will and Gilan, who had never heard this story before, erupted in laughter. Maddie grinned, but decided that, in Halt's current mood, it might be best to appear sympathetic.

"You should have had your cowl up!" Will said.

"I did," Halt replied. "The damn nanny goat nuzzled it aside and started chomping."

Their laughter grew louder. Gilan finally got control of himself and said, straight-faced, "I've often wondered how you came by that haircut. This explains a great deal."

Halt had the reputation in the Ranger Corps of cutting his hair with his saxe knife. The results were often ragged and uneven.

"So, what happened then?" Maddie wanted to know.

"Obviously, I leapt up to get away from the nanny goat. The Temujai nearest me was thrown from the saddle when his horse reared in surprise. I grabbed the other one by the leg and tossed him out of the saddle as well. Then I ran for it. I only just got away. Fortunately, Abelard was close by, and he outran their ponies. I circled back for the rest of the horses that night."

He looked steadily at Maddie. "The point of this is, accidents happen. People tread on you. Nanny goats chew your hair. You have to be ready for the unexpected. It's all part and parcel of staying hidden. Remember it in future. Learn from this experience. You never know what's going to happen."

Maddie nodded meekly. "Yes, Halt. Thank you."

"Now," said Halt, turning back to Will and Gilan, "do either of you grinning apes want to ask me what brought me here? Why I've ridden all the way from Castle Redmont and my cozy fireplace to visit you?"

Halt had been an irregular visitor to the Gathering this year. He had coached some of the younger apprentices, helping them improve their shooting technique. And from time to time he had assessed them in various tasks. But that side of his activity had ended as the Gathering came to a close.

Gilan shrugged. "I assume you came for the farewell ceremony."

Halt nodded. "Well, that's true. But that's not until tomorrow. A dispatch came for you from Horace. I thought I'd better bring it out, since nobody at Redmont knew where the Gathering Ground was."

The Gathering Ground moved each year, and its exact whereabouts were kept a strict secret. The Ranger Corps had made many enemies over the years, and some of them would have been keen to know where the entire Corps would be for these two weeks.

Halt reached inside his vest and brought out a rolled scroll, held with a ribbon, which was in turn sealed with a large blob of wax. He passed it to Gilan, who studied the seal, recognizing Horace's symbol.

"Have you read it?" he asked Halt. The old Ranger was notorious for his ability to open and reseal communications. He had an extensive kit of instruments with which he could lift wax seals without disturbing the impression or breaking the wax. And, in case of accidents, he also kept a stock of counterfeit seals with which he could replace the original. They weren't always exact replicas, but they were close enough to fool most people at a cursory glance.

Halt looked affronted. "It's sealed," he said, with some dignity. Will grinned to himself as he realized that Halt hadn't actually answered the question.

"When has that ever stopped you?" Gilan muttered, breaking the seal and unrolling the parchment sheet to read it. After a few seconds, he glanced up at Maddie. "Your dad sends his love," he said. "He hopes you're doing well at your assessments."

Maddie smiled. Typical of her father. He would send her a personal message even in an official communication. She and Horace had a close relationship, which had become even closer when she began training as a Ranger. It took her further into her father's world and gave them a lot in common.

Gilan went back to the dispatch, frowning slightly as he read on.

"Bad news?" Will asked, noticing the frown.

Gilan waved the question aside, waiting till he'd finished reading the message. Then he looked up, fixing his gaze on Halt. "Have you heard anything about a group called the Red Fox Clan?"

Halt made a small moue. "Not a great deal. Anarchists, aren't they?"

Gilan shook his head. "A bit more than that. We've been getting reports about them at Castle Araluen for some months now. They're a group who oppose the current laws of succession to the throne. They want to revert to a patriarchal system."

Araluen law said that any true descendant, male or female, could inherit the throne. Thus, in the event of Duncan's death,

Cassandra would become queen, and ruler, in her own right. Horace would not become King simply because he was married to her. He would be her consort. And, in time, Maddie would inherit the throne from her mother. But if the Red Fox Clan had their way, the kingdom would revert to an old law, where the throne could be passed down only to a male descendant. If this happened, it would throw the current succession into chaos.

"Any reason why they feel that way?" Will asked.

Gilan shrugged. "Most likely because someone wants to use it as a pretext for taking the throne himself," he said. "In any event, they mean trouble for Cassandra and Maddie here, and Horace thinks it's time we put a stop to it."

"What's he got in mind?" Will asked. He noticed that Halt wasn't asking questions, which seemed to indicate that he had read the dispatch.

"We've finally located their headquarters near the east coast," Gilan said. "Horace plans for him and me to take a company of troops and put an end to their nonsense once and for all." He hesitated, looking at the other two Rangers. "At the same time, there are rumors that another group of them has formed on Redmont's northwest border. He's asked if you two will investigate, see what they're up to, and bring them to heel as well."

"So, you'll be heading back to Castle Araluen tomorrow?" Halt asked.

Gilan regarded him, head cocked to one side. "That's what it says here," he said, tapping the dispatch. "But how could you have known that?"

Halt smiled. "Just a lucky guess," he said.

4

THE CLOSING CEREMONY OF THE GATHERING WAS ALWAYS A bittersweet affair. The Rangers and their apprentices gathered for a farewell banquet, with kitchen and serving staff brought in from Castle Redmont and its adjoining village. Now that the Gathering was almost over, there was no need to keep the location a secret. It would be moved somewhere else the following year.

The Rangers feasted and talked long into the night, until the poignant moment when they joined together to sing their traditional farewell song, "Cabin in the Trees."

Rangers lived a dangerous, adventurous life, and there was no knowing how many of those assembled here would be present in a year's time. So they mingled and embraced and wished each other well and looked deep into one another's eyes, knowing that in some cases this could be the last time they saw their comrades.

Gilan had decided to stay for the ceremony, in spite of originally declaring his intention to return immediately to Castle Araluen in response to Horace's message.

"One night won't make any difference," he told Halt. "And

Horace will be busy assembling his troops anyway. I'll leave early in the morning."

Most of the others followed his example, packing up and leaving camp before dawn. Now that the Gathering was over, they were keen to return to their respective fiefs and catch up on events that had transpired while they had been away. Will and Maddie, with only a short distance to travel back to Castle Redmont, took their time, staying for a late breakfast and watching the catering staff pack up their wagons and head out. There was something sad about the patches of bare earth where the Rangers had pitched their tents for the past ten days—evidence that they had been here but now were gone.

Will looked around the near-silent ground. "Good-byes are always sad," he said, more to himself than to Maddie. But she replied anyway.

"Mother told me you always felt that way—that when you left, you never looked back."

He smiled sadly. "That's true. I could never bear to see who or what I was leaving behind. These days, I tend to look back in case it's the last time I see the people I'm leaving." He shrugged. "Put it down to my advancing years, I suppose."

Maddie laughed. "Advancing years indeed! You're in your prime."

"It'd be nice to think so," he replied. Then he noticed a figure approaching through the empty tent lines. "Hullo, I was wondering if Jenny would drop by."

His old wardmate Jenny had been responsible for the catering the night before. Master Chubb, her longtime mentor, had recently retired. In spite of Baron Arald's best efforts, Jenny had resisted all offers to move to Castle Redmont and take over the kitchens there. She was an independent character, and she enjoyed having her own establishment in the village. Instead, she had trained one of her own apprentices to replace Chubb in the castle kitchens. On special occasions, she took over the cooking at Redmont. Baron Arald treasured those occasions and tried to arrange as many as he could.

Will rose to greet her as she came closer. He grunted slightly as he stood, uncoiling his legs, and glanced down at Maddie.

"See what I mean about advancing years?" he said, feeling slightly envious of the way she rose smoothly to her feet. Even the old injury to her hip didn't seem to bother her most of the time. Then he turned to his old friend. "Morning, Jenny. I'm sorry we didn't have time for a long chat last night."

"I was a little busy," Jenny replied. She was a stern and demanding taskmaster to her kitchen staff, and she insisted that the Rangers be provided with only the best food and drink. They had had time for a brief word the previous night, but no more than that.

Will looked at her appreciatively. There were a few lines of gray in her blond hair these days, and her waist might have thickened a little—one of the hazards of being a chef and having a keen appreciation of the fine food she prepared—but she'd always had a rounded figure, and the extra inches looked good on her.

"You're as pretty as ever," he said, but she waved the compliment aside.

"And you're as grim as a gray old wolf," she said. "Whatever became of that fresh-faced boy I grew up with?"

"Weight of responsibility," Will said. "After all, now I have this dreadful apprentice to keep in check."

Jenny smiled warmly at Maddie. In the early days, when Maddie had first arrived at Redmont, they had got off to a rocky start because of Maddie's haughty suggestion that Jenny address her as "Your Highness." But the two were good friends these days.

"How are you, Maddie?" she asked.

Maddie grinned in return. "I'm fine, Jenny," she said. "Would you like some coffee?" She gestured at the pot sitting in the hot embers at the side of the fire, but Jenny shook her head.

"I'll have to keep an eye on my kitchen staff while they pack up. Otherwise they'll leave my best pots and ladles behind and I'll have to come back and find them."

"Gilan left early this morning," Will said.

She nodded. "Yes. He came by early and we had some time together. Good to see him." She smiled at the memory.

Will cocked his head to one side. "So . . . any chance that you'll be moving your restaurant to Castle Araluen?"

But she shook her head firmly. "No. I've suggested that Gilan move his headquarters to Redmont. No reason why he shouldn't, after all."

Jenny and Gilan had been "an item," as people said, for years now. But their relationship was limited by geography. Jenny had spent years building up her business in Wensley Village near Castle Redmont, and Gilan was based at Castle Araluen.

Will shrugged. "I suppose he thinks he needs to be close by Horace and Evanlyn," he pointed out, but Jenny made a derogatory sound at that suggestion.

"There are always pigeons to carry messages," she said. "And it's only a couple of days' ride—less on one of your fabled Ranger horses. There's no reason why he couldn't be based here."

Will made a defensive gesture with both hands, not wishing to be dragged into that debate—although he tended to agree with Jenny. Gilan could quite easily work out of Redmont, and he'd be close to his two senior Rangers, Halt and Will, if he did so.

"I'll leave that to you two to work out," he said.

Jenny stepped forward and embraced him. "We'll get there eventually," she said. "Take care of yourself. Gilan tells me that you two are off to the northwest in the next few days?"

"I am," Will said. "Halt and I want to have a look around up there. Maddie will be heading back to Castle Araluen." He sensed Maddie's quick reaction as she turned to look at him.

"I thought I'd be coming with you and Halt," she said.

But he shook his head. "Your mother is expecting you back at Araluen," he said firmly. "She hasn't seen you in a year." He noted the stubborn set of her jaw. He knew he'd be in for a long argument.

"But why?" Maddie asked for the fifteenth time. "Why can't I come with you and Halt? I'm a Ranger, aren't I?"

"Because your mother wants you to visit her," Will told her patiently. "You go home for a vacation every year after the Gathering."

"So, if I go every year, will it matter if I miss once? Besides, I can come with you and Halt, then go home."

"We don't know how long we'll be on the border," Will said. "We could be weeks, even a month."

"Oh, come on! Gilan said they're only vague rumors. Chances are there's nothing to them and you'll be back in a week or two at most."

"No," said Will firmly, hoping that his refusal to discuss the matter further would put an end to their disagreement. But Maddie fell back on old ground.

"Why?" she said. "Just tell me why."

And that made sixteen and seventeen times, he thought. He sighed heavily.

"Your mother still hasn't forgiven me for recruiting you into the Rangers," he said.

She made a dismissive gesture. "That wasn't your fault. Gilan and Halt did that."

"Maybe. But I'm the one who trains you, so I'm the one who gets the blame when you keep passing each year."

"She doesn't want me to fail, does she?" Maddie asked.

"No. Not exactly. She's very proud of you. But initially, she thought you would only remain as an apprentice for one year. So she wouldn't be totally devastated if you failed and had to go home. As it is, she insists on your coming home for a month each year, and I'm not about to get in the way of that."

Maddie thrust her jaw out pugnaciously. "You mean to tell me you're scared of my mother?" she challenged.

Will met her gaze very evenly. "You'd better believe it," he told her.

Back at the cabin in the woods near Redmont, the two of them began packing their gear for their respective trips. As usual, Will simply crammed his spare clothes and equipment higgledy-piggledy into his saddlebags, shoving them in to make them fit. Maddie carefully unpacked them, folded them neatly, and replaced them in the bags so that they took up half the space they had previously.

"No need to bother with that," Will told her, and she gave him a long-suffering look.

"They'll be all crushed and wrinkled when you take them out if I don't," she told him.

He shrugged. "If I wear them for half an hour, the wrinkles will come out," he said. Then, considering for a moment, he added, "Well, maybe an hour."

Her own packing took considerably longer, as she had to take with her not just her Ranger uniform, but also the gowns and dresses and cloaks she would wear as the royal princess. She would change identities halfway to Castle Araluen.

Maddie's position as a Ranger was kept a strict secret in the kingdom. The Rangers knew, of course—but Rangers were notoriously tight-lipped. A few others, such as Baron Arald and his wife, were also aware of her activities with the Corps, but the general population was kept in the dark. Her Highness Princess Madelyn was, after all, second in line to the throne, and it would be risky for her identity as a Ranger to be widely broadcast. There was always the chance that enemies of the kingdom might seek to capture or kill her. As the apprentice Ranger Maddie, she kept a lower profile and was not in the public eye. Most people thought she was at Castle Redmont, learning the fine arts of diplomacy and hospitality under the careful eye of Lady Sandra.

The other person who was privy to the deception was her maid, Ingrid.

When Maddie had first arrived for her training, she brought a lady's maid with her, along with a staggering amount of luggage. Will had promptly dispatched the girl and most of the baggage back to Castle Araluen, saying that a Ranger's apprentice did her own cleaning and clothes mending. In subsequent years, however, they realized that Maddie would need a maid as a traveling companion when she went home at the end of the year, and Ingrid had been given the task. During the year, she stayed at Castle Redmont and worked for Lady Sandra. Then, when Maddie left for home, Ingrid would accompany her.

The day they were due to leave, Ingrid arrived from the castle, leading Maddie's Arridan gelding, Sundancer. It would never do for the heir to the throne to be seen riding a shaggy Ranger horse. The fine-boned Sundancer was a far more fitting mount for her. Of course, Maddie would ride Bumper until she resumed her identity as a princess. Then the little horse would masquerade as a pack pony.

"I'm sorry about that," she told Bumper, rubbing his silky nose. "I know it's beneath your dignity."

Bumper came as near to shrugging as a horse can manage. *If you can dress up like a glorified dressmaker's dummy, I suppose I can carry a few parcels.*

5

GILAN AND HORACE LEANED OVER THE MAP SPREAD OUT ON Gilan's desk. Horace was using the point of his dagger to indicate features on the map as he spoke.

"Our spies tell us that the Red Fox Clan have gathered somewhere in this area." He traced the dagger point along a winding river, indicating a spot four days' ride north of Castle Araluen.

"The Wezel River," Gilan commented, noting the name. He touched a marked feature on the north bank, by a long curve in the waterway. "What's this?"

"It's an old hill fort," Horace told him. "Hasn't been inhabited in centuries."

"Are the Foxes using it?" Gilan asked.

Horace shook his head. "No. So far as I know, they have a camp somewhere on the south bank, along this long, curving stretch."

"So, if we approach from the south, we'll have them hemmed in against the river."

"That's right. The river is deep and there aren't many fords. It's not a particularly good tactical position for them. But then, they seem to be pretty low on tactical sense."

"They're not trained warriors, then?" Gilan asked.

"Not from what I've heard. They're mainly brigands and thugs who have been recruited to the Red Fox Clan by the promise of payment and easy pickings. There may be half a dozen or so trained men among their leaders, but the rest appear to be a rabble."

"Numbers?"

Horace rested the point of the dagger in the rough wood of the desktop. "Thirty to forty. No more than that," he said. Then, preempting the next question, he added, "I figure we'll take twenty cavalrymen and twenty archers with us." He glanced up. "They're trained men and they've all been in battle before. I don't think forty raggle-tailed rebels will give us too much trouble."

Gilan grinned. "Particularly not with you and me along," he said. He was joking, but there was a strong element of truth in the joke. Horace was the preeminent warrior of the kingdom, skillful, fast and strong. His amazing ability had been noted when he was barely sixteen years old. Now, many years later, he had added a wealth of experience to his natural skill. And Gilan, of course, was the Ranger Commandant, and as such he was one of the most capable Rangers in the Corps.

"We'll be taking rations for ten days," Horace told the Ranger. "Dried meat and fruit, and flatbread. Each man will have two canteens. Once we're on the way, I want to move quickly and get to the Wezel River before they hear word that we're coming. The sooner we wrap this up, the better. We'll bivouac at night and avoid towns and villages on the way."

"Good thinking. The fewer people who see us, the better. When do we leave?"

"The cavalrymen are still mustering their remounts—the

horses have been out in the fields for several months, and it'll take a few days to get them settled and retrained for carrying riders. They go half wild when they're left alone for any length of time. So we should be ready to go by the end of the week. That way I'll get a chance to see Maddie before I leave." Maddie was due to arrive the following morning.

"I'll get you to check over the archers' equipment tomorrow, if you would," Horace continued. "You know what to look for better than I do."

Gilan nodded assent. He reached down and slid the map across the desk, unrolling it a little more to find the area where Castle Redmont was situated.

"Halt and Will should be well on their way by now," he said. "Do you expect them to find anything?"

Horace shrugged. "The intelligence was sketchy—more rumor than hard fact. But I can't afford to ignore it. I'll sleep better if I know those two have had a good look around. This Fox cult may be a bunch of blowhards, but an idea like this can gain momentum all too quickly, and before you know it, we could have a full-scale uprising on our hands. We need to nip it in the bud right away."

Gilan released the edge of the map, allowing it to roll closed once again. "Best way to handle it," he said. "Strike fast before things get out of hand."

Horace straightened from where he'd been leaning on the desktop. He rerolled the map into a tight cylinder and slipped a loop of brown ribbon over the end to contain it.

"It should take us three or four days to reach the Wezel," he said. "Then a couple more days to locate the Foxes' camp, and we can put an end to this nonsense."

Gilan grunted agreement. But he was frowning slightly. One fact was causing him concern.

Horace noted his expression. "Is there a problem?"

Gilan hesitated. "Forty cavalrymen and archers," he said. "That's more than half the standing garrison here. Are you worried that you might be leaving Cassandra shorthanded if there's trouble?"

Horace shook his head. "Araluen is easily defended," he said. "Even a small garrison can hold it. And Cassandra is a good commander. She's seen her share of combat."

Gilan nodded. "That's a fact," he said. Cassandra had proved her worth in battles from the coastal plain of Skandia to the desert wastes of Arrida and the rugged mountains of Nihon-Ja. Given a virtually impregnable position like Castle Araluen, there was no doubt that she could mount an effective and successful defense against any foreseeable threat.

Maddie and Ingrid had made good time after leaving Redmont. The weather was good, and the roads were clear.

Ingrid looked at the sun, gauging the time by its position in the sky. "You'll need to change clothes soon," she warned. "Time for you to become a princess again."

Maddie wrinkled her nose distastefully. She was still dressed as a Ranger, although she rode with her cowl back and her head bare. She enjoyed the comfort of the Ranger clothes. They were loose fitting and unrestrictive. By contrast, the riding gown she would soon put on would be tight and uncomfortable, designed for style rather than function.

Bumper sniggered. *Dressmaker's dummy.*

"Don't you laugh, pack pony," she said softly.

Ingrid glanced her way. "Did you say something?"

Maddie hurriedly shook her head. She wasn't sure how her maid would react to the fact that she spoke to her horse and believed he spoke back to her. Ingrid would probably think her mistress was crazy. But then, Ingrid was half convinced of that anyway, not understanding how Maddie could prefer the rough-and-ready life of a Ranger's apprentice to the soft comforts and fine clothes of a princess.

Then the matter was forgotten, and Ingrid gestured down the track. "We have company."

They had left the open country on the far side of the river, and the road at this point led through a section of Alder Forest. The trees were tall and grew close together on either side of the path, which had narrowed down until it was just wide enough for two riders to travel abreast.

About thirty meters ahead of them, two men had stepped out of the trees to block the path. They were both heavily built and dressed in rough, stained clothing. Both were armed.

The man on the right held a bow, with an arrow fitted to the string but not yet drawn. The flights of more arrows were visible over his shoulder, where they were held in a rough quiver. He had a long knife at his waist.

The other, a slightly taller man, had a heavy cudgel in his right hand. It was made from a piece of hardwood, tapering down from a wide head to a narrower handgrip, wrapped with a leather strap. The heavy head was liberally studded with spikes. Altogether, it was an unpleasant sight—as was its owner.

Instinctively, both girls had drawn rein and brought their horses to a stop. Beneath her, Maddie felt Bumper's body vibrate as he sounded a warning rumble.

"Maybe we should have brought an escort," Ingrid said quietly, although Maddie noted that she didn't seem too concerned about the situation.

"For these two drabs?" she replied. "You've got to be joking."

Maddie lifted her right leg over the pommel and slid to the ground beside Bumper. As she did, she reached for the sling that was coiled under her belt, shaking it loose, and feeling in her belt pouch with her other hand for several of the smooth, heavy lead shot she kept there. Her bow was in its bow case, tied to the right-hand rear of her saddle, but she wasn't concerned about that. The sling was her weapon of choice anyway.

Not needing to look, she loaded a slug into the pouch of the sling. The practiced ease with which she did this should possibly have sounded a warning to the two brigands. But they were overconfident, seeing no possible danger from two young women. She stepped a pace away from Bumper, giving herself room to wield the sling.

Ingrid looked down at her. "Anything particular in mind?"

Maddie shook her head. "Let's see how things turn out," she said, letting the sling hang to full length beside her. Bumper was continuing to rumble deep in his chest, a low, warning note that was audible only for a few meters.

The man with the bow raised it now, although he still didn't draw the arrow back. "Don't keep us waiting, girls," he called out. "Just come forward and hand over your valuables. It'll go easier for you if you do."

There was a note of amusement in his voice. Maddie sensed that he was very satisfied with the situation. Ingrid was well dressed and was sure to have money and jewelry on her. Her horse was a well-bred mare and was obviously worth money as well. As was Sundancer, who was bringing up the rear, carrying their baggage. Bumper, of course, appeared unimpressive—a rough, little barrel-shaped horse that was probably sturdy and hardworking, but not worth a great deal. All in all, the two girls looked like ideal prey for the robbers. Relatively helpless and unprotected by guards, they would offer little resistance to two armed men.

"We'll stay here, I think," Ingrid replied. In a quieter voice, she said to Maddie, "We could always turn back."

Maddie shook her head. "They wouldn't make it so easy. By now, you'll probably find there's a third member of the band who has worked his way behind us."

Ingrid glanced over her shoulder and saw that Maddie was right. A third figure, equally roughly dressed and armed with a heavy staff surmounted by a spearhead, was standing at the point where the track led into the trees, silhouetted against the bright sunlight behind him.

"You're right," she said. She took a firmer grip on her riding crop. Ingrid never used it on her horse, keeping it instead as a concealed weapon. It was a piece of stout ashwood, fifty centimeters long, wrapped in leather and with a polished stone pommel at one end. The other end tapered down to the whip section—a flat piece of braided leather. In addition, as was the custom for ladies, she wore a dagger on her belt.

"I'll take care of the bowman first," Maddie said in an undertone. "With any luck, the others will run once he's down."

"And without any luck?" Ingrid asked.

Maddie grinned. "It'll be their bad luck," she said.

6

THE MAN WITH THE BOW WAS BECOMING IMPATIENT. THE girls had been standing immobile for several minutes now. He had seen Ingrid cast a look over her shoulder and knew she was aware that any possible retreat was cut off.

"Come along!" he ordered. "We've wasted enough time here. Come forward and hand over your valuables!"

To emphasize the point, he began to draw back on the arrow. The bow and the string creaked as they came under strain.

Maddie's eyes narrowed as she studied the bow. It was a poor weapon, unlike the beautifully fashioned bows that Rangers used. It was made from an unevenly shaped stave, with one limb narrower than the other, so the top half of the bow bent more than the lower. She seriously doubted he could hit anything beyond fifty meters with a bow like that. But then, he would be well used to its peculiarities and would probably allow for any uneven flight.

And besides, they were inside fifty meters, so she decided that it wasn't worth letting him take a shot.

Moving swiftly and smoothly, she took a long step forward with her left foot, letting the sling in her right hand hang down to its full length behind her body. Then she whipped it up and over, stepping into the shot with her right leg as she did so. It was a smooth, coordinated movement, putting her leg, body and arm into the force behind the sling. The lead shot whizzed away, too fast for the eye to follow, and smashed into the upper limb of the bow, halfway up its length. The upper limb was the weaker of the two, and it was bent more than its fellow. The sudden impact of the lead shot shattered it, so that the bow seemed to explode in the man's hands as the tension on the string was suddenly released.

The broken limb flew loose, and then, stopped by the string, flicked back and smacked the man across the jaw, raising a bleeding weal there. He cried out and staggered back, dropping the broken bow and throwing a hand up to stem the sudden flow of blood. He wasn't quite sure what had just happened. Things had moved too fast for him to see clearly. But he knew it had been the fault of that slim girl standing beside the shaggy little horse. Determined on revenge, he reached for the long knife at his belt and started toward her.

"They never learn," Maddie said. She loaded another slug into her sling and whipped it toward him. It hit him on the point of the shoulder, smashing the bone and bruising the flesh. The knife dropped from his fingers, and he stood, swaying, sobbing with the sudden shock and pain. Slowly he sank to his knees, his left hand reaching to try to ease the agony in his broken shoulder. He doubled over until his head touched the ground, little moaning sounds escaping from his lips.

"You witch!" his companion screamed. He brandished the cudgel above his head and ran at Maddie. She calmly loaded another shot into her sling and stood waiting for him. But Ingrid acted first.

Ingrid spurred her horse forward, reversing her grip on the riding crop as she did. The man saw her coming and turned to face her. He swung wildly with the cudgel, but she nudged her horse with her knees and it gracefully sidestepped, avoiding the blow. Then it lunged back in before he could recover, and Ingrid leaned out of the saddle, wielding the riding crop and bringing the heavy stone pommel crashing down on top of his leather cap.

He looked up at her, startled. Then his eyes glazed and he simply folded up like an empty suit of clothes, collapsing to the leaf-strewn forest path, stone-cold unconscious.

With two of their attackers taken care of, Maddie turned her attention to the third member of the gang. He hesitated, seeing his companions disabled within a matter of seconds. Then he turned and ran.

"Bumper," said Maddie quietly, and pointed at the retreating figure.

The little horse took off like an arrow released from a bow. Maddie, as always, was fascinated by the acceleration that Ranger horses could manage. Within a few strides, he was at top pace, rapidly gaining on the floundering figure before him.

If the robber had had the wit to cut off into the trees to either side, he might have had a better chance. But he chose to remain on the path, then on the open ground beyond the forest. He'd barely covered ten meters of the latter when Bumper caught up with him and, true to his name, slammed his shoulder into the robber's side.

The impact sent the man tumbling in the grass, rolling over several times before beginning to rise, groggily, to his feet. He shook his head to clear his vision—his head had thudded heavily into the ground when he fell, and he was a little dizzy. The small, shaggy horse stood a few meters away, ears pricked, watching him with a curious expression on its face, as if to say, *What are you planning to do now?* The robber had the distinct impression that the horse was amused by the situation. His hand dropped to the knife at his belt. He had lost his spear in the fall, and it was out of sight in the long grass.

He slid the knife from its sheath and began to advance on the horse, muttering a curse as he did so.

"That's far enough." He heard Maddie's warning call and glanced back toward the point where the track led into the trees. She had followed Bumper at a more leisurely pace and was standing now at the edge of the forest. Her sling, loaded with another lead ball, hung unobtrusively from her right hand, swinging slowly back and forth, level with her right knee.

When Maddie had hit his companion with two casts of the sling, the third bandit hadn't seen exactly what had happened. His view of the scene, and of Maddie's actions, had been blocked by the horse. Not appreciating the threat offered by the innocuous-looking weapon, he began to advance on Bumper, whose ears twitched slightly.

"Last warning," Maddie called. Her voice was sharper now.

He glanced at her and snarled. "Best call your horse away, missy," he said. "Else I'm going to gut him."

Maddie sighed. She had given him a chance. But Will had spent years drumming into her the rule of thumb in situations like this. *Give an enemy one chance to surrender. But one chance only. After that, take action.*

The robber took another pace toward Bumper, cooing softly in what he intended to be a soothing voice.

"Come on, horse . . . good horse. Stand still while I plunge this blade into your belly. . . . Stand now, that's . . . Aaaaiiiyaaah!"

The scream was torn from him as the lead shot slammed into his forearm, breaking the bones there. The knife fell from his suddenly nerveless fingers, and he clutched at his arm with his left hand, bending over in reaction to the unexpected impact and searing agony.

Maddie casually folded the sling and placed it under her belt, then drew her saxe as she advanced on the stooped-over, moaning figure. He heard her approaching and looked up, tears of shock and pain running freely down his grubby, unshaven face.

"You broke my arm!" he said in an accusing tone.

Maddie couldn't help smiling at his indignation. Here he was, a would-be robber intent on preying on two seemingly defenseless girls, and he had the gall to act as the injured party. It never failed to amuse her how so many thugs on an occasion like this would assume that same attitude of injured innocence.

"Could have been your head," she said unsympathetically. She prodded him in the rump with the point of her saxe. He skipped away from the contact, sniveling as the movement sent waves of pain coursing through his broken arm.

"Get moving," Maddie ordered him crisply, gesturing toward the path into the forest. Continuing to moan and protest, the robber complied, leading the way back up the trail to where his two erstwhile companions were seated at the base of a large oak. Ingrid stood over them, her reversed riding crop in one hand and her dagger in the other. But the men were thoroughly cowed and offered no resistance to their intended victims. They looked up as Maddie shoved their companion down beside them, eliciting another groan of pain from him as she did so. The man Ingrid stunned had regained consciousness, although a certain dazed look in his eyes told Maddie that he was probably concussed.

She tapped her saxe against her leg as she studied them, figuring out what to do. They could hardly take the men with them, but she certainly wasn't going to turn them loose.

"All right," she said abruptly. "Strip."

None of them moved. They all stared at her, uncomprehending. Finally the former bowman spoke.

"Our clothes? All of them?"

Maddie shook her head impatiently. "I don't think so. Ingrid doesn't deserve to see such an unpleasant sight. Just your breeches and your shirts. Down to your underwear."

They still didn't move, so she added crisply, "Get on with it!"

This time, they obeyed, moving awkwardly in the case of the two with broken arms, and shrugged off their stained and dirty outer clothing. Their underclothes were no more attractive. They had obviously gone unlaundered for many days, and they were holed and ragged. Maddie kicked the discarded clothes away from the men, into a rough pile.

"Shoes as well," she ordered, and they reluctantly obeyed.

Ingrid watched curiously. "Is there any reason for this?" she asked quietly.

Maddie nodded, glancing up at her. "Makes them feel vulnerable and less likely to disobey orders. Having them strip tends to take the starch out of them—particularly in front of two girls."

"Makes me feel light-headed," Ingrid commented. "They are rather on the nose, aren't they?"

She was right. With their clothes removed, the strong odors from their unwashed bodies were all too apparent.

"Not much we can do about that," Maddie commented. She

leaned down and caught hold of the concussed man's wrists, pulling them behind his back and tying his thumbs together with a length of leather thong. Then she quickly did the same for his companions, resulting in more cries of pain as she moved their injured arms into position—something she did without excessive gentleness.

"Oooh, by the gods, that hurts!" the third member of the gang whined.

Maddie eyed him unsympathetically. "Serves you right for attacking helpless girls."

Ingrid smiled. Anyone less like a "helpless girl" than her mistress she couldn't imagine.

"Now scrooch up against the tree," Maddie continued, gesturing for them to shuffle backward so that they were sitting with their backs to the trunk of the big oak. Once they were in position, she ran a length of rope around the tree, looping it around their throats and pulling tight so there was barely any slack. They were now fastened to the tree, unable to move without choking themselves and their companions, and unable to reach up to untie the rope.

"Are we going to leave them here?" Ingrid asked. She had been watching the procedure with interest, wondering how many times Maddie had performed similar actions in her career as an apprentice Ranger. She certainly seemed to know what she was doing, the maid thought. It was probably not the first time she had secured prisoners this way.

Maddie tested the rope, then stepped back, satisfied that there was hardly any slack in it. She smiled as she considered Ingrid's question.

"I'm tempted to," she said. "There are wolves and bears in the

forest here, I'm sure. They'd take care of them for us." She
noticed the startled, worried looks on the three men as she
spoke. "But perhaps we should be merciful. There's a manor
house half an hour's ride from here. We'll ask the local lord to
send back men to bring these three beauties in and find a nice
warm jail cell for them."

They rode on for fifteen minutes, at which point Maddie
dismounted and changed clothes, packing away her Ranger
uniform and cloak into a large saddlebag and donning a neat,
divided riding habit, linen shirt and fine leather jacket more
befitting her identity as a princess of the realm. She unsaddled
Bumper, removed the packsaddle from Sundancer and changed
the two over.

"Sorry about this," she told Bumper. She felt it was beneath
his dignity to act as a beast of burden.

He snorted.

Sundancer, by comparison, seemed delighted to be free of the
packsaddle and to resume his proper identity as a saddle horse.
He nickered appreciatively as Maddie swung up astride him.

A few kilometers farther on, they rode through a neat little
village and stopped at the impressive manor house at its out-
skirts. The local lord, an elderly knight, hurried out to greet
them when Maddie identified herself to his butler. He had obviously been halfway through his midday meal. A large white
napkin was still tucked into his collar, and there were crumbs in
his beard. He bowed hurriedly as Maddie dismounted, noticed
the napkin as he did so and dragged it loose, trying belatedly to
conceal it behind his back.

"My lady," he said, "welcome to Tonbridge Village. I'm Sir

Gerald Wollden, and this is my manor house. Can I offer you food and refreshments? A bed for the night, perhaps?"

Maddie shook her head. "Thank you, no. I'm in a hurry to reach Castle Araluen. But there is a service you can perform for us," she said.

Ingrid noted how easily she assumed the confident, commanding manner of a princess. The elderly knight bowed several times in acquiescence.

"Anything, my lady," he said eagerly. "Anything at all!"

"We left three injured men a few kilometers down the track. I wonder if you'd take care of them for me."

"Of course, my lady! I'll send some servants to look after them straightaway."

Maddie pursed her lips. "I'd rather you sent your guards to arrest them," she said. "They're brigands. They tried to rob us."

The gentlemanly old soul was aghast at her words. "Rob you? Are you all right, my lady? Are you injured?"

"No," Maddie reassured him. "My companion here took care of them. She's a very capable young woman."

The knight looked at Ingrid in some confusion. She was a slightly built girl. He couldn't imagine her besting three robbers.

"I'll deal with them, my lady," he assured Maddie. He rubbed his chin thoughtfully, loosening a few of the crumbs in his beard. "Usually, we hang robbers."

Maddie frowned. "That might be a little extreme. I'd say put them in a cell for a few days, then keep them for, say, three months, and have them perform all the hard labor that's needed round the village. That should teach them a lesson."

"I'll take care of it, my lady," he said. "Rest assured, we'll find plenty of work for them to do." His eyes glittered as he thought about the three ruffians accosting the princess. "Hard work," he added.

"Thank you, Sir Gerald. I appreciate your help. Now I'll be on my way." She moved back to the horses and, unthinking, went to mount Bumper. He edged away from her, snorting a reminder, and she changed direction to swing herself up into Sundancer's saddle.

"Going to have to watch that," she said under her breath as they rode out of the manor house yard.

7

Maddie drew rein as they emerged from the tree line. The sight of Castle Araluen never failed to take her breath away. The beautiful castle, with its soaring turrets and gracefully curving walls, dominated the landscape for miles around. Sited at the top of a long, gradual rise, it seemed at times to be floating in the air. Banners and flags stood out from its many flagstaffs, supported by the breeze that seemed to be a constant in this part of the kingdom. She reflected for a moment. She couldn't recall ever seeing the flags and banners hanging limply on their staffs.

"I never get sick of seeing it again when I've been away," Ingrid said, noting the rapt expression on her mistress's face.

Maddie nodded slowly, her eyes still riveted on the beautiful building before them. "It's stunning, isn't it?"

Castle Araluen had none of the uncompromisingly solid lines of a castle like Redmont. But its beauty belied its strength. The tall walls and deep moat kept attackers at bay, and the towers and battlements afforded the defenders with a host of positions from which they could rain down arrows, spears, rocks, hot oil and boiling water on those below.

They sat for several minutes, admiring the sight of the

graceful building. Then Maddie touched her heels to Sundancer's flanks and urged the horse forward. Ingrid followed suit, and they rode at a slow canter up through the beautifully landscaped parklands and carefully mown grass. There were only occasional clumps of trees to provide shade and shelter from the wind for people relaxing in the parklands. This was done intentionally. There was no way a large body of men could approach the castle unseen. The ground was open and the view unrestricted for half a kilometer around the castle, preventing any surprise attack in force. Even half a dozen men would be seen quickly from the numerous vantage points on the castle walls. So even though the parkland was pleasing to the eye, it served a far more serious purpose than mere aesthetics, keeping the castle safe from invaders and attackers.

They weren't halfway when they saw movement at the main gate. The massive drawbridge was down, because it was the middle of the day and there was no perceived threat to the castle. Maddie, watching carefully and knowing what to expect, saw the two sentries on duty at the outer end of the bridge come suddenly to attention as a lone rider emerged from the castle, already moving at full speed.

"I wonder who that might be," Maddie drawled with a slow smile as the rider galloped headlong down the hill toward them, her long blond hair flying behind her in the wind, and the scarf round her throat billowing out to match it.

"Could it be your mother, do you think?" Ingrid said in the same amused tone.

"Her Royal Highness the Princess Regent?" Maddie replied. "Surely you don't think she would behave with such a lack of dignity and sense of occasion."

"She did last year," Ingrid told her.

"And the year before that," Maddie agreed. She halted Sundancer and stood in her stirrups to wave a greeting to the flying figure rapidly approaching them.

Cassandra reined in as she came close, hauling on the reins so that her horse went back on its haunches and slid, stiff legged, to a stop beside them in a cloud of dust and flying grass. She threw her leg over the pommel and slid lightly to the ground, rushing toward her daughter, arms outstretched.

"Maddie! Maddie! You're home at last!" Her voice was high-pitched with excitement.

Maddie swung down from the saddle in a more conventional movement. She had barely disentangled her foot from the stirrup when she was overwhelmed by her mother, who squealed with incoherent delight and collided with her daughter as she threw both arms around her and sent the two of them staggering.

"Steady on, Mum!" Maddie cried breathlessly. "You'll knock me over!"

Ingrid watched with amusement as Maddie's prediction became a fact. The two women, mother and daughter, lost their balance under the impetus of Cassandra's rush and went sprawling in the neatly mown grass, rolling over and dissolving into gales of laughter. Cassandra was the first to recover, rising to her feet and holding out a hand to help Maddie up.

"What a trip!" Maddie said, laughing still as she brushed stray strands of grass from her hair. "First we get stopped by bandits, then my mother barges into me like an angry bull when I think I'm safe home."

Instantly, the laughter fled from Cassandra's face as she realized what Maddie had said. It was replaced by a look of concern.

"Bandits?" she repeated. "You were held up by bandits? What happened? Are you all right?"

"No, Mum," Maddie said, straight-faced. "They killed us both. You're looking at our ghosts. Of course we're all right."

"But what happened? Were you in danger? When did this happen? Where are they now?" The questions poured out of Cassandra nonstop, her words running together. Maddie held up a hand to stop the flow, but her mother looked up to Maddie's companion.

"Ingrid, what happened? For goodness' sake, someone give me a sensible answer!"

Ingrid smiled reassuringly at the worried Princess Regent. "Really, my lady, we were never in any real danger. Your daughter handled the situation easily."

"How many were there? Where are they now? Are you sure you're both all right?" Ingrid's unflustered answer did nothing to ease Cassandra's worry.

"Honestly, my lady, we're fine. We were never in any real danger."

"But what happened?" Cassandra repeated. The pitch of her voice was getting higher and higher as she tried to get answers to her questions. She was actually hopping from one foot to another, a sure sign of the agitation any mother feels when she hears her child has been in danger.

Maddie put a hand on her shoulder to calm her. "Mum, it was fine, really. We were half a day's ride from here, passing through Alder Forest, and these three raggle-tailed ruffians decided they'd rob us. They stepped out onto the track and told us to hand over our valuables."

"Were they armed?" Cassandra asked anxiously.

Maddie shrugged. "Barely. One had a club. The other had a rather sad-looking bow, and the third had a spear."

"He was behind us, cutting off our retreat," Ingrid put in.

Cassandra glanced up at her quickly. "So you couldn't run away?" Nothing the girls were telling her was making her feel any more reassured.

"There didn't seem to be any need," Maddie told her. She really couldn't understand why her mother was carrying on so. But then, she wasn't a mother.

Ingrid took up the tale again. "Lady Maddie used her sling and smashed the bow. Then she smashed the bowman's shoulder," she said. When she and Maddie were alone, she simply referred to her as "Maddie," but in front of her mother, she thought she should show a little more respect.

"Then Ingrid whacked the second one with her riding crop," Maddie said. She looked up at her maid. "That's a very handy piece, by the way. I must get one."

"You hit him with a riding crop?" Cassandra asked. It didn't sound like a particularly effective way to deal with an armed bandit.

Ingrid held up the crop for her to see, pointing to the heavy stone pommel. "It's not an ordinary crop," she said. "It's weighted with lead in the handle and has this heavy stone at the end."

"And then Bumper took care of the third man," Maddie continued. "Sent him flying head over heels. He turned nasty at that, so I broke his arm with my sling shot. Couldn't have him hurting Bumper." She turned to smile at the little horse. He pricked his ears as he heard his name, and whinnied softly.

She saw that Cassandra had calmed somewhat, and patted her mother's shoulder again. "Mum, they were just three ruffians. And remember, I've been training for three years now as a Ranger. I've faced much worse situations than this."

Cassandra passed a hand over her face. "Don't tell me that. I really don't want to hear that." She put her hands on her daughter's shoulders and looked deep into her eyes. "You're sure you're all right?" she asked, her tone serious.

Maddie grinned at her. "I'm fine, Mum. Really. Ingrid could have handled them by herself. She's very capable."

Ingrid shook her head, smiling at the statement. When it came to capable, she thought, nobody was more so than her mistress. It amused her that Cassandra didn't realize that her daughter was a highly trained warrior, skilled in the use of bow, sling and knife. She might be an apprentice still, but an apprentice Ranger was a very dangerous person. Particularly if you were an oafish, poorly armed ruffian who relied more on bluster and threats than actual skill at arms.

Finally, Cassandra seemed to be convinced. She smiled wearily at her daughter and embraced her once more—this time more gently than the first.

"Well, if you're sure you're all right . . ."

Maddie hugged her warmly. "I'm sure, Mum. Really." She stepped back from her mother and held her hands out from her sides for inspection. "See? There's not a mark on me."

Even though she was joking, she noticed that Cassandra did examine her closely, looking for any possible sign of injury. Finally, the Princess Regent seemed satisfied. She nodded and turned to retrieve her horse, where it was grazing nearby.

"Well then, in that case, let's go home," Cassandra said. "People are waiting to greet you."

They remounted and, riding side by side, with barely a meter between them so they could reach across and hold each other's hand, continued in a contented silence up the grassy hill toward the castle. As they came close to the sentries at the outer end of the drawbridge, Cassandra released Maddie's hand and turned to face her.

"I wouldn't mention that little matter to your father," she said in a low voice. "You know how he tends to worry."

"How *he* tends to worry?" Maddie repeated incredulously. Then, realizing that her mother was deadly serious, she nodded acquiescence. "He'll never hear a word from me."

Because, knowing her mother, she had a pretty good idea where and when her father would hear about the encounter on the track.

There followed several hours where staff and old friends welcomed Maddie home as she did the rounds of the massive castle, greeting people she had known for years. First and foremost, of course, was her father. Horace swept her off her feet in a massive bear hug as she dismounted in the courtyard, holding her well off the ground and spinning her round, saying her name over and over.

Finally, having greeted just about everyone, with the exception of her grandfather, King Duncan, she and her parents retired to their apartment in the central keep tower for a private family dinner.

"You can say hello to Father tomorrow," Cassandra told her. "He's very weak these days, and he's resting."

"I had hoped he might be feeling better," Maddie said, sadness touching her voice.

But Horace shook his head. "He's not recovering at all. He's getting worse each day. I'm glad you came home. This could be your last chance to see him."

She felt tears burning against the back of her eyes. She had known for some time that Duncan's health was deteriorating—which was why her mother had assumed the role of Regent in his name. But recognizing that they could soon lose him saddened her immensely. She was quiet for a few minutes, dealing with the knowledge.

Horace put his arm gently around her shoulders. "But you're home now, and who's to say he won't make a recovery," he said.

She forced the tears back and managed a smile. She was genuinely delighted to see her parents once more and looked forward to exchanging stories with her father—and finding out more about his and Gilan's planned expedition to deal with the mysterious Red Fox Clan. In the back of her mind, she was already scheming to see if she could accompany them.

They sat down to one of her favorite meals—slow-roasted lamb shoulder, flavored with rosemary and wild garlic, accompanied by crisp-roasted potatoes and steamed greens. The richly flavored meat had been roasting in a covered iron camp kettle for almost three hours, and it simply fell from the bone as she plunged her knife and eating fork into it.

"Mmm. That's good," she said. "That's as good as Jenny makes it."

Her mother smiled. She had actually prepared the meal herself. "It's Jenny's recipe," she said. "But I'm glad you approve of my cooking."

They ate in pleasurable silence for several minutes, and then Horace set down his eating implements and studied his daughter. She looked older, he thought, and then realized that she *was* older—and that at her age, a year was a relatively large amount of time. She looked fit and healthy, and there was a new air of confidence about her—one that he approved of. Unlike his wife, he was more than happy that Maddie was training as a Ranger. She was learning tactical and strategic skills, and the ability to analyze a situation quickly and intelligently, which would come in handy when she finally took the throne.

"So, what have you been up to?" he asked.

Instantly, Cassandra unleashed a pent-up torrent of words. "What has she been up to? I'll tell you! She was set upon by robbers barely a half day's ride from here! Attacked, and had to fight for her life. We're lucky to have her with us still, and it's your fault!"

"My fault?" Horace said mildly.

She nodded vigorously, pointing an accusing fork in his direction so that he recoiled slightly. "Your fault for encouraging her to go ahead with this Ranger business, instead of staying safe at home with us!"

He looked at her steadily until she subsided, a little red-faced and embarrassed by her outburst.

"So what happened?" he asked Maddie.

"It was nothing, Dad, really. They were three clumsy thugs who tried to hold us up. I took one down with my sling, Ingrid brained the second and Bumper took care of the third."

"Then what did you do with them?"

Maddie shrugged. "We tied them up and handed them off to a manor lord along the way—a Sir Gerald Something-or-Other."

"That'd be Sir Gerald Wollden," Horace said. "I'll send him a note of thanks." Then he grinned. "You say Ingrid brained one?"

Maddie returned the smile. "With her riding crop. Knocked him cross-eyed with the hilt."

Horace looked impressed. "Well, good for her." He caught Cassandra's eye and nodded toward the platter of lamb. "I wonder, could you serve me a couple more slices?" he said. "It's very good."

Cassandra sighed and shook her head at his total lack of concern.

"You're obviously not a mother," she said.

Horace raised his eyebrows. "Thank goodness for that."

8

THE FOLLOWING DAY, CASSANDRA HOSTED A FAIR IN THE
parklands outside the castle walls so that the entire district
could welcome Maddie home properly. All of the castle staff
were there, along with those of the guards who were off duty,
and the residents of the local village, who turned out en masse.
In addition, local nobles and other villagers from ten kilometers
around made the journey to Castle Araluen for the big day.

They weren't disappointed, even though some of them
walked all the way to get there. There were massive cooking pits,
full of glowing charcoal, with lambs, boar and sides of beef turning slowly on spits over them, operated by muscular, sweating
castle kitchen staff, who paused in their labor only long enough
to allow the cook's apprentices to slice juicy pieces of roasted
meat from the outside of the slowly turning carcasses. A few
meters away, racks of brown, crusty pastries and pies were on
offer as well.

There were stalls selling fruit and brightly colored puddings
for those with a sweet tooth, and barrels of wine and ale were
propped up on trestles to ease the collective thirst. For the
younger attendees, there was lemon-flavored water, sweetened

with sugar—a rare treat for many of the village children, and one that they took full advantage of.

There was entertainment as well, with jugglers, acrobats, jongleurs and musicians scattered at intervals throughout the park. And, of course, there was the usual array of sideshows and stalls offering tests of skill, such as hoopla, where a careful observer might have noticed that the wooden hoops looked suspiciously smaller than the prizes they had to be thrown over to win. Apples floated in a barrel for people to dunk for, blowing bubbles and snorting water as they attempted to secure one of the slippery, bobbing pieces of fruit from the water, often immersing their entire head in the barrel as a result.

Young men from the village could test their strength against a huge, heavily muscled bald man in a ragged leopard-skin loincloth. They would sit on opposite sides of a bench and arm-wrestle him. But he was a cunning competitor, with skill exceeding even his brute strength, and a sense of timing that invariably allowed him to launch the first attack in the contest. He rarely lost.

A Punch-and-Judy tent provided shamefully violent entertainment for the younger children, who shrieked with laughter as Judy belabored her unfortunate husband with a cudgel made of layers of split wood, which gave off a very satisfying *CRACK!* whenever she made contact.

More shrieks came from a stall where older children were invited to pin the tail on a donkey. The contestants found it more entertaining to peek below their blindfold and stab the pin violently into the oversize backside of the fat knight who was leading the donkey in the colorful illustration. One contestant, overcome with the spirit of the whole thing, managed to shove her pin into the behind of the unfortunate carnival worker who was running the stall. More shrieks greeted that effort, including a very loud one from the victim, who didn't see it coming.

Among the visiting noblemen and knights, Horace spied Sir Gerald Wollden of Tonbridge Manor. He approached the elderly knight and nodded a friendly greeting.

"Sir Gerald," he said, "I owe you my thanks for assisting my daughter."

Sir Gerald, who had just bitten into a hot pie, held up a hand in apology as he negotiated the hot meat and gravy and the delicious, flaky pastry. He gulped, burning his tongue and the roof of his mouth as he swallowed the mouthful, then had to take a deep draft on the tankard of ale he held in his left hand before he could reply.

"Your pardon, my lord!" he mumbled, wiping his mouth with the back of his hand.

Horace smiled and waited patiently. He'd had no intention of embarrassing the older knight. "Take your time, Sir Gerald. There's no rush," he said easily.

Sir Gerald swallowed another mouthful of ale to cool his scalded mouth, then made a small bobbing movement that was halfway between a bow and a curtsey.

"I meant to say, my lord, I was delighted to be of service to Princess Madelyn," he finally managed to enunciate.

Horace gave him moment or two to settle down before continuing. "If you like, I'll send some men to take those ruffians off your hands. I wouldn't want you burdened with them."

"No burden, my lord. They're more than earning their way. We have a lot of heavy laboring that needs doing round the village, and they're taking care of it. My people are enjoying having their services available. Only this morning, they cleaned out the cesspit by the inn. Hasn't been done for some time, and my villagers were happy to have somebody else do it for them."

Horace had been impressed by Maddie's intelligent solution to the matter of punishment for the would-be robbers. Far better to have them performing menial and necessary tasks round the village than undergo the more drastic punishment of hanging or removing a hand from the guilty party.

"Very well," he said. "But make sure you let me know if they become a nuisance—or if you run out of cesspits to empty."

"I'll do that, my lord," Sir Gerald replied, taking another bite of his pie, which had cooled sufficiently to make that a more comfortable matter.

Horace reached out and touched his forearm. "No need to 'my lord' me, Sir Gerald," he said. "I'm no lord. I'm a simple knight like yourself. You can address me as Sir Horace."

Horace was a staunch egalitarian. He had no use for high-flying titles that he considered he hadn't earned.

Sir Gerald nodded several times. "Yes, my l— . . . Yes, Sir Horace," he amended. He found it difficult to believe that a man married to the future queen of the realm wouldn't adorn himself with titles and decorations. But he'd heard that Sir Horace was, at heart, a simple, unassuming man. Unassuming, perhaps, but still the deadliest knight in the kingdom.

Horace nodded and moved off. He'd seen Maddie through the crowd, heading for the archery range at the foot of the slope, where the ground leveled out and allowed room for targets and butts to be set up.

Maddie had paid the stallkeeper a five-pennig piece for three shots and was studying the bows and arrows available for use with a critical eye. Several of the bow limbs were warped, the weapons being not much better than the one that had been used to threaten her the previous day. The arrows were missing fletching—most of them had only two vanes attached, and many of the shafts were twisted.

Most of those paying to compete didn't seem to notice. Their eyes were on the array of rich prizes that were available for a good score.

Bows twanged and arrows skittered off toward the targets thirty meters away. Many of the arrows twisted in flight and slid past to impact the straw bales acting as a backstop behind the targets. Others plunged downward after only a few meters, burying their points in the soft turf. The married couple running the stall looked highly pleased with the results so far. No good archer would attempt to shoot with the shoddy bows they had on offer, which meant their customers were all people who knew little or nothing about archery.

Maddie selected a bow that had more or less even limbs, with only a slight warp in the lower one. She scanned the arrows on offer, and quickly chose three that were almost straight and had full sets of flights. She tested the draw weight to the bow. It couldn't have been more than thirty pounds. She'd need to aim high over a thirty-meter range. She set an arrow on the string.

"Three arrows in the red circle to win a prize, my lady," said the stallkeeper's wife. The red circle was the innermost circle of the target.

"Don't show off," said a voice close by.

She turned and saw her father standing just behind her.

"Remember," he continued, "you're supposed to be a helpless

young maiden, not a dead shot."

She smiled lazily. Then, barely seeming to aim, she drew and shot in one clean movement. The arrow thudded into the center of the red circle.

"Oooh! I hit it! I hit it!" she squealed in what she imagined sounded like girlish excitement, dropping the bow and clapping her hands with joy.

Horace raised his eyes to heaven. "Ham," he said softly.

She grinned at him and took up her second arrow, noting that while she had been looking away, the stallkeeper had substituted a very warped example in place of the shaft she'd selected. She nocked and drew back, holding the bow awkwardly and pinching the nock of the arrow between her forefinger and thumb. She let her bow hand waver with the strain, frowned heavily and aimed for a dead-center shot, trusting that the arrow would never manage such a result.

She shot. The arrow flipped away, twisting in the air so that it flashed past the right side of the target, burying its head in the wall of straw bales behind it.

"Oooh! I missed!'" she squealed in disappointment. Horace rolled his eyes again. "Is there a prize for hitting the hay bales?" she asked hopefully.

"Three arrows in the red circle for a prize, my lady," intoned the stallkeeper's wife stolidly. Surreptitiously, her husband was reaching for the remaining straight arrow, hoping to substitute another bent shaft. Without seeming to notice, Maddie reached down and picked up the arrow before he could take it. Smoothly, she nocked it and shot. This time, the arrow thudded into the red circle—of the target next to hers. She turned a winning smile on the stallkeeper.

"Is that worth anything?" she asked.

He shook his head. "Three arrows in your own red circle for a prize, my lady," he said, offering her three more shafts. "Care to buy another three?"

She shook her head. "I think I had beginner's luck," she said, smiling sweetly. "And the bows seem awfully dangerous."

Beside her, Horace groaned. She gave him a conspiratorial smile, and they walked away, arm in arm, heading back up the slope toward the castle. The afternoon was drawing on, and the shadows were growing longer. There was a cool nip in the air as well.

"Enjoying yourself?" he asked.

She nodded. "Yes. It's fine to see everyone again. A lot of old faces I've been missing." She looked around the crowded park, smiling happily. She knew that in a couple of days, she would become bored with the restrictions of castle life and her position, and be longing for the freedom and activity of life as a Ranger. But for now, she was content.

"You look as if you've used a bow before," a voice said behind her.

She turned to see the speaker and was pleasantly surprised. He was in his mid-twenties, tall and lean, with broad shoulders. He was clean-shaven, with a strong, square jaw, straight nose and even, white teeth—which she could see because he was smiling. He was handsome, undoubtedly so. His hair was dark blond and slightly shorter than was fashionable. His eyes were clear blue, with a mischievous twinkle to them. It was that, she thought, more than anything else that made him attractive. She noticed he was dressed in the uniform of the palace guard—a captain, judging by the silver rank insignia on his right shoulder.

Instinctively, she liked him.

"Just luck," she said, returning the smile. "Beginner's luck."

He cocked his head to one side, and those eyes told her he didn't believe her but he'd let her get away with the pretense.

"If you say so." He nodded a respectful greeting to Horace. "Good afternoon, Sir Horace," he said. "I take it this is the Princess Madelyn we've been waiting for?"

"Afternoon, Dimon," Horace replied. "Yes, this is her. Maddie, this is Dimon, one of our brighter young officers. Dimon, this is Princess Madelyn."

Dimon came to attention and bowed his head briefly in her direction. Maddie was pleased he didn't perform an elaborate sweeping bow with one leg pushed forward and his arm tracing a half circle in the air. She was always vaguely suspicious of such overblown actions.

"Delighted to meet you, Your Highness," he said. His eyes continued to twinkle, as if he were sharing some secret joke with her. His manner was friendly but respectful. He wasn't overawed by her rank or the presence of her father. She liked that. Dimon was obviously a young man confident in his own abilities.

"Call me Maddie," she said, inclining her head to him in return. "All my friends do."

"Then I'm pleased to be included among them," he said. "I hope I'll see more of you while you're back with us."

"I'm sure you will," Maddie said.

Horace had been eyeing the two of them during all this. They were obviously attracted to each other. Not surprising, he thought. They were both attractive young people. He felt a surge of fatherly protectiveness. He hadn't had to deal with Maddie and boys before. It was a new experience for him.

"Perhaps Dimon will find time to take you hunting while I'm gone," he said.

"I'll make time," the young captain said. "I'm eager to see you shoot again—with a decent bow next time."

"That first shot was the merest fluke," she said. "Actually, I prefer the sling as a weapon."

Dimon nodded reflectively. "Like your mother," he said. "I hear she's an excellent shot."

"I'm better," said Maddie boldly. "But then, I have more time to practice. I'm not busy running a kingdom."

"I hope to see you demonstrate your skill," Dimon said. He looked to Horace. "If you'll excuse me, sir, I'm on duty at the fourth hour, so I'd better get back to the castle. Princess Maddie," he said, "I'll be seeing you again."

"I look forward to it," Maddie told him.

Dimon turned and strode away toward the castle, his long legs eating up the distance. Maddie looked at her father, noticing the slightly bewildered look on his face.

"He's nice," she said. "Where did he come from? I don't remember him."

"He joined us about six months ago," Horace told her. "He's very bright. He's already been promoted twice."

"Will he be going with you and Gilan?"

"No," her father said. "He'll be here in command of the garrison."

Maddie's smile widened. "Good," she said.

9

THERE WAS A LOT OF CATCHING UP FOR MADDIE TO DO OVER the next few days. First and foremost, she wanted to see her grandfather. He was in a sunny room on the fourth floor, where he stayed bedridden for most of each day. She checked with the medical orderly on duty in his anteroom to make sure he was awake and she wouldn't be disturbing him. Then she tapped lightly on the door and entered.

She was shocked at how old he looked. Duncan had always been a big, cheerful presence, with a personality that seemed to fill any room he was in. But the weight had fallen off him so that he was a shadow of his former robust self. His cheeks were hollow, and his eyes were sunken in his face. And his hair, which she remembered as a distinguished salt-and-pepper color, was now white.

But the smile was the same. He was delighted to see her. They had always been close. She perched on the edge of his bed and they talked for an hour or so. He quizzed her keenly about her training and her progress in the Ranger Corps. She discovered that he heartily approved of her decision to stay with Will after her first year.

"You'll rule this country one day," he told her. "Your time as a Ranger will be more use to you than any amount of needlework and ladylike skills. You'll need to be able to lead men, to command in battles and to plan strategy. Nothing will teach you that better than Ranger training."

Duncan had a high regard for Will and Halt. Halt, of course, had been one of the first Rangers to support him in his battle with Morgarath long ago. And Will, as an apprentice, had been instrumental in foiling Morgarath's final attempt at taking the throne.

She spent a pleasant hour with him, regaling him with tales of her adventures with Will—of brigands and highwaymen outwitted and captured, and Hibernian pirates who insisted on using the west coast of the kingdom as a sanctuary from their own officials, and who had to be discouraged from time to time. She told the stories with a rich vein of self-deprecating humor and was pleased to see the light in her grandfather's eye and hear his deep laughter as she made herself the butt of many of the stories.

Eventually, she noticed that he was tiring. He smothered a yawn once or twice, and she realized she should let him rest. She kissed him lightly on the forehead and took her leave. As she reached the door, he called her and she turned back. He waved a hand at her.

"Thanks for coming, Maddie. Come again anytime."

"I will, Grandpa," she promised. Then his eyes slid shut and his breathing became deep and regular.

Back in the royal apartments, she found a brief note from Gilan.

Riding kit. Stables. Eleventh hour.

She glanced at the water clock set by the window and realized she had less than ten minutes before the deadline he had set. She quickly changed into riding gear—as befitted Princess Madelyn, not Ranger Maddie—and made her way down the stairs in a rush, erupting from the main doorway into the courtyard and running full tilt across the cobbles to the large stable building.

Gilan was waiting for her in the dim, shady interior. She noticed with some surprise that he had Sundancer and Bumper both saddled, along with Blaze, his own Ranger horse.

He gestured for her to mount Sundancer and swung up easily into Blaze's saddle. Bumper, ears pricked and alert, followed them as they trotted out of the stables and across the courtyard.

"Where are we going?" she asked.

Gilan held a finger to his lips in a signal for silence. "When we're outside," he said.

They trotted across the drawbridge, the hooves of their horses clopping and clattering in their three separate rhythms. Then Gilan swung southwest.

"I thought you'd want to ride Bumper while you're here," he said.

She nodded confirmation of the fact. "Of course."

Once they were in the trees and hidden from the castle, she switched horses, swinging into Bumper's saddle with a satisfied sigh. She had missed her horse over the past few days.

"Right," Gilan continued. "Well, we could hardly have people querying why you'd ride such a scruffy little barrel when you had a perfectly good Arridan at your disposal." He nodded toward Sundancer. True to his name, the Arridan's glossy coat gleamed in the late morning sun.

Bumper snorted indignantly. *Scruffy little barrel indeed!*

Gilan turned and looked suspiciously at him. Like all Rangers, he talked to his horse and believed the horse talked back. But like all Rangers, he never mentioned it to anyone else, and he wondered if other Rangers and their horses had the same communication. He suspected that Maddie and Bumper did, but it would never do to ask.

"So?" Maddie said, prompting him. She'd noticed he was distracted from his train of thought, but didn't know why. He recovered himself hastily.

"So I've arranged for a farmer and his wife who live nearby to keep Bumper in their barn while you're here. You can ride out to their farm on Sundancer, switch horses and explore the district on Bumper."

She grinned, delighted by the idea. She had been wondering how she would spend time riding Bumper while she was here. As he'd said, it would appear suspicious if she ignored her supposedly superior Arridan to ride what appeared to be a shaggy pack pony.

"Who's this farming couple?" she asked.

"Warwick is a little more than a farmer," Gilan said. "He's actually one of my intelligence agents, and he keeps an eye on things in the area, lets me know if anything suspicious is going on. He's a very useful fellow. Louise, his wife, is a skillful observer as well." He paused a few seconds, then added, "They know you're with the Corps, but they'll never tell anyone."

"Interesting," she said. She'd suspected that Gilan had a network of agents keeping him informed. But this was the first time she'd had the suspicion confirmed.

Five minutes later, they reached the farm, and as they rode

into the home yard, Warwick and Louise hurried out to greet them.

If Maddie had had any preformed idea about what a secret agent looked like, Warwick definitely didn't fit it. He was short and stocky, in his mid- to late thirties, with a cheery, welcoming grin that seemed to be always present on his face. His eyes crinkled above the smile, and above that he was completely bald on top, with only a fringe of brown hair around his ears and the lower back of his head. He looked very fit and moved with an obvious agility. His forearms, bare beneath the short sleeves of his linen shirt, were thick with muscle.

His wife was a few centimeters taller than him, slim and darkly pretty. She had a lazy, knowing smile that constantly touched the corners of her mouth. Her dark eyes looked steadily at Maddie as she studied her. The younger girl guessed it would take a lot to surprise Louise.

"Louise, Warwick, this is Maddie, the fellow Ranger I spoke to you about," Gilan said.

Warwick gestured for Maddie to dismount. Good manners dictated that one always waited to be invited to do so. She swung down from Bumper's saddle and Gilan did likewise.

"Welcome to our farm, Maddie," said Warwick, his grin wide and friendly. He reached up and rubbed Bumper's soft nose gently. "And I'm guessing this is Bumper?"

Bumper tossed his head at the sound of his name. Warwick laughed and reached into a pocket to produce a carrot, which he fed to the little horse from the flattened palm of his hand. Bumper crunched the vegetable, then swung his eyes to Maddie.

I like this one.

And that was enough for Maddie. The surest way to her

heart was to win over her horse, which Warwick had done easily. She smiled at him.

"You've made a new friend," she said.

Warwick nodded happily. "He's a beauty," he said. "Reckon he could run all the day if you asked him."

"And half the night," Maddie agreed.

"I'll unsaddle him and settle him in the barn," Warwick told her. "Lou has some coffee just made. Go on into the house and have a cup."

"Never been known to refuse." Gilan grinned. "Lou makes great coffee."

Maddie tethered Sundancer to a post by the front door of the farmhouse. Blaze, of course, didn't need to be secured. She would wait patiently for Gilan, with her reins dropped loosely onto the ground before her. They entered the farmhouse, Maddie blinking in the sudden dimness after the bright sunshine outside.

It was a typical small farm building, with the ground floor divided into areas for eating, cooking and relaxing. A short ladder led to an upper loft, which Maddie assumed was their bedroom.

The rooms were furnished with simple but well-made furniture. Two comfortable-looking wooden armchairs were set on either side of the fireplace, with thick cushions in place to soften the hardwood seats. There was a small dining table, with benches on either side to seat four people. Louise led them to this now and gestured for them to sit. She fetched the coffeepot from the edge of the fire and poured them a mug each. Then she pushed a pot of honey forward.

"I know you Rangers have a sweet tooth," she said with a smile.

Maddie returned the smile and helped herself to a generous dollop of honey in the steaming, fragrant coffee. She took a sip. Gilan was right. The woman made excellent coffee.

A few minutes later, Warwick rejoined them. He patted Maddie's arm. "Your boy is settled in nicely, with a big bin of oats and some fresh water. He's looking very happy."

"And you can come and see him anytime you like," Louise added. "Stay the night if you want to."

"Thanks," Maddie told them. "It's nice to know he's in good hands."

"Oh yes, oh yes," said Warwick, rubbing his hands together. "We like Ranger horses on this farm." He took a sip of the coffee Lou had poured for him and smacked his lips in appreciation. "Good brew, Lou," he said. Then he laughed. "I made a rhyme!"

"We noticed," Lou said dryly. But she gave him an affectionate look all the same.

"So, Warwick," Gilan said, "has anything been going on in the area?" Warwick gathered his thoughts before he spoke. Maddie noticed that the easy grin disappeared from his face as he did. This was official, she realized.

"They say there've been lights up in that old abbey again," he said. "I've been out several times to check, but they've never been there when I've been watching."

"Are your informants reliable?" Gilan asked.

Warwick shifted on his bench. "I wouldn't say they were totally reliable," he said. "But they've mentioned it several times over the past month. There may be something going on."

"Or nothing," Lou put in cynically. "People can talk themselves into seeing things, and seeing lights in an old building can easily be a trick of the moonlight."

Gilan rubbed his chin. "Possibly," he said. "Or maybe travelers passing through have been sheltering there. But keep an eye on it anyway. If you get definite news of something odd while I'm away, pass the news on to Maddie here."

Maddie looked at him in some surprise. He saw the look and shrugged.

"You're a fourth-year apprentice now. I trust your judgment and Will says you're more than capable of handling tricky situations. In fact, I've been planning to ask you to keep an eye on the fief while I'm away. Maybe patrol the area two or three times a week." He switched his gaze to Warwick. "But if you do see something up there, don't go and investigate by yourself. I don't want you taking risks."

Warwick looked serious for a moment, and then the grin spread across his face again. "You don't want me taking risks, but you'd send a slip of a girl up there to investigate?"

Gilan nodded seriously. "This 'slip of a girl,' as you call her, can knock the eyeballs out of a gnat with her sling without even having to think about it."

Warwick regarded her with new respect, as did Lou. Maddie felt herself reddening.

"That might be a bit of an exaggeration," she said. "I can really only knock the head off a gnat. We don't do eyeballs until fifth year."

"I find that more believable," Lou said, with a slow smile. "Anyone for more coffee?"

10

ON THE WAY HOME, THEY PASSED THE TRAINING GROUND where the cavalry were exercising their remounts. Each trooper traveling with Horace and Gilan would take two horses, so that the troop could travel more quickly without tiring the horses unduly. As Horace had observed, the bulk of the herd had been out to grass for several months and had been skittish about being saddled and ridden once more. The troopers were getting them accustomed to the necessary discipline.

"Looks like they're nearly ready," Maddie remarked. Gilan nodded, eyeing the horses as they formed fours and then an extended line, then went to a trot, increasing tempo to a canter and then a full gallop while maintaining their formation.

A few of the horses still shied and tugged at the reins, tossing their heads against the restricting bits. But overall, they were well behaved. After all, you never wanted a cavalry horse to become too docile. A bit of wildness could be a good thing.

"So you'll be leaving tomorrow?" Maddie said. There was a note of wistfulness in her voice.

Gilan turned his attention from the horses to her.

"Mid-morning," he said. "That'll give us time to get well on the way before we camp for the night."

"Don't suppose I could go with you," she said a little plaintively. "I could be quite useful, you know."

"Yes, you could. And no, you can't," Gilan replied, smiling. "I don't want your mother mounting my head on a spike over the battlements. You're here to see her. Not to come traipsing off with us to the northern part of the fief."

"I'm here to see Dad as well," she said. But her halfhearted tone said she knew she was arguing in vain.

"And you'll see him when we come back. We should only be a couple of weeks. Besides, I'll feel better knowing you're looking after things here."

"You're not just saying that to make me feel better about staying here?"

He shook his head firmly. "I don't do that. And I meant what I said. You're going into your fourth year of training. You should be able to cope with anything that crops up." Not that he expected anything out of the ordinary. Araluen was a well-organized, well-disciplined fief, as befitted the seat of the capital. But you never could be sure, as the incident with the three brigands had indicated.

"Don't worry. You'll have plenty to do to keep you busy," he said. "And if you get bored, you could always spend your time trying to find the old secret tunnels in the castle."

Maddie pricked up her ears at that. "Tunnels? What tunnels?"

He waved a hand vaguely in the air. "Oh, possibly just rumor and old wives' tales," he said. "The castle is supposed to be honeycombed with tunnels and secret stairways behind the walls. Duncan's grandfather was reputed to have a secret exit that led under the moat. He apparently used to pop out secretly to visit his girlfriend in the village. That was before he was married, of course," he added, in a very proper tone.

Maddie said nothing further. But she was thoughtful for the rest of the ride home. Secret tunnels and stairways sounded like a fascinating subject to explore. Gilan noticed her preoccupation and smiled at her. He'd known that mention of secret tunnels would fire her imagination. She was a Ranger, after all, and Rangers had an active curiosity and interest in such matters.

The small force left the following morning, as Gilan had predicted. Maddie and Cassandra both embraced Horace and Gilan, and stood by the portcullis gate as the horsemen and archers filed through in pairs. Each pair nodded a salute to Cassandra as they passed, and she favored them all with a brilliant smile. Maddie, watching her, realized how popular she was with her soldiers—probably as a result of her background as a fighter and adventurer herself. They respected her courage and her fighting ability, and her grasp of tactics and strategy. They knew she would never set them a task they couldn't perform.

The two women watched as the small force disappeared into the tree line at the bottom of the hill. For a few moments, a slight haze of dust marked where they had passed, and then the breeze dispersed it and all was silent.

"Well, that's that," Cassandra said, and turned to go back into the castle keep.

"I suppose you're used to seeing Dad ride off to battle," Maddie said as they strolled back across the cobbles. She knew that Horace had ridden out many times over the years to suppress local rebellions or hunt down bands of robbers and outlaws.

Cassandra nodded. "Used to it. But I never like it."

"He can look after himself," Maddie said. After all, she knew her father was the foremost knight in the kingdom. His achievements and abilities were legendary.

"I know," her mother replied. "But there's always the chance something can go wrong—a broken stirrup leather or a loose saddle girth, for example. Some things are outside his control."

Maddie's expression grew worried. "Thanks," she said. "You've just ruined my day for me."

Cassandra smiled. Her negative frame of mind was more the result of knowing she would miss Horace over the next few weeks. The two were very much in love. And in truth, she knew he could look after himself, broken stirrups or saddle girths notwithstanding.

"He'll be fine, don't worry," she said reassuringly. "I'm just a little blue because he's going. And besides, he has Gilan to look after him." Conscious of the need to keep her daughter occupied, knowing that palace life could become boring and restrictive for her, she added casually, "I have a session with Maikeru in fifteen minutes. Care to come and watch?"

"I'd love to," Maddie said enthusiastically. "Dad said he's remarkable, and I've never seen a Nihon-Jan swordsman in action."

When Cassandra had first visited Nihon-Ja, the Emperor had been fascinated by the fact that both she and Alyss, Will's future wife, were trained in swordsmanship, arming themselves with lightweight sabers. There was no tradition of female

warriors in Nihon-Ja, and the Emperor, Shigeru, had decided
that perhaps it might be a good thing if there were. The Emperor
had sensed that the Nihon-Jan form of swordsmanship, which
relied on speed and agility more than brute force, might well be
suited to a woman's abilities.

Cassandra and Horace, of course, had a large estate in
Nihon-Ja, a wedding gift from the Emperor. But with Duncan
ill, they had not had an opportunity to visit their lands in the
far-distant kingdom for many years. To make up for their inabil-
ity to travel, and knowing Cassandra's interest in martial arts,
two years ago the Emperor had decided to send Maikeru to her.

Maikeru was a slightly built, wiry man. There wasn't an
ounce of fat on his body. His hair was gray and he was obviously
in his sixties. Yet he moved lightly and without difficulty, and
his swordplay was a wonder to behold.

"I bring you two gifts from Emperor Shigeru," he'd said
when he first met Cassandra. He had held out a long parcel
wrapped in oilcloth.

She had stepped forward to take it from him and unwrap the
oilskin. Inside was a Nihon-Jan *katana*, the long sword favored
by the Senshi warriors of the sunrise land. It was sheathed in a
beautifully lacquered black scabbard of polished wood, inlaid
with mother-of-pearl shell. The blade, when she withdrew it,
had a blue tinge to it, and curving lines along its length, showing
where several rods of iron had been beaten together, shaped and
tempered by a master swordsmith. It had a single edge, which
was sharper than the sharpest razor, and a two-handed handle
with a small, flat rectangular crosspiece to protect the user's
hands. It was somewhat shorter than a conventional Araluen
cavalry sword, and much lighter to wield. But the blade was far

harder than any in the kingdom, save for the saxe knives carried by Rangers or the sword Horace wore—which had itself been fashioned by a Nihon-Jan craftsman many years before.

"This is beautiful," she had said, sliding the blade back into its scabbard and looking around curiously. There had been nothing else in the oilskin package. "But you said two gifts. Where is the second?"

"I am the second," Maikeru said gravely, inclining his head to her. "I am a Swordmaster of the fourth rank, and my lord Shigeru has charged me with the task of teaching you the use of the *katana*."

Cassandra had been startled by the statement. "But it can take years to master the *katana*."

Again, Maikeru had bowed to her. "Then I will remain here until you are skilled," he said.

And so Cassandra had begun her instruction under the amazing Swordmaster, learning the cuts and thrusts, when to retreat, when to attack, how to face an Araluen swordsman armed with sword and shield, how to use speed and cunning to defeat a more powerful warrior. She was an apt student, and Maikeru was pleased with her dedication and her progress.

He was made welcome by Cassandra and Horace, as well as Gilan and the other warriors in the castle, and became a valued and respected member of the Araluen court. Several of the more mature ladies of the court, most of them widows, found his upright bearing, impeccable manners and formal approach to be more than a little attractive. Maikeru had left behind no family in Nihon-Ja. His wife had passed away many years before, and they had no children. His loyalty was to Emperor Shigeru—but, gradually, he transferred that to the slim princess who ruled the island kingdom. And, as the first year turned into the second, Maikeru began to think of Araluen as his home.

Maikeru spent time each day with Cassandra—her other duties permitting—instructing her in the use of the *katana* and improving her technique. Now, she would be capable of holding her own with all but the finest swordsmen in Nihon-Ja.

Today, she was to practice with Dimon, as Maikeru dictated that she must learn to fight against a style dissimilar to her own. Dimon was a capable swordsman—not as skilled as Horace or Gilan, but a good match for her and a good training partner who would not feel it necessary to hold back. For the bout, they met in the armory hall—a long, bare room on the first floor of the keep. One wall was lined with tall windows that let the daylight flood into the room, providing excellent lighting for the practice bouts that were held here. There were tiered benches along the opposite wall, and Maddie found a seat there.

Her mother was donning her padded practice jacket and protective leather helmet when Dimon arrived, similarly attired. He selected a wooden practice sword and shield from the rack and walked over to greet Maddie, smiling. Cassandra was armed with a wooden weapon, shaped like her *katana* and replicating its weight and balance.

"Nice to see you again," he said.

Maddie returned the smile. Dimon had been on duty since the day of the fair, and they hadn't seen each other in the intervening days—save for the occasional quick, friendly nod as they passed.

"Good to see you," she said.

"I have the day off tomorrow," he said. "Would you like to go hunting?"

"That'd be great," she said.

His smile widened. "I'm keen to see how you manage a proper bow."

"I told you," she replied, "my weapon of choice is the sling." She frowned slightly, looking at the shield on his left arm. "Speaking of weapons, isn't my mother at a disadvantage here? She doesn't have a shield."

"So she has less to carry," he said.

But Maddie turned to Maikeru and called out across the hall. "Maikeru-san, my mother has no shield. This isn't an even match."

She was concerned that Cassandra might be hurt. She knew Dimon was an excellent swordsman and it seemed that he had an advantage over Cassandra's slim, wooden practice *katana*.

Maikeru crossed the hall, his thin slippers whispering on the timber floor, scarred and marked by generations of practice weapons that had missed their mark and rebounded off the floorboards. He stopped a few meters away from Maddie and bowed briefly.

"Your mother has a shield," he said. "You just can't see it. It is half a sword length in front of her and is activated by the movement of her *katana*."

Maddie frowned, not understanding.

Dimon, who had been through this exercise before with Cassandra, smiled encouragingly. "Wait and see," he said.

"If you injure my mum," she said, "I won't go hunting with you tomorrow."

Dimon acknowledged the statement with a shake of his head. "If I injure your mum, I won't be going anywhere tomorrow myself."

Maikeru motioned the two combatants to the center of the hall. They faced each other and took up their respective positions. Dimon had his shield raised and his sword projecting halfway over the top of it. Cassandra faced him, her feet widely spaced, her *katana* held back over her right shoulder.

Maikeru had a wooden rod in his hand. He began tapping it on the floor in a steady rhythm. Then he called:

"Commence!"

11

Maikeru continued to tap his wooden rod on the floor. Maddie realized he was setting a tempo for the practice bout. Suddenly, Dimon took a half pace forward and darted his sword out at Cassandra, chest high.

Cassandra brought her sword forward and moved its tip in a small circle, catching the blade of Dimon's weapon and deflecting it to one side with the circular motion.

Recovering quickly, Dimon lunged once more. The *katana* moved in the opposite direction now, deflecting his wooden blade to the other side. Then, as he was slightly off balance, Cassandra leapt forward and delivered three rapid cuts at him. He took the first two on his shield, then narrowly managed to block the third, a horizontal sweep at thigh level, with his own sword.

The crack of their swords as they came together echoed in the armory hall. They stepped apart, resumed their ready positions and eyed each other carefully.

Maikeru increased the tempo with the wooden rod on the floor. "Begin!" he said.

This time Cassandra was the first to attack. She swept

forward, her wooden blade flashing in the air. A series of staccato *CRACKS!* marked its impact with Dimon's sword and shield. The young warrior backed away, defending desperately against the ever-changing direction and blurring speed of Cassandra's onslaught. Cassandra pursued him down the length of the armory hall, their feet shuffling and squeaking on the floorboards.

But even though she was driving Dimon back, she could find no gap in his defenses. His sword or shield blocked her cuts—overhead, side on, and even sweeping up from knee height. Sometimes he only managed to get his sword or shield into position at the last moment—but he managed nevertheless.

Cassandra, knowing that speed was her best weapon, continued the assault, searching for an opening, seeking a relaxation in his defense. She didn't find one.

Eventually, Maikeru cried, "Enough!"

The two combatants lowered their swords and stepped back. Both were breathing heavily from their exertions, and from the flood of adrenaline that coursed through their bodies. They eyed each other balefully. There was no room for friendship in this contest. They were practicing for war. The time might come when such a competition was a matter of life and death. Maikeru had dinned into their brains the basic message of weapons practice.

"Practice as you mean to fight," he had told them. No quarter. No sporting gestures. Just a single-minded dedication to winning the bout. Here, losing might mean a painful bruise. In a real battle, the result would be death.

"Come," Maikeru said to them, pointing to the floor in front of him.

They made their way back from the end of the hall, where Cassandra had driven Dimon, and stood attentively before him. Cassandra wiped perspiration from her forehead with the sleeve of her padded jacket. The jacket was stained and grimy, and Maddie wondered if the armorers ever thought to launder them.

Maikeru frowned, studying the princess for several seconds, then spoke. "Your speed is excellent. You gave your opponent no time to begin his own attack."

Dimon nodded agreement. "She's wickedly fast. Several times there, I barely managed to get my sword or shield in position in time."

Maikeru looked at him, his dark eyes steady and unblinking. "Yet manage you did," he said simply, and Dimon shrugged. The Swordmaster turned his attention back to Cassandra.

"You see, my lady," he said, "your speed is your best weapon. But the longer a combat lasts, the more it will be reduced. You become tired. Your arms are heavy. The *katana*, once so light and easy to wield, begins to weigh down your arms so that the muscles ache." He paused and raised an interrogative eyebrow at her.

"That's a pretty good description of the way I feel," she admitted.

He nodded. "Your speed and agility are not infinite resources," he said. "They only serve you for a certain time. Then they begin to deteriorate. And *then*," he emphasized the word heavily, "your opponent's greater strength and force become the dominant factors in your fight."

Cassandra frowned. "But—"

Maikeru held up his hand to stop her. "When you are facing a skilled opponent like Dimon-san, you must find a way to end the bout quickly. Before his advantages—his weight, his strength and his power—become the dominant ones."

"Well, I was trying to do that," Cassandra said. Her face was reddening a little, Maddie noticed. Her mother had always had a quick temper, as Maddie knew only too well.

"You were trying the same thing over and over," Maikeru told her. "If it didn't work the first time, why should it work on subsequent attempts?"

"But you've told me that speed is my best weapon," Cassandra said, an argumentative tone in her voice.

Maikeru nodded. "But not your only weapon. Dimon-san found a way to counteract your speed, and to make you waste your energy against his defenses, until you became tired and your speed was diminished. When this happens, you must look for something unexpected. Otherwise, as the bout goes on, it becomes more certain that he will be the victor."

"Unexpected," Cassandra repeated. "What do you mean by that?"

"Remember your three best allies. Speed. Agility. And surprise. Faced with a foe like this, you have to surprise him, before it's too late. Your overhand, side cut, and diagonal cuts were not fast enough to break his defense. Look for something else."

"Such as?" Cassandra asked. Dimon and Maddie watched keenly, sensing that this was a new plateau in the Princess Regent's swordsmanship.

"One example might be a single-handed thrust," Maikeru told her quietly.

She opened her mouth to speak, stopped and thought. Then she said slowly, "But you say I must always fight two-handed."

Before she had finished, Maikeru was shaking his head.

"There is no 'always,'" he told her. "You must be ready to change, to adapt, to try something new and unexpected."

In a sudden blur of motion, he dropped the wooden rod and drew his own *katana* from its scabbard. Then he lunged forward, holding it in one hand, the single cutting edge facing upward. The point stopped a bare two centimeters from the startled Cassandra's face.

Instantly, in a continuation of his first movement, Maikeru withdrew the weapon and re-sheathed it. He bowed an apology to Cassandra. She waved it aside, looking at him with renewed interest.

"By using one hand, you increase your reach by almost half a meter," he said. "This alone will take your opponent by surprise, as well as the fact that most of your attacks to this moment have been with the edge, not the point."

He paused, to see if she was following. She nodded.

"It's a risky move for you because it leaves you open to a counterattack. You must be ready to recover instantly if the thrust doesn't go home."

Again Cassandra nodded. Then she gestured at the sword in its scabbard.

"You reversed your wrist so that the cutting edge was uppermost," she said. "What was the reason for that?"

Maikeru nodded approvingly. "You notice small details," he said. "That's good."

He drew his sword again, more slowly this time, and demonstrated the reversed wrist position, with the cutting edge on top. The *katana*'s blade had a slight curve, imparting a downward direction to the thrust.

"By reversing my wrist, I make the point of the *katana* travel slightly downward, because of the curved blade. That means the sharp cutting edge can shear more easily through your opponent's chain mail. The edge is sharp enough to do that," he added.

Cassandra nodded, eyes narrowed as she studied the gleaming blade. "I see," she said slowly.

"Practice it with me," Maikeru told her. He stood beside her, demonstrating how to progress from an obliquely angled cut into the thrust, releasing the left hand from the grip, turning the wrist and stepping forward, all in one smooth movement. Cassandra copied the sequence several times, gradually moving faster and faster. As her movements became more confident, Maikeru stepped away, re-sheathing his *katana* and watching her closely. He bent and retrieved his wooden rod and began to tap a tempo on the floor once more. Then, with his free hand, he gestured down the length of the hall.

"Move," he instructed her. "And change to the thrust every three strokes. Vary the sequence so you become used to thrusting after any other stroke."

She shuffled down the hall, her light slippers whispering on the boards. Then, with every third stroke, she stamped her right foot forward and lunged, point down and cutting edge uppermost. Maikeru let her reach the far end of the hall before he called out.

"Now back again."

The tapping of the rod on the boards became more rapid and Cassandra moved toward them, the *katana* like a striking snake. Cut, cut, slash, thrust! Cut, cut, sweep, thrust. She stopped in front of him and he nodded approvingly.

"Now try it with Dimon-san."

Dimon held out a hand, protesting. "But I'll know she's going to do it every third stroke."

Maikeru smiled grimly. "But only she will know when those three strokes begin," he said. Dimon nodded his understanding.

They assumed their ready positions, and Maikeru once more called for them to begin. This time, Dimon struck first, aiming an overhead blow at Cassandra. Her wooden blade flickered out and she deflected his stroke so that the practice sword rebounded from the floorboards, throwing him slightly off balance.

Seizing her opportunity, Cassandra delivered a barrage of cuts, slashes and sweeps. Then, after six of these, she suddenly lunged one-handed. Dimon only just managed to recoil away from the tip of her blade, stumbling slightly but bringing his shield up to block the thrust.

Once more, she began to cut and slash at him. This time, she waited four strokes, then lunged. But he was ready. His shield caught her sword and deflected it away from him. Then, as she was still leaning forward, unbalanced and open to his reply, his sword flashed forward and struck her on the outer thigh.

They stepped back. It had been a winning blow. In a real fight, it would not have killed her outright. But even if it hadn't severed any of the major blood vessels in her leg, it would have taken her right leg out from under her and left her at his mercy.

"Again," Maikeru said quietly, and once more the hall resounded with the rapid impacts of wood on wood. Then, Cassandra essayed another thrust—with the same result. Dimon's shield blocked her *katana*. His sword whipped out and caught her on the hip.

Cassandra stepped back, her cheeks flaming with effort and

frustration. She rubbed her left hand against her hip. There would be a bruise there tonight, she realized.

"This is hopeless!" she said angrily.

Maikeru regarded her with a half smile. "You think so?"

"I know so!" she replied, still angry. "The thrust leaves me open to a reply, as you said. And Dimon has no trouble avoiding it. Why bother with such a useless tactic?"

Maikeru turned his impassive gaze to Dimon. "You noticed?" When the young captain nodded, Maikeru indicated Cassandra. "Tell her."

"You're signaling the thrust," Dimon said apologetically. "I know when you're going to try it." He paused, then elaborated. "Actually, I didn't know the first time, but after that it was obvious."

"What was so blasted obvious?" Cassandra knew it wasn't fair to vent her anger on a subordinate like Dimon. He couldn't respond in kind. Nonetheless, her quick temper overcame her sense of fairness.

"Before you thrust, you raise your chin slightly," Dimon told her.

She drew breath for a heated reply, then realized he might be right. She looked at Maikeru for confirmation, and the gray-haired Swordmaster nodded.

"Every time," he said. "It's a habit you'll have to break. Otherwise it could cost you your life."

Cassandra considered his words, glanced at Dimon and nodded. "Thanks," she said. "I'll have to work on that."

12

THE DAYS PASSED AND TIME BEGAN TO HANG HEAVY ON MADdie's hands. She went hunting with Dimon, which was a welcome diversion. The young captain offered her the use of a bow but she declined. It wasn't a good idea to let anyone, even a captain of the castle guard, know about her skill with a bow. Most young women of her age and social station could shoot, but her ability was far beyond what might be expected, and that could lead to questions. It was vital that she protect her secret life as an apprentice Ranger, so she thought it best not to show any skill with the bow at all. And since she wasn't sure that she could fake being less of an archer than she was, the best way was to use her sling exclusively. At least that wasn't known as a weapon of choice for Rangers.

Dimon was a capable shot, but she could see that she was far better, and she was glad of her decision. She bagged two large hares with her sling, and he shot a young deer, bringing it down after stalking it for half an hour. The deer would go to the castle kitchens, as would the two hares, and would provide meat for the main dining hall. Maddie was glad he elected to end the hunt then, rather than continue on, killing for the sake of killing.

Dimon hunted only for the table, not for sport or for trophies. She liked that in him. Additionally, she enjoyed his cheerful company, and they spent three pleasant hours together while they hunted.

But with Horace and Gilan absent, and more than half of the castle garrison with them, Dimon's free time was limited. He was in command of the remaining troops, and he took his responsibility seriously. Maddie regretted that they had little time to spend together, but appreciated that he attended so conscientiously to his duties.

Her mother, too, was busy. Horace's absence meant that a lot of the administrative work he usually undertook now fell to her. Maddie regretted that they had no time for more practice bouts with Dimon and Maikeru, although she knew her mother did manage to fit in several sessions with the Swordmaster.

She rode out to Warwick and Lou's farm several times, switching over to Bumper to patrol the area. Warwick reported that there had been no sign of lights in the old abbey since she had been there last. She rode up to inspect the building once, but aside from the cold ashes of an old fire, doubtless left by travelers, there was no sign that anybody had been there in recent days.

The fact was, Araluen was a far more peaceful fief than Redmont. This was in part because of the relatively large garrison at Castle Araluen and that the area around it had been settled for many years. Redmont, by comparison, was on the outer fringe of the kingdom, closer to the Hibernian sea with its pirates and smugglers, and the border with Celtica. There was far more going on in Redmont Fief—more action, more activity. There was more to keep a Ranger and his apprentice occupied and on the alert.

Araluen Fief was boring by comparison—especially for an adventurous young woman like Maddie. The result was that after a few more days, she became restive and unsettled, and was looking for something to occupy her mind.

The answer came in a conversation with her grandfather, whom she visited most days—sometimes for an hour or so, at other times, if he was tired, for a few minutes.

"Have you explored the castle?" he asked her one day after she complained of being bored by the enforced inactivity.

She shrugged. "I grew up here," she reminded him. "I think I've seen everything there is to see."

He smiled and tapped his finger against the side of his nose. "Ah, but what about what isn't to be seen?"

She frowned. "What isn't to be seen?" she repeated, not understanding.

"It's rumored there are lots of secret places within these walls—some inside the walls themselves."

"Secret places? You mean tunnels?" she asked, her interest sparked.

"Tunnels, yes. And stairways. It's rumored that my grandfather had a secret way out of the castle—a tunnel that led under the moat." Duncan smiled. "Seems he had a girlfriend in the village and he liked being able to sneak out to see her."

"Gilan said something about that. Where is it?" Maddie asked.

He shook his head. "I never had time to look for it when I was younger," he said. "But it strikes me that it might be useful to know about such things. I imagine it would begin somewhere in the cellars. But where?"

"You said secret stairways as well?" Maddie prompted him.

"Most of these old castles had secret ways to access the towers.

Usually by a narrow stairway built inside the walls. Can't see why Araluen would be any different. They must be here somewhere." He looked around the room, indicating the thick stone walls.

Maddie rose and prowled around the room, stopping to tap on the walls every few meters or so. They sounded disappointingly solid, she thought.

"How would one go about finding such things?" she mused, half to herself.

Duncan shrugged, the movement causing him a slight twinge of pain in his injured leg. "The castle library might be a place to start," he said. "Ask for old plans and sketches of the castle. Look for anomalies."

"Such as?"

He rubbed his stubbly chin. His servant hadn't shaved him so far this morning. "Well, look for rooms that should be the same dimensions but aren't. Walls that are shorter than the rooms above and below them, or adjoining them. Look for variations in their measurements. Sometimes that will indicate the presence of a hidden chamber."

"And in the cellars and lower levels of the castle," she said.

Duncan nodded. "That's where I'd start."

She stayed with him for another half hour. The conversation turned to other matters, but she was distracted by the idea of secret stairways and tunnels continuing to pop into her mind. Finally, she rose and took her leave. She kissed him gently on the forehead and moved to the door. As she laid her hand on the latch, he stopped her.

"Give my regards to Master Uldred," he said.

She looked back at him, her head cocked to one side. "Uldred?"

"The head librarian. Been here for years. He should know where to lay his hands on the old charts and plans of the castle."

The library was on the first floor of the keep, in a large, well-ventilated annex set on the western side. High-level windows admitted the sun, letting it shine down on the stacks of books and scrolls that were packed into shelves twice the height of a man.

Uldred was a thin wisp of a man, with long, unkempt gray hair, cut short in the front but hanging halfway down his back. He was dressed in a monklike scholar's robe, with a long hood hanging at the back and a belt made of silken cord. It occurred to Maddie that most scholarly types were small in build. Heavier-set or taller men tended to become warriors.

When Maddie entered, Uldred was presiding over the library from a mezzanine balcony that overlooked the rows of shelves, sitting at a large table that had several volumes and scrolls stacked neatly on one side.

"Your Highness," he said, smiling a welcome, "what brings you to my domain?"

"Please, call me Maddie," she said, smiling in reply. "'Your Highness' is far too formal."

He inclined his head, pleased by her friendly and informal approach. "Maddie it is then," he said. "What can I do for you?"

"The King said you might be able to show me the original plans and sketches of the castle," she said.

He regarded her with a knowing look. "Looking for secret tunnels, perhaps?"

She raised her eyebrows in surprise. "Yes. How did you know that?"

Uldred sighed. "It's why most people want to study the plans.

So far, nobody's found anything," he told her. "Not that too many of them kept at it for long. They become bored and skip through the plans quickly. Never find anything that way."

"Well, I'll try to stay focused. Can you show them to me?"

He shook his head. "I've got too much work right now but I can show you where to find them."

"That'd be fine," she told him.

"Then follow me," he said, rising from behind his worktable and leading the way to the wooden stairway that descended to the library floor. He moved quickly, and she had to hurry to keep up with him. He preceded her to the eastern corner and stopped, indicating a section of shelves packed with rolled scrolls and large, leather-bound volumes.

"They're all there," he said. "I'm sorry I can't let you take them out of the library. But there's a table and chair here you can use to study them. Oh, and a pen, ink and paper if you want to make notes."

She walked to the shelves and studied the array of scrolls, hesitating as she sought a place to start.

"They're labeled," Uldred told her, seeing her uncertainty. "I'd start with the lower levels. Doubt you'll find a tunnel at the top of a tower, after all."

She grunted a reply and peered more closely, seeing the labels on the shelves under the scrolls. She reached out for one.

"'Cellar Level One,'" she read aloud. "That's as good a place as any."

"I'd say so," Uldred told her. Then he turned away. "I'll be back at my desk if you need anything." He paused. "Oh, and put everything back where it came from, won't you?"

Maddie nodded, taking the heavy, rolled scroll from the shelf and blowing a little dust from it. Obviously, nobody had looked at it for some time. She moved to the table he'd indicated, untied the ribbon securing the scroll and rolled it open. There were half a dozen lead weights on the table, and she used four of them to hold the scroll open, then bent over it to study it.

Engrossed in her task, she didn't hear Uldred as he walked quickly back through the shelves toward his lofty perch.

She pored over the chart, initially not fully understanding what she was seeing. She lowered herself into the chair and thought for several minutes.

"I guess the best way is to get accustomed to all these drawings and measurements," she said quietly to herself. "After all, it's not likely that there'd be a label saying 'Tunnel here.' I'll need to suss it out."

She spent the next hour and a half going over the charts and plans until she was familiar with the style of them. By the end of that time, her eyes were watering with the effort of concentration. The lines, measurements and notes were beginning to swim before her eyes. Reluctantly, she rolled up the parchment scroll she had been studying and retied the ribbon around it. She replaced it in the shelves and picked up her sheets of notes, then retraced her way through the shelves to the ladder stairs that led to Uldred's office. Mounting them quickly, she coughed to gain his attention and he looked up, smiling.

"Finished?"

She shook her head. "Just starting. I'll be back tomorrow. Thanks for your help."

She turned and left the room, and he watched her as she walked briskly through the rows of shelves to the entrance.

"Well, good for you," he said softly.

13

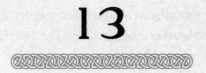

THE FOLLOWING MORNING, AFTER BREAKFAST, SHE WAS BACK at the library, waiting for Uldred to open up. He arrived after a few minutes and smiled to see her there.

"Getting an early start?" He unlocked the big double doors and let her in.

Maddie went immediately to the shelves where the plans were kept and took out the scrolls for Cellar Level One and Cellar Level Two—the upper and lower cellars beneath the keep. She had thought about her task as she lay in bed the previous evening, and today she had a plan of action.

She set out her pen, ink and sheets of notepaper. Then she laid a graduated scale beside them—one she had taken from her father's desk. It was a flat rule, marked in centimeters, and about thirty centimeters long. He used it to measure distances on his scale maps when he was planning a journey or a campaign.

She studied the plan of the upper cellar. It was a rectangular room thirty meters long and ten wide. At one end were racks for wine barrels and storage bins for dried fruit and vegetables. Along each of the two longer walls, half a dozen indentations were marked—small rectangular rooms that she knew were used as cells for prisoners. In some castles, they would be called dungeons and they'd be poorly lit and ventilated, with water dripping down the walls. Here, she knew, they were at least clean and dry. At the moment, none of them was occupied.

She placed her scale rule along the long side of the cellar and measured it. The thirty-meter length corresponded to fifteen centimeters on the scale. She made a note of the fact, then rolled the scroll up, refastened it, and reached for the plans of Cellar Level Two, the rooms directly below.

At first glance, it appeared identical to the room above. But then her eyes narrowed and she frowned thoughtfully as she noticed an anomaly.

Ranged along the two long walls of the cellar were the same rectangular indentations denoting cells. But whereas the upper cellar had six on each side, Cellar Level Two had only five. Quickly, she placed her rule against the longest side and measured it. Twelve and a half centimeters. That indicated that the lower wall was twenty-five meters long—five meters shorter than the room above it.

"How come nobody's noticed that before?" she mused aloud. Then she realized that the two plans were on separate sheets. Chances were, nobody had ever placed them side by side to compare them, or measured the length of the walls for comparison. Or maybe they had and had simply accepted the fact that the lower cellar was shorter. It was significant to her only because she was looking for a concealed passage.

But now that she had noticed it, the question was, why was Cellar Two five meters shorter than Cellar One?

"One way to find out," she said to herself. She rolled up the second set of plans, refastened them and placed both scrolls back on the shelves. She planned to come back to the library, so she stacked her notes, pen and rule neatly on the table and hurried to the door. She debated saying good-bye to Uldred, then decided against it. He'd only ask her if she'd found something, and she didn't want to appear foolish if her idea turned out to be a wild-goose chase.

She made her way down to the cellars underneath the keep.

Since there were no prisoners in the cells, there was no call for anyone to be stationed down here. But the area was well lit with torches in brackets on the wall and three lanterns hanging from the low stone ceiling. Obviously, members of the castle staff came in each morning and lit them all. As she'd noted earlier, the cellar was well ventilated and dry. A slight breeze blew through it, coming from a ventilation shaft somewhere, installed to stop the air from going stale and musty. She walked to one end of the room, placed her back against the wall and paced carefully to the far end.

One of the skills she had learned with Will was how to pace out distance, taking long steps that were consistent in length. She knew from her practice and training that twelve of these elongated paces were equivalent to ten meters. She counted aloud now as she measured the length of the room.

"...thirty-four, thirty-five...and a half," she said as her right foot butted against the base of the far wall. That was close enough to thirty-six, which would coincide with the thirty meters marked on the plan in the library. She examined the wall. It was made of large blocks of sandstone fitted together and cemented in place. She rapped on several of them with the hilt of her saxe. They sounded solid enough.

"Hmm," she muttered, casting her glance around the long,

low-ceilinged room. There was nothing remarkable about it. The walls were bare. The room was unfurnished, aside from the racks of wine barrels and the wooden bins of vegetables at the far end.

"Let's see downstairs," she said, and headed for the staircase that sloped down to the next level.

Cellar Two was not as well lit as the upper level, and there were no wine barrels stored here. But it was still relatively dry, although there was a faint hint of mustiness in the air. The ventilating breeze upstairs was not evident here. Maddie took a few minutes to study the long, shadowy room. It appeared to be identical to its upper neighbor.

Once again, she moved to the far wall, placed her back against it, and began to pace, counting aloud as she did. Her voice echoed off the stone walls on either side. The open doors of the cells were dark holes, like eyes watching her.

". . . twenty-eight, twenty-nine, thirty, thirty-one . . . and that's it," she said as she fetched up against the wall once more. She rubbed her chin.

"Near enough to twenty-five meters," she said reflectively. "Definitely shorter than the room upstairs."

She turned and paced once more, measuring the length of the room in the other direction. Again, she managed thirty-one paces before her toe stubbed against the base of the wall. There was no doubt about it. This room was five meters shorter than the one above. But why should it be?

She took down one of the hanging lanterns and moved to the far wall again, studying it in fine detail. Like the wall upstairs, it was made from large sandstone blocks. The mortar between them was old but firm. It hadn't begun to deteriorate with age.

She inched her way along the wall, peering closely at it, holding the lantern high to shed its light on the stone, then holding it at an angle so that any anomalies might be highlighted. Nothing.

Then she noticed something on the end block, at the base. She bent for a closer look. Three words were written there—or rather, the same word was written there three times.

Sinister. Sinister. Sinister.

The lettering was small. It had been carved into the stone, presumably with a sharp-pointed tool, and if she hadn't been looking so closely, with the light angled to throw the words into relief, she might well have missed them.

"Sinister," she said to herself, then shrugged. "Not a bad description for a dungeon."

Although, as she'd noticed earlier, it wasn't a particularly appropriate description of this dungeon. It was dimly lit and low ceilinged, yes. But it was dry and free of vermin or the sort of tools of torture that were features of many dungeons.

No rack. No chains or fetters in sight.

She pushed open the door to the last cell in line and went inside, holding the lantern high to throw its light into the farthest corner. The walls were rough but dry. A battered, old wooden bed frame stood along the longer wall, and the door, made of ironbound wood, had a small barred window in its upper half, allowing light and air into the cell.

A small wooden table and stool completed the furnishings. There was even a stub of a candle, old and yellowed with age, on the table.

It certainly wasn't luxurious, she thought. But it could have been a whole lot worse. The worst you could say about it was that the hard wooden cot might be somewhat uncomfortable.

But sinister? Not really.

She exited the cell and looked around, wondering why someone had carved those words into the stone. Wondering who had carved them.

"A prisoner?" she said, then discarded that idea. A prisoner would have been in the cell itself. If he wanted to carve a message, he would have done it in there. She couldn't see any jailer allowing a prisoner out to vent his feelings on the wall itself.

It was a puzzle, and she sighed as she contemplated it.

"Put it out of your mind," she told herself. She knew that was the best way to find an answer to puzzles like this. But, of course, as soon as she tried to push the thought aside, it crowded back into her consciousness.

Why was it written there?

And why was this room five meters shorter than the one above it?

Was there another room behind that stone wall? And if so, how did one gain access to it? She studied the wall again. She could see no sign of a door in the wall, or any kind of opening. The mortar was all solid, with no cracks visible.

Her stomach rumbled loudly, reminding her that it was getting close to the time for the midday meal.

"Going hungry won't solve the puzzle," she said, and mounted the stairs, heading for the buttery on the ground floor of the keep. "Maybe a full stomach will help you solve the riddle."

As it turned out, it didn't. But it solved the problem of her rumbling stomach.

After a substantial lunch, she decided to leave the puzzle of the cellars for a few hours. She hadn't seen Bumper in two days.

She collected her belongings from the library and thanked Uldred.

"Giving up?" He smiled, although there was a tone of disappointment in his voice.

She shook her head. "Taking a break. I need some fresh air to help my thinking."

She left the library and headed for the stables to saddle Sundancer, cramming several apples into her jacket pocket as she went.

She rode to the farm, where Lou greeted her warmly. Warwick was working on one of the outlying fields. Leading Sundancer to the barn, she unsaddled him, gave him a brief rubdown and an apple, then tossed the saddle over Bumper's back.

Wondered where you'd been.

"Sorry, I've been busy."

She was preoccupied as she rode through the fields toward the hill where the old abbey was situated. She inspected the building once more, but it was unchanged. After patrolling the surrounding area for an hour and finding nothing to arouse her interest or suspicion, she returned to the barn, deep in thought, changed her saddle over, and rode back to Castle Araluen, waving a farewell to Lou as she left.

She clattered across the drawbridge, nodding a greeting to the sentries stationed there. At the stable, a stable boy took Sundancer's reins from her.

"I'll settle him down, my lady," he said cheerfully. She was going to demur, then shrugged. One of the perks of being a princess was that people tended to do this sort of menial task for you. She left Sundancer in his care and mounted the stairs to her rooms, where she asked the servants to draw her a bath. Again, it occurred to her that, had she been back at Redmont, she would have had to perform this task for herself.

"I didn't ask to be summoned here," she said. "May as well take advantage of it."

Her shoulder and neck muscles were stiff—a result of sitting hunched over the charts in the library. She lay back in the hot, soothing water for half an hour, feeling the tension in her muscles release and her limbs relax. Then she clambered out of the bath, wrapping herself in a full-length towel and spilling a substantial amount of the now-lukewarm water on the flagstones as she did so.

She contemplated mopping it up and grinned. Normally, she would do that. But here, she was a princess, with servants just waiting to look after her every need. She compromised by apologizing to the maid who hurried in at her call to dry the floor and empty the bath.

"No trouble, my lady," the girl said cheerfully.

"See?" said Maddie to herself, to assuage the guilt. "She *wants* to look after you."

She had an early dinner by herself. Her mother was attending to the details of an upcoming official visit by the newly appointed Iberian ambassador, and Maddie didn't want to bother her. Dimon was on duty—again—so she was left to her own devices.

Which suited Maddie as she pondered the mystery of that five-meter discrepancy and the apparent lack of any way through the stone wall. Eventually, with no solution coming to her, she decided to go to bed. It had been a long day, poring over charts and measurements, descending into the cellars, then riding to Warwick and Lou's farm and beyond.

It was warm and cozy under her blankets. Leaving the window open so that the chill night air would cool the room, she pulled the blankets up to her chin, luxuriating in their warmth. She stretched her legs out, yawned twice and let her eyes close. Her breathing became deep and regular.

Then, suddenly, she sat up in bed.

"*Sinister* means 'left'!"

14

It was close to midday when the little company rode out of the trees onto grassy flatland. Beyond the knee-high grass that waved gently in the breeze, Horace could see the silver sparkle of water stretching for several hundred meters to the north.

"That's the Wezel," he said.

Gilan nodded acknowledgment. "And there are our two scouts," he replied, indicating the two mounted troopers waiting by the riverbank.

Horace turned in his saddle and beckoned the troop leader forward. The lieutenant trotted his horse up to them. Protocol dictated that while they were marching, he would stay a reasonable distance from the two commanders, allowing them to speak in relative privacy. He saluted as he drew rein alongside them.

"Wait here," Horace told him, then indicated the two scouts several hundred meters away. "We'll check with the scouts, and if it's all clear, we'll signal you forward."

"Are you planning to stop here for a while, sir?" the lieutenant asked.

Horace squinted up at the sun, almost directly overhead.

"We might as well rest the horses—and the archers," he added with a grin. The archers, being unmounted, marched in the rear of the cavalry. "But wait till we hear what the scouts have to say."

"Yes, sir." The lieutenant touched his hand to the rim of his iron helmet, then turned away and issued commands to his troop. "Stay mounted, but sit at rest," he told them.

The troopers eased their tired legs, standing in their stirrups and stretching their muscles. The archers who accompanied them simply sat or lay on the grass at the edge of the track, with sighs of relief. Horace and Gilan urged their mounts into a canter and rode toward the two scouts.

"Looks as if everything's all right," Gilan observed. Had the scouts intended to warn them of danger, they would have signaled so by now. As it was, they sat at ease and waited for the two commanders to come up with them. It was Horace's operation, so Gilan left it to him to question the two riders.

"Where are the Foxes?" Horace asked.

Since early that morning, following a tip-off from a village they had passed through, they had been shadowing a small group of members of the Red Fox Clan. There were half a dozen of them, and they had been moving at a brisk pace through the wooded country, consistently heading north.

"Must be going somewhere," Gilan had noted.

Horace had grunted assent. Obviously, the Foxes were going somewhere, he'd thought. But he realized that Gilan had meant they had a definite destination in mind. In spite of the vagaries of the tracks through the forest they had been following, they had maintained a base course that traveled consistently north. Now the broad, deep waters of the Wezel prohibited any further progress in that direction. The Foxes must have turned either east or west, and presumably the two scouts had waited to apprise Horace and Gilan of their quarries' new course.

The senior of the two scouts, who wore corporal's rank insignia on the chest of his jerkin, saluted briskly. Horace nodded acknowledgment and briefly touched his forehead with his forefinger. He wasn't much for parade ground drill, Gilan noted with a private smile.

"Sir," said the corporal briskly, "we followed them here, to the river's edge. Then they turned east, following the bank." He indicated the direction they had taken with a pointing arm.

"Do they know you were following them?" Horace asked.

The corporal hesitated. "Hard to tell, sir," he said. "They didn't *seem* to know we were behind them. We stayed well back. Of course," he added, "it was easier to stay concealed when we were in the trees. They could have spotted us when we reached this open ground."

Horace considered the man's answer for a few seconds. Short of having the six Fox members spur off at full gallop, there was no way of ascertaining whether they had spotted their followers.

"Hmm," he said. "How long since they reached this point?"

The two scouts exchanged a glance, and then the corporal replied. "Half an hour, sir. Twenty minutes at least." He looked back at his companion again. "Would you say so, Ned?"

The second trooper nodded. "Twenty minutes, at least, sir."

Horace glanced to the east, in the direction the small party had gone, and came to a decision. "Very well, get back on their tail," he said. "Stay well back." He indicated the tree line several hundred meters away. "You can stay back in the trees."

"Yes, sir," the corporal replied.

Horace continued with his orders. "We'll take a ten-minute break here and follow on after you. If there's anything to report, or if they change direction again, one of you ride back to tell us."

"Yes, sir!" the troopers chorused.

Horace waved them away. "Right. Get moving. But be careful. Odds are they're heading for some meeting point or rendezvous, and we don't want to frighten them off."

The two troopers cantered slowly away, their horses' hooves thudding dully on the soft grass. Horace turned in his saddle, whistled, and then waved for the rest of the party to join them. Gilan unhooked his canteen from the saddlebow in front of him and took a long drink.

"Might as well stretch our legs," Horace told him. Then, as the troop arrived, with the archers straggling loosely behind, he addressed the lieutenant. "Ten minutes, Burton," he told him. "Let the men dismount and loosen saddle girths. Check the horses for any signs of lameness or galling."

The lieutenant nodded, then turned and issued his orders to the troop. The cavalrymen swung down from their saddles and began to check their mounts. It was standard procedure to make sure the horses were in good shape before they attended to their own needs. Each man was leading a spare horse and they were checked as well—although without being burdened by a saddle or a rider, there was little chance that they would need any form of treatment.

As before, the archers simply sprawled on the grass where they stood. There were, after all, some advantages to traveling on foot.

Horace grinned at them. "Undisciplined lot they are," he said.

Gilan followed his gaze and replied seriously. "Maybe. But they're good men in a battle."

"Let's hope so," the tall knight replied. "We might need them before long."

After the ten-minute break was over—measured by the troop sergeant with a small sandglass—the men tightened their saddle girth straps and remounted. Grumbling, the archers came to their feet and stood ready in a loose formation. Horace raised his right hand to shoulder height, then lowered it in the direction he wanted them to travel.

"Move them out, Lieutenant," he said, and once again the little force was on the move.

They traveled for another hour, walking the horses so that the archers could keep up. There were no complaints from the bowmen. They were used to going on foot. Their feet and leg muscles were hardened to the task, and they managed a brisk pace that kept them level with the horsemen.

They paralleled the riverbank. As Gilan and Horace had predicted back at Castle Araluen, it formed an effective barrier, keeping the party ahead of them from crossing.

Gilan held up a hand and the column stopped.

"What is it?" said Horace. Then he saw for himself as his eyes followed Gilan's outstretched arm. The two scouts were reined in on the bank of the river, waiting for them. They were about three hundred meters ahead.

"You've got sharp eyes," he told the Ranger Commandant.

"Something's happened. Wonder why one of them didn't ride back to warn us," said Gilan. The reason soon became apparent as they spurred their horses to join the scouts.

"They got away, sir," the corporal said apologetically.

Horace's brows drew together in annoyance. "Got away? How? I told you to stay back out of sight, didn't I?"

"And we did, sir. But I think they've been on to us the whole time, only they never let on. There was a boat waiting for them here." He indicated a shallow sandy beach at the river's edge. "Took them on board and rowed them across the river. We couldn't do anything about it, sir. We were staying back and they'd got on board before we knew what was happening."

Horace let his breath out in an exasperated sigh. "Can't be helped, Corporal," he said. "Not your fault. As you say, it seems they've been on to us the whole time."

He twisted in his saddle. "Lieutenant!" he called, beckoning for the officer to join them. As the man rode up, Horace indicated the cavalrymen.

"Any of your men raised in these parts?" he asked. "I'd like to know if there's a ford anywhere close by."

The lieutenant looked doubtful. "Not sure, sir. Most of them came from the south originally. But I'll ask around."

"No need," Gilan said. "One of the archers grew up here. Used to be a poacher before he signed up with the archers. He should know the area." He raised his voice. "Archer Ellis! Come here, please!"

Ellis, a nuggety man in his mid-thirties, heaved himself to his feet. Like the others, he had taken the opportunity to sprawl on the grass by the riverbank. He hurried forward now. Gilan noted approvingly that he brought his longbow with him. No archer worth his salt would ever leave it behind when on campaign.

Ellis saluted, touching the knuckles of his right hand to his forehead.

"Yes, Ranger!" he said smartly. Gilan commanded the respect of the archers. As a Ranger, Gilan's skill with the bow was far superior to their own, and they recognized the fact.

"You were raised around here, weren't you? Used to be a poacher, I'm told?" Gilan said.

Instantly, Ellis assumed a look of shocked innocence. "Me, sir? A poacher, sir? Nay, I never touched one of the King's animals. It's a wicked lie folks tell about me, it is."

Gilan said nothing, simply stared down at the man with a look of utter disbelief on his face.

Ellis shifted his feet uncomfortably, then eventually admitted, "Well, maybe once . . . twice even. I might have accidentally shot a rabbit or a hare. Accidentally, I say. And once it was shot, weren't no sense to leaving it lying around, were there?"

"Oh, get over yourself, Ellis. I don't care if you shot half a hundred deer while you were at it. The question is, how well do you know this area?"

Ellis glanced around, as if seeing the river, the grassy plain and the forest for the first time. "Why, like the back of my hand, sir," he said, relieved that the question of his former illegal activities was not Gilan's main interest.

"So are there any fords close by?" Gilan asked.

Ellis pursed his lips, considering. "Not particularly close, sir. Nearest is a good two kilometers from here. And it's a difficult crossing, sir."

"How's that?" Horace interposed.

Ellis turned his gaze to the tall warrior. "It's fast running, sir—like the rest of the river—and it's quite deep. Maybe chest high." He indicated with his right hand a point just below the collar of his jerkin. "Man can get swept off his feet easy as blinking," he added.

"But if you could hold on to one of the horses while you crossed, would that be easier?" Horace said.

Ellis considered his answer for a few seconds, then grinned. "Yes. Be easy as pie then, I'd say." If the horse were upstream, it would break the force of the current. And it would provide a stable handhold for a man crossing beside it.

"Good," said Horace. He nodded his thanks to Ellis. "Well, I suggest you lead the way to this ford of yours. We need to get across the river and pick up the trail of those Foxes again." He looked at Gilan. "I trust you'll be able to manage that?"

Gilan shrugged. "Shouldn't be a problem."

Behind them, the cavalry lieutenant coughed discreetly. "Sir Horace?"

They turned to look at him. He was pointing to the tree line, several hundred meters distant. Armed men were emerging from the trees and forming up in three ranks. A lot of armed men.

"I think we're in trouble," Horace said.

15

For a few seconds, Maddie was tempted to throw off her bedclothes and hurry to the lower cellar. Then she reconsidered.

It was cold. It would be colder still below ground level. And it would be dark and difficult to see anything. Furthermore, if she went exploring down there now, she was liable to disturb the night watch and cause an alarm. Questions would be asked about what she was doing, and she preferred not to have to answer them. She pulled the blankets back round her chin.

"It'll still be there tomorrow," she said, yawning, and settled back under the blankets.

She ate breakfast hurriedly the next morning. There were only a few others in the buttery, members of the castle staff who were either coming on or going off duty. She was grateful there was nobody there with whom she needed to talk. Her head was too full of the possibilities in the lower cellar, and she would have been a poor conversationalist. Her mother was a habitual early riser, she knew, but she was probably having her breakfast in her room or in her office.

Maddie didn't quite understand why she was so intent on not

discussing the possible existence of a secret tunnel or a concealed stairway with anyone. Maybe it was because she felt that the tunnels and stairways, if they were there, had been kept secret for a reason. Even Uldred's attitude seemed to indicate that he didn't really believe they existed—that they were more the subject of myth.

Or perhaps it was her training as a Ranger that made her reluctant to discuss the matter. Rangers were notoriously secretive and closemouthed. They liked to possess knowledge that others didn't, to be aware of matters that others weren't. You never knew, after all, when such knowledge might give you an advantage.

From habit born at the little cabin in Redmont Fief, she took her dishes to the kitchen, rinsed them in the big sink and stacked them to be washed. The scullery maid looked at her in surprise. She wasn't used to members of the nobility doing menial work.

"Thank you, my lady," she said, but Maddie barely heard her, her mind intent on what she was about to do.

She found a lantern in a store cupboard, ascertained that the reservoir was full of oil and headed for the stairs down to the cellar. She checked that she had her saxe in a scabbard and her sling rolled up and tucked beneath her belt. A pouch of shot for the sling weighed heavily on her left hip. She didn't think she'd need weapons, but you never knew.

Once again, there was nobody in the upper cellar, and she was glad to see it. The housekeeping staff had renewed the torches and lanterns and gone on to their next task. The same held true for the lower cellar. She walked up to one of the torches set in a bracket on the wall. She had noticed the previous day that a supply of waxed tapers was kept close to hand, presumably for lighting the central lamps. She raised the glass in her own lantern now, wound the wick up a centimeter or so, and lit a taper from the torch, carrying the tiny flame to the wick.

Soaked with oil from the reservoir, it flared up immediately in a bright yellow flame, tinged with black smoke at the top. She lowered the wick so that it was burning more cleanly, and the black smoke disappeared. Then she closed the glass front of the lantern. The light, reflected from the polished metal disk behind the wick, shone out strongly, throwing a pool of light ahead of her. She took the lantern and moved to the end wall, crouching to look at the words scratched into the stone there.

Sinister. Sinister. Sinister.

"Left, left, left," she muttered to herself. "Or three left. Or left three." She tried variations to see if they made more sense. "Left three," she decided, after a moment's thought. She placed her hand on the inscribed stone, then counted three stones to the left, touching each with her forefinger.

There was absolutely nothing remarkable about the stone she was now touching. It was identical in every way with its neighbors. She pushed it experimentally, placing the flat of her hand in the middle of its rough surface.

Nothing.

She tried pushing on the edge of the stone, searching for any slight movement there. In keeping with the instructions so far, she pressed the left-hand side first. Then the right.

Again, nothing.

She tried pushing the top and bottom, with no result. Then she wedged her fingers in the shallow gap between the stone and the next in line and tried pulling the top. Then the bottom.

Nothing budged.

She sat back on her haunches, thinking. As she often did in such a situation, she spoke her thoughts aloud.

"Left, left, left," she said softly. "What else can it mean?"

Of course, she realized, it could mean any stone in the row that was third from the corner. She let her gaze run up the row, seeking any sign of a crack or a fault in the mortar. But there was nothing. She'd try the others in that row in a minute. But for now, there was another possible interpretation.

"Maybe it means three left from the first stone, not the corner itself," she said. That would make it the fourth stone in the row. She moved her attention one more stone to the left, bringing the lantern close to study the seams, the mortar and the stone itself.

She pushed on the middle of the stone. Nothing happened.

"Solid as a rock," she murmured.

She was going through the motions now, dispirited and more than half convinced that she had misinterpreted the meaning of the three words gouged into the rock. She pressed halfheartedly against the left-hand side of the stone.

There was a resounding metallic *CLACK!* from inside the wall and a section three stones wide, with the keystone in the center, swung smoothly out from the wall, traveling a distance of half a meter before stopping. She inserted her fingers in the wide gap at the left-hand edge and heaved. The door, one and a half meters high by a meter wide, swung easily, pivoting on a central hinge and revealing a dark cavity behind it.

She rose to a crouch and, holding out the lantern so it began to illuminate the dark space behind the door, peered in round the edge that now stood out from the wall.

She could see stone walls inside—in a space about three

meters by three meters. Gingerly, she turned sideways and squeezed through the opening, holding the lantern up to let its light fill the space and dispel the shadows.

The walls were rough-hewn stone, not dressed and trimmed like the outside. The ceiling was more roughly worked rock, and there was barely room for her to stand erect under it. The small room was littered with cobwebs.

The floor was dirt—dry clay, she thought, studying it more closely. It was rough and uneven underfoot as she moved a few paces into the cavity.

The wall behind her, through which she'd just passed, was to the north. In each of the three walls that faced her, she could see the dark outline of an entrance—or an exit. One east. One west. One south. She went to the western exit and held the lamp inside at arm's length.

There was a narrow tunnel there, barely a meter wide, leading off in a straight line and descending gradually downhill. She frowned, orienting herself. The moat lay in that direction, she realized. The moat and the outer walls. She felt a surge of excitement, and her breath came faster as her heart rate accelerated.

Duncan said that his ancestor had used a tunnel to pass in and out of the castle without anyone seeing him. Could this be that tunnel?

Holding the lantern high, she took a step into the tunnel. Tiny feet skittered and pattered somewhere in the darkness. Rats, she thought. Their presence didn't bother her unduly. She had a saxe and a lantern, and chances were they'd stay away from the light.

She took another pace, then hesitated, realizing she'd left the concealed door wide-open behind her. If anyone came down to the cellar, they'd see it, and the secret would be out. She retraced her steps hurriedly and pushed against the inner edge of the door, so that it pivoted shut with that same loud *CLACK*.

"Maybe I shouldn't have done that," she said doubtfully. She went down on her knees and felt along the bottom row until she reached the fourth stone from the left. To enter, she had pushed against the left side, which now would be on the right. She placed her hand on the right side now and pushed again.

CLACK!

The door swung open again, and she breathed a sigh of relief. The thought of being trapped in here was not a pleasant one. Now she knew she would be able to get back out the way she had come in, and the sense of foreboding that had been growing in her chest was eased.

"Nothing to it really," she said, mocking herself.

"Then let's see where this tunnel goes," she replied. She closed the door once more. Holding the lantern up, she stepped carefully into the dark tunnel, her feet slipping on the uneven clay beneath them.

A tangle of cobwebs brushed her face, and she shoved them aside impatiently. As she moved farther into the tunnel, she felt it sloping sharply beneath her feet. Again, she heard the skitter of paws and claws on the rock and clay. But she saw nothing.

"They're more afraid of you than you are of them," she said. Then she replied, *"Are you afraid of them?"*

This time, she didn't answer. She preferred not to lie to herself.

She went on, stepping carefully as she felt the ground become softer underfoot. She held the lantern low and studied the tunnel floor. The clay was wet here as water forced its way through the roof and walls and dripped down. Her shoulder brushed the wall—there really wasn't a lot of room down here—and left a smear of wet clay on her jerkin.

The air was chill and smelled of damp. More water dripped from the ceiling, and she pulled her collar up to shield herself from it.

"I must be under the moat," she said, with some wonder in her tone. She tried to remember how wide the moat was. She seemed to recall it was eight to ten meters across, and she shuffled on, placing her feet carefully and counting her steps. The floor of the tunnel was level now. It was no longer sloping down.

Then it began to slope up once more and the dripping water gradually tapered off. Something was hanging from the ceiling of the tunnel, and she brought her lantern up to study it more carefully. It was a dense tangle of roots. She recognized it as the root ball of a sizable bush.

"I'm outside the walls," she said. She looked along the length of the tunnel ahead of her, where the darkness swallowed the dim light of her lantern, and wondered how far it went. "Only one way to find out," she said. And set out into the dark tunnel.

16

"HOW MANY DO YOU THINK?" GILAN ASKED. HORACE HAD been studying the enemy force, his eyes narrowed.

"At least a hundred," he said, the anger evident in his voice. "Someone's been lying to us," he added. More troops were emerging from the trees and forming up with their comrades.

"That's closer to a hundred and fifty," Gilan said. "Three times the number we were told to expect." The enemy formation was almost complete, he saw. They had formed in two ranks, spreading across the edge of the cleared ground. As they came closer, Gilan knew, the two ends of the line would advance ahead of the center, to enclose the small force on the riverbank. He turned and called an order. "Archers, two ranks. Here!"

He indicated a spot a few meters to their front. The archers ran to form up in two ranks of ten men each. Their equipment rattled and jingled as they moved, then fell silent when they were in position.

"Open order. Go," Gilan said quietly, and the front rank stepped forward two long paces. They moved as one. Archers might not be much for parade ground drilling and moving like mindless puppets while a sergeant called the step. But this was different. This was part of their fighting technique, and they had practiced it over and over.

Horace nodded approvingly as they turned side on, each man with his bow ready in his left hand and his right resting on the nock of an arrow in his belt quiver. He turned to the cavalry officer.

"Lieutenant. Form your men on either side of the archers, please."

As the lieutenant shouted his orders, the cavalry split into two parties. Half of them rode to the left flank of the archers, the others to the right. They formed in a single line, waiting.

"Shields," the officer called. They had all been carrying their shields on their backs, and now they shrugged them around to the side, slipping their left arms through the arm and hand straps. Each man carried a long lance and they held them upright now, the butts supported in the small leather buckets on their right stirrups. The horses, bred to fight, moved restlessly, snorting and sniffing the air, sensing that a battle was imminent.

"They're keen to go," Gilan said easily.

Horace shrugged. "Horses can't count," he said. They were outnumbered more than three to one, as he'd noted earlier.

"So what now?" Gilan asked.

"We let them come to us," Horace said. "No sense in charging them. They'll simply form a shield wall and we'll lose men trying to break it. Let's use the archers to discourage them."

Gilan nodded. Across the open ground, they could hear a series of orders being shouted.

"They sound like Sonderlanders," he continued. "Whatever happened to 'fifty men, untrained and poorly armed'?"

"At least there's no cavalry," Horace observed. "That's something to be grateful for."

Each of the men facing them carried an oblong shield made of wood, covered with hardened leather and rounded at the corners. Some were armed with spears, some with axes and the remainder with long swords. Most of them wore metal helmets. The others made do with hardened leather caps studded and banded with metal reinforcement.

"I'd say they're mercenaries—at least some of them. Maybe half. And they've provided weapons and armor for the rest. As I said, somebody's been lying to us."

"Yes. We've been sold a pup. That looks certain," Gilan agreed. "And it's obvious that the six we've been following knew we were behind them and led us here into this ambush."

"I can't wait to speak to that villager who set us after them," Horace said. "That is, if he's still in the village. Odds are he's rejoined his friends in the Foxes. Here they come." He added the last as a command rang across the grassy space and the enemy line started to move forward.

"Archers!" Gilan called. "Five shafts each, alternating volleys. Ready!"

There was a whispering sound as twenty arrows were drawn from sheepskin-lined quivers and nocked onto bowstrings.

"Not yet," Horace warned.

Gilan smiled sidelong at him. "I have done this before, you know."

Horace made a small pacifying gesture with his right hand. "Sorry," he said.

The Ranger Commandant let the enemy force advance another half dozen paces, then began to call his orders.

"Front rank, shoot!"

The front rank of ten men brought their bows up, sighted and released. They immediately sank to their knees. Before the arrows had reached their targets, Gilan called again.

"Rear rank, shoot!"

Another ten arrows whipped away, flights catching the air and creating a whistling sound as they did so.

"Front rank, shoot!" The front rank had stood once more as soon as the rear rank's arrows were away. Now they drew and shot another volley. As they released, the sound of their first volley striking shields and men echoed across the field. Two of the enemy went down. Another three staggered from the heavy impact of the arrows on their shields, opening gaps in the line. At the same moment, the second rank's volley smashed home and more gaps appeared.

"Rear rank, plunging volley, shoot!" Gilan called, and the second rank raised their aim point so that their arrows soared high into the air and plunged down onto the enemy's rear line. Too late, the men behind the front line raised their shields overhead. Four of them screamed and fell.

"Pick a target!" Gilan shouted. "Don't just let fly! Front rank, shoot!"

Another volley slammed into the enemy formation. More men fell.

"Rear rank, shoot!"

The enemy advance hesitated, then stalled. Individual soldiers crouched and cowered behind their shields in the face of this deadly, implacable shooting. The archers were the pick of the Araluen bowmen. They had trained under the eagle eye of a retired Ranger and, aside from the members of the Ranger

Corps itself, were probably the finest bowmen in the kingdom.

"Front rank, shoot!"

More arrows whimpered away, slamming into shields, helmets, and exposed arms and legs. Having the two ranks shoot alternately meant that the enemy was facing a continuous hail of arrows, a withering blizzard of death and injury. It was too much. One of the men in the front rank rose from his crouched position and shoved his way through the men at the rear, holding his shield behind him to protect him from those pitiless arrows. Then another joined him. Then three more. Then the entire force was running back toward the tree line and their furious commander.

"Cease shooting!" Gilan called, and the deadly hail stopped. But it was too late for the enemy to reform their men. They ran blindly back into the trees, past their officers, who leaned down from their saddles to strike at them with the flat of their swords.

"Nestor!" called Gilan to the commander of the archers—who he knew to be an above-average shot. "See if you can hit that fellow on the black horse for me."

One of the mounted men at the tree line was obviously the leader of the enemy force. He was shouting abuse and insults at his men as they ran past him. The archer whom Gilan had addressed grinned as he nocked an arrow to his bowstring. He narrowed his eyes, estimating the range, then raised his bow past the horizontal, leaning back at the waist to do so, drew and released in one single movement.

They could follow the flight of his arrow until it disappeared against the bright sky. Gilan, with the skill of long experience, counted it down.

"Three . . . two . . . one . . ."

The enemy commander gave a sudden yell of pain and twisted in his saddle as the arrow plunged into his left shoulder. Caught by surprise and unbalanced by the heavy impact, he swayed, then fell heavily to the turf. Two attendants ran forward and half lifted him, dragging him back into the safety of the tree line.

"Well done, Nestor!" called Horace, and the others, cavalrymen and archers, applauded the shot. "You'll have an extra ration of meat tonight." He paused, studying the enemy, demoralized and cowed, their disciplined formation totally broken.

"Don't think they'll try that again." He urged his horse forward and addressed the archers.

"How many of you can ride?" he asked, and all but five raised their hands. "Bareback?" he added and the hands remained raised.

"Us can't afford fancy saddles." One of the men grinned and the others laughed. After routing the enemy as they had, any joke would gain an appreciative reaction.

"What have you got in mind?" Gilan asked.

Horace indicated the troopers' remounts, tethered to a rope line between two trees. "We've got twenty spare horses," he said. "If we're all riding, we should beat that rabble"—he gestured contemptuously at the enemy force—"to this ford your man told us about."

"What about the five who can't ride?" Gilan asked.

Horace pointed to the small cart that carried their provisions, camping equipment and spare weapons. "They can ride on the cart. It'll be quicker than walking. But we should move now, before the enemy manage to reorganize their men."

Quickly, they set about assigning horses to the men who had

said they could ride. The five who couldn't clambered aboard the supply cart.

"Your troopers are all expert horsemen," Gilan pointed out. "They could let the archers have the saddled horses."

But Horace shook his head. "If my men have to fight, they'll need saddles and stirrups," he said, and Gilan nodded, understanding. A man on horseback needed the support of stirrups and a saddle if he was going to use his lance and sword effectively.

"Good thinking," he said. "Better detail two of your men as horse holders if the Foxes attack again. My archers will need to dismount and form up in a hurry, and we don't want their horses getting away."

Horace agreed and passed the order on to his troop commander. A few minutes later, the force was mounted and he signaled to Ellis to lead the way to the ford. The party trotted off, then increased speed to a canter, hooves thudding dully on the grass.

Horace glanced back over his shoulder at the Foxes. They were nursing their wounds and reluctant to move from the cover of the trees. On the green field between the trees and the river, eleven of their comrades lay where they had fallen.

17

IT WAS COLD IN THE TUNNEL, AND THE DARKNESS SEEMED TO swallow the light of the lantern after a few meters. Maddie walked in a slight crouch, because the roof was low—although occasionally it seemed to open upward for at least another meter. Judging by the way the ground underfoot became unsteady and uneven, she guessed that these were places where the tunnel ceiling had collapsed.

"Hope it doesn't choose to do that while I'm down here," she muttered. The possibility of being buried down here was an unpleasant one, and she realized, with a twinge of discomfort, that nobody knew where she was. If anything went wrong, she could be buried permanently. Maybe Uldred would remember that she had said she wanted to find the secret tunnels. But before any rescue party could set out after her, they'd have to solve the mystery of the concealed chamber in the lower cellar, then figure out how the secret door opened.

Then the ceiling became lower and the path became less cluttered and uneven, and she pushed the thought aside.

It was awkward making her way in the restricted space. With no light other than the glow of her lantern, she had no reference points to tell her how far she had come, and none to indicate how far she might have to go. Too late, she realized that she should have been counting her paces, to give her a rough idea of the distance she had covered.

"Some explorer you are," she sniffed with disgust.

At least the walls and floor were dry, unlike the section that went under the moat. That had been unpleasant in the extreme, with water dripping down from the roof and the ground squishing underfoot with each pace.

Abruptly, she came to a blank wall of rock. It loomed out of the darkness, lit by her lantern, massive and unyielding. She felt a deep sense of disappointment. The journey ended here, in a dead end. There was no secret way out. The original diggers must have felt the same sense of despondency when they realized there was no way they could tunnel through this solid wall of granite that confronted them. She stepped forward, raising the lantern to study the rock more closely, and realized that this wasn't the end after all.

The tunnel took a ninety-degree turn to the right to avoid the massive boulder that barred the way. The resultant path was narrow, and she had to turn side on and hold her breath to squeeze past it. But then the tunnel opened out and gradually curved back to resume its original direction. Her confidence grew once more as she followed the cleared path. Then the tunnel began to incline upward.

She stopped. After at least half an hour of stygian darkness, she thought she could see something up ahead. Unthinking, she advanced her lantern, and the brightness of its tiny yellow flame overpowered whatever it was she had seen—or imagined—in the distance. She lowered the lantern and held it behind her body to shield the light. Gradually, her eyes became accustomed to the near-total darkness around her, and then she could see it again.

A faint circle of light.

She held the lantern forward again, and the small gray circle disappeared. She trudged on, stumbling occasionally on the rough floor of the tunnel, saving herself from falling with her free hand against the cold rock walls.

Ten paces. She had begun to count now. Then twenty. And now, the gray circle in the distance seemed to be clearly visible. She hid the lantern again and the grayness stood out more strongly, becoming almost white.

And it was twice the size it had been originally.

She had no way of knowing how far it was. She just kept trudging and stumbling over the uneven ground, trying to avoid staring directly at the lantern. Whenever she did that, it took several minutes for her vision to recover and become reaccustomed to the gloom.

She knew she must be getting close. The gray circle of light was growing larger with every pace. Gradually, it lost its circular shape and became oblong—more like a wide slit than a hole. The bottom was wider than the top, which tapered sharply.

She knew she was looking at the end of the tunnel now, and she increased her pace, stumbling once or twice in her impatience. Suddenly, she just wanted to be out of this dark, gloomy hole in the ground. She wanted to breathe fresh air and see the bright sunlight once more.

The exit didn't open directly to the outside world. It made another right-angle turn—this time to the left—around a rock outcrop. She squeezed around the rock and found herself confronted by a thick mat of foliage, overgrown branches and leaves that hid the tunnel exit's existence from passersby. She drew her saxe and began to hack at the tangle of leaves and branches, then stopped.

No point in cutting haphazardly, she realized. If she did that, she'd leave the entrance exposed. She worked more discreetly, cutting only enough of the bushes to allow her passage through. Then she forced her way between the thick vines and the unyielding rock and shoved herself out into the open air.

Breathing heavily, she looked around to get her bearings. She was in one of the small groves of trees and bushes that dotted the landscape of the castle park. It was large enough to provide privacy and shelter for couples who wanted to picnic here or spend quiet time together. But not big enough to shelter an attacking force of any kind. A few meters away from the concealed entrance, a wooden table and benches had been placed. It was typical of at least a dozen secluded spots in the parklands. She stepped clear of the entrance, dragging her foot free of the branches and vines that wrapped around it and tried to hold her back, and moved to the table to sit down.

From there, she could see no sign of the entrance when she looked back at it. The rock outcrop concealed it almost completely, and any further sign of it was obscured behind the tangled bushes.

Rising, she moved out of the grove, and suddenly she could see Castle Araluen rearing high above her. She was at least 150 meters from the castle gates. Looking back to where she knew the tunnel exit was, she nodded in admiration of those old tunnelers. They had come a long way, she thought.

She turned and looked downhill, to where she could see the

roofs of the local village rising above the treetops, and a glimpse of sunlight on water that marked the stream that ran through the village. She recalled Duncan telling her that his ancestor had a girlfriend in the village and used the tunnel to sneak out and see her.

"Well, Great-Great-Grandfather," she said, smiling, "you were a naughty boy, weren't you?"

On reflection, she realized, the tunnel must have been intended for a more serious purpose than her great-great-grandfather's secret trysts. Perhaps it was intended as an escape route in times of danger. Or a means of secret access to the castle itself. If the latter were the case, she thought, it was no wonder its existence had been a closely guarded secret. Castle Araluen was regarded as virtually impregnable, but the tunnel under the moat provided a dangerous flaw in that invulnerability. As a result, the fewer people who were aware of it, the better.

"Well," she said reluctantly, "best be getting back."

The thought of leaving this pleasant world of green grass, sunlight and fresh air for the dark, airless confines of the tunnel was decidedly distasteful. She picked up her lantern from where she had left it on the table and realized that she had neglected to extinguish it. She shook it experimentally and the oil reservoir splashed with a hollow sound. She had checked that it was full that morning, but she had been using it extensively since she descended to the cellar. The lantern felt less than half full now, and the thought of running out of oil halfway through the tunnel, and being plunged into darkness, did not appeal to her. She glanced at the sun. It was after the noon hour, and she knew the drawbridge guards changed at noon. That meant there would be nobody to question how she had gotten outside the castle walls if she went back in that way.

Coming to a decision, she raised the lantern glass and blew out the tiny flame. Then she set out up the grassy hill for the castle gates.

That afternoon, after a hurried lunch, she explored the remaining two tunnels. Both of them remained within the castle walls. The one that led east was relatively short. It led to a passage below the courtyard and up a concealed stairway to the massive gatehouse that contained the machinery used to raise and lower the drawbridge. The stairway emerged at a point halfway up the walls, close to the mighty cogwheel that was turned to operate the drawbridge. It was in a cleverly concealed alcove behind the huge heavy wooden beams and chains. Unless someone climbed up there—and there was no reason why anyone might—the stairway would remain undetected.

The third tunnel was considerably longer. Its original direction was to the south and it seemed to run straight, but without any outside reference she had no way of knowing whether it veered to the left or the right. The only way of knowing would be to follow it to its end and see where it took her.

It took her, after several hundred meters, to a chamber some three meters square. Set against the side wall was an angled ladder—or a steep set of a dozen wooden stairs. Holding the lantern high, she peered upward. At the top of the first set of stairs was a second ladder. Beyond that, the darkness prevented her from seeing more. She tested the stairs, gradually letting more and more of her weight settle on one of them, then climbing up a few steps, moving slowly and carefully. They seemed solid enough, so she began to climb in earnest. At the top of the first set, there was a small platform, allowing her to step to the side and align herself with the next flight. After more testing, she mounted that and went up again. As she climbed, she looked up and could make out a third flight, aligned with the first, reaching higher and higher inside the wall. Above that, more darkness. She guessed, from the height she had covered, that she was ascending inside the outer wall of one of the towers—presumably the south tower.

After she climbed two more flights, she could make out a glimmer of daylight high above her. She found herself looking out a narrow slit of a window, high enough and narrow enough to be virtually invisible from the ground. The view from the window confirmed that she was climbing the south tower. She recognized the ground below her, and a partial view of the western tower to her right.

Now that she was able to orient herself, she could see that this concealed set of stairs was on the southwestern side of the tower, and parallel to the large spiral staircase that led upward on the southeastern corner, which provided the main access to the upper floors.

Here, high above the ground, the lighting on the stairs was more even, with those narrow slit windows positioned at every second flight of steps.

She climbed all the way to the top, where she found a door. There was a small spyhole in the door, obvious because of the ray of light it emitted into the dimness of the hidden staircase. She peered through it and could make out a large chamber inside. It seemed deserted. There was a table and a dozen chairs in the room and, on the opposite wall, a weapons rack where spears and halberds were stored.

The door handle was in plain sight on this side. She guessed it would be concealed on the other side—as would the door itself. She placed her hand on the lever, tempted to lift it and let herself inside. Then she hesitated. The room seemed to be deserted, but her field of view was restricted and there could well be somebody in there. If that were the case, it would not be a good idea for her to go blundering into the room, appearing through the wall as if by magic. She took her hand away from the lever. She'd need to find out more about this upper room. She'd never been here before. In fact, she had spent little time in the south tower of the castle.

"I'm going to need to do more research," she muttered under her breath. Then, reluctantly, she headed back down the narrow stairs and retraced her path through the tunnel to the cellar.

All in all, she thought, it had been an interesting day.

18

As Ellis had warned them, the ford across the river was chest deep and the current was strong. Horace and Gilan reined in to study the crossing. So far, there was no sign that the Foxes had followed them. After their demoralizing defeat earlier, they would be in no hurry to get close to those deadly archers again.

"We should get half the archers across first, to set up a defensive line on the far bank and cover the rest of the force while they cross," Gilan said after a few minutes. The river was just over one hundred meters wide at this point, so the bank they were on would be well within range.

"Good thinking," said Horace. "We don't want them catching us while we're floundering around mid-river. I didn't see any archers among them, did you?"

Gilan shook his head. "If they had any, they would have used them," he said. He called to the commander of the archers. "Nestor, get half your men paired up with the cavalry and set up a line on the far bank."

The senior archer nodded and touched his forehead with his knuckles, then began calling orders to his men so that half of them slipped down from the backs of the horses they had been riding. They handed the reins of the unsaddled horses to the cavalrymen they were paired with and stood beside the mounted men, gripping the harness leathers tightly. They handed their bows up to the riders, who slung them across their shoulders.

"Why not let them ride across?" Horace asked.

But Gilan shook his head. "They can ride, but they're not experts. And it'll be tricky controlling a horse in that current. Better to let your men keep the horses in place so they can provide support for the archers walking beside them."

The first of the cavalrymen were urging their horses forward into the river, the archers clinging to the downstream side, where the horses would provide a bulwark against the current. They surged out into the stream, the water rising rapidly until it was lapping at the riders' knees. The archers, clinging desperately to the harnesses, pushed on with them, nearly chin deep in the river. Two of them lost their footing, and their legs floated up to the surface. But they maintained their grip on the stirrup leathers and, with their mounted companions leaning down to heave them upright, regained their feet once more.

Gilan watched until they were halfway across the river. Then, satisfied that the plan was working, he turned his attention back to the tree line, several hundred meters away. He walked to where the second group of archers were standing ready, facing the trees, bows in hand.

"Any sign of them?" he asked the second in command of the force.

The man shook his head. "Not so far, Ranger."

The terrain here was similar to the spot where they had first engaged the Foxes—several hundred meters of open grassy plain before the thickly wooded forest began again.

"Call out as soon as you see them," Gilan said.

The man nodded, his eyes fixed on the shadows beneath the trees.

Behind him, Gilan heard a whip cracking, accompanied by loud splashes and shouts of encouragement. He turned to see the supply cart as it entered the water, with the five archers who couldn't ride still clinging to it. It lurched sideways under the initial thrust of the current, then the wagoner whipped up his horses and they bent to the traces, pulling it straight. The wagon rocked and shuddered as it coped with the uneven river bottom and the force of the water shoving against it. For a moment, Gilan thought it might tip over, and he opened his mouth to shout a warning. But it was solidly built, with a low center of gravity, and it regained its balance, gathering speed as the horses pulling it grew in confidence.

The wagon lurched violently as one wheel sank into a hole in the riverbed. One of the archers was nearly dislodged from his precarious perch, saved only by a quick hand thrown out by one of his companions, who dragged him back to safety. Gilan heard a quick peal of laughter from the men on the cart, including the one who had nearly fallen. He nodded to himself. Morale was good if they could laugh about the near mishap, he thought.

He touched Blaze's sides with his heels and trotted up to rein in beside Horace, who was watching the progress of the small force across the river.

"What have you got in mind once we're across?" he asked.

The tall warrior grinned ruefully at him. "Well, there's no further need to track down those six Foxes we've been following," he said. "We've found the main force we've been looking for."

"And there are more of them than we bargained for," Gilan said. "We'll need to find shelter—somewhere we can set up a good defensive position."

"I was thinking we should head for that old hill fort we saw on the map. It's only three or four kilometers downstream from here."

Gilan nodded agreement. "Thought that might be what you had in mind," he said. "They're nearly across," he added, indicating the men in the river.

The first three horsemen were urging their horses up the shallow slope on the far bank, the archers releasing their hold on the horses' harness and walking unsteadily away from them. The cavalrymen who had assisted them handed their bows back and the archers sat on the grass, wringing out their sodden breeches and jackets. As he watched, the remaining archers waded clear of the river. The supply cart plunged up the bank, the archers riding it jumping clear and running to re-form with their comrades.

"Ranger!"

It was the archer Gilan had spoken to who was calling. Gilan looked at him now and saw the man pointing to the tree line in the distance. There was movement there as men began to emerge from the forest.

"Looks like our friends have arrived," he said.

Horace looked to the far side of the river, where the archers who had already crossed were still recovering from the effort of wading chest deep in the fast-running current, and from the soaking they had received.

"Be a couple of minutes before they're ready," he said.

Gilan pursed his lips. His friend was right. "The lads on this side will have to discourage the Foxes," he said. He slipped down from Blaze's saddle. "Think I'll give them a hand."

He strode across the grass to join the small band of archers. There were eight of them in the line. Seven had crossed with the cavalry and five had ridden on the supply cart.

Horace turned to the waiting cavalrymen. "Form up on the riverbank," he said. "Be ready to help the archers when they make a run for it."

In the distance, he could hear orders being shouted. The Foxes were beginning to form up—a single extended line this time.

"Archers, stand to," Gilan ordered quietly.

The bowmen, who had been lounging on the grass, rose to their feet to form a line, spaced two meters apart, standing side on, each with his right hand on an arrow in his belt quiver, his left holding the bow loosely, in a relaxed position. There was no sign of nervousness or anxiety among them. They were confident in their own ability and knew they were about to deal a deadly rebuff to the advancing troops.

From the far side of the river, a piercing whistle cut the air. Horace turned and saw that the twelve archers who had already crossed were now formed up as well. Their commander waved his bow over his head to signify that they were ready.

"Nestor has his men in position," Horace called to Gilan.

The Ranger acknowledged the information with a wave of his hand. His eyes were still fixed on the approaching troops, now striding with growing confidence, since the expected hail of arrows had not materialized.

Their spirits were further bolstered as they saw that the

force of archers facing them had been halved. Eight bowmen, they thought, couldn't do much to stop them.

They were about to find out how wrong they were.

An officer rode among the advancing infantry, leaning down to drive them forward with blows from the flat of his sword. The men recoiled from him, but he was keeping them moving, not allowing them to shirk or hesitate.

Gilan allowed himself a humorless smile. "Never a good idea to draw attention to yourself in a battle," he said. "Particularly when there are archers around." He raised his voice so the line of archers could hear him. "All right, lads, I'm going to take down that nuisance on the bay horse. When I do, that's your signal to start. Shoot fast, but aim your shots. Ready?"

There was a feral growl from the waiting archers in response. Eight hands drew eight arrows from their quivers and nocked them ready on the bows. Gilan nodded approvingly. Their discipline was excellent, he thought.

Then, the enemy line passed a point he had already selected. He nocked an arrow to his own string, raised his bow, sighted and shot in one smooth movement, barely seeming to aim.

The arrow flew in a whimpering parabola, then struck home in the center of the rider's chest, hurling him backward over the horse's rump and leaving him lying still on the grass. The men around him parted, looking fearfully at him as he lay there. Nobody had seen the arrow coming. Nobody had seen any of the men facing them shoot.

Then the first flight of arrows from the near riverbank hit them, slamming into shields and helmets and exposed arms and legs. One man fell. Two others staggered under the impact.

And the second flight of arrows hit them, causing more damage, creating more gaps in the advancing line.

And then a new rain of arrows was upon them as Nestor and his men on the far bank added their contribution to the mayhem. Arrows plunged down from a higher angle, an almost ceaseless shower of hardened steel points that slashed through chain mail, tore holes in leather and metal breastplates, and sent men crashing to the ground on all sides.

One sergeant looked along the line, seeing the neatly ordered rank being disrupted and torn apart. They still had seventy meters to go before they reached the small force of archers facing them. At this rate, few of them would make it. As he had the thought, the man next to him fell with an arrow through the top of his leather helmet.

He glanced back to see their commander, safe and secure in the tree line, screaming at his men.

"It's easy for you," he muttered. "You're not out here." He stopped and held his sword over his head, waving it in a circle in an unmistakable gesture, then letting the point descend and indicate the ground behind them.

"Fall back!" he yelled, his voice carrying across the battlefield. "Fall back! Close up and fall back!"

Better to have them retreat now, while they still had some vestige of discipline, than wait till the arrows had decimated them and destroyed their will to fight.

Gilan saw the lone figure calling orders. As he watched, he saw the line close up, sealing the gaps torn by his archers' arrows, and he raised his own bow to shoot the sergeant who was restoring some sense of discipline to their attackers. Then he stayed his hand. The man was ordering the Foxes back, ordering them to retreat. He might be saving some of their lives by keeping them in formation, but it made no sense to cut him down now. He was doing the work of the Araluen force.

The line of attacking infantry began to withdraw, leaving a score of huddled shapes on the grass behind them. Once they began to retreat, Gilan knew they wouldn't attack again in a hurry.

"Cease shooting!" he called, and the last few arrows hissed away. Nestor's men had already stopped. The Fox line was out of range now.

"Back to the riverbank!" he ordered. "Partner up and get across the river!"

19

THE NEW IBERIAN AMBASSADOR WAS AN INCREDIBLY TALL and thin man, standing well over 190 centimeters. He was aged around forty and had thick black hair slicked back from his face with a scented pomade. His skin was swarthy and he had a large hooked nose set between prominent cheekbones. His eyes were dark—almost black, Maddie thought—and his eyebrows were thick and bushy. They too were black, with no trace of gray in them. She wondered if he perhaps dyed his hair.

He wore a richly brocaded red-and-gold tunic, with the national symbol of Iberion, a griffin, on the left breast. He was accompanied by a retinue of only four attendants, since he had been warned that the official dinner was to be a small affair only.

"My apologies again for such a small gathering, Don Ansalvo," Cassandra said as they were all seated at the dining table in the large hall. "Normally I would have arranged a larger group to welcome you. But as you know, my husband and our Ranger Corps Commandant are absent at the moment, so it's just us."

"Just us" was Cassandra herself, Maddie, Dimon and Lord Anthony, the Castle Araluen chamberlain.

Don Ansalvo waved the apology aside. "A smaller gathering

gives us the opportunity to get to know each other more closely," he said. "And besides, who could complain about a gathering that contains two such beautiful ladies?"

He made a graceful hand gesture that encompassed Cassandra and Maddie, at the same time contriving to bow forward from the waist, in spite of the fact that he was seated.

Maddie caught Dimon's eye and rolled her own eyes. Dimon hid a grin behind his napkin. Iberians, Maddie had been told, were well-known for their effusive compliments and exaggerated sense of gallantry. Don Ansalvo looked at her now, his perfect white teeth showing in a smile, and she bowed her head toward him in recognition of his remark.

"You're too kind, Don Ansalvo," Cassandra said.

He looked back at her. "Tell me, my lady, what is it that has taken Sir Horace away from the castle?" He had been informed of Horace's absence when he arrived, but the reason hadn't been stated.

Cassandra shrugged. "It's a relatively minor matter, but one that requires his attention."

Don Ansalvo tilted his head to one side. "A relatively minor matter?" he repeated. "What is it exactly?"

Cassandra wasn't keen to discuss Araluen's internal politics with the new ambassador. Araluen and Iberion were at peace, but the Kingdom of Iberion had a reputation for meddling when other countries were having problems. She indicated for Dimon to answer, feigning disinterest in the matter.

"A small group of hotheads and rabble-rousers are trying to stir up the people," he said. "It's not a big problem but Sir Horace thought it best to stamp it out before it became one."

Don Ansalvo nodded, leaning back in his chair while he

considered the answer. "And he is right," he said. "Any sign of rebellion must be stamped out quickly. We have a problem of our own in Iberion."

"And what might that be, Don Ansalvo?" Maddie asked. She sensed her mother's reluctance to discuss the Red Fox Clan and thought this was a way to steer the conversation away from them.

Don Ansalvo favored her with a rather patronizing smile. "It's nothing that need worry such a gem of female pulchritude," he said smoothly.

She smiled back, forcing the expression onto her face. "And yet I'd be interested to know," she said.

He shrugged. "As Sir Dimon says, hotheads and rabble-rousers. Two of our southern provinces are seeking to secede from Iberion and form a separate nation. Naturally, we can't allow this to happen."

"Naturally," Maddie said dryly. She was willing to bet that the provinces in question were rich in farmland or natural resources. Don Ansalvo studied her briefly. He didn't seem to notice the cynical attitude behind her reply. But then, Maddie thought, he was a diplomat and had years of experience in masking his true feelings.

She shifted slightly in her seat. In spite of her misgivings about wearing formal clothes once more, Maddie was enjoying the dinner. The blue gown that her mother had chosen for her was an excellent choice and she knew it suited her. But it was a fraction tight around the shoulders.

Don Ansalvo took a sip of his wine and turned his attention back to Dimon. Maddie had the distinct impression that he preferred to discuss important matters with a man, rather than with a girl like herself, or even her mother, the Princess Regent.

"But tell me, Sir Dimon, what is the nature of this rebellion of yours?" he asked.

Dimon hesitated. He seemed to share Cassandra's reluctance to discuss internal politics with an outsider. But Don Ansalvo had been frank and forthcoming about the problems Iberion was facing, so it was difficult for Dimon not to go into a little detail. He glanced quickly at Cassandra, who nodded, almost imperceptibly.

"There's a small group of agitators who object to the law that says a daughter may inherit the throne. They wish to return to the rule of male succession," he said. His tone indicated that he would give no further details on the matter.

The ambassador nodded slowly. "Ah, of course. Your country is one of the few that allow female succession, isn't it?" he said thoughtfully. "You say they wish to return to the old way. So this has not always been the law in Araluen?"

"My grandfather changed the law," Cassandra told him, with a note of finality in her voice.

Don Ansalvo stroked his waxed mustache. "It would never do in Iberion," he said. "My people wouldn't stand for it."

If they're anything like you, I'm sure they wouldn't, Maddie thought. She glanced quickly at Dimon and was surprised to see the stony, set expression on his face. It was there for only an instant, and then he realized she was watching him, and smiled brightly at her. She assumed his look of distaste was triggered by the Iberian's unmistakably superior attitude to all things Araluen. Cassandra interrupted Maddie's train of thought with her next question.

"So, Don Ansalvo, when do you plan to move into your residence?"

As ambassador, Don Ansalvo was provided with a large manor house as his official residence. It was a few kilometers south of the village that sheltered under the castle's protective shadow. Cassandra's question, and the deliberate change of subject, indicated to him that any further questions about the trouble in the north would be unwelcome—and probably go unanswered. He was diplomatic enough to concede.

"I thought we would leave at mid-morning tomorrow," he said. "If that suits your arrangements?"

"As a matter of fact, that would suit me perfectly," she said. "We're about to let most of the castle staff go and keep only a skeleton staff on duty."

Don Ansalvo's raised eyebrows posed an obvious question, and Lord Anthony leaned forward to explain.

"At this time of year, the farms in the district are plowing the stubble into the fields and gathering food and firewood for the winter—salting meat and bringing in the late harvest of vegetables," he said. "Most of the castle staff come from local farms. We usually let go as many people as we can spare to help out. And this year, with Sir Horace and most of the garrison absent, we only need a skeleton staff in the castle—no more than twenty people. Even I will be leaving early tomorrow. My daughter and her new baby are coming to visit and staying at our house in the village." Anthony smiled at Cassandra. "The princess has kindly given me leave to spend time with them."

"Of course," Don Ansalvo replied. Then he turned those dark, penetrating eyes on Maddie once more. "But what will you do, Princess? Won't it be boring for a lively young woman like yourself to be stuck in a half-empty castle?"

"Oh no," Maddie replied, with expertly feigned enthusiasm.

"I'll have my sewing and needlework to keep me busy and entertained. You've no idea how diverting petit point can be."

Don Ansalvo sniffed delicately. "I'm sure I haven't," he replied.

Maddie quickly glanced at her mother and read the warning expression in her eyes.

Don't push it.

But Maddie was still irritated by the ambassador's earlier comment about Araluen's laws of succession. She smiled sweetly now. "Tell me, Don Ansalvo, you said a female ruler would never be accepted in Iberion. What makes you say that?"

The Iberian leaned back in his chair and made a languid gesture with one hand. "Iberians believe it is not a woman's place to rule. That is a man's role."

Maddie saw the quick warning glance from her mother but ignored it. With the smile still fixed to her face, she continued. "And what, precisely, is a woman's role?"

"It's an important one," the ambassador said condescendingly. "A woman nurtures and teaches. She is the emotional center of the home. She creates an atmosphere of gentility and affection so important for the family."

"And stays barefoot in the kitchen?" There was a hard edge to Maddie's voice now, but Don Ansalvo didn't seem to notice. He considered her statement and nodded.

"We have nothing against shoes, but preparing meals is an important part of a woman's function—either cooking them herself or overseeing the efforts of servants." He nodded toward Cassandra as he said this. Then, seeing Maddie's obvious disagreement, he continued.

"But a woman cannot lead a country in time of war. That is a man's job. No woman has ever done so."

"My mother has been involved in more than one battle in her time," Maddie said doggedly. The smile was long gone now. Cassandra made a gesture for her to desist, but Maddie had the bit between her teeth and Don Ansalvo's reply had only served to fan her anger further.

"Yes," he said, "before I accepted this appointment, I studied your mother's past accomplishments and they are admirable. But the battles she fought in were small skirmishes, not full-scale wars." He bowed toward Cassandra. "No offense intended, my lady."

"I think the Temujai invasion of Skandia might count as a full-scale war. I'm sure the Skandians thought so," Maddie said.

He raised an eyebrow at her in polite disdain. "And was your mother in command of the Skandian army?" he asked.

She flushed, realizing she had trapped herself with her hasty words. "Well, no. Not exactly . . ."

"As I read the account, the commander was the Skandian Oberjarl Ragnak. And his chief strategist was one of your Rangers."

"That's true. But—"

"In fact, in all of her battles, Princess Cassandra was assisted by one or more of your redoubtable Rangers. And her husband, of course, a champion knight. Fighting and commanding armies is not something a woman is cut out for."

"Yet my mother is practicing with the sword," Maddie said.

Don Ansalvo tilted his head to one side, considering the statement. "Ah yes. Many Iberion ladies of noble birth learn to use the foil or the épée. It develops coordination and balance. But I think a woman with a light sword, facing a fully armored knight, would be at some risk. Don't you agree, Sir Dimon?"

Dimon, not expecting to be drawn into the conversation, hesitated awkwardly. He had no wish to offend the ambassador, or Cassandra.

"I think," he said reluctantly, "that in such a case, the advantage would lie with the man."

Don Ansalvo nodded, a superior expression on his face. Cassandra hurried to change the subject before Maddie could speak again.

"Well, that's enough talk of wars and fighting," she said. "Don Ansalvo, I'm told you are an expert performer on the lute?"

The ambassador bowed slightly from the waist. "I do have some small skill in that area."

"Then perhaps you'd favor us with a song?" Cassandra said.

Don Ansalvo shook his head modestly, making a disclaiming gesture with both hands. "No, no. I couldn't possibly bore you," he began.

But one of his entourage had already produced a lute case from beneath the table and was opening it and passing it to his master.

"Oh, well," said Don Ansalvo, accepting the instrument. "Perhaps one song—an Iberian song about a beautiful lady and a noble knight who dies defending her honor . . ."

And more fool him, Maddie thought grimly. She settled back in her chair, her anger at the smooth-talking, condescending Iberian still smoldering. Don Ansalvo smiled at her with what he thought was overwhelming charm, struck a few preparatory chords and began to sing. Maddie leaned back in her chair.

This could be a long night, she thought.

20

⟨⟨⟨⟨⟨⟨⟨⟨⟨⟨⟨⟨⟨⟨⟨⟨⟨⟩⟩⟩⟩⟩⟩⟩⟩⟩⟩⟩⟩⟩⟩⟩⟩

THE FOLLOWING DAY, MADDIE AND CASSANDRA WERE strolling around the battlements, enjoying the expansive views below the castle. Cassandra was taking a welcome break from her desk and its litter of paperwork.

"Well, you managed to survive the ordeal of dining with the Iberian ambassador," Cassandra said.

Maddie frowned. "He's a pompous, condescending git," she said spitefully.

Her mother smiled. "Such courtly language," she said. "He seemed very taken with you."

"He seemed very taken with himself," Maddie replied. "But he certainly kept himself busy passing oily compliments on my 'unsurpassed beauty.'"

When he had finally set the lute aside—after not one but half a dozen numbers—Don Ansalvo had spent the rest of the evening plying Maddie with effusive, overstated compliments, all of them based on his appreciation of her physical charms.

"Well, he's a diplomat, and an Iberian. There's an old saying, *When you've learned to fake sincerity, you're ready to become an Iberian diplomat.*"

Maddie pushed out her bottom lip in a moue of mock disappointment. "You mean he wasn't being sincere?"

Cassandra grinned. "I'm afraid not. In case you were wondering, your eyes don't really *shine to match the full moon low over the horizon*," she said, quoting one of Don Ansalvo's more exotic compliments.

"I'm devastated to hear it," Maddie said, in a tone that indicated she was anything but. "I felt sorry for Dimon. He was sort of caught in the middle there, wasn't he?"

"Yes. He apologized later for not sticking up for you. But there wasn't a lot he could say. You seem to be getting on well with him," Cassandra added, a questioning note in her voice.

Maddie nodded. "Yes. I like him. He's good company."

"You know he's a distant relative, don't you?" her mother said.

"Dimon?" Maddie looked up in surprise.

Cassandra nodded. "Pretty distant. I think he's your cousin six or seven times removed on your grandmother's side," she said. "It gets a little hard to keep track after four or five removes."

"So we're related. No wonder he's such a nice person," Maddie said.

"It's not a close enough relationship to form any barrier if you were . . . interested in him," Cassandra said, studying her daughter's reaction.

Maddie snorted derisively. "Oh, please!" she said. "I like him. He's good company. But I'm not interested in him romantically!"

Cassandra shrugged. "Just saying, if you were," she said. It was a new experience for her to think about her daughter forming attachments with personable young men. She wasn't totally sure how she felt about the sensation.

But Maddie waved the idea aside and changed the subject. "So what's been keeping you busy?"

Cassandra sighed and stretched. "I'd forgotten the amount of paperwork involved in accepting a new ambassador," she said. "King Carlos of Iberion sent a twenty-page missive for me to answer in detail—and in suitably florid court language. I should have kept Lord Anthony on for a few more days to draft the reply for me. It's taking me ages."

"Why not call him back?" Maddie asked, although she suspected her mother would never do that.

Cassandra shrugged. "His daughter arrived with her new baby daughter. He's settled happily at home with his family. And with the visitors, he has a lot of work to do stockpiling food and firewood for the colder months. What about you? What have you been up to?" she asked.

Maddie waved a hand vaguely in the air. "Oh, just poking around the castle. I've been out to Warwick and Lou's farm a couple of times to see Bumper. Patrolled the area to see if anything's happening. Gilan asked me to do that," she added, in case her mother might think she was interfering where she wasn't wanted.

Cassandra nodded. She knew about the arrangement with Warwick and Lou, knew they were part of Gilan's intelligence network. And she was aware that Gilan had asked her daughter to keep an eye on the fief in his absence.

"Gilan said something about the old abbey above the farm," Cassandra said.

"Yes. Apparently they had seen lights up there. Or thought they had. I checked it out but there's been nobody there for some time. If anything, it was probably travelers passing through and using the building for shelter."

She paused, then changed the subject abruptly. "Mum, tell me about the south tower."

Castle Araluen had four towers, one at each of the four corners of the crenellated outer wall. In the center was a fifth, the keep. The main administration offices, formal dining halls, audience rooms, throne room and apartments were there, along with floors of accommodation for visiting guests and senior castle staff. Cassandra's and Horace's work spaces were there as well, in addition to the royal apartments.

The keep was lower than the four towers. But it was joined to them at the fourth-floor level by four arched stone walkways, which gave the entire structure the appearance of being ready to spring into the air.

"You grew up here. Don't you know?" Cassandra replied.

Maddie shook her head. "I never spent much time there when I was a kid," she said. "But I was in there today and . . . it seems kind of empty. There are no rooms or apartments—well, hardly any—in the lower floors. It just seems sort of superfluous. Maybe that's why it never interested me when I was growing up."

"I suppose not," Cassandra replied. "Actually, it's what we call our 'retreat of last resort.'"

That phrase caught Maddie's attention, Cassandra thought, seeing her daughter sit up straighter. It had implications of adventure and action and, as such, it would inevitably fire her daughter's interest in martial affairs.

"That sounds fascinating," Maddie said.

Cassandra elaborated. "In the event that Castle Araluen's outer wall were breached," she said, "we would fall back to the keep as our penultimate line of defense. But if that fell in its turn, the defenders could access the south tower by way of the arched stone bridge. The south tower is much more defensible and is set up to survive a long siege."

"How so?" Maddie asked.

"The top levels are served by a single spiral staircase, which could be easily defended by a few men. It's the only access."

Not quite, thought Maddie. But she said nothing.

Cassandra continued. "The upper two floors are kept stocked with food and weapons. And within the spire there's a large cistern that collects rainwater—that would be even more important than food supplies in the long run. Even a small force could hold out there for months."

Maddie nodded thoughtfully.

Cassandra mistook her expression for concern and added reassuringly, "Not that it's ever likely to come to that, of course. The outer wall has never been breached."

"Of course," Maddie said.

That explains why it's the only tower served by a secret staircase, she thought. If all else failed, the occupants could escape down to the cellar level and out through the tunnel under the moat.

Cassandra rose from the table. "Well, I'm afraid I still have work to do," she said.

Maddie looked up at her. "Don't stay up too late."

Cassandra smiled. "I'm supposed to say that to you," she said. She started toward the door that led to her office, then, as a thought struck her, turned back. "Oh, by the way, don't disappear tomorrow. I have people arriving that I want you to meet."

Maddie grinned at her. "Not more smooth-talking Iberians?"

Cassandra gave a short laugh. "Not these people. They're quite rough and ready."

"Rough and ready?" Maddie replied. "They sound like my sort of people."

"They are. I'm pretty sure you'll like them. They're Skandians."

21

THE EIGHT ARCHERS BROKE RANKS AND RAN FOR THE RIVER-bank, where horsemen were waiting to help them across the ford. Handing their bows up to the riders to keep them clear of the river, they seized hold of the horses' harnesses, grabbing stirrup leathers or girth straps. Some of the horses had leather harnesses around their necks as well, and these made excellent handholds. The riders waited until their "passengers" were settled, then urged their horses forward at a walk into the river.

Seeing that his men had started crossing, Gilan paced backward to the riverbank, keeping a keen eye on the Foxes.

As he had expected, their discipline and their willingness to fight had evaporated. They skulked among the trees, seeking protection from the deadly arrows—even though they were well out of range. Their commander, his left arm in a sling and a bloodstained bandage around his shoulder, railed at them in vain, challenging their courage, threatening to withhold their pay and have every fifth man whipped.

They avoided his furious gaze, turning away and sinking to the long grass, physically and mentally exhausted by the ordeal they had just gone through. Reflecting the opinion of the sergeant who had led them back to safety, they occasionally cast angry glances at their shouting commander. It's fine for you to shout and threaten, they thought. You stayed safe here in the trees while we were providing target practice for those cursed archers.

A leader who refused to share the discomforts of campaigning and the risk of combat with his men rapidly lost their respect and their willingness to obey his orders. But their commander was too obtuse to realize that. He thought bluster and threats could take the place of respect.

Eventually, by dint of threatening and punishing those who disobeyed, discipline would be restored among the Foxes—to a certain extent. But it would take time, and in that time, the enemy were escaping across the ford.

Gilan waited on the southern bank, keeping a keen watch on the enemy force, until the second group of archers were almost across the river. Then, seeing no sign that the Foxes had rallied, he turned Blaze's head and urged the mare into the river.

She pushed strongly, half walking, half swimming. She wasn't as long in the leg as the taller cavalry horses, and the water came up almost to the saddle. But Gilan was an expert rider, and he maintained his balance against Blaze's lunging progress, staying in the saddle as the horse forced her way across the ford. Then he felt the water level dropping away as the river shallowed.

Blaze's gait steadied and she trotted up the bank, pausing to shake herself, sending a shower of water that gleamed silver in the sunlight.

Horace, who had been waiting for Gilan, took the brunt of

it. "Thank you very much," he said sarcastically, wiping river water from his face.

Gilan grinned easily at him. "If you don't know that's the first thing a horse does after it's been swimming, don't blame me."

Horace shielded his eyes with one hand and peered back across the river. "No sign of movement there?"

Gilan stood in his stirrups and followed the tall warrior's gaze. "It'll be a while before they get them moving again," he said. "They've taken two drubbings from our archers, and they won't be keen for a third."

"Of course, things might change once they see we've moved out," Horace said.

Gilan considered the statement. "You think they'll keep after us then?"

Horace nodded. "Don't see why they wouldn't. They lured us here for a purpose, and so far they haven't accomplished it."

Gilan scanned the ground around them. The terrain here was similar to the side they had just left, with relatively open ground for a hundred meters or so, then thick trees. Forty meters from the river, he saw a line of low bushes—fifteen meters long and about chest high—that would provide concealment for a small group of men.

"I'll keep four men here, under cover," he said, indicating the bushes. "Once the Foxes get their nerve up and try to cross, we'll do what we can to change their minds."

"And what happens when you leave?" Horace asked.

Gilan shrugged. "With any luck, they won't know that we've gone. I'll get the men to fall back one at a time, staying low until they reach the trees. If you leave some horses tethered there for us, we should get a head start on them."

Horace considered the plan. "That should work," he said. "Without horses, they're going to have to try to get ropes across the river so that their main body can cross. So the first men to cross will have to swim, carrying the ropes."

"And they should be easy targets," Gilan agreed. "If we pick off three or four of them, the rest will be reluctant to try crossing. By the time they realize we're gone, we should have a good lead."

"I assume you'll be the last to leave?" Horace said.

Gilan met his gaze evenly. "Of course," he said. "I'm not going to ask someone else to stay behind. Besides, I'm the best shot, so it makes sense for me to stay till the end."

"Just checking," Horace said mildly. In Gilan's place, he would have done the same. Besides, as the Ranger said, it made sense for the best shot to be the last to leave.

"You'd better get moving," Gilan told him now, in a brisker tone. He gestured toward the far bank, and the small figures moving among the trees. "They won't stay moping around over there forever." He dismounted and strode quickly to where the archers were waiting. Most of them had stripped off their soaked outer clothing and were working in pairs to wring the water out. They looked up as he approached.

"All right, get dressed and move out. Find the horses you were riding and mount up. Nestor, Clete, Gilbert and Walt, you stay with me. Have you all got full quivers?"

Two of the men nodded. The others indicated their quivers. One had three shafts left. The other had five. "Right—collect more from the supply wagon. In fact, get extra for the rest of the men. On the double!" he snapped, and the two archers trotted off to the supply wagon, where two thousand spare shafts were stored in arrow bags.

A few minutes later, Horace led the force into the tree line and turned to the west. Horses for the four archers who would remain with Gilan were tethered in the trees, out of sight of the far bank. Horace led Blaze into the trees and let the reins fall to the ground once they were in the shadows. The Ranger horse would wait there until Gilan came for her. Staying low to avoid being seen, he then returned to the line of bushes, where the others were waiting. They crouched in the cover of the bushes while he outlined the plan.

"Stay out of sight," he told them. "We don't want them to know we're here until we start shooting. Then, one by one, make your way to the trees and follow the main party. Try to stay out of sight. I want the enemy to think we're still here, even after we're long gone."

The four men nodded. They grinned at one another. They were enjoying this fight. Usually a battle meant they stayed in a line and shot shaft after shaft into the air in a solid hail of arrows. It was fairly impersonal, and most of the time they couldn't really see the effect their shooting was having. This encounter was different. They had seen their shafts taking down the men who were advancing on them, seen the havoc and uncertainty their shooting caused.

And so far, they had been untouched themselves.

"Might as well make yourselves comfortable while we're waiting," Gilan told them. "I'll keep an eye on our friends across the river."

They settled down on the soft grass. Like all soldiers, they were experienced in taking any opportunity to rest. In the space of a few minutes, two of them were even snoring gently, their heads resting on their packs. Gilan looked at them and smiled.

Nestor, the oldest of the group, saw the look. "They'll sleep anywhere," he said, grinning. "If they'd stopped halfway across the river, they probably would have dozed off there."

The sun was warm on their backs, and their clothes were quickly drying. Not that they'd be completely dry, of course, but they were no longer heavy and sodden. Gilan pulled his cowl up to put the pale oval of his face in shadow and crouched behind the line of bushes, finding a gap through which he could watch the far bank.

A mayfly buzzed around his head. He was tempted to swipe at it but resisted the urge. The movement might be seen by the enemy. Instead, as it hovered close to his face, he screwed his lips up and tried to blow it away. The mayfly ignored the attempt.

Time passed, and the faint noises of Horace's group—the jingle of harness, rattle of weapons and thudding of hooves on the soft grass—gradually died away. The mayfly became more persistent, and in spite of himself, Gilan found his eyelids drooping heavily. He shook his head and changed his position into a less comfortable one, kneeling on one knee. Clete and Walt continued to snore softly.

He saw movement across the river and came more upright, looking closely, although remaining concealed behind the bushes.

A dozen or so men were advancing from the tree line, heading for the riverbank. They moved cautiously, expecting any minute to be assailed by a hail of arrows. As this didn't happen, they became more confident. Initially moving in a crouch, they stood and began to move faster. Gilan, from his hiding place, could see that three of them had heavy coils of rope around their shoulders. He nodded to Nestor, indicating the two sleeping men. The old archer reached behind him and shook the two men gently. Experienced warriors that they were, they came awake without any undue noise, instantly ready for action.

"They're coming," Gilan whispered. "Get ready."

The four archers slowly changed position until they were kneeling on one knee behind the covering bushes. They had each slipped an arrow from their quivers and had them ready on the bowstrings. They looked expectantly at the Ranger, now half concealed in the bushes, where he had moved forward for a better view.

"Not yet," he said softly.

The three men carrying the ropes had reached the river's edge. They shrugged the rope coils off their shoulders and began to attach the loose ends to anchor points on the bank—sturdy saplings or deeply embedded rocks.

They stripped down to their undergarments and tied the ropes around their waists.

"They're going to swim the ropes across," Gilan whispered. "We'll wait till they're halfway across and start shooting."

Watched by their comrades, who were crouched behind their shields on the bank, the three rope carriers waded into the river. One of them cried out in surprise as he felt the unexpected strength of the current. Then he recovered and continued to wade out.

Within a few meters, they were shoulder deep in the water and forced to begin swimming. As soon as their feet left the bottom, they began to drift quickly downstream. But they were all strong swimmers, and Gilan could see they were making good progress across the ford. He selected the first man who had entered the water. He was obviously the strongest swimmer of the three and had gained a lead of several meters over the others.

"I'll take the nearest one," Gilan said, rising slowly to his feet. "You take care of the others."

His four archers also rose, their heads and shoulders now above the screening bushes. But they went unnoticed. Understandably, the men on the far bank were watching the swimmers, slowly paying out the rope behind them as they fought their way across the river. The fact that they had been unmolested so far had given them a false sense of confidence.

Gilan brought up his bow and sighted on the leading swimmer. Beside him, he sensed the other shooters were doing the same.

"Now," he said softly, and released.

22

MADDIE RODE OUT EARLY THE NEXT MORNING ON SUNDANCER, heading for Warwick's farm. Mindful of Cassandra's instruction not to "disappear," she had checked with her mother and ascertained that her Skandian guests wouldn't be arriving before midday.

"But that means you have to be back here by half past the eleventh hour," her mother warned her. "I want to ride down to the dock to welcome them."

Maddie promised that she would be back well before that time, and went to saddle her horse.

She rode through the portcullis and across the drawbridge, nodding a friendly greeting to the sentries there, who came to attention to salute her. Once she was in the parkland, she set Sundancer to a gentle canter, enjoying the wind in her hair as the Arridan loped across the neatly tailored grass, his hoofbeats sounding a dull tattoo on the soft ground. When she entered the forest, she had to slow down to a trot. The trees grew too close together here to permit any higher speed, unless in the case of a dire emergency.

She whistled as she rode, and Sundancer, sensing her

cheerful mood, tossed his head and shook his mane at her. She leaned forward and patted his neck. He was a good horse, but her mood was caused by the fact that she would be seeing Bumper. She hadn't visited the farm in several days, and she was missing her shaggy little companion.

"If it weren't for him, you'd be my favorite horse," she said, and Sundancer tossed his head once more at the sound of her voice. Unlike Bumper, however, he didn't reply.

Warwick was working in the barn when she rode into the farmyard. He had the big doors open to admit light and was repairing the leather traces on a plow. He strolled out to meet her as she dismounted and then tethered Sundancer to the post by the farmhouse door.

"Morning, Maddie," he said cheerfully. "Come to see Bumper, have you?"

"That's right, Warwick. And you, of course," she added with a grin, which he matched. She had her Ranger cloak rolled up and tied behind her saddle. She took it down now, shook it out and swung it around her shoulders. The simple act of wearing it made her feel more positive, more confident. The cloak was a symbol of who she was and what she did.

"Thought I'd scout around the area," she said. "Has anything been going on?"

Warwick screwed up his face thoughtfully before answering. "Not sure," he said. "Barnaby Coddling at Coddling Farm says he thought there'd been people up at the abbey again the other night. But Barnaby's inclined to imagine things. Once he hears there's been activity there, he's bound to think he's seen it. Likes a bit of drama, does Barnaby."

"Maybe I should take a look," Maddie said. She had loosened

the girth straps on Sundancer's saddle and was heading for the barn to saddle Bumper. "Can you feed and water Sundancer for me?" she asked.

Warwick nodded. "Be pleased to," he said. He had set down his tools and moved to where the Arridan was standing patiently. He rubbed the velvet nose. Sundancer snuffled and nuzzled his jacket, searching for the apple that was always there for a hungry horse. Warwick chuckled and fed it to him.

In the barn, Bumper nickered a welcome to Maddie, his ears pricked and his eyes alert as he put his head over the half door to his stall. She fetched his saddle and bridle from their pegs and lifted the saddle up over his back.

Where have you been? he demanded. He became quite touchy if Maddie left him to his own devices for too long. She patted his neck, then swung up into the saddle.

"I've been busy," she said softly. "I'll tell you about it when we're out of here."

Well, that's all very well, but I've been worried about you. Never know what might happen to you if I'm not around.

"Sundancer would look after me," she said, and Bumper snorted loudly, rattling his mane at her.

Sundancer? That overbred excuse for a horse? What could he do if you got into trouble?

"Sundancer has excellent bloodlines," she told him.

But he was unimpressed. *All thoroughbreds tend to be hysterical and far too excitable for their own good—or for yours.*

Ranger horses, of course, were bred from many different bloodlines. The Corps horse breeders selected horses for their differing qualities—some for speed, some for stamina, some for intelligence—and bred the best of those qualities into the shaggy little horses they provided to the Corps. As a result, horses like Bumper, who was nothing if not outspoken, tended to be somewhat snobbish about the merits, or otherwise, of thoroughbreds.

Maddie sighed. "No wonder some people call horses nags."

Bumper jerked his head up and lapsed into silence. She smiled to herself. She'd finally got the best of him in a verbal duel, she thought. And she'd been saving that quip for some time now, looking for a chance to use it.

"Talking to someone?" Warwick asked as they emerged into the sunlight.

She shook her head. "Just myself. Bad habit I've gotten into."

Warwick nodded understandingly. "First sign of madness," he said cheerfully. He had a shrewd idea that Rangers talked to their horses. He'd heard Gilan do it several times. But it would never do to let on that he knew, of course.

"I'll take a look around up at the abbey," she said. He waved a cheerful farewell to her as she urged Bumper into a trot and headed out of the farmyard into the surrounding forest. They were halfway to the abbey before Bumper relented and spoke to her again. He was a garrulous little horse, and he couldn't stand to be silent for too long, even if he was pretending to be offended.

What do you expect to find up here? he asked as they negotiated the steep track that led to the abbey.

"Probably nothing," she admitted. "Warwick didn't place too much faith in the reports that there'd been people up here."

The ground around the abbey, a two-story stone building with a bell tower at one end, had been cleared of trees, leaving an open space roughly fifty-by-thirty meters. The wind was stronger up here on the hilltop, and the treetops bent and waved in the breeze. There were several pines among them, and the wind created that strange surflike sound that pines make as the wind passes through their branches.

She twitched the reins lightly, and Bumper came to a stop. She surveyed the area. It seemed unchanged since the last time she had been here.

"No sign of anything," she said. The ground was hard and rocky, and she knew it had rained the previous night. That and the constant wind would remove any faint trace of tracks that might have been here. Any sign of activity would likely be inside the building. She swung down from the saddle, grunting slightly at the ever-present twinge in her hip as her feet touched the ground and took her weight.

"Stay here," she told the horse. He pricked his ears but said nothing.

Even though she didn't expect trouble, she had been trained to always be ready for it. She took her bow from the leather bow case fastened behind Bumper's saddle, unclipped her quiver from the saddlebow and clipped it onto her belt. The bow and quiver stayed out at the farm with Bumper. A relatively powerful recurve bow and a quiver full of arrows fitted with warheads might create unwanted curiosity around Castle Araluen.

She nocked an arrow to the string and advanced toward the abbey. The double doors were closed, although the left-hand one showed a gap of several centimeters between it and its neighbor. She tried to remember if it had been unlocked on her previous visit, but couldn't.

"Some Ranger you are," she muttered to herself. It was her constant expression of self-criticism. She stretched her left leg out, placed her foot against the slightly open door and shoved hard. There was a loud creak from the rusty hinges as the door swung farther open. The stiffness of the rust in the hinges stopped it before it slammed back against the door frame, but it left an opening big enough for her to pass through.

She waited, listening for any sound of movement inside. Her heart rate was up, and her breathing came a little faster. To enter the abbey, she'd have to expose herself in the doorway, silhouetted by the outside light. She'd be a perfect target for anyone inside.

If there were anyone inside.

Moving quickly and silently, she slipped through the opening, stepping immediately to her right to clear the doorway, filling the opening for only a second or two before she slipped into the concealing shadows inside the old building.

Nothing moved, except for a few dry leaves that stirred in the open doorway, swirling around as the wind blew in. Gradually, her eyes became accustomed to the dimness and she searched the interior, ready for any sign of danger. But there was nothing.

The abbey was a large single room, with a small choir gallery against the rear wall. The bell tower rose above this gallery. A rickety old wooden ladder provided access to the gallery, which stood three meters above the floor of the main room. The high arched ceiling provided the extra height required to accommodate it. There was a window set in each of the walls beside it.

The door was set midway along one of the long side walls, so she could see both the gallery and the altar and pulpit. Several rows of pews were still standing in the church, but at least half of them had been taken by local inhabitants over the years. They were made of good-quality timber, and there was no sense leaving it here to rot. She guessed that if she inspected the farm-houses in the area, she'd find where the old pews had been converted to household furniture—settles, chairs, bedsteads and the like.

The door creaked softly as a stronger-than-usual gust of wind moved it a few more inches on its stiff hinges. She realized she'd been holding her breath and let it out now in a long sigh. She lowered the bow and released the tension she'd held on the string.

Then she saw the fox face.

At first sight, it appeared to be nothing more than random scratch marks in the hard-packed earth floor. But then she realized that the marks formed a definite shape. It was upside down from her viewpoint, but as she moved closer, she made it out for what it was—a rough outline of a fox's mask. It was on the floor between two of the surviving pews, and she guessed that it must have been scratched onto the hard earth with the point of a stick or a metal spike of some sort. Possibly the artist had been sitting on the pew idly passing the time, amusing himself while he waited for the meeting—if that was what had transpired here—to begin.

One thing was sure. It hadn't been here on her previous visit.

"So . . . ," she said thoughtfully, "it looks as if something has been going on here after all."

She searched the rest of the floor and found no further sign of activity. But a fox's face scratched into the earth was a good indication of who had been here. It was too big a coincidence to be anyone other than the Red Fox Clan. And as Will was fond of telling her, *We don't believe in coincidence.*

Satisfied that there were no further clues to what had been

going on, she retraced her steps to the door, pulling it closed behind her as she went out, leaving it as she had found it when she arrived.

Bumper raised his head curiously. *Find anything?*

"Yes. It seems that Barnaby Coddling wasn't imagining things," she told him. "We're going to have to come back here and keep an eye on the place."

Bumper flicked his tail at an errant horsefly. *Suits me.*

Maddie stroked his neck idly as she considered her options. There was no way of knowing when the Foxes might meet here again. That meant she would have to keep a constant watch on the abbey, and that would mean slipping out of the castle each night via the tunnel.

"I'm going to have to move you closer to the castle," she said. "I'll find a spot for you where the forest begins." She could be spending hours on watch at the abbey, and the thought of walking each night to get here didn't appeal. And she could hardly ride Sundancer out and switch horses at the farm as she'd done today. She'd be seen leaving and arriving back. If people knew she was absent from the castle for hours each night, questions would be asked—by her mother, among others.

"And I don't have any answers for her yet," she admitted to herself. "Just a vague hunch that something underhanded is going on."

She rode back to the farm, where Warwick had finished repairing the plow traces and was now replacing a broken hinge on the home paddock gate.

"Don't you ever have a day off?" she asked.

He shook his head cheerfully. "A farmer doesn't know what that means," he said. "Find anything up at the abbey?"

She told him about the fox face scratched into the floor.

He rubbed his chin thoughtfully as she described it. "I never noticed that before," he said. "Why would someone do that?"

She shrugged. "I guess to pass the time while they were waiting. Anyway, I'm going to be coming out here for the next few nights to keep watch. I'll find a spot for Bumper closer to the castle. Can you lend me a bucket and a horse blanket for him?" She looked at the sky, with white clouds driven by the gusting wind. The rain seemed to have passed. "And a sack of oats if you have them," she added.

Warwick nodded and strode into the barn to collect the items she needed. As he handed them to her, he asked, "Want me to come with you to watch the abbey?"

She shook her head. "I'll be better alone. Two of us will be twice as easy to spot. And I'm used to staying out of sight."

She swung up onto Bumper's back and, leaning down, unhitched Sundancer's reins from the post.

"I'd better get back and meet those Skandians," she said.

23

LEADING SUNDANCER BEHIND HER, SHE RODE BUMPER INTO the forest and headed at a brisk trot toward the castle. She had surveyed the land around the castle over the past few days and had earmarked a spot where Bumper would be out of sight.

It was a small glade set about twenty meters inside the forest, below Castle Araluen. There was a clearing about eight meters across, surrounded by thick-growing trees that would conceal it from anyone passing by. The trees would also provide shelter for her horse in the event that the weather turned bad—although Bumper was a hardy little animal and used to spending time in the open. Still, there was no need for him to be any more uncomfortable than he had to be, which was why she had asked to borrow a blanket for him.

They reached the spot she had selected and she dismounted. She tethered Sundancer to a low-lying branch and then led Bumper through the foliage that grew up between the trees, shoving the thicker branches to one side. The Arridan whinnied uncertainly as they disappeared into the trees, and she called to him.

"I'll be back. Don't panic."

Thoroughbreds, Bumper sniffed. *They're so hysterical.*

She ignored the statement, looking round the clearing. It was an ideal spot for him, and she quickly unsaddled him, laying the saddle and bridle over a horizontal branch. She unstrung her bow, unclipped the quiver from her belt and slid them both into the waterproof bow case attached to Bumper's saddle. She threw the blanket over his back and fastened the straps around his shoulders and under his belly.

"That should keep you cozy," she told him. He looked at her sidelong, and she gestured to a narrow gap between the trees on the side of the glade farthest from the castle. "There's a stream through there, about five meters away," she said. They could hear the water bubbling and splashing cheerfully. "And I'll leave you some oats. Don't eat them all at once."

Bumper snorted. Such an injunction was beneath his dignity. She poured half the oats into the bucket and set it under a tree for him. Bumper was trained to eat sparingly. She knew he wouldn't simply munch down the oats as soon as she was gone. And he would remain in the glade without needing to be tethered—except when he needed water. If there were any passersby, he would stay silent and unmoving. She didn't like leaving him here when he could have been in Warwick's warm barn, but there was no alternative.

"I'll be back tomorrow night," she told him. She and Warwick had discussed her plan to keep watch at the abbey, and they both agreed that it was unlikely the Foxes would gather there tonight— so soon after they had been there. Previously, signs of activity at the abbey had been at least five or six days apart. So, it would likely be close to a week before they reconvened. But to be on the safe side, she would begin watching the following night.

"I'll take a quick look up there tonight just to make sure," Warwick told her, and she had agreed to that.

She patted Bumper's neck, and he bumped his head against her shoulder affectionately. Then she slipped back through the trees, untied Sundancer's bridle and swung up into the saddle.

"Stay out of sight," she called back to Bumper, and he whinnied briefly, which she took as *Tell me something I don't know.* Then she touched her heels to Sundancer and trotted out of the trees and onto the open parkland. Once on clear ground, she touched him again and set him to a fast canter up the hill.

He wasn't Bumper, she thought, but he was an excellent horse. He had a smooth, easy gait and an exceptional turn of speed. She increased the pace to a gallop and he stretched out, covering the ground in long, easy strides, his hooves barely seeming to touch the ground. As she came closer to the castle, she saw her mother, mounted on her black gelding, waiting outside the walls at the end of the drawbridge. Dimon and another rider were with her, standing a few meters away.

She reined in beside her mother, Sundancer scattering tufts of grass and clumps of mud as she did so. She laughed with the sheer exhilaration of the dash up the hill.

Cassandra glanced meaningfully at the sun, almost overhead. "You're nearly late," she said.

Maddie grinned at her. "Which means I'm on time—or even a little early," she replied.

Cassandra shrugged, then turned as a stable boy led a string of three ponies across the drawbridge and handed the lead rein to Dimon's companion. All of the ponies were saddled, and, she noticed, all of them were quite elderly and docile.

The young captain saw Maddie's curious gaze and gestured

to the horses. "They're for the Skandians," Dimon told her, answering her unasked question.

"Couldn't we find them something a little more lively?" she asked. One of them, a dappled gray, looked in danger of falling asleep in mid-stride.

Her mother answered her. "Skandians aren't keen riders," she said. "They'll ride when they have to, but they'd rather not."

"You're coming with us?" Maddie asked Dimon.

He nodded. "Of course. I can't let the princess ride off without protection—although I'd rather have a half troop."

"Two of you will be enough," Cassandra said easily. "After all, I'm armed." She tapped the polished wood hilt of the *katana* in her belt. "And Maddie and I both have our slings." Like her daughter, Cassandra always carried her sling and a pouch of shot with her when she traveled anywhere.

She paused for a second to make sure the trooper had the horses ready to move, then pointed to the northeast, the direction where the River Semath lay. "Let's get moving," she said.

They proceeded at a gentle trot—the best pace the three tubby old ponies could manage, Maddie assumed. Halfway down the slope, they angled to the east. They rode into the trees, following a wide bridle path. After fifteen minutes, the trees began to thin out until they were riding on a clear grassy area, with only occasional growths. The river gleamed silver in the middle distance. It was wide and slow flowing at this point. From here, it wound down to the coast, some fifteen kilometers away. Inland, it cut back to the south, emerging by the picturesque village that lived under Castle Araluen's protection, then disappearing into the wooded flatlands that lay in that direction.

They reined in at the sturdy wooden jetty on the banks of

the river. Cassandra stood in her stirrups, shading her eyes as she peered downstream. Half a kilometer away from their vantage point, there was a sharp bend in the river. As yet, there was no sign of the wolfship—Maddie assumed the Skandians would be in a wolfship.

"There she is," Dimon said, pointing. A small, graceful craft was rounding the bend, traveling at a considerable speed, in spite of the light wind. Maddie was surprised to see that it wasn't a wolfship—at least not one like any that she had seen in pictures.

It was smaller than she expected, with four oars on each side instead of the normal ten to fifteen. And the sail was a triangular shape, set along the line of the hull instead of a square sail set crosswise. As she watched, the ship reached the northern bank of the river and turned to the left to tack toward them. As its bow came round, she was surprised to see the triangular sail lose its taut shape and slide down the stumpy mast. In its place, another sail slid up on the downwind side, caught the wind and filled into a smooth, swelling shape. The ship, which had lost a little speed in the turn, accelerated once more, a distinctive white bow wave forming under its forefoot.

A long banner rippled out from the tall sternpost and Maddie frowned. The device on the banner was a red hawk, stooping after its prey.

"That's your banner," she said, slightly scandalized.

To her surprise, her mother grinned. "Yes. Erak flew that banner on *Wolfwind* when he brought Will and Halt and me home. And Hal has continued the tradition, flying it from the *Heron* whenever he visits. They're a cheeky bunch," she added with a smile. She didn't appear to mind that her personal insignia was being usurped.

"Hal?" Maddie asked. She knew who Erak was. After all, he was the Oberjarl, the ruler of the Skandians. Everyone knew who he was.

"Hal Mikkelson. He's one of their most successful skippers—skirls, they call them. A brilliant navigator and shipbuilder. He designed that ship. Gilan sailed in it with them when they flushed out a band of assassins who were targeting me some years back."

Maddie wrinkled her nose. "It's kind of small, isn't it?"

"It's small. But according to Gilan it's very fast and amazingly maneuverable. Something to do with the shape of the sail."

Dimon was watching the fast-approaching ship with interest. "So this is the famous Heron brotherband," he said, almost to himself.

"What's a brotherband?" Maddie asked. "And how come this one's famous?"

"The Skandians train their young men in groups of ten or twelve," Dimon said. "They learn to live together, fight together and handle their ships. A brotherband becomes the basis of a ship's crew when they graduate. They stay together for life."

"And this one is famous," Cassandra chipped in, "because they've traveled from one end of the known earth to the other. They pursued a pirate named Zavac down the Dan River to the eastern end of the Constant Sea. He'd stolen a precious artifact from Hallasholm, their capital. They caught up with him, sank his ship and killed him. After that, they fought and defeated the assassin cult I mentioned in the eastern part of Arrida. And they rescued a group of young Araluens who were taken by slavers in Socorro."

"They're even rumored to have discovered a new land way to the west. But that's probably a myth," Dimon put in.

Maddie noticed a slightly dismissive note in his voice as he made the last comment, almost as if he was reluctant to sing the Skandians' praises too enthusiastically.

Maddie turned her gaze back to the pretty little ship that was drawing up to the jetty. She heard a command shouted from the stern, and the sail suddenly collapsed and slid down the mast, crewmen hurrying to gather it in. The ship turned slightly to run parallel to the jetty, speed falling off her. She had almost stopped as she reached the structure. A tall figure leapt lightly ashore and passed a hawser round a bollard, looping it twice round the worn timber for purchase. He set his heels and slowly brought the ship to a halt. The bow swung in against the jetty, the impact absorbed by cane fenders that were hanging over the sides of the ship. Another crewman jumped ashore to do the same thing at the stern end. In the space of half a minute, the ship was secured snugly to the jetty.

"Come on," Cassandra said, grinning widely. "Let's go say hello."

She slipped down from the saddle and strode toward the jetty. Maddie hastened to follow her. Behind them, Dimon paused uncertainly, then turned to his trooper.

"Mind the horses," he said, and dismounted, hurrying to catch up with the two women.

"Stig!" Cassandra cried, holding out her arms to embrace the tall Skandian who had jumped ashore first. "Welcome to Araluen!" He engulfed her in an enthusiastic bear hug, lifting her off her feet. Dimon started forward, then stopped as he heard Cassandra's delighted peal of laughter.

"Put me down, you great ape!" she said. Eventually, the Skandian did, and she turned to beckon Maddie forward.

"Stig, this is my daughter, Maddie. Maddie, this is Stig."

Maddie studied him with interest. He was tall and broad shouldered and athletic in build. He reminded her of her father in the way he moved—gracefully and always in balance. He was handsome, there was no denying it, with sparkling blue eyes, even features and a short, neatly trimmed blond beard and mustache. His hair was blond as well and cut short. He shook her hand, grinning as he saw her wary reaction. She wasn't sure that he mightn't envelop her in a bear hug as well. Although, on reflection, she thought that mightn't be altogether too unpleasant.

Cassandra continued with introductions. "Stig, this is Dimon, captain of my guard."

The Skandian stepped forward, smiling and offering his hand. Maddie was somewhat surprised to see Dimon hesitate momentarily, then take it. She put it down to his overprotective attitude toward her mother.

"Good to meet you!" Stig said cheerfully.

Dimon replied, a little stiffly, "Welcome to Araluen."

Maddie had no further time to reflect on Dimon's awkwardness. Her mother was drawing her attention to two more of the Skandians, who were advancing up the jetty, their faces wreathed in smiles.

"And here are two more old friends: Hal Mikkelson, skirl of the *Heron*, and Thorn, the biggest rascal you're ever likely to meet."

24

AT THE LAST MOMENT, GILAN CHANGED HIS POINT OF AIM. Somehow, it went against the grain to kill an unarmed, unsuspecting man—even an enemy.

However, the swimmer had to be stopped and the target area he offered was small. Only his head and shoulders showed above the surface of the river. Gilan selected his right shoulder as an aiming point and released.

He heard the other four bows shoot almost at the same time, following his lead. His arrow plunged down in a shallow arc and struck the lead swimmer in the right shoulder. The man let out a cry of agony and stopped swimming. Almost immediately, he sank beneath the water, only to surface again a meter downstream, churning the water to foam with his left arm and crying out in pain. His comrades on the riverbank stared at him in panic for a few seconds. Then, as his cries continued, they began to haul in on the rope, dragging him back toward the bank. He turned on his back in the water, feebly kicking with his feet, thrashing the surface, in an attempt to get back to the bank.

The other archers didn't have the luxury of choosing to wound their targets. Gilan was a superlative shot, and he could aim at the swimmer's shoulder with confidence. His companions couldn't hope for that sort of accuracy and the swimming men offered them only small targets. One of them was hit in the chest, the arrow plunging through the water almost unimpeded to strike him twenty centimeters below the surface. He cried out once, threw up his hands and sank without a further sound. The rope handlers hauled on his rope and he reappeared after a few meters, lying on his back, limp and unmoving as they pulled him back to the bank.

The third swimmer yelled out in fear as three arrows whipped viciously into the water around him. One of them was close enough to graze his arm with its razor-sharp warhead, and blood started reddening the water around him. In response to his frantic cries, his companions began dragging him back through the water as fast as they could. A sizable wave built up around him as the current ran over his fast-moving body. Inevitably, some of it went into his mouth, and he began coughing and gagging.

"Stop shooting," Gilan ordered quietly. "Stand down."

There was no point in wasting further arrows. The swimmers had been turned back, and once again the enemy were in disarray. The men tending the ropes shouted to their comrades to cover them with their shields—a request their friends weren't overly keen on fulfilling, since they planned to stay protected by the shields themselves.

Seeing an opportunity to demoralize the men further, Gilan loosed an arrow at the group on the bank, targeting one of the rope handlers. The arrow hit him in the leg and he fell awkwardly to the grass, clasping both hands to the wound and appealing to his friends for help. They ignored him, working harder to drag the injured swimmer to the bank. As he rolled into the shallows, two of them dashed forward and, grabbing him by the arms, began to drag him backward toward the tree line, heedless of his cries of pain.

The second swimmer, hit in the chest, was obviously dead when he grounded in the shallows. He made no move to rise, and his arms and legs moved weakly in the current. His rope handlers, after a moment's hesitation, cut the rope attached to him and ran for the trees, one of them pausing to assist the man with the leg wound. The current continued to move the dead swimmer until he gradually drifted away from the bank and downriver. He rolled over once so that he was floating facedown. Then he was lost to sight as the river took him round a slight curve.

The third swimmer, blood flowing down his arm, scrambled to his feet as he reached the shallows and splashed ashore. He wasted no time on his friends, setting out at a dead run for the safety of the trees. The rope trailed behind him, snaking through the long grass. Gilan sent an arrow hissing past his ears to speed him along. Surprisingly, the man found extra reserves of speed and redoubled his efforts to reach safety.

Then the inevitable happened. The trailing rope snagged round a low tree stump and jerked tight, bringing him crashing to the ground. He rolled around frantically, yelling in fear and thrashing at the ground as he sought to cast the rope loose. Then, finally free, he lurched to his feet and took off again.

The watching archers chuckled. Gilan narrowed his eyes, scanning the rope-handling party still on the far bank. Huddled behind their shields, they began to retreat slowly away from the river. He could see that they had no idea where the sudden hail of arrows had come from. None of them was looking at the row of bushes. They were all scanning the riverbank directly opposite them.

He gave them a few more minutes as they retreated cautiously. As before, when no sudden hail of arrows eventuated, their confidence grew and they stood more upright, still with the shields in front of them as they backed away and began to move faster.

"Walt, Gilbert, get going," Gilan said. "Stay low and keep these bushes between you and them. When you reach your horses, walk them for the first twenty meters. Don't suddenly gallop away or you'll be heard."

The two archers grunted their understanding and, staying in a crouch, duckwalked on their haunches away from the bushes, staying low until they were inside the tree line. Once he was assured they were on their way, Gilan resumed his watch on the far bank.

The enemy were milling around the two injured swimmers, now that they had assisted them back to the tree line. The one Gilan had shot looked to be in a bad way. They laid him on the ground, and he could see several medical orderlies bringing a litter for him. As before, their leader raged impotently. But after several minutes, sensing the silent animosity of his men, he moderated his behavior, trying to be more conciliatory.

Nestor, the senior archer, moved up alongside Gilan to watch, and chuckled quietly. "Think they'll try again, Ranger?" he asked.

Gilan shrugged. "I don't know how they'd go about it. They're sitting ducks once they get into the water, and they know it. He'll have a hard time persuading them to try it again.

The only thing I can think of is for them to try to cross wearing armor."

"They'll sink if they do," Nestor replied.

Gilan shrugged. "Maybe a heavy breastplate and helmet might keep a man on his feet," he said. "If they can stop being swept away, it might give them a chance."

Nestor patted his quiver, where the feathered ends of his arrows rustled as he touched them. He withdrew one, fitted with a hardened, tapering bodkin point.

"That is, until we put one of these beauties through his breastplate," he said. Bodkin arrows were designed to penetrate armor. The archers carried a mixed selection of bodkins and leaf-shaped barbed warheads in their quivers.

"True," Gilan agreed. "They may not know we have armor-piercing arrows. We haven't used them so far."

"Be another nasty shock for them, won't it?" Nestor said. He sounded as if he was very pleased with the idea of surprising the enemy yet again.

Gilan continued to watch the Foxes. Now that the first flurry of activity looking after the injured swimmers had passed, they appeared to be having an animated discussion. Faintly, the Ranger could hear shouted comments and voices raised in anger, although he couldn't make out the words themselves. Whatever they were discussing, it was going to be a while before they could organize a further attempt on the ford.

"Nestor," he said, "you and Clete might as well get going. Remember, stay low until you're in the trees. Then move off slowly once you're mounted."

Nestor sniffed. "Happy to stay here with you if you like, Ranger," he said.

Gilan grinned at him. The old warhorse was enjoying this, he thought. But he waved him away. "I appreciate the offer, but you'd better be on your way. I can hold the fort here for a while longer."

"That's true enough," Nestor agreed. He had no misconceptions about Gilan's skill. He knew the Ranger was a better shot—a far better shot—than himself or any of his men. And Gilan was fast. He could send a hail of arrows, all aimed shots, whistling through the air at the enemy, making them think they were facing three or four shooters. "All right, Clete," Nestor said, turning to the other archer. "Let's make a move. Stay low now."

Like the others, they crept out of the bushes while doubled down on their haunches to stay concealed. Gilan watched them go, then looked back to the Foxes. They were still debating, still moving around uncertainly. There would be no further threat from them for some time, he thought. He settled down to wait, wondering what they would try next.

When they did make a move, his earlier prediction, spoken half in jest, turned out to be correct. A group of five men, huddled behind hastily constructed wooden man-high shields, advanced on the riverbank. Among them was a man wearing a helmet and metal breastplate, and carrying a smaller, circular shield. He was a squat, stocky figure, made even more so by the fact that he was wearing the armor. Gilan assumed that there was a layer of chain mail underneath the breastplate. He selected a bodkin point arrow from his quiver and waited.

The small group stopped a few meters from the riverbank. Hastily, one of them wound the end of a rope around the armored man's waist, tied it off, then retreated behind the makeshift shield wall. Another stayed beside the would-be crosser, protecting him with a long shield.

The shield bearer walked with him to the water's edge, scanning the far bank anxiously, trying to see some sign of movement, some indication that they were about to be shot at. Then, as the armored man slipped into the river and waded quickly forward until he was waist deep, the shield bearer skipped back to the relative safety of the shield wall behind him.

The armored man now raised the small shield he carried, so that it covered his head and upper body. He steadied himself, testing the strength of the current as it pushed at him, then took a tentative few steps forward.

It appeared that Gilan's supposition had been correct. The weight of the armor and helmet helped stabilize him against the fierce tug of the current. But that was somewhat offset by the uneven nature of the riverbed. Three times in the first ten meters, he had to stop to regain his balance as the river threatened to topple him. Then he continued, walking slowly, testing each step.

"Mind how you go," Gilan said softly. "If you fall, they're going to have to drag you out in a hurry."

Three more paces. The man swayed, then recovered. He advanced farther. He was now a third of the way across the river, the shield held up in front of his face and upper body. Gilan nodded in admiration. This was a brave man, he thought. He was also an intelligent one. Unlike those who had gone before him, he wasn't growing overconfident when there was no sign of opposition. He continued to move deliberately, expecting a volley of arrows at any minute.

Halfway across.

Still he continued his steady, patient progress. Occasionally, as his footing became uneven, the shield would dip momentarily as he regained his balance. But it was impossible for Gilan to predict when this would happen, and there was never enough time to release a shot while the shield was down. He recovered quickly each time.

Three-quarters of the way.

The river began to shallow at this point and he crouched, staying low so that the water reached almost to his neck, with the circular shield protecting his exposed face and shoulders.

On the far side, his companions shouted encouragement as they saw him wading closer and closer to the bank without any sign of resistance. Back in the trees, the rest of the Foxes joined in the chorus of support, cheering and whistling.

He was in the shallows now, still crouching behind the cover of the shield. Gilan selected a second arrow from his quiver, holding it loosely between the fingers of his bow hand. Then, rising to his feet, he aimed and shot.

The armored man was wading up the bank, water cascading from him, draining out of the metal breastplate. He stayed low, with the shield held protectively before him.

Until Gilan's first arrow hit it and knocked it sideways.

The second shot was already on its way while the first was in the air. As quickly as the man tried to recover, bringing his shield back in front of his body, the arrow was even quicker. It slammed into the unprotected breastplate with the full force of Gilan's massive bow behind it. At such a short range, the armor had no chance against the hardened steel point. It ripped through the breastplate and into the man's body.

He reeled back into the shallow water. As it reached up to his calves, it tripped him and he toppled backward into the shallows. The shouts of encouragement from the far bank fell silent as the Foxes watched their comrade lying still in the river.

Gilan studied him carefully. He was weighed down by the breastplate, helmet and shield. The current didn't seem to be moving him as it had moved the previous crossers. There was always the chance that he might be heavy enough to anchor the rope on this side and allow another swimmer to cross.

Coming to a decision, Gilan loosed a volley of six arrows at the men on the opposite bank. The arrows rained down in rapid succession, thudding into shields and exposed limbs. It was too much for the men to bear. They had been lashed by these arrow storms twice before, and now they simply broke and ran.

Knowing that all eyes would be on them for a few minutes, Gilan slipped around the end of the line of bushes and sprinted for the riverbank, drawing his saxe as he went. He stooped over the body of the armored man and quickly slashed the loop of rope around his upper body. The loose end of the rope floated away in the current. Satisfied, Gilan turned and ran back to the bushes. He'd wait awhile longer, then head out after Horace and the rest of the party.

It would be some time, he thought, before the Foxes attempted another crossing.

25

HAL MIKKELSON WAS A DISTINCT CONTRAST TO HIS CREW-
man Stig. He was slighter in build and not as tall, although he
was well muscled and fit. His hair was light brown, worn long
and tied back from his face in a neat queue. He was clean shaven
and, Maddie noticed with interest, very handsome. His brown
eyes were friendly as he reached to take her hand.

"Princess Madelyn," he said, and she took his hand. His eyes
showed slight surprise for a second as he felt her firm grip.

"Call me Maddie," she said.

He nodded, pleased with her lack of formality. Skandians
didn't go in for that sort of thing. She heard Dimon clear his
throat, a disapproving sound. She assumed it was because of
Hal's casual approach. The skirl, as she now knew him to be,
turned to Cassandra, a wide grin on his face. He relinquished
Maddie's hand and stepped forward to embrace her mother.
Again, Dimon shifted his feet awkwardly.

"Cassandra," Hal said, "it's good to see you again."

"And you, Hal. It's been too long," Cassandra said. When
she was free from Hal's embrace, she touched Maddie's arm
lightly and indicated the third Skandian.

"This is Thorn," she said, pausing before adding, "I'm not sure if I ever heard your second name, Thorn."

Thorn was unlike anyone Maddie had ever met. He was older than the other two, tall and heavily built—bearlike, she thought—though the bulk was all muscle, not fat. His iron-gray hair grew in wild tangles, and he had it set in two loose plaits. His beard and mustache were equally unkempt. His mustache, in fact, was uneven, one side being longer than the other by several centimeters. This was because a few days prior, working on tarring a seam on the ship's deck, he had inadvertently gotten a large dollop of tar on the right side of his mustache. Unable to clean it off, he had simply taken his saxe and removed the offending section.

Thorn was dressed in the leggings and sealskin boots that Skandian sailors habitually wore. And his upper body was covered by an amazing sheepskin vest. At least, Maddie thought it might have been sheepskin originally. Now it was covered with variegated patches, sewn on haphazardly wherever they were needed. Studying him, Maddie thought there might be more patches than original garment.

His eyes were blue and had a far-seeing look to them. He seemed to view the world with a constant sense of amusement, and she found herself instinctively liking him.

But the most notable feature of the man was his right hand—or rather, the lack of it. His arm ended halfway down the forearm, and the hand had been replaced with a polished wooden hook. He brandished it now in answer to Cassandra's implied question.

"It's Thorn Hookyhand, Your Royalty," he told her, grinning

hugely. Thorn's disregard for protocol and royal titles was even stronger than that of most Skandians.

"Actually, he's usually known as Thorn Hammerhand," Stig told them.

Maddie frowned. The wooden hook was substantial, but it didn't look at all like a hammer. "Hammerhand?" she queried.

Stig explained. "When we go into battle, he changes the hook for a huge club that Hal made for him. It fits over the end of his arm, and he can smash helmets, shields and armor with it." His grin widened. "He's terrible in battle."

"He's terrible anytime," Hal interposed, and all three Skandians, and Cassandra, laughed heartily. Hal indicated the ship moored a few meters away.

"Come and meet the rest of the crew," he said, adding to Cassandra, "They'll be pleased to see you again, Princess."

They crossed the jetty to the little ship, Hal assisting Cassandra down onto the bulwark and then the deck. Stig held out his hand to Maddie, but she didn't notice, negotiating the gap from the jetty to ship's railing easily, then stepping down lightly onto the deck.

Thorn eyed her astutely. She wasn't the usual simpering, giggling princess that you might expect, he thought. But then, of course, she was Cassandra's daughter. Like her mother, she was slim and moved with an easy athleticism—aside from a slight limp, he noticed. His keen eyes noted the sling coiled neatly under her belt, and the pouch of lead shot. He also noticed that she had a sheathed saxe at her side—hardly the sort of thing one would expect a young woman at court to be carrying.

Altogether, a fascinating character.

As she met the other members of the crew and chatted with them, Thorn noted her easy confidence and self-assurance. She wasn't daunted or overawed in the presence of this group of capable, tough men. She seemed quite at home in their presence, in fact. He also noted that the Herons seemed to react well to her, treating her as an equal, albeit one to be respected.

There's more to this one than meets the eye, he thought.

Cassandra was looking round the ship, a slightly puzzled expression on her face. "Where's Lydia? Is she no longer with you?"

Stig offered a sad smile. "She's still a Heron," he told her. "But Agathe, the old woman who took her in when she first came to Hallasholm, is very ill. Agathe's been like a surrogate mother to Lydia since she's been with us. The healers don't give her a lot of time, and Lydia thought she should stay with her this time, instead of coming on this trip."

"More's the pity," said the huge man who wore strange dark patches of tortoiseshell over his eyes. He had been introduced as Ingvar. "We all miss her."

Cassandra turned to her daughter, her disappointment obvious. "That's a shame. I really wanted you to meet her. She's an amazing woman, just as much a warrior as any of this lot."

She made an all-encompassing gesture that took in the rest of the crew. Her smile robbed the words of any insult, and several of them grunted assent.

Thorn frowned thoughtfully. Why would Cassandra be so keen to have her daughter meet a girl warrior like Lydia? He looked at Maddie again. Ingvar had taken her for'ard and was showing her the workings of the Mangler, the massive crossbow that *Heron* had mounted in her bows. The young woman was studying the weapon with what appeared to be professional interest.

There's *definitely* more to her than meets the eye, he told himself for the second time.

Cassandra led the way back to the jetty, Stig, Hal and Thorn following her as she stepped ashore. Maddie smiled a farewell to Ingvar. The dark tortoiseshell covers over his eyes were disconcerting at first, but once you became used to them, he was a likable character.

"I've organized a luncheon in the park outside the castle," Cassandra said as she led the way to the horses. She stopped and turned back, looking at the ship. "The whole crew are welcome to join us, of course."

Hal shook his head. "Kind of you. But the lads can stay here. We hit a storm on the way over and there are a few repairs that have to be done—ropes spliced and rigging replaced."

"I'll have food brought down to the ship, in that case," Cassandra said.

"Lots of it," Ingvar called, and they all laughed.

They mounted the horses. Hal and Stig seemed reasonably comfortable riding. Thorn showed a little more trepidation. He held the reins tightly in his left hand, looking warily at the sleepy horse he had been given.

"You don't like riding?" Maddie asked with a grin.

"If it doesn't have a rudder and a tiller, I don't trust it," the shaggy old sea wolf replied. "Besides, I can never find the anchor on one of these when I want to stop it moving."

"You'll have a bigger problem *starting* that one moving," Maddie told him. He was riding the horse that had looked as if it could fall asleep in mid-stride.

"That suits me fine," Thorn replied between clenched teeth.

Normally, the Araluens would have cantered easily back up the hill to the castle. Out of deference to their guests, they maintained a stately walk.

"*Heron* looks in good shape," Cassandra said to Hal.

He smiled a little sadly. "Yes. But she takes a lot of maintenance these days. She's feeling her age, I'm afraid. I suppose I'll have to build a new ship one of these days, but I can't bear the idea of parting with her. This may be her last voyage."

"Speaking of which, what brings you here this time? The message I got said it was something to do with the archers we send you."

In a treaty arranged by Will many years before, Araluen sent a force of one hundred archers to Skandia each year to help protect them against the threat of the Temujai riders. In return, Erak provided a wolfship for the King's use—in carrying messages and helping suppress smuggling and piracy along the coast. Another part of the treaty had been Erak's agreement to stop raiding the Araluen coast.

"Erak was wondering if we could increase the number of archers this year," Hal told her. "Another twenty men would be welcome."

Cassandra raised her eyebrows. "Shouldn't be a problem," she said. "Are you expecting trouble of some kind?"

Hal's horse stumbled slightly over a protruding tree root. He instantly dropped the reins and gripped the pommel of his saddle in both hands. Cassandra smiled and gave him a few minutes to recover the reins and his equanimity.

"He's got four feet. Why can't he stay on an even keel?" Hal asked.

"You Skandians fascinate me," Cassandra said. "You can walk around quite calmly on a ship heaving and plunging through four-meter waves for hours on end. But if a horse so much as sneezes, you think you're in danger of falling off."

"You can trust a ship," Hal told her. "Horses can turn nasty. And they bite." He added the last darkly. Maddie, listening, wondered if there was a story behind that particular statement.

"But to answer your question," Hal continued, "we're a little concerned about the Temujai. They've been sniffing around the border in the past few months, and Erak thinks they might be planning something. Their Sha-shan has never forgiven us for taking him prisoner years ago."

Cassandra looked at him with interest. "I didn't know about that."

Hal grinned. "It's quite a story," he said. "Kept them quiet for some time, but now they're getting restless again, and Erak would like to beef up the archers' numbers. He's offering you an extra supply of timber and hides in exchange. I'm authorized to negotiate the amounts."

"I'm sure we can sort out the details," Cassandra said. "Although we may have to wait until Horace returns with the men he's taken."

It was Hal's turn to look disappointed. "Horace isn't here?"

She shook her head. "He's gone north chasing down a bunch of nuisances called the Red Fox Clan," she said. "He should be back within ten days or so."

"Pity," Hal said. "We'll probably be gone by then. By the way," he added, "when we rounded Cape Shelter a few weeks back, we sighted a Sonderland ship crammed with soldiers and heading south. They haven't bothered you, have they?"

Cassandra shook her head. "Not that I know of."

Dimon, riding behind them, answered the question. "They were probably headed for Iberion," he said. "We had dinner with the ambassador this week, and he said they were hiring Sonderland mercenaries to put down a revolt in one of their provinces."

Hal nodded. "No problem for you then," he said. "In any event, once we've agreed on the changes to the treaty, and restocked the ship with provisions, we'll head back to Skandia."

"Speaking of provisions," Cassandra told him, "we've planned a hunt for tomorrow. There are plenty of deer in the forest, and quite a few boar. And the lake is full of geese and ducks."

"That'll make Edvin happy. He's always keen to replenish our stocks of fresh meat whenever he can."

"It'll make Ingvar happy too," Stig put in. "He's always keen to eat it."

26

ONCE HE WAS AWAY FROM THE IMMEDIATE VICINITY OF THE riverbank, Gilan urged Blaze into a steady canter. By the time he caught up with the rest of the party, they were a few hundred meters from the old hill fort.

"Any developments back at the ford?" Horace asked as Gilan rode up and drew rein beside him.

"Nothing unexpected. Three of them tried to cross and we beat them back. That set them to thinking for a while as they realized how vulnerable they were once they were in the river. Then they sent one man wearing armor to try to get a rope across. He made it to the bank, but got no farther."

"You shot him?" Horace said.

Gilan regarded him with an even gaze. "Well, I didn't walk down and hand him a bunch of jonquils."

"What do you think they'll do next?"

Gilan paused. He'd been considering that while he was riding to catch up with the mixed force of cavalry and archers.

"I think they'll wait for nightfall," he said. "It'd be harder to pick them off in the dark."

Horace glanced at the sun already dipping below the treetops to the west. "That gives us another hour at least," he said. "What time is moonrise tonight?"

"Somewhere between the sixth and seventh hour, I think. That'll delay them even further. The moon would give us plenty of light to shoot by."

"If you were still there to shoot at them," Horace said.

Gilan nodded. "If we were still there to shoot at them," he agreed. Then he gestured toward the ancient structure looming before them. "Let's take a look at this hill fort."

As the name suggested, the fort had been built on the site of a natural feature—a low but steep-sided hill. A path spiraled around the hill, leading up to the summit, where a wooden structure had been built—a palisade of logs two meters high. There would be a walkway constructed inside it for the defenders.

The sides of the hill were covered with long grass, making the hill difficult to climb—especially for men burdened with armor and weapons. Gilan had a mental picture of men slipping and stumbling as they tried to battle their way upward. They'd be badly exposed to arrows, spears, rocks and other missiles from the fortifications at the top.

Horace gave the order for the archers and troopers to remain at the base while he and Gilan climbed the hill to survey the fort. He sent two troopers back down the path that led to the river to give early warning if the Red Fox Clan had managed to cross in pursuit. Then he and Gilan urged their horses up the narrow, winding path.

Even on the path, the going was steep and difficult. The ground underfoot was packed earth, and the track followed the contours of the hill, spiraling upward. The path was three meters wide, and at irregular intervals there were barriers of rock and wood, designed to further delay an attacker's progress. Eventually, of course, an attacking force could outflank the stone and timber barriers across the path. But it would take time for them to do so.

They dismounted at the first of these obstacles and heaved the old, rotting panel that served as a gate to one side.

"Should we man some of these?" Gilan asked.

Horace shook his head. "We don't have enough men. Better to hold the very top—make the Foxes climb all the way, then shove them back down."

They rode on, circling round to the far side of the hill, then returning once more, always angling upward, and passing two more barricades as they did. They circled the hill one more time and came to the end of the track. The very top of the hill had been dug out so that they were confronted by a sheer earth wall, a meter and a half high, that ran all the way round the hilltop. Above that, the timber palisade stood another two meters high. A heavy gate was set into it.

They dismounted. Horace tethered his horse to a nearby bush, and they set about scrambling up the packed earth wall on their hands and knees. At their first attempt, they simply slid back down. Then Gilan drew his saxe and drove it into the hard earth to provide a secure handhold. Horace did likewise, and they gained the upper level beneath the palisade.

They studied the gate. The timber was old and warped, but it appeared solid. There was no sign of rot.

"Good hardwood," Horace said appreciatively. "Lasts for years. That'll keep them out."

"It appears to be doing the same to us," Gilan observed mildly.

Horace looked around, seeking some other form of entrance,

although he knew there wouldn't be one. Then he stepped close to the wooden wall, standing with his back to it, and held his hands cupped together at thigh height.

"Come on," he said. "I'll boost you up."

Gilan slung his bow around his shoulders and slid his quiver around to the back of his belt. Then he took a few paces forward and stepped up into Horace's stirruped hands.

As Gilan straightened his knee, Horace heaved upward and their combined thrust propelled the Ranger to the top of the wall. He hauled himself over the rough timbers, pausing with one half of his body inside the wall and the other outside while he studied the wooden walkway running around the interior of the wall. It looked solid enough, so he rolled himself over the parapet and dropped lightly to the old planks.

"All okay?" Horace called from below.

Gilan rose to peer over the top of the wooden wall, grinning. "Fine," he said. "I'll slip down and raise the locking bar on the gate."

"Watch your step," Horace cautioned him. "The timbers in there mightn't be as solid as the walls."

Gilan waved acknowledgment and made his way along the catwalk to where he could see a flight of stairs leading down into the interior of the fort. He paused at the top to look around. The timber wall enclosed a circular area approximately twenty meters in diameter. It wasn't a very large space, he thought, but it would be easier to defend with their small body of men. There were three large huts and one smaller one in the inner compound. They were constructed from timber and seemed the worse for wear. Originally, the roofs had been thatched, but the thatching had long since rotted away. The huts themselves, built from lighter timber than the fort, had deteriorated badly. They leaned and sagged precariously, looking as if one good push would send them crashing to the ground.

He studied the steps for a few seconds, testing them with his weight before he committed himself. The stairway moved slightly under his weight, and two of the risers groaned and creaked as he made his cautious way down to ground level.

"Have to repair them," he muttered. But on the whole, he was relieved to see that the stairs were sound. Obviously, the defensive, utilitarian parts of the fort had been built to last, using solid hardwood. The accommodation huts were another matter.

He hurried to the gate, where a heavy wooden bar was secured in two massive iron brackets. The brackets were rusted, but still sound. He lifted the bar and set it to one side. Then he laid hold of the handle on the door and heaved. It opened a crack. Then the old hinges screamed a protest and it stopped moving.

"Give it a shove!" he called to Horace. He felt the tall warrior's weight pushing against the door and redoubled his own efforts to pull it open. Reluctantly, the hinges succumbed to their combined efforts and the door groaned halfway open. Then it stopped completely.

"Needs a bit of oil," he said.

Horace stepped inside, his eyes darting around as he took in the interior of the fort. "Those huts have had it," he said, and Gilan nodded agreement.

"Yes. They're rubbish. But the wall and the walkway look to be pretty solid. The steps need a little strengthening but they look all right. In fact, it should suit us quite nicely."

Horace put his shoulder against the gate and shoved hard.

It gave another meter, then stopped. "As you say, this needs some oil."

Gilan shrugged. "Do we want it to open any farther?"

Horace shoved the door again and opened it an additional few centimeters. "We'll need to get the horses inside," he said.

Gilan pursed his lips. He had forgotten that detail. Then a thought struck him. "How do we get them up that final vertical wall?"

"By dint of much pushing and heaving and scrambling," Horace told him. "If all else fails, we'll dig out a ramp for them."

Dismissing the matter of the gate, he strode into the inner compound. He drew his sword and held it casually beside him.

Gilan raised his eyebrows. "I don't think there's anyone here," he said mildly.

Horace inclined his head. "Never hurts to be sure," he said. He stopped by the smaller of the huts. Its walls sagged and the roof timbers had largely collapsed. The door, warped and full of gaps, hung haphazardly by one hinge. He set his foot against the doorpost and pushed. There was a creaking of old timbers and a groan as the fastening pegs gave way, and the entire front wall crashed down in a cloud of dust and splinters.

"That, of course, was the commander's quarters," Gilan said.

Horace sniffed disdainfully. "I'll make do with a tent," he said. "In fact, we all will."

They took another ten minutes to explore the interior of the fort—not that there was a great deal to see. It had obviously been unused for many years. There was a well in one corner, close to the gate, surrounded by a low stone parapet and covered with a circular wooden hatch. When Gilan slid the old, rotting wooden cover aside and tossed a pebble down, they heard a

splash of water far below. Horace leaned over the dark hole and
sniffed the air. There was no smell of corruption or rot. He saw
an old wooden beaker hanging on a frayed cord beside the parapet and carefully lowered it down, mindful that the cord could
break at any time. He felt the beaker touch the water and moved
the cord gently so that the container tipped and filled. Then he
retrieved it, sniffed the half-full contents and tasted it.

"Water's clean," he said.

"That's handy," Gilan replied. He peered over the edge of the
well's parapet. He thought he could see a tiny circle of light
reflecting from the black surface far below. He stepped back.
There were four large barrels standing close by. He checked
them but they were empty.

"What are these for?" he asked.

Horace shrugged. "Maybe for taking supplies of water to different points around the wall," he said. He set the beaker down
and looked around once more, satisfied with what he saw.

"We'll set up our tents in here," he said. "Let's bring the
others up."

Gilan smiled. "You can do that," he said. "I'll stay here and
keep watch."

Horace eyed him. "In other words, you don't feel like going
down that steep path and scrambling back up again."

Gilan held out his hands ingenuously. "You're the commander. It's your prerogative to lead the troops," he said.

Horace rolled his eyes. "As you say, I'm the commander. I
could order you to do it while I take it easy up here."

"You know us Rangers," Gilan replied. "We're notoriously
bad when it comes to obeying orders."

But Horace was already striding back toward the gate.

27

THE HUNTING PARTY ASSEMBLED IN THE CASTLE ARALUEN courtyard the following morning, just as the sun was rising over the tops of the trees at the base of the hill. The three Skandians were already waiting when Maddie and Cassandra emerged from the keep tower.

Maddie and Cassandra were accompanied by Dimon. He was armed with a hunting bow—a solid weapon but not as long or as powerful as the war bows carried by the castle's archers or the Ranger Corps. The two princesses were armed with their slings, and each had a bulging pouch of lead shot at her belt. In case of emergencies, Maddie was also carrying a bow slung over her shoulder. With a draw weight of only forty pounds, it was not as powerful as the recurve bow she used as a Ranger, so it didn't have the range and hitting power. But it would be useful enough for hunting. The sling wasn't suitable for all forms of game, she knew.

Dimon smiled when he saw the bow. "What do you expect to hit with that?" he asked. He had seen the standard of Maddie's archery. Or at least, he thought he had.

She shrugged. "You never know. I might get lucky."

He shook his head. "Not sure there's that much luck in the world."

Stig and Thorn were both armed with heavy spears. Hal had a crossbow slung over his back. Cassandra had arranged for it to be fetched from the ship by the servants who took food to the rest of the *Heron's* crew.

"Good morning, gentlemen," Cassandra said cheerfully, and they replied with a chorus of greetings. "I trust you slept well?"

Stig grimaced cheerfully. "I find it hard to get used to the fact that my bed isn't moving when I come ashore after a long voyage," he said. "Although it feels as if it is."

Hal agreed with Stig. "It takes a while to get your land legs back. By contrast, when we're on board the ship, it feels as if it's not moving at all," he said. "We'll be rolling around as if we're drunk for a day or so."

"Why is that?" Maddie asked. She had no experience of sailing or ships and was finding their observations interesting.

The two Skandians shrugged. "Nobody knows," Stig said. "It just happens that way. I guess we get used to the ship rolling, and when that's not happening anymore, we somehow think it is."

The seventh member of the party was Ulwyn, a grizzled old forester who had hunted the woods around Castle Araluen for the past thirty years. He would act as their guide on the hunt, seeking out and following the tracks left by game—deer, rabbits and hares, and wildfowl. He carried a bow and had a long-bladed hunting knife in a scabbard on his belt. He was accompanied by his hunting dog, Dougal, a rather scruffy beast of indeterminate lineage, who lolled his tongue at them. Dougal was getting on in years, and he had a stiff rear leg, but that didn't dampen his enthusiasm for hunting, fetching game and tracking. Ulwyn had known Cassandra since she was a girl and was totally devoted to her. He nodded a greeting as he joined them.

"Morning, Yer Highness," he said.

Cassandra smiled at him as she leaned down to scratch Dougal's floppy ears. "Good morning, Ulwyn. I trust you'll be able to find us some game today?"

He nodded several more times. "That'll be so, my lady. We'll strike out down to the lake, where we should find geese and ducks." He nodded at the sling coiled under her belt. "You should be able to bring down a few with that sling of yours. Then we'll angle over toward Sentinel Hill. There's been deer sighted there in the last few days."

"Sighted by whom?" Maddie asked.

He grinned knowingly at her. "Why, by me, my young lady," he said.

She nodded to herself. She would have expected him to go out the previous day and search for the best hunting spots for them.

Ulwyn looked around, making sure everyone was ready. "Shall we go?"

Out of deference to the Skandians, they had elected not to ride. They walked across the drawbridge and headed downhill toward the forest, Ulwyn leading the way. The grass was still wet with dew, and looking behind them, Maddie could see the dark tracks they were leaving as they displaced the moisture from the grass. They passed the small grove that masked the entrance to the tunnel under the moat, and she surreptitiously studied her companions to see if anyone noticed anything unusual about the spot. Nobody did, of course. People had been walking past that hidden tunnel for years without seeing anything out of the ordinary. Ulwyn led them slightly to the right, and she was relieved to see they would pass well clear of the glade where Bumper was tethered. She doubted that anyone else would sense his presence, but she couldn't be sure of Ulwyn. Or Dougal.

She started suddenly as she heard the whir of Cassandra's sling beside her, and the hiss of her shot as she let fly. A hare had broken cover in the grass ten meters ahead of them. It had barely reached half speed when the lead shot smacked into it and bowled it over.

"Stay awake," her mother told her.

Maddie made an appreciative gesture with her hands. "Good shot," she said, and the Skandians chorused their agreement.

Cassandra smiled a little smugly, it has to be admitted. "Even with my faulty technique?"

Maddie shook her head with a tired grin. She and her mother used totally different techniques with their slings, and Maddie had always held that Cassandra's was less efficient, and slower, than her own. Her mother was obviously delighted that she had scored before her daughter, beating her to the shot.

Ulwyn gathered the hare into his game bag and they moved on into the trees.

"What's wrong with Cassandra's technique?" Hal asked.

Maddie sniffed. "Just about everything. She makes up for bad technique with extraordinary good luck."

"Ha!" Her mother snorted and gave her a superior smile.

Maddie held her tongue. We'll see what's what when we reach the lake, she thought to herself.

But to her chagrin, when she and Cassandra let fly at two rising ducks, her shot grazed the tail of the one she aimed at, doing no more than knocking a feather loose, whereas her mother's target dropped like a stone into the lake as her shot hit dead center. In spite of his stiff rear leg, Dougal bounded away, hurling himself into the lake and churning the water to retrieve the fallen bird.

"Ha!" said Cassandra again, as Dougal dropped the duck at her feet.

Maddie reddened but said nothing. Again, Ulwyn gathered the prize into his game bag.

Thorn watched the byplay between the two women with amusement. "So," he said to Maddie, "your mother whirls her sling around her head horizontally two or three times and then releases. You don't do that. You let it fall back behind your shoulder, then you step forward and whip the sling overhead to release it." He looked at Hal, who was always interested in the mechanics of weaponry. "Sort of like the way Lydia uses her atlatl, isn't it?"

Hal agreed. "No whirling," he said.

Maddie regarded them both, not sure if they were teasing her, and felt the heat rising in her cheeks.

"It's more efficient my way," she said, trying to sound objective. "All that whirling and whirring wastes time and gives game a chance to escape—or an enemy to shoot first."

"I can see that," Hal replied solemnly.

"Yet," said Cassandra, "here am I with a duck and a hare in the bag and you, with your superior method, have downed . . . how many? Oh, that's right," she said, "precisely none."

"The day isn't over yet, Mother," Maddie told her, speaking very precisely.

They moved on from the lake—the other ducks and geese

there had all taken flight, and it would be some time before they settled to the water again. The hunting party headed toward Sentinel Hill, and Maddie began to see signs that deer had passed this way recently. She didn't let on that she'd seen the tracks—that would be a little out of character for a princess. But it was evident that Ulwyn had noticed them, and she saw him nodding contentedly to himself.

He appeared to have missed something else, though, and she thought it might be important that he knew about it. She pointed to several long gashes in the bark of a tree, low down and close to the ground.

"What caused this, Ulwyn?" she asked ingenuously.

"Why, that was well spotted, my lady!" Ulwyn said. He went down on one knee and touched the slashes. Maddie could see from where she stood that the sap on the disturbed bark was dry. The marks were many hours old.

Ulwyn looked up at her. "I saw these yesterday when I was scouting," he said. "A boar did this, my lady."

She made her eyes widen. "A wild boar?" she asked breathlessly.

The old hunter smiled grimly. "Well, we don't have any tame ones around here, Lady Madelyn. But he'll be long gone by now," he said reassuringly.

But Maddie had noticed something that the old hunter seemed to have missed. There were several more slashes on an adjacent tree, and the sap was still oozing wetly in them.

"What about those?" she asked.

Ulwyn looked, then frowned. "Hmm," he said thoughtfully. "Those were made today. And not so long ago." Then he raised his voice to speak to the rest of the group. "Eyes open, everyone. We don't want to come upon this one without seeing him first."

Thorn had watched the interplay between the young princess and Ulwyn. He wasn't taken in by her pretended ignorance. *You knew perfectly well what those marks were,* he thought. *And you wanted the rest of us to be on the alert for the boar.*

Maddie turned suddenly and caught him looking at her. He grinned and tapped one finger along the side of his nose. She frowned at him, suspecting that he'd seen through her playacting, then shook her head and turned away.

They moved on through the trees. Conscious that the boar might be close to them, and knowing that the sling would be virtually useless against it, she had coiled up the weapon and tucked it into her belt. Instead, she nocked an arrow to the bowstring and held the bow loosely, ready to shoot if necessary. Dimon saw the movement and smiled to himself once more, shaking his head.

They were working in a large half circle, planning to return to the lake, where the ducks might have resettled. Hal sighted a small deer and shot it with his crossbow. It was a good shot. The little animal leapt into the air, ran half a dozen paces, then fell dead. Ulwyn quickly field dressed it, and Thorn and Stig tied its four legs over a stout sapling, carrying it between them.

Maddie estimated they were halfway back to the lake when Dougal began barking frantically, and darted forward toward a dense thicket of bushes at the far side of the clearing they were crossing. The hunters stopped, startled by his sudden outburst. From the thicket, they could hear the movement of a large, heavy body crashing into the bushes and branches, and hear an enraged, threatening squeal.

"It's the boar!" Ulwyn yelled, then called to his frantic, near-hysterical dog, "Dougal! Back away now! Back away!"

But Dougal paid him no heed. The old dog darted forward toward the thicket, shoving his head between the dense-growing bushes and barking nonstop. The noises from within the thicket increased, and then suddenly Dougal turned tail and retreated as a shaggy, dark figure erupted from the bushes and charged after him.

The little dog tried to dodge, but his stiff back leg betrayed him, and he stumbled so that the boar was upon him. It butted its head into his ribs, and he squealed in fright and pain as the impact threw him several meters.

The hunters began to move in. Stig and Thorn dropped the carcass of the deer and moved forward, spears raised. Hal brought up his crossbow, and Dimon nocked an arrow to his bow. Ulwyn was panicking, terrified that his dog would be injured. Luckily, the boar had not used its tusks so far.

The boar dashed forward, and Dougal managed to leap awkwardly to one side, evading the slashing tusks. As the two animals moved round each other, one slashing and squealing, the other dodging awkwardly, none of the hunters had a clear shot or cast at the boar.

Except Maddie.

For three years, she had been trained to recognize and take advantage of a split-second opportunity. Now she had one as Dougal backed away and the boar hesitated, drawing back on its haunches and preparing for a final charge. She drew, sighted and released in one fluid movement. The arrow flashed across the clearing and thudded home, penetrating deep behind the boar's left shoulder and tearing into its heart.

The savage beast squealed once, reared onto its hind legs, then fell dead on the grass, its legs sticking out stiffly.

Instantly, Maddie let out a panicked squeal of her own and let the bow drop to the ground in front of her. When the others realized where the arrow had come from, they turned to face her. But she was standing, shaking, her hands covering her eyes, and calling frantically.

"What happened? What happened? Did I hit it?"

Her companions heaved a collective sigh of relief. The tension went out of the clearing as they looked again at the dead boar.

"You hit it all right, my lady!" said Ulwyn. "Killed it stone dead." Stig and Hal echoed his words of praise. Dimon looked on in utter disbelief.

Maddie took her hands from her eyes and looked at Ulwyn, wide-eyed. "I did?" she said in tones of total surprise. "But I had my eyes shut."

"She did at that," said a voice behind her. "Had them shut tight the whole time."

It was Thorn. She realized that the old Skandian had been standing behind her and had likely witnessed the entire event—had seen her cool, disciplined handling of the bow, then her pretense at panic as she hurled it to the ground. She met his gaze now as Dimon knelt beside the boar and shook his head.

"If that's the case, that was the luckiest shot I've ever seen," Dimon said slowly.

As Maddie studied the old sea wolf, he let one eye slide shut in a surreptitious wink. *If you don't want 'em to know, I'm not saying anything,* the movement said.

✦ ✦ ✦

They circled back to the lake, with Dimon and Hal carrying the boar and Stig and Thorn with the deer between them. They'd be hard put to carry any more large animals, and Hal looked appreciatively at the two carcasses.

"Edvin will be pleased," he said. "That's plenty of fresh meat for the trip home."

They added to their bag at the lake, with Cassandra bringing down three more ducks and Maddie accounting for a goose and a mallard. Dougal, thoroughly chastened now, brought the birds ashore for them.

"And there's tonight's dinner taken care of," Cassandra said with a satisfied smile.

They dined on roast goose that night in the refectory adjoining the kitchens. The rest of the *Heron*'s crew were summoned to join them, and it was a festive and cheerful occasion, marred only slightly by the fact that Dimon hurriedly excused himself, on the pretext of duty. Maddie noted again that he seemed somewhat uncomfortable around the Skandians. She puzzled over it for a few minutes, then dismissed it. Hal and his crew were excellent company—boisterous and cheerful, with a fund of exciting stories to tell. If Dimon chose to be prickly around them, that was his problem.

They were demolishing a fig pudding after the main meal when a servant entered and spoke quietly to Cassandra. She listened, then pointed out Hal. The servant moved down the table to where the skirl was waiting expectantly.

"Captain Hal, there's a messenger here for you. He's a Skandian and he says it's urgent."

He nodded toward the door leading to the stairway, where a figure could be seen waiting just outside. Hal glanced interrogatively at Cassandra, who nodded. Then he beckoned to the waiting man.

"Come in," he said. And, as the newcomer moved out of the shadows into the light, he recognized him. "Is that you, Sten Engelson?"

"Yes, Hal. It's me all right."

Hal turned to Cassandra and explained. "Sten is the first mate on *Wolfbiter*."

"*Wolfbiter*?" Cassandra said. "Isn't she the—"

"The current duty ship, yes," Hal told her. "Jern Icerunner is her skirl. We spoke with Jern two days ago when we reached the mouth of the Semath, where she was patrolling." He turned his attention back to Sten.

"Is there a problem?" he asked, although as he said it, he realized that Sten would hardly be here if there wasn't.

"*Wolfbiter* is damaged, Hal," Sten said. "She went onto Barrier Rocks, south of the Semath. A rogue wave picked her up and dumped her heavily. Jern managed to get her to the beach, but he thinks her back might be broken. He wants you to take a look before he decides to abandon her."

Stig leaned toward Maddie and said in a low aside, "Hal is an expert shipbuilder as well as a skirl. If *Wolfbiter* can be repaired, he'll be able to tell them."

Hal was rubbing his chin. "I'd best go and take a look," he said. Then he turned to Cassandra. "We'll leave straightaway, my lady," he said. "That way, we'll just catch the outgoing tide. I don't like the idea of the duty ship being out of action any longer than it has to be."

Cassandra nodded. "Neither do I, with this Red Fox Clan disrupting things," she said. "How long do you think you'll be?"

Hal paused, screwing up his eyes while he considered the problem. "A week, maybe ten days at the most. If we have to abandon her, I'll need to bring her crew back with us—and we'll need to provision the ship for the trip home. We can finalize the details for the archers then too," he added as an afterthought.

"I'll have the papers ready to sign, Hal. And I'll have the boar and your deer salted and ready to go as well," Cassandra said.

Hal nodded his thanks, then turned to his crew. "Right, lads, we'd better be moving. The tide won't wait for us, and it'll be hard rowing if it turns."

There was a clatter as benches were pushed back from the table, and the *Heron*'s crew rose to their feet and began making their way toward the door.

Stig paused halfway and turned back, reaching across the table to tear a leg from the carcass of the goose. He ripped a large chunk off with his teeth and grinned at Maddie.

"I never waste good food," he said.

Hal snorted derisively. "You never waste any food," he said. "Now let's get moving."

28

By dint of much pushing, pulling and swearing, they got the horses up the last part of the hill and into the fort. The supply wagon was a different matter. The vertical wall was too high and too steep, and Horace was disinclined to waste time building a ramp for the wagon. In the end, he had it unloaded and left it on the path below the gate.

"If the Foxes try to mount an attack, we can always push it over the edge and let it run down on them," he said.

While Horace had been bringing the rest of the force up the hill, Gilan had discovered the use intended for the barrels. There were four drains dug along the front wall of the palisade, two on either side of the gate, spaced five meters apart. He experimented by pouring a bucket of water down one of them. A minute or so later, he saw a stream of water spurt from the edge of the path.

"If we pour water down them, it'll wet the grass slope below the last section of path," he told Horace. "That'll make it even harder for the enemy to climb."

Horace nodded, grinning at the ingenuity of the original designers. He had the barrels moved so that they stood by the four drains, then set a party of men to filling them with water.

Initially, the old dried-out seams leaked profusely. But as the water soaked into the staves and expanded them, the leaks slowed to a trickle.

Night fell and the men lit cooking fires. The supply wagon had carried bags of grain for the horses. If they rationed it carefully, it would last a week or so. The horses would be hungry, and their fitness and strength would suffer. But they were unlikely to be mounting a cavalry charge while they were in the fort.

Horace posted sentries around the walls, with strict instructions to wake him if there was any sight or sound of the enemy arriving. He considered it unlikely, however.

"If you're right," he told Gilan, as they sat by a small fire nursing mugs of hot coffee, "they will have waited for nightfall to cross the river. My guess is that they would have camped on the meadow by the river for the night. They'd hardly want to go blundering through the forest in the dark in case we were waiting in ambush for them."

"Maybe that's what we should have done," Gilan suggested, but Horace shook his head.

"Night battles are too risky. Too many things can go wrong. We might thin their numbers out, but we could lose a lot of our own men. And we don't have a lot to lose."

"So we wait here for them."

"We wait here for them, and see what they have in mind."

"You think they'll attack?" Gilan asked.

Horace looked deep into the fire before he answered. "I think so," he said. "They'll have to test our strength at least once. But they'll take a lot of casualties if they do. My guess is, once they've tried, they'll pull back and surround the hill. We don't have enough men to mount a frontal attack on them, so we can hardly break out."

"Which means if we don't get help, we'll be bottled up here," Gilan said thoughtfully.

His friend nodded. "And I'm beginning to think that's what they've had in mind all along."

Gilan frowned. "What makes you think that?"

"There are a lot more of them than we expected," Horace replied. "And they're better organized than we were led to believe—and better armed. Maybe this whole thing was designed to get us out of Castle Araluen, and leave the garrison weakened."

Gilan took a deep sip of his coffee and thought about what Horace had said. "That makes sense," he said at length. "But Araluen is a tough nut to crack, even with half the garrison missing. Dimon is a good man, and of course, Cassandra has been in her share of fights over the years. If there's an attack, they'll be able to hold out."

"I suppose so," said Horace. But he didn't sound happy about the prospect. "And in the meantime, we're stuck here, sitting on top of a hill and out of the way."

Neither man said anything for a few minutes, and then Horace added, "And nobody knows we're here."

The enemy column arrived an hour after first light. Horace and Gilan stood on the catwalk inside the palisade, peering down the hill to the flat land below as the files of men marched out of the forest and formed up on the open grassland.

"There's a few less than there used to be," Gilan remarked.

Horace grunted. "Still more than a hundred and thirty of them. They still outnumber us more than three to one."

Three officers rode forward, stopping at the base of the hill, where the track began its sinuous path upward. Gilan could make out the leader from the day before in the center. The white bandage and sling on his right arm stood out in the early morning light. The man urged his horse forward and started up the steep spiral path, shading his eyes with his unwounded hand and peering up at the fort high above him.

"Think he knows we're here?" the Ranger asked, not really expecting an answer.

But Horace gestured to the smoke from their cooking fires, thin gray columns that rose unwaveringly in the still morning air. "Oh, he knows all right," he said. He glanced across the fort, making sure there were lookouts on all four walls, ready to keep an eye on the enemy leader as he spiraled upward, with the other two officers following his lead.

The three riders pushed on, leaning forward in their saddles against the slope, and disappeared from sight around the first curve in the track. Horace called to a sergeant on the west wall.

"Got them in sight, Sergeant?"

The sergeant waved acknowledgment. "In sight, sir. Still coming up!"

A few minutes later, his opposite number on the rear north wall raised a hand. "Enemy in sight, sir! Still climbing!"

Then, as the three riders continued up and around the hill, a similar warning came from the eastern wall. There were five men stationed at each wall, three troopers and two archers. As the enemy came into sight, one of the archers on the east wall held up a hand.

"Try a shot, sir?" he called.

But Gilan motioned for him to stand down. The enemy leader would be within long bowshot now. But he would be aware of the danger and would certainly have his shield in position to intercept any arrows from above.

"Save your arrows," Gilan called back.

The archer shrugged, a little disappointed.

Gilan turned to Horace. "Pity Maddie's not here with her sling. A lead shot bouncing off his helmet might give him pause."

Horace grunted noncommittally. He didn't share Gilan's wish that Maddie were here with them. This was a dangerous situation and not one he wanted his daughter to be involved in.

"Coming into sight now, sir!" called the lookout at the eastern end of their wall, and within a few seconds, the trio of riders appeared around the bend. They were on the second-top tier of the path. One more pass around the hill would bring them up to the top level.

"Get ready to put a warning shot past his ear," Horace said, and Gilan stepped forward, drawing an arrow from his quiver.

"That's far enough!" Horace shouted.

A second later, Gilan drew back and released. The arrow hissed down, passing within half a meter of the Fox leader's face. He jerked hurriedly on the reins and brought his horse to a stop. As Gilan had predicted, his long, triangular shield was deployed on his right side—the side facing the fort—covering most of his body and legs. His head was covered by a full-face helmet. He reached awkwardly with his left hand, now holding the reins, and pushed up his visor.

"I'll give you one chance to surrender!" he shouted. His voice was surprisingly high-pitched, although that might have been because of the tension he was feeling. "One chance only!"

"And then?" Horace replied.

The man gestured to his troops, at the base of the hill. "You can't hope to escape!" he said. "We outnumber you four to one. You're stuck here on this hill."

"And we're quite content to stay here," Horace told him, although, after the thoughts he'd expressed earlier, that wasn't true. "If you have so many men, why don't you come and drive us out of here?" His best chance was to goad the enemy into making an attack. The hill was an excellent defensive position, and Gilan's archers could decimate any attacking force.

"I've got a question for you," the Fox leader shouted, anger evident in his voice. "While you're twiddling your thumbs up here, what do you think is happening at Castle Araluen?"

Horace's expression darkened. That was what he had been worried about. He was being held here, unable to do anything constructive, and Castle Araluen was left vulnerable to attack. But he wasn't going to play into the enemy's hands by debating that position.

"I've got a question for you," he called in return. "How are you planning to get back down that hill?"

The rider was stunned into silence for a second or two.

In a quiet voice, Gilan spoke to the two archers on the south wall. "Archers, forward."

The two archers stepped forward to the edge of the palisade.

Below them the rider saw the two heads appear above the wooden wall, their bows in plain sight. His horse snorted, sensing his sudden fear, and tried to rear. He held it in check, cursing it. Then he called to Horace.

"You can't shoot me! I came here for a parley!"

Horace smiled grimly. "I didn't invite you," he said. "And I don't see any flag of truce. I'm perfectly within my rights to order my men to shoot."

The Fox leader, having got his horse under control, was backing it nervously down the path. If he turned, his shield would be on the downhill side, exposing him completely to arrows from the wall. He would have to switch the shield to his left arm again, and that would be a slow, clumsy movement, with his right arm injured and bandaged.

Gilan knew that Horace would never order his men to shoot at a virtually helpless man—even an enemy.

"Might save us some trouble if we did kill him," he suggested mildly.

But Horace shook his head. "Someone else would take command," he said. "And he might know what he's doing."

"So we let him go?" Gilan asked. He had been trained by Halt, who had no false illusions about honor or fair treatment for an enemy. So far as Halt was concerned, if you had your enemy at a disadvantage, you didn't let him off the hook.

Horace turned a hard look on him, knowing what he was thinking but refusing to be swayed from what he knew to be right.

"We let him go," he said. Then he added:

"For now."

29

LIFE AT THE CASTLE WENT BACK TO ITS UNEVENTFUL ROU-
tine after the departure of the noisy, irreverent Skandians.
Maddie found herself wishing that they had stayed longer. They
had brought a breath of fresh air to the castle.

However, she had work to do, and the following evening she
set out to keep watch at the old abbey.

She waited till the castle had settled down for the evening,
then crept surreptitiously down to the cellars. As before, she
took a full lantern with her. She also took her sling and her saxe,
and she wore her Ranger cloak over her normal daywear of
jerkin, leggings and boots.

She let herself into the concealed chamber at the end of the
cellar, pausing to light her lantern from one of the lamps that
were kept burning there. She eased the concealed door shut
behind her, confident now that she would be able to open it on
her return the following morning.

Then, holding the lantern high, she set out down the sloping, uneven path that led under the moat. Knowing what to
expect this time, she was unfazed by the dripping water that ran
down the tunnel walls as she passed beneath the moat.

As before, she felt the tunnel angling upward as she passed beneath the moat and out onto dry ground once more. There were still bundles of roots hanging through the ceiling of the tunnel, and she used her saxe to clear them away. She'd almost certainly be passing through here again on subsequent nights, and she didn't enjoy the sensation of having them suddenly loom out of the darkness and clutch at her face and hair.

This time, with only dim starlight outside, she didn't see the circle of light shining as she approached the end of the tunnel, and it came as something of a shock to reach the tangle of bushes at the exit. Realizing that her lantern would shine like a beacon in the dark, she quickly extinguished it before exiting the tunnel. She pushed the bushes back into place across the entrance, concealing it from outside view, then set off down the hill to the spot where she'd left Bumper.

Conscious that there were lookouts posted on all the castle walls, she moved carefully, in a half crouch, making use of all available cover. She also kept her camouflaged cloak wrapped around herself and her cowl up.

In the dim light—the moon was yet to rise—it was highly unlikely that anyone would notice the indistinct figure moving slowly and silently through the knee-high grass of the park. Still, she breathed a sigh of relief when she reached the tree line and disappeared into the concealing shadows there. She stood upright and made her way to the hidden glade where Bumper was waiting for her, his ears pricked. He had obviously heard her coming, but, as he had been trained to do, remained silent until she spoke first.

"Pleased to see me?" she asked, rubbing his silky nose and handing him the carrot he knew she would be carrying. He nickered softly, then crunched the carrot contentedly. She glanced around the small clearing. Everything here seemed to be in order. His feed bag hung from a branch, and when she checked it, she saw it was still half full. The water bucket was nearly empty. She'd fill it when they returned. He could always make his own way to the small stream nearby, of course. But she preferred to leave water handy for him.

Quickly, she saddled him and swung up into the saddle. Her bow was in its bow case, strapped to the saddle. She took it out to check that it was undamaged and the string was still firm, with no sign of dampness or unraveling. Satisfied that all was well, she slid it back into the bow case. Then, touching her heels lightly to Bumper's sides, she set out down the twisting game trail for the abbey.

She dismounted when they were twenty meters from the clearing where the abbey stood, and left Bumper behind as she crept silently forward through the trees.

There was no sign of anyone in the clearing, and she turned her head this way and that, listening carefully for any sound, any hint that there were people inside the abbey.

Nothing.

She walked back to Bumper and held her finger to her lips, then pointed to the ground at his feet. The message was clear: Be silent and stay here. He tossed his head in acknowledgment, and she turned to creep back to the abbey.

There was open ground for fifteen meters between the edge of the forest and the building. She felt an almost overwhelming temptation to cross it slowly and furtively, but that wouldn't serve any purpose. Slow movement wouldn't conceal her from any potential observer.

Taking care to make no noise, she stepped lightly across the clear ground until she was beside the door. She noted that it was now closed, yet she remembered leaving it slightly open last time she had been here.

Could have been the wind, she thought, but she doubted it. It was more likely that someone had closed the door behind them. And that meant that Warwick's informant had been right. There had been people here recently.

Question was, were any of them still here?

Only one way to find out, she thought. Leaning forward, she pushed against the door with her left hand, her right hand touching the hilt of her saxe.

The door gave easily. Someone had obviously oiled it. And that indicated that they planned to use the abbey again in the future. She let it swing open, hanging back and waiting to see if there was any reaction from inside.

Again, nothing.

Drawing her saxe, she stepped quickly through the door opening and moved to one side, out of the doorway. There was no sound from the abbey. No challenging voice. No urgent scuffling of feet as someone moved to take cover. She waited until her eyes were accustomed to the gloom and peered around, searching the interior in sections.

There was no sign of anyone.

Aware that she had been holding her breath, she let it out in a long sigh and re-sheathed her saxe.

The old farmer who had reported seeing people here had said he had seen them around midnight, and Warwick's previous observations agreed with that timing. That meant she had at least an hour to wait to see if anyone turned up. She moved

down the body of the church and climbed the rickety stairs to
the choir gallery. From there, she'd have a good view of the entire
building and still be able to remain concealed.

She settled down on the floor beside the front bench in the
gallery, behind the solid timber balustrade, made herself as comfortable as possible, and settled in to wait. The moon had risen
now and was shining at an oblique angle through the window set
beside the gallery.

She woke with a start, realizing that she must have dozed off. She
looked at the window. There was no sign of the moon, yet she
knew it had risen. She had been awake when that had happened,
watching the pale silver light flood through the window across
the interior of the old church. Cautiously, she raised her head,
making sure the abbey was still deserted.

"Fine Ranger you are," she said, thinking of the scathing
rebuke she would have received from Will for falling asleep on
watch. On the wall opposite the gallery window was a high slit
in the stonework—no more than an arrow slit, really. She looked
at that now and could see the moon's light sending a narrow,
high-angled shaft across the building. The moon had risen,
passed across the church and was now descending on the far
side. She estimated that she had been asleep for at least two
hours.

At least she could be confident that there had been no sign
of the Red Fox Clan while she had been asleep.

"I'm not so dopey that I could sleep through the noise made
by a whole bunch of people gathering there below me," she said.
But it was scant comfort. The unavoidable fact was, she had
fallen asleep while she was supposed to be on watch.

She rose now, stretching her cramped limbs. She had slept with her head at an angle, without any proper support, and her neck ached. She rolled her head and shoulders, trying to ease the stiffness, but without much success.

She climbed down the ladder stairs to the floor of the abbey and headed for the door. She made one last inspection to make sure that the building had remained unoccupied and there was no sign that anyone else had been in here in the past few hours. Nothing seemed to have changed, and the rough sketch of the fox mask was still in place. She checked around the doorway, but there was no sign of the dust and dirt there having been disturbed, no sign of footprints anywhere.

"Just as well for you," she muttered. Even though she was sure there was nobody else around, she checked carefully before she left the abbey, then moved quickly across the open ground to the shelter of the trees, where Bumper waited patiently for her.

Fell asleep, did you? he asked, and she wondered how he knew.

"Just resting my eyes," she said. "Just for a few minutes."

Ha! She knew she could never fool her horse, so she said nothing, resigned to letting him have the moral victory—yet again. She swung up into the saddle and turned his head for home. There was no point in waiting here any longer. All reported sightings of activity at the abbey had taken place before midnight, and she judged it was well after that now.

"We'll just have to come back again tomorrow. And the night after that if necessary," she told Bumper.

So long as you get a good night's sleep, he replied.

She chose to ignore him.

30

FOR THE NEXT TWO NIGHTS, MADDIE KEPT WATCH IN THE abbey, but with no result. There was no sign of the Red Fox Clan, no sign of any movement in the forest around the old abbey. No sign of anything.

She wondered briefly if she should tell Cassandra of her suspicions, but decided against it. Not yet, anyway.

She wasn't completely sure why she didn't want to tell Cassandra. Possibly, she realized, her mother would quiz her about how she was leaving the castle at night without being seen or challenged by the sentries. And that would lead to her revealing the existence of the tunnel under the moat, which her mother would want to examine and, being a mother, would probably put off-limits. Besides, once Cassandra knew about the tunnel and explored it, it was inevitable that others would learn of its existence, and Maddie wasn't ready for that to happen yet.

Additionally, she had in mind an incident that had taken place eighteen months previously. She had been convinced that she had stumbled upon a robber's lair in the forest close to Redmont. But when she had sounded the alarm and led a patrol of the castle guard to the spot, the robbers had turned out to be innocent tinkers. She didn't want to risk the same embarrassment this time. She was determined to make sure of her facts before she involved other people.

It would be better to have something definite to report.

On the fourth night, Maddie waited in her room until the castle had settled for the night. It took a little longer than usual. For a start, Cassandra had wanted to talk when they were having their usual after-dinner coffee together. Then, for some reason, there was a lot of movement in the castle, with a lot of people on the stairs and in the public rooms. Once things had calmed down, she crept quietly into the cellar and made her way through the tunnel again.

You're late. Bumper's tone was mildly accusatory as she made her way into the little clearing where he waited for her.

"I dozed off," she explained. "It's fine for you—you can sleep all day if you want to."

Sleep is overrated, Bumper told her. It occurred to her that he found quite a few things overrated.

"Only for those who can sleep all day," she replied. She saddled him quickly and mounted, moving off through the trees at a brisk trot to make up lost time. They were familiar with the track now and could move more freely. They reached the abbey and she dismounted, leaving Bumper in the trees. There was no need to instruct him to wait now. He knew the routine.

Take care. He sensed that she was becoming accustomed to having nothing happen at the abbey. That could lead to inattention.

"I will," she replied, and ghosted through the trees to the edge of the clearing where the old stone church stood. As before, she stopped and listened before gliding silently across to the entrance. The previous night, she had placed a leaf in the door-jamb as she closed it. It was still in place, telling her that nobody had entered the abbey in her absence. She opened the door and slipped inside.

She didn't need to pause to let her eyes accustom themselves to the dimness now. The interior of the building was familiar to her, and she made her way quickly to the stairs up to the gallery.

As she had done on the previous three nights, she sank to the floor in front of the first pew, concealed from the body of the church by the solid oak balustrade at the front of the gallery. Previously, she had pierced a hole in the paneling with the point of her saxe. This gave her a way of viewing what was going on in the church without revealing herself.

She settled herself, finding an uncomfortable position where the arm of the pew dug into her back. She had discovered that this kept her awake as she sat, unmoving, for several hours each night. She checked the moon position. It was considerably higher tonight than it had been originally, shining down through the gallery window at a steep angle. It wouldn't be long before it passed over the building and shone down through the—

Below her, she heard the door ease open. Someone was here.

31

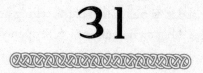

INSTINCTIVELY, EVEN THOUGH SHE KNEW SHE WAS CON-
cealed from anyone in the body of the church, Maddie shrank
down even lower behind the wooden balustrade. She could
make out a number of voices, talking in low, conversational
tones. And she could hear the shuffle of multiple feet on the
floor of the abbey below.

Cautiously, she placed her eye to the small hole she had
drilled in the wooden board that formed the front of the balustrade. She had to move her head to find the optimum viewing
position, but once she did that, she could see that the church was
beginning to fill with people.

They shuffled in—fifteen to twenty of them, she estimated—and took their places in the front four rows of pews,
before the old wooden pulpit where the abbot would have read
their sacred lessons to them when the abbey was a functioning
church. The last three rows of pews were left empty, and she
breathed a sigh of relief. She had experienced a sudden jolt of
panic as she wondered if this mysterious congregation might
decide to occupy the gallery as well as the main church itself.
That, she thought, would have been awkward in the extreme.

The mumble of conversation continued, although she couldn't distinguish any individual remarks. Chances were, it was mere inconsequential chatter. Occasionally, she heard suppressed laughter, which seemed to bear out the theory that the speakers were merely catching up on events with each other.

Her eye, glued to the spyhole, was beginning to water as she strained to see beyond its limitations and get a better sight of the people below her. She leaned back, rubbing it with the back of her hand, and blinking several times to clear it. Then she leaned into the spyhole once more, choosing a different angle so she could see more.

She started as a sudden flare flashed below her. Switching her angle, she looked to where one of the people had struck a flint on steel, sending sparks into a small pile of tinder. As she watched, he blew, and a tiny tongue of yellow flame blossomed. It grew larger as more of the fuel was lit. Eventually, the small flame was held to the oil-soaked body of a torch. There were a few seconds where nothing seemed to happen, and then the flames took hold on the torch, feeding on the oil. A yellow light filled the abbey, and there was a murmur of satisfaction from those around the torchbearer.

Several other men, all holding torches, crowded close and lit them from the first flaming brand. The light inside the abbey grew stronger, and shadows leapt grotesquely across the walls. Now she could get a clearer view of the people who had entered.

They were all male—or at least, all the ones she could see were. They were dressed in everyday clothing—breeches, jerkins and cloaks. And they were all armed, with a variety of swords, long knives, axes and spears.

On their heads, they wore strange caps, and it took her a few

minutes to realize that they were made from fox fur—more correctly, from the masks of foxes.

The eyeholes were dark and empty, but the ears and snouts
were still in place, sitting on top of the wearers' heads. From
above, they appeared like a small troop of foxes bobbing around
below her. The overall effect was a little grotesque, and she
shivered.

She was now in no doubt that she had infiltrated a meeting
of the mysterious Red Fox Clan.

The door, which the last person to enter had closed to seal
out the cold wind, was suddenly pushed open and the subdued
chatter of voices died away, leaving an expectant silence. She
heard the firm strike of heels on the hard flagstones as someone
entered. She shifted her head this way and that, trying to get a
clear view of the doorway and the new arrival. But her limited
field of vision through the spyhole didn't allow it.

Finally, deciding to take the risk, and reasoning that the
upper level of the abbey was in relative darkness compared with
the torchlight below, she raised her head above the level of the
balustrade for a brief glance.

A tall figure, clad in a full-length, fur-lined red cloak, was
striding to the lectern in front of the assembled group. His face
was concealed in the shadow cast by his cowl so she couldn't
make out his features. But there was something vaguely familiar
about him—about the way he moved and stood. Will had taught
her to pay attention to body language and the way a person held
himself.

It's the hardest thing to disguise, he had told her. *You can change
your features and your clothing. But the way you move will all too
often give you away.* To this end, he had instructed her in small

subterfuges, like putting a pebble in one shoe, or building up the heel of one boot to alter her gait when she moved. Or of intentionally holding her shoulders and head at an angle different from the norm.

You have to be particularly aware of this, he had told her. *You have that slight stiffness in your hip that defines the way you move or stand.*

So she watched the newcomer carefully. There was definitely something familiar about him, she thought. He moved with an easy, athletic grace. He was obviously a warrior—she could see the long sword in a scabbard at his left side. The hilt was visible, projecting forward from beneath the cloak. And the tail of the cloak was held up at one point, where it draped over the end of the scabbard.

She lowered herself slowly back behind the balustrade—any sudden movement might draw his attention. He was almost directly in front of her now, and she could see him easily through the spyhole. He stood behind the lectern. Slight movements of the cowl showed that he was scanning the assembled audience from side to side. After a minute or so, he made a discreet hand gesture toward someone in the church, obviously signaling them to open proceedings.

A deep voice intoned from the space underneath Maddie. "All stand and hail, *Vulpus Rutilus.*"

Vulpus Rutilus. She recognized the form of the words as being in the ancient Toscan language. Before she had been recruited into the Rangers, she had studied it at Castle Araluen, hating every minute of it.

Now, however, she recognized those two words from her long-distant lessons.

Vulpus Rutilus. Red Fox. The leader of the cult was obviously assigned this title. There was a general shuffling of feet as the men below her stood. The leader remained unmoving at the lectern while they rearranged themselves. Then, in a loud chorus, they spoke.

"Hail, *Vulpus Rutilus*! Hail, leader of the Red Fox Clan!"

There was a rustle of movement, and through the spyhole, she saw the group all raise their right arms, held straight, above shoulder level, in the traditional ancient military salute of the Toscans. Their leader raised his own right hand in reply.

"Hail, members of the Clan. Hail Red Foxes."

His voice was muffled by the cowl, but her heart froze as she recognized it. Then, after a few seconds, he swept back the heavy cowl so she could see his face in the torchlight, and she knew for sure who he was.

Vulpus Rutilus, leader of the Red Fox Clan, was none other than Dimon, her mother's trusted commander of the guard.

Stunned by the realization, she dropped back from the spyhole into the narrow space between the gallery's front pew and the balustrade, leaning against the rough stone wall of the abbey for support. Vaguely, she heard the sound of shuffling bodies as the Foxes took their seats once more, waiting for their leader to address them. How could Dimon, of all people, be a traitor? He was a trusted officer in the castle guard. He was even said to be a distant relative. Maddie had a deeply ingrained sense of loyalty and honor, and it simply made no sense to her for such a person to be a turncoat—to abrogate his position and his responsibilities so badly.

Then, as he spoke further, she began to understand.

"For some weeks now, you've been gathering here with your

men, traveling from all corners of the kingdom," Dimon said. "Now the time for action has come. Tomorrow, we will launch our attack on Castle Araluen." There was a murmur of surprise from the assembly. They obviously hadn't been expecting this. She put her eye back to the tiny hole drilled through the balustrade and saw him holding up his hands for silence. Gradually, the voices died away.

"I know. I know. This is sooner than we had planned. But conditions for the attack are favorable, and I believe we are ready." He looked around the faces before him, making sure that everyone was paying attention, then continued.

"The plan to lure Sir Horace and the Ranger Commandant away from the castle has been more successful than we had expected," he said.

Maddie felt her heart skip a beat. The plan to lure them away? So it had been a ruse to remove Cassandra's two most experienced and renowned warriors, and half the garrison, and prevent them from playing a hand in the defense of the castle against the Red Fox Clan.

"They are currently trapped in an old hill fort on the northern banks of the Wezel River. Our Sonderland allies have them surrounded. They are effectively out of action."

"Lord Vulpus, how long can the Sonderland mercenaries hold them?" a voice asked.

The tone was respectful, and Dimon nodded at the speaker, acknowledging it as a fair question. "Indefinitely. But knowing Sir Horace and the Ranger, I expect they will try to break out. If they do, they will almost certainly be overwhelmed and killed by our superior numbers. But it would be a bad idea to underestimate those two. On the slim chance that they might survive,

I want to have occupied Castle Araluen. We all know what an impregnable stronghold that is. They can destroy themselves against the walls of Araluen while we sit safely inside."

He paused, his gaze traveling round the room. "Of course," he continued, "we won't have to assault the castle. You will all be disguised as members of the garrison. I have uniforms outside for you and your men. You will form up under my command and we will simply march into the castle. Nobody will try to stop us. Once we're inside, we'll have the remaining garrison outnumbered. We'll kill them, and the Princess Regent, and take control. Then we'll spread the rumor that the princess was murdered by assassins from the Red Fox Clan, in spite of our efforts to save her. Once we're inside the castle, I'll remain masked so that the staff and servants don't recognize me.

"With Duncan and his immediate family out of the way, I will be the next in line to the throne. I am related to the royal family, as you all know. It's a distant relationship, but a perfectly legal one—and one I can prove. Best of all, from our point of view, I'm a male heir. The people will accept me. After all, I will be seen as the heroic victor over the Red Foxes. Then, once I am in power, I will rescind the law passed by my ancestor and restore the law of male succession to the throne of Araluen. Male succession only," he added with grim emphasis, and there was another murmur of agreement.

"What if the Ranger Corps rises against you?" It was the same voice that had spoken before, and Maddie had the sudden realization that this conversation had been orchestrated to raise and then demolish any possible objections to Dimon's plan.

"Why should they? They won't know of my association with the Clan, and I will be the legitimate heir to the throne. There'll be nobody to tell them otherwise. We'll simply claim that a loyal group remained trapped with me in a section of the castle, and we eventually broke out and defeated the Red Fox members—unfortunately too late to save Cassandra."

"There's always the young princess." This was a new voice, and several others called out, agreeing.

"Madelyn? She's a flighty young girl. And she's in the palace with her mother. I expect she'll suffer the same fate."

Maddie smiled grimly. Without her willing it, her hand touched the sling coiled under her belt. For a moment, goaded by his derisive reference to her, she was tempted to rise from her hiding place and place a lead ball between his treacherous eyes. Then sanity prevailed. Throwing away her own life wouldn't help matters.

"What about the King?" another voice called.

Dimon made a contemptuous gesture. "He's weak and sick. I'd say he doesn't have much longer for this earth."

Maddie felt a prick of tears at the description of her grandfather. And at Dimon's scornful dismissal of him. The leader of the Red Foxes was going to pay for this, she told herself.

"We heard there were Skandians in the castle. Will they take a hand in all this?" This was yet another voice.

Dimon replied with a nod. "They've gone," he said. "That's why I want to act now. They'll be gone for at least four or five days, maybe a week. They might have helped Cassandra—but if we act now, we'll be in control of the castle by the time they return. And, like Horace and Gilan, they'll have no idea that we were behind the princess's death."

Maddie found herself nodding slowly. This explained Dimon's antipathy toward the crew of the *Heron*. He had seen them as a possible obstacle to his revolt. A dozen tough, battle-hardened Skandians under the command of a resourceful leader might well throw his carefully planned coup off balance.

"Are there any more questions?" Dimon was asking. He looked around the room, searching the faces before him. There was no reply. "In that case, we'll adjourn this meeting. We'll assemble tomorrow at noon in the forest below Castle Araluen. Collect your uniforms outside. We'll simply march up the hill, across the drawbridge and into the castle. Kill anyone who shows any resistance."

There was a stir of movement from below, and Maddie rose carefully, intent on getting one more look at the conspirators before the meeting broke up. It might be handy to be able to recognize some faces the next day, she thought. Dimon, of course, she would know. But she might need to be able to identify the other ringleaders.

As she cautiously drew herself up to peer over the balustrade, she supported herself with one hand on top of the wooden rail.

But the old timber was rotten and worm ridden, and as she put her weight on it, a piece broke away beneath her hand with a splintering *crack*. Two dozen pairs of eyes turned toward the sound, and she dropped back out of sight. In the sudden panic of the moment, she forgot her training, forgot the need to move slowly. And the sudden movement betrayed her presence.

Below her, she heard Dimon shouting.

"The gallery! There's someone up there! Get him!"

32

THEY HAD BEEN IN THE OLD HILL FORT FOR THREE DAYS before the Red Fox Clan launched their attack.

An hour after dawn, Gilan was patrolling the walls, as was his custom each morning, when he heard the sound of whistles and bugles coming from the enemy camp. The Fox troops had set up tent lines at the bottom of the hill. Now their men were pouring out of them and forming up on the open space between their camp and the beginning of the winding track that led up to the hill fort.

"So they're moving at last," said a voice from close behind him.

He turned quickly to see that Horace was there. "Looks like it," he replied. He glanced around the walkway and saw a group of archers a few meters away, watching the preparations below with interest. His senior archer was among them.

"Nestor!" he called, and as the man looked up, he said, "Over here, please."

The grizzled archer walked smartly to him, knuckling his forehead as he drew close.

"Looks like they've made up their minds, Ranger," he said.

The small garrison of the hill fort had been wondering when the Foxes might gather sufficient courage to attack.

"Indeed it does. Deploy your men, Nestor. My guess is the enemy will use the spiral track until they're close to the top, then try to come up the grass slope for the last of the climb."

Nestor nodded. He'd come to the same conclusion.

Gilan continued. "Problem is, we won't know which part of the hill they'll choose for the final assault until they're committed."

"Makes sense for them to attack here at the main gate," Nestor said, jerking his thumb toward the gateway before them. "It's a shorter climb up the grass slope here, and there's no way through the wall on any of the other sides."

"You're probably right. But let's put five archers on each wall, just to keep an eye on them. If they try to come up the grass slope, they'll be sitting ducks. Rapid shooting from five men should slow them down until reinforcements arrive. And if they make their way round to this side, the men from the other walls will have time to reinforce us here."

"I'll get on it right away," Nestor said. He touched his forehead again and turned away, calling orders to his men and shouting down into the courtyard below to summon the remainder of his small force.

"That's good thinking," Horace said. He had been listening while Gilan issued his orders. "I'll put two troopers with your men on each wall as well."

He turned and walked away, calling for the lieutenant in command of the cavalry troop. As word of the impending attack spread among the garrison, the yard below became full of men hurrying to their stations on the wall, or buckling on armor and weapons. There was almost a sense of relief among the garrison now that the fight was finally about to start. The uncertainty of waiting for the enemy to attack had been grating on their nerves for the past two days.

Gilan smiled grimly as he remembered an old saying: *Waiting for the fight is worse than the fighting itself.*

He checked his own equipment, making sure his quiver was full of arrows and his saxe and throwing knife were loose in their scabbards. Then he set the end of his bow on the planks and, using his foot as a brace, bent the stave while he ran the string up to slip into the notch at the top of the bow. He flexed the bow once or twice, making sure the string was securely set and that the string itself was in good condition, with no sign of fraying or unraveling.

It was an automatic reaction and quite unnecessary. Rangers were trained to keep their equipment and their weapons in perfect condition at all times. Still, he remembered Halt telling him many years ago, *It's the time you don't check when something will go wrong.*

Satisfied that he was ready, he moved up to the wall once more. He heard the sound of running feet and felt the vibration through the planks of the catwalk beneath him. Glancing round, he saw the small groups of archers and troopers running to take up their positions on the other three walls, spacing themselves out to cover the widest area possible.

On the south wall, where he stood, was the largest concentration of defenders. Five archers and himself—that should provide a suitably lethal storm of arrows—and the remaining cavalry troopers formed a strong defensive line along the wall. As he watched, he saw Horace detailing six of the latter to empty the ready water barrels down the drains by the gate. The men ran to do his bidding, and several minutes later, Gilan saw jets of water spurting out of the hidden pipes under the track and showering down to wet the grass on the steep slope.

"That should slow them up," Horace said, grinning, as he returned to Gilan's side.

There was a trumpet blast from below them, and the two ranks of enemy troops turned right and began to march toward the beginning of the spiral trail. Gilan noticed that they were all carrying body-length shields, made from timber, and a group halfway along the column were burdened with long ladders, made from roughly trimmed saplings, with the rungs lashed in place with leather thongs and creepers. Obviously, the delay in their attack had been caused by their constructing the ladders and the new shields. They had learned their lesson about the deadly accuracy of the Araluen archers.

He counted five ladders and estimated their reach. They looked long enough to scale the wall of the hill fort. He checked along the length of the catwalk, where Horace had organized work parties over the past two days to pile up stocks of large rocks every couple of meters, ready for use.

Glancing round, he studied the men on the other three walls. Their numbers were depressingly thin, he thought. If the attackers were well led and persistent, they had a good chance of getting inside the fort. It would depend on where the attack was focused. The defenders simply didn't have enough men to cover all four walls.

"How many do you think?" he asked Horace, who had been watching the column through slitted eyes.

"Maybe eighty," he replied. "They're not committing their full force."

"They're not being led by their commander, either," Gilan replied. He had seen no sign of the officer with his arm in a sling who had been so vocal several days previously. The man leading the column was younger—more of a warrior than a talker, he thought. He was mounted, and he urged his horse up the steep, uneven track, casting constant glances at the defenders above him, waiting for the onslaught that he knew would come eventually.

The head of the column had passed around the hill, out of sight. The rest of the attackers straggled after it. There were gaps in their formation, and they were making heavy work of the uneven ground of the trail—particularly the ladder carriers in the middle of the column.

The spiral trail wound clockwise round the hill, and as the tail of the column passed out of sight, the leader of the men on the west wall called a warning.

"They're in sight now! Still staying on the trail!"

A few minutes later, the north wall repeated the cry. Gilan nodded quietly. They were still several levels below the top of the trail, faced by steep and slippery grass slopes. They wouldn't attempt to leave the trail yet.

"In sight! Still coming!" That was the east wall.

A few minutes later, the column appeared, rounding the hill, on the next tier of the spiraling trail they were following. He sensed someone moving to stand beside him and glanced round to see it was Nestor.

"Try a few shots, Ranger?" he suggested.

Gilan considered the idea, then shook his head. "Save your arrows," he said. "When they're on the next tier, we'll hit them with a volley, then rapid shooting."

Nestor nodded. He could see the sense in waiting until the enemy were well within range before hitting them with a concentrated rain of arrows. By that stage, they'd be mentally preparing themselves for the final uphill assault. The sight of half a dozen of their comrades tumbling backward, transfixed by arrows, would be a demoralizing one—all the more so because they would have been expecting it for some minutes.

The column went round the hill again, and the warning cries from the other three walls rang across the empty courtyard. Then the marching men appeared once more, now on the penultimate level below the gate.

"Ready, archers!" called Gilan, and the five archers assigned to the south side stepped forward to the palisade, nocking arrows to their bowstrings. Gilan did likewise.

"Troopers, stand to!" Horace called, and the cavalrymen stepped forward as well, each holding his long lance upright. Designed for use from horseback, they would be well suited to repelling men climbing up the assault ladders, catching them on the iron points before they could use their own close-range weapons—axes, swords and clubs.

The attacking force hesitated. Suddenly, the wall high above them seemed to be filled with armed men. The early sunlight glinted on the steel heads of lances and the helmets worn by the troopers.

"Archers!" Gilan called. "One volley, then four shafts rapid! Ready!"

Six bows groaned slightly as the shooters drew back their

shafts, each picking a target in the mass of men below. The attackers saw the movement and brought up their shields to cover themselves.

"Aim for the gaps!" Gilan called. "Shoot!"

The bows thrummed with the ugly sound of release, and a few seconds later, six arrows slammed into the men crouched downhill. Two of the shafts found their way through gaps in the improvised shield wall and two of the Foxes staggered backward, toppling over the edge of the track and tumbling down the grass slope below. The other shafts struck against the shields, but the impact staggered the men holding them. Normally, in a properly formed shield wall, they would be supported by two or three ranks of men behind them, all adding their weight and thrust to the task of keeping the front line stable. But here, they were on their own and on uneven, sloping ground. Inevitably, several of them staggered and opened the shield wall to the next four rounds of shafts, loosed in rapid succession from the wall above them. More men cried out in pain and staggered back, clutching at the cruel barbed shafts that transfixed them.

"Re-form the wall!"

It was the mounted officer Gilan had noted. He urged his horse back through the struggling mass of men. Gilan took a shot at him, but the man was an experienced fighter and he had his shield held high to deflect any arrows coming his way.

"Face uphill!" the mounted man ordered, and the attackers turned to obey his command. "Forward!" he yelled, his voice cracking with the strain, and his men began to struggle up the grassy slope.

They slipped and stumbled on the wet, treacherous grass,

and more of them were cut down by the archers above as they floundered and struggled, trying to get a foothold. Then the officer, seeing their plight, showed an admirable talent for improvisation.

"Ladders here!" he shouted, waving a heavy-bladed ax toward the grass slope. The men carrying the ladders struggled along the track and, under his direction, lay the ladders down on the slope. Instantly the attackers, now with firm footholds, began to swarm up the ladders at four points, gathering on the narrow level section below the gate. Sheer weight of numbers told. As more and more men clambered over the wall, the archers lost their cool precision and began to shoot wildly, as fast as they could nock, draw and release. But too many arrows were striking shields, held high for protection.

In vain, Gilan sought a clear shot at the man directing the attack. But he had dismounted and was protected by his own kite-shaped shield as well as the milling mass of soldiers around him.

Once the attackers had gained the top level, they dragged the ladders up after them. Gilan peered over the palisade, but beneath him all he could see was a roof of shields protecting the men below.

Then a ladder slammed against the wall a few meters away, and one of the Foxes began to mount it, its limbs trembling under the impact of his feet. He was halfway up when a trooper leaned over and speared him with his lance, sending him toppling down onto the roof of shields below. Another attacker began climbing the ladder, with a third in place at the foot, ready to follow. Gilan leaned out and shot the man on the ladder. But the next man was already on his way up.

Now Gilan could see four ladders against the wall. He had no time to look for the fifth, as the attackers, ignoring the rain of rocks and missiles, swarmed up them, swinging weapons wildly at the defenders as they reached the top of the wall. Desperately, the troopers and archers stabbed and shoved at them, driving them back. But the attackers were beginning to get the upper hand.

"We need more men!" Horace yelled at him, then gestured to the other three walls. "Get the other archers over here!"

Gilan nodded and ran to the inner edge of the catwalk, yelling to his men to join the defenders on the south wall. They came at a run, the increase in numbers easing the burden of the men pushing and struggling at the top of the ladders. Gilan peered over the wall again and saw a now-familiar figure mounting the ladder. It was the enemy leader. His shield was held high to protect him. In his other hand he clutched a heavy ax. He was agile and well balanced, barely needing to keep a hand on the sides of the ladder as he ran lightly up the treads. Gilan dropped his bow and reached for his sword. But he felt himself shoved aside as Horace took his place.

"Let him come," said the warrior. "I want them to see him fall."

He had his round buckler on his left arm, the oakleaf motif on it already dented and scarred by multiple impacts from enemy weapons. He waited for the Fox leader to reach the top of the wall, his sword, made by Nihon-Jan swordsmiths many years before, back over his right shoulder.

The Fox leader suddenly lunged up over the top of the palisade, sending two of the defenders flying with a wide, looping swing of his ax. Behind him, more attackers were poised to swarm over the top of the wall once he had cleared a space for them.

As Gilan watched, a movement from the western wall caught his eye, and now he saw what had become of the fifth ladder. It was protruding over the top of the western wall's battlements, and already attackers were clambering over it, driving back the two troopers who had remained behind when Gilan had summoned more men to the south wall.

There were already three of the Foxes on the walkway and more mounting the ladder behind them when Gilan stepped to one side to clear his line of sight and nocked an arrow to his bow. With almost nonchalant ease, he drew, sighted and shot, then sent another arrow after that one, and then a third.

In a matter of seconds, the three attackers sprawled lifeless on the catwalk. The fourth to mount the ladder appeared over the wall and another arrow slammed into him, sending him toppling back. The fifth peered cautiously over the top of the wall, saw his comrades lying dead and promptly dropped out of sight. The two defenders darted forward and shoved the ladder away and to the side, sending it clattering back to the ground below. Gilan let out a long breath. It had been a close call.

In the meantime, Horace had stepped forward to meet the leader of the attackers. The man swung the huge ax in a horizontal cut that could have beheaded the tall warrior facing him.

If it had hit him.

Instead, Horace brought his buckler up, holding it on a slant so that it deflected the ax, rather than directly blocking it. The result was that the axman, not meeting solid resistance, slipped off balance to one side. Now Horace stepped forward again and brought his sword up and over in a vertical cut. The axman managed to bring his own shield up in defense, but the massive force of the blow staggered him again. He reeled back against the wall. As Horace went to follow up on his advantage, the man hurled his ax at him.

Again, Horace's buckler saved him, sending the heavy weapon spinning away, clattering to the ground below the catwalk. But the delay gave the Fox leader time to draw his own sword. Recovering his feet, he hacked wildly at Horace. There was a ringing clash of steel on steel as the two blades met. The Fox leader grimaced in surprise as his sword met a seemingly unmoving barrier. The shock of impact ran up his arm, and his blade dropped—only slightly, but enough to give an expert swordsman like Horace a killing advantage.

Horace's sword darted out, fast as a striking viper. The super-hardened, razor-sharp blade cut through the man's chainmail overshirt as if it weren't there. He straightened up and staggered back against the wall once more, and then Horace jerked his sword free and rammed his shield into him. The Fox commander fell backward, toppling through the gap between two of the crenellations and crashing onto men on the ladder behind him.

There was a loud cry of despair from the men gathered at the base of the wall. Seeing their best warrior, and their leader, dispatched with such ease, the attackers lost heart. If he couldn't make it up the ladder, what chance did they have?

The Foxes began to fall back from the walls, leaving their ladders leaning against them, with the defenders immediately shoving the ladders away. The Foxes began to stumble down the grass slope to the next level of the trail. They ran, they slid, they staggered down the wet grass, now wet with blood as well as water. Within minutes their retreat had become a panicked rout.

Eagerly, the archers took up their bows again and began to pick them off as they slipped and staggered down the hill. Gilan shook his head wearily, sick of the slaughter.

"Stop shooting!" he called. "Save your arrows."

He turned to Horace, who was cleaning his sword with a piece of cloth. "That was a little too close for comfort," he said.

Horace said nothing for a moment, surveying the fleeing army and the litter of bodies on the ground at the base of the wall.

"Maybe. But I don't think they'll try it again in a hurry," he said.

33

PANDEMONIUM REIGNED IN THE CHURCH BELOW MADDIE AS the Foxes started to move toward the stairway leading to the gallery. There was a clamor of voices, all shouting at once. Dimon screamed at them, his voice cracking with the strain.

"Up there! In the gallery! Catch him!"

With a sense of horror, Maddie realized she was cut off. There was no way she could reach the door with the flood of men mounting the stairs.

It was their haste that gave her a little breathing space. Too many of them tried to climb the old stairs at the same time, forgetting that the timbers might not be sound. There was an ugly, cracking noise as two of the steps gave way and collapsed, sending four of the climbers tumbling down. They, in turn, brought down several more men, and for some moments there was a jam of bodies at the foot of the stairs.

Then, one of them, with more sense than the others, took control. He shoved the struggling bodies away from the steps, reached up to the railing and hauled himself carefully over the two broken risers.

"Take it easy!" he shouted. "One at a time! Move slowly!"

She could hear the more measured sounds of feet on the stairs now and looked around desperately, seeking a way out. For a moment, she considered lowering herself over the balustrade and dropping down into the main part of the abbey. But she discarded the idea. There were still men milling about down there, and she'd be captured in an instant.

The only alternative was the window on the far wall. It was a fixed window, made from small glass panes, tinted several colors and arranged to create a pattern on the floor of the church when the light shone through them. At the moment, with the inside of the church lit, the glass appeared dark and forbidding. The glass sections were held in place by a framework of lead strips, she knew. But the window was old, and she hoped that the lead strips would be weak and fragile.

Otherwise, she would be badly injured when she tried to break through—which was what she planned to do.

There was no time to think about it any further. It was her only avenue of escape, and already she could see the head and shoulders of the first of her pursuers appearing above the floor level, where the stairway opened into the gallery.

She rose to her feet, gathered her cloak around her and ran full tilt at the window. At the last minute, she tucked her head in, protecting it with her folded arms and her cloak, and drove herself headfirst at the center of the window. Vaguely, she heard the man who had come up the stairs shouting a warning to his companions below.

Then she hit the panel of stained glass.

The spiderweb of lead strips holding the glass in place was old and brittle, as she had hoped. She burst through the window with a splintering crash, showering glass and lead fragments out into the night.

It was a three-meter drop to the ground below, and she felt herself toppling as she fell. She tucked her head in and twisted so that she struck the ground on her shoulder and rolled to absorb as much of the impact as she could. Even so, she was badly winded by the impact, and it took her several seconds to come to her feet and regain her breath. Above her, the man who had led the way up the stairs leaned out through the shattered window, yelling for those below to cut her off.

The door was five meters away from her, and as she dragged huge gulps of air into her lungs, four men burst out into the open. They hesitated, their eyes not accustomed to the darkness outside after the bright torchlight in the abbey. Then one of them saw her and pointed.

"There he is!"

They were between her and the spot where she had left Bumper. She had no choice. She turned and ran for the back of the abbey as they came after her. Going this way was taking her farther and farther away from her horse, but there was no alternative. She heard the man at the window yelling more instructions as she rounded the back of the building, but she couldn't make out the words. The rush of blood in her ears and her own ragged breathing drowned them out.

She paused, leaning against the stone wall, and tried to whistle for Bumper. But her mouth was dry and her breath came raggedly, and she could make no sound. Then three more of the Foxes burst around the other corner of the wall ahead of her, and she realized what the man at the window had been shouting. He had been directing them to cut her off.

The church was built close to the trees on this side, with only a narrow gap between the stone walls and the dense forest growth. She was hemmed in to a narrow space barely five meters wide, and there was no way she could cut around them. She reached for her saxe and drew it, determined to take some of them with her. She couldn't hope to defeat the three men facing her and the other four coming from behind her.

The three men blocking her way hesitated for a second or two, then charged toward her. Two of them had swords, and the third was armed with a heavy club. She set her feet, the saxe ready, although she knew she had little hope of fending off three attackers at once, all armed with weapons with a longer reach than her own.

Then a shaggy form burst around the corner of the church, behind the men. The first of them heard the hooves drumming behind him and began to turn, but Bumper slammed his shoulder into him and sent him flying. He dealt with a second in the same way, crashing into him with a sickening thud. The man went down and stayed down.

The third man was armed with the club. He turned and crouched, swinging wildly at the horse as it danced around him. Then Bumper saw his chance and, pirouetting neatly, set his front feet on the ground and kicked out with his back legs, driving them into the man with a solid *WHUMP!* The force of the impact picked the man up and hurled him against the stone wall of the church. He slid down the rough stones and lay senseless on the ground. Bumper, looking extremely pleased with himself, trotted to where Maddie leaned against the wall, her shoulders heaving as she still sought to refill her tortured lungs.

"Good boy. Good boy!" she groaned as he stood alongside her. She reached up and caught hold of the pommel, but for the moment she simply didn't have the strength to mount.

"There he is!"

Her original four pursuers came into sight. Wary of a possible ambush, they had held back from chasing her too closely, content for their companions to cut her off from the other direction. Now, seeing her leaning against the stocky horse, they came after her with renewed energy.

"Run!" she ordered Bumper. He turned and accelerated away as only a Ranger horse could. She lifted her feet as she clung to the pommel, hanging beside him as he galloped down the narrow passage between the church and the trees.

Two more men appeared before them, and the little horse simply shouldered them aside as he'd done to their comrades. They cried out in surprise and pain as he sent them sprawling on the ground. There were other men confronting them now. But they had seen what had happened to their comrades, and they leapt out of the way, registering only at the last minute that the horse, which appeared riderless, was actually carrying their quarry, clinging desperately to the saddle.

You'd better get mounted.

"I'm trying, believe me," she gasped. Judging his speed and the rhythm of his movement, she let her feet come down to touch the ground and thrust upward with her bent knees, at the same instant heaving herself up with her arms.

She rolled up and across his back, clinging desperately to the saddle while she managed to get a leg on either side of his stocky body. Her feet found the stirrups, and she settled more firmly into the saddle. The reins were somewhere on his neck, but she didn't have time to find them. She grabbed a handful of his mane and bent low over his back as they sped out of the clearing and into the trees.

Dimly, she registered that they were heading south—away from the castle. But there was nothing she could do about that. Behind her, she could hear Dimon's voice, shouting for his men to get their horses and go after her.

We can worry about the castle later, she thought. For now, we've just got to get away.

She made no attempt to direct Bumper, trusting to his instinct and eyesight to guide them through the close-growing trees without reducing speed. Low branches whipped at her, two of them slashing across her face and bringing tears to her eyes before she could crouch down over his neck to avoid them. She clung on grimly as he swerved through the trees at a dead run— faster than she would have had the nerve to drive him. Eventually, she found the reins, the ends knotted together round his neck. But she held them loosely, not wanting to turn him one way or the other, content for him to choose his own path.

He nickered appreciatively. *Just hold on. I'll get us out of here.*

Behind her, she could hear her pursuers shouting instructions to each other and the thunder of hooves as they rode through the trees behind her. But none of their horses was as sure-footed or sure-sighted as Bumper, and from time to time she heard the crash of collisions and shouts of pain and alarm as they blundered into the trees. The sounds seemed to be falling away behind her, and eventually she twitched lightly on the reins to slow down her horse's breakneck speed.

"All right," she said. "We've left them behind."

Bumper instantly slowed from his headlong gallop to a fast

trot. Now she could see the trees around them, and she sat up straighter in the saddle, scanning the ground in front of her. At last she saw what she was looking for—a narrow game trail that led south through the trees.

"We'll follow this," she said, nudging him toward the trail with one knee. He grunted and responded, shoving aside the low undergrowth as he made his way onto the trail.

The shouts and hoofbeats were still behind them, but not too close. She heaved a sigh of relief.

"We'll keep going south until we're in the clear. Then we'll circle around them and head back to the castle," she told her horse. Again, he grunted, concentrating on following the narrow game trail.

Dimon had told his men that they would launch their attack on the castle the following day. It was imperative that she get back there tonight, so she could warn her mother of his treachery. Then they could forestall his bold plan to simply lead his men across the drawbridge and into the castle. She realized that he had no idea that she had been the one hiding in the gallery. He had repeatedly called on his men to catch "him." He might even think that she had been an itinerant tramp seeking shelter there—although the presence of her horse tended to work against that assumption.

She was in a part of the fief she hadn't seen before, and realized that the ground beneath her was rising gradually. The trees were becoming more widely spaced as well, and she was conscious of low hills rising on either side of her as she rode on. They became progressively steeper and higher, and she realized that she was riding up a valley—wide at first but becoming narrower the farther she went, as the steep hills on either side closed in.

Then Bumper came to an abrupt stop and she looked up. A sheer rock wall barred the way in front of them. She swung Bumper to the right and cantered along it, seeking a way around. But there was none. The rock wall facing her abutted the steep side of the valley, leaving no way out. Desperately, she cantered back the other way, but found the same situation on the left side. The sides of the valley formed a solid U shape, too steep to climb.

With a sinking heart, she realized she was in a blind valley, with no way out other than the way she had come.

She turned Bumper's head back downhill, but as she did so, she saw the flare of torches among the trees below her. Dimon and his men were at the wide end of the valley.

She was trapped.

34

A LINE OF SEARCHING MEN WAS DEPLOYED ACROSS THE WIDE end of the valley. Every third or fourth man was carrying a torch, and the flickering light they cast shone among the trees as they made their way up the valley.

It was a search line, Maddie realized, intent on finding her. They had followed her along the game trail and made up some of the distance between her and them while she was searching for a way out of the dead end she had ridden into. Her pursuers were dismounted now, their horses back in the trees while the men moved steadily up the narrowing valley, scanning the ground for any sign of her.

She gnawed her lip anxiously, assessing the situation. With any luck, she could slip past the cordon of searching men. The light was bad, even with their torches, and the ground was uneven, with lots of low undergrowth for cover. But not with Bumper. There was no way she could conceal him.

Coming to a decision, she slid down from the saddle and patted his neck as he turned his head to look at her.

"You're going to have to run for it," she told him.

He shook his mane disdainfully. *I can do that. Get back in the saddle and we'll go.*

"You're going alone. I can slip past them on foot. They won't bother you once they see I'm not riding you."

Bumper pawed the ground uneasily. He didn't like the idea of being separated. He saw it as his duty to protect her. But she knew it was the safest way. If they rode headlong into a line of armed men, all on the alert for them, there was too great a risk that her horse would be wounded or killed—too great a risk that she would be captured. If that happened, there'd be no way of warning Cassandra about the imminent attack on Castle Araluen.

And that, now, was her most important task.

If she and Bumper separated, there was danger for both of them. But the danger was less this way than if they stayed together. And there was always the chance that Bumper would provide a diversion for her as she tried to break through the search cordon.

She patted his neck affectionately. "Trust me," she said, "this is the best way. Once you're through, head back to the forest below the tunnel entrance. I'll meet you there."

Again, he shook his mane uncertainly. She looked downhill and saw the line of torches coming closer. She would have to move soon. As the valley narrowed, the distance between the searchers became less and less. And that would make it easier for them to spot her. She slapped the little horse lightly on the rump.

"Go!" she ordered him and he reared slightly, raising his fore-feet a meter off the ground, then set off at a canter, heading diagonally across the valley to the left.

"Good boy!" she whispered. He would draw the searchers' eyes to that side of the valley. Accordingly, she wrapped her cloak around herself and set off in a crouching run for the right side.

The undergrowth was waist high and she slid easily through it, the cloak helping her blend into the background. Crouched as she was, her head came up just above the bushes and she knew she would be all but invisible to the approaching line of men.

She heard shouts of alarm as they saw Bumper cantering toward them. Instinctively, they all turned toward the horse and began to close in on him. Realizing their attention was totally distracted, she put on a burst of speed and ran, still crouching low, toward the mouth of the valley.

"Let him go! It's just his horse!" she heard a voice calling, and the men withdrew as the stocky little horse cantered past. Then there was more shouting, confused at first. But one voice, Dimon's, cut through above the others.

"He's on foot. He'll be trying to hide farther up the valley. But he can't get out. Re-form the line and let's move!"

She realized that her pursuers were familiar with the terrain here. Dimon's words indicated that he knew it was a blind valley and that their quarry would be trapped somewhere ahead of them. But it didn't occur to him that Maddie might have turned back toward her pursuers, intending to slip through the cordon. There were very few men in the kingdom who would have the skill or the daring to attempt such a course, and Dimon had no idea that they were pursuing a Ranger.

The men began to spread out again—they had gathered together at the point where Bumper had cantered through their line. She had hoped that she might be past them by the time they were back in position, but soon saw that that wouldn't be the case. As the search line rapidly re-formed, they were barely twenty meters short of her current position. She could see that she was halfway between two of the searchers, who were moving up the valley with a five-meter gap between them. Then the angle of the ground beneath them changed and they inadvertently swung a little to their left, so that the nearest of them would pass by her with less than a meter to spare. Now silence and absolute stillness would be her best allies. Slowly, she slid to the ground, lying flat and letting the cloak spread over her body.

As luck would have it, the undergrowth here was sparser than in any other part of the valley. She lay still, feeling horribly exposed and obvious, as she heard the nearest man stumbling and crunching his way through the low bushes toward her. Fortunately, he wasn't one of the torchbearers, although the man on her right was. She lay, her face pressed to the ground, seeing the flaring light becoming stronger as they moved ever closer to her position.

Surely they must see her. She cringed mentally, forcing herself not to move, holding her breath, covered by the cloak and its irregular patterns of gray and green that blended into the undergrowth.

Trust the cloak.

The familiar Ranger's mantra echoed in her head. She was sure they must hear the frantic pounding of her heart. A foot crunched through the undergrowth close by her head. It must have been barely half a meter away, she thought. Then the searcher paused. She heard a muttered curse, then a slapping sound, right on top of her.

"What's up now?" The voice came from her right as the torchbearer queried his comrade.

"Mosquito," said a voice, right beside her. "I got it," he added.

"Good for you." The torchbearer's reply was heavy with sarcasm. "Now let's get a move on. We're falling behind the line."

Then, suddenly and unexpectedly, she felt a sharp pain in her left wrist as a heavy boot trod directly onto it, grinding it into the hard ground and pebbles beneath it. It was so sudden, so unexpected and so painful that she nearly cried out, nearly pulled her hand away. She felt an immediate sense of déjà vu, her mind instantly going back to that time weeks before during her assessment. She bit her lip, holding back the unbidden cry of pain that sprang to her lips, using every last ounce of willpower to leave her hand where it lay, unmoving.

The man above her stumbled and swore.

"What is it now?" The torchbearer's voice reflected the impatience he felt with his clumsy, tardy companion.

"Trod on a root," the man said. "Shine your torch over here for a moment."

She felt her skin crawl with terror as he said it. Surely now they would see her. Then she heaved a sigh of relief at the other man's exasperated reply.

"What for? You've already trodden on it. Why do you want to look at it? Now get a move on. You're holding up the line."

"Oh, get off my back," the man close to her grumbled. But the pressure came off her wrist as he stepped away and began moving again. She heard the crunch of his boots and the swishing sounds as he pushed through the low bushes. The sounds began to recede and she realized, with a sense of triumph, that they had passed her by.

She was beyond the search line.

She lay unmoving, waiting, straining her ears to hear any

sound of a follow-up line coming behind the first line of search-ers. But there was nothing, and she realized that these men didn't have the skills of the Rangers who had searched for her at the Gathering. They were an impromptu search party, and the idea of having sweepers behind the line hadn't occurred to them.

Still, she lay silently, letting them move farther away from her. The sound of their voices became less and less—although she noted that the man who had trodden on her continued to whine and complain as he moved forward. She realized she had been lucky that he was the one who had come closest to her. He was obviously unmotivated, more inclined to complain about the situation than to apply himself to the search. A more conscien-tious searcher might well have spotted her, she thought.

Now she had to gauge the right time to move. Before long, the search line would reach the end of the valley. Then they would head back, over the ground they had already covered. By the time they did that, she would need to be well on her way.

But not too soon. She forced herself to count to fifty, then slowly rose to her knees, her head just reaching above a nearby bush. She glanced up the valley and could see the line of search-ing men, revealed by the flaring light of the torches they carried.

Downhill to her left, she could see more torches among the trees. But these were static, and occasionally she saw a large dark shape move in front of them. She listened and heard an occa-sional snort and stamping of hooves. These were the men detailed to hold the horses as the rest of the group searched.

Angling away to her right, she slipped through the under-growth in the thigh-burning crouch she had practiced for hours at a time during her training. Her nerves were strung to breaking point as she waited for a shout that told her she had been sighted. But her skill at movement and her training stood her in good stead. She slipped silently in among the closer-growing trees at the beginning of the valley. Glancing back over her shoulder, she could see the wavering line of torches farther up the hill. They were almost to the end of the valley.

Time I wasn't here, she thought. Glancing up at the stars to get her bearings, she began to run, jogging lightly through the trees, heading north again. As she looked at the sky, she could see the first pale rays of dawn beginning to show. She was tempted to increase the pace, but she knew that if she kept to a steady jog, she would cover more ground. Grimly, she moved on, knowing she was in a race against time.

Behind her, she heard a horn blowing. The Foxes must have reached the end of the valley, and Dimon, finding no sign of her, was now sounding the recall. Some minutes later, she heard the low rumble of hooves as the Foxes regained their horses and began cantering back toward the castle. There was no way she could outdistance them, and the sound of their horses passed her by and gradually died away.

She jogged on, grimly determined to reach the tunnel before Dimon could enter the castle.

It took a few minutes for her to realize she was lost. She was in among the trees again, and couldn't see the stars. Even if she could, she had no idea where she was. When she had escaped from the abbey, she had given Bumper free rein to take her wherever he could. He had zigzagged wildly through the trees, then moved onto the game trail, which wound erratically back and forth.

She had a vague feeling that the abbey lay somewhere to her

right. Her best bet was to make her way back to it. From there, she would know what direction to take. She stopped, pondering her next move. Her instincts told her that the way to the castle lay ahead and slightly left, and she was tempted to trust them. But she knew she needed to get her bearings first, to get to a location she was familiar with and start from there. And the only place she could do that was the abbey. Otherwise, there was a good chance that she would blunder through the forest, losing her way completely.

Grimly, she recalled the words of an old joke about a traveler asking for directions to a town from an old farmer.

"Well," said the farmer, "if I was going there, I wouldn't start from here."

That was her predicament now. To get to the castle, she had to find a start point she knew. She wished that she had been able to keep up with Dimon and his mounted men in order to follow them. They knew the countryside and they would know the best way back to Castle Araluen.

"Wishing doesn't get it done," she said. It was a favorite saying of Will's—which he had learned from Halt in his turn.

Glumly, she headed to the right to look for the abbey. Her heart sank as she realized she had just lost the race back to Castle Araluen.

35

MADDIE HEAVED A SIGH OF RELIEF AS SHE SAW THE ABBEY'S tall tower looming over the treetops. A few minutes later, she reached the clearing where the crumbling old stone building was situated, approaching carefully in case there was anyone around.

The clearing was deserted, however, and she glanced around quickly. The door hung open on its hinges once more, and she could see the gaping hole where the stained-glass window had been, and the litter of broken glass and lead strips on the ground below it, evidence of her violent exit.

She heaved a sigh of relief. She finally had a familiar location from which to head back to Castle Araluen. Then she looked up at the sun, now rising over the treetops, and her heart sank. She knew the daily routine at the castle. The drawbridge would be lowered and the portcullis opened each morning between the eighth and ninth hour, once the garrison had surveyed the surrounding countryside and ensured there was no enemy in sight. Judging by the sun, it was nearly that time now. Any minute, the huge cogs would turn and the bridge would come down. Dimon had said they would assemble at noon for his treacherous entry into the castle, but he would waste no time now that the Foxes' secret was known to an outsider. Already, she assumed, his men would be in the forest below the castle, donning the uniforms that would identify them as members of the garrison.

"No alternative," she said to herself, and, turning away from the abbey, she began to jog through the forest. As before, she resisted the temptation to run at full speed. Better to maintain a steady pace and eat up the miles. There was always the chance that Dimon could be delayed and she might make it back through the tunnel in time to raise the alarm.

Unconsciously, she began counting her paces in her head to measure the distance she had traveled. She would reach one hundred and begin again, the silent cadence matching the rhythm of her feet pounding softly on the forest floor.

Her mind kept going over the words Dimon had uttered the night before—specifically the threat to her mother. He would kill her, she knew, without the slightest compunction. He intended to seize the throne and could leave no other claimant alive to thwart him—or to provide a rallying point for any resistance to his rule. He would kill her grandfather as well, and the thought of Dimon's threat to the helpless old man made the anger burn brightly within her.

She thought about his intention to claim that he had defeated the Red Fox Clan and driven them off—unfortunately too late for Cassandra and her family. Would her father and Gilan believe the story? Regretfully, she concluded that they probably would—at least initially. They would have no reason to suspect Dimon of treachery. He had established himself as a loyal officer, and a protector of the Crown Princess. Horace would be devastated by the death of his wife and daughter, but he would see no reason to disbelieve Dimon's story.

Neither would Gilan, she thought. His loyalty and his oath was to the crown, and he would continue to serve Dimon as Commandant of the Ranger Corps. Perhaps neither man would like the situation, but they would probably accept it.

"Not while I'm around," she repeated grimly. Her presence, and her knowledge of his treachery, was the one factor that Dimon hadn't reckoned on. He assumed she was still in the castle with Cassandra. And he assumed that she would be an easy victim. For the first time, she understood the value of maintaining secrecy over the fact that she was a trainee Ranger. Before this, she had thought of it as somewhat melodramatic and unnecessary. But she had gone along with it for the sake of peace and quiet. Also, she had realized that if she resisted the idea of maintaining the secret, she might be barred from her Ranger training. At times, the subterfuge had been a nuisance and even something of an encumbrance, with the whole rigmarole of changing clothing, horses and identities. But now she was grateful for it.

Then she went back to counting the paces as she jogged through the trees. She might arrive too late. But she had to try.

Cassandra was training with Maikeru. It was the first time in days she had had the time to work on her swordsmanship, and she was enjoying the physical and mental exertion that it required. She had sent a servant to look for Dimon and to ask him to join her, but the man returned saying the guard commander was nowhere to be found in the castle.

"That's odd," she mused. "I wonder where he's got to?" Then

she dismissed the question. With a reduced garrison, Dimon was kept busy organizing the watch and the daily routine of the soldiers under his command. She couldn't expect him to be available to drop everything and attend to her when it suited her.

Maikeru's wooden practice sword tapped her painfully on the shoulder.

"Pay attention to your drills," he rebuked her. "A wandering mind is dangerous. You must concentrate. Now begin again."

She rubbed her shoulder and bowed in apology for her distraction. Then she assumed her fighting stance and advanced on him, striking left and right in a sequence of high, low, low, high attacks. Then, after the final high, she smoothly reversed the sword and leapt forward, stepping with her right foot and following up in a one-handed thrust.

Maikeru's sword just managed to deflect the point of hers at the last moment. He stepped back, indicating the sequence was over, and lowered his sword. He nodded approvingly.

"That was good, my lady," he said gravely. "You have eliminated the movement that warns you are going to thrust. I take it you have been practicing in private."

"You still managed to parry it," she said, slightly aggrieved.

His lips moved in a thin smile. "I have been a student of the *katana* for over forty years, my lady," he said. "Your strike would have succeeded with most opponents."

She grunted. She knew he was right, but she had a competitive personality. Just once, she wanted to best her mentor in a mock duel. Then she laughed at herself, knowing "just once" wouldn't be enough. If she managed it once, she would want to do it again and again.

She stripped off her gloves reluctantly. She had enjoyed the workout but knew she couldn't stay away from her desk any longer. She felt the floorboards trembling slightly beneath her feet and was aware of a low background rumble that told her the massive gears controlling the drawbridge had been disengaged and the bridge was coming down. That reinforced her decision to get back to work.

"Must be past the eighth hour," she said. "It's high time I was at my desk."

Maikeru eyed her thoughtfully. "You work too hard, my lady," he said. She looked tired, he thought, and he could see a few gray wisps in her blond hair.

She laughed. "The work doesn't do itself."

Maikeru took both practice swords and returned them to the rack along the wall. Then he gathered up the padded vests and gauntlets they had worn for the session. "There's been no word from the north?"

She shook her head. "Nothing so far," she said. "We all assumed they'd be back within a few days. Obviously, it's taking longer than we expected."

The door to the practice hall opened and a young page entered, looking nervous in the presence of the Princess Regent and her inscrutable instructor. The castle staff told wildly imaginative tales among themselves about the unsmiling Nihon-Jan warrior and his uncanny skill with the *katana*. Not all of them were inaccurate.

"What is it, Richard?" Cassandra asked, smiling to put him at ease.

"My lady," he said, addressing her but with his eyes constantly flicking to glance at Maikeru, as if expecting him to perform some amazing feat of swordsmanship while he watched. "The sergeant says to tell you there are men approaching the castle."

"Men?" Cassandra asked, instantly on the alert. "Are we under attack?"

Richard smiled reassuringly. "No, no, my lady. My apologies for alarming you. They're castle garrison troops."

Cassandra's face lit up. She looked at Maikeru. "It's Horace and Gilan," she said happily. "They're back!"

But again Richard demurred, his face thoughtful. "I don't think so, my lady," he said, and he was sorry to see her face fall, the glad expression extinguished. "They're coming from the south. Captain Dimon is leading them," he added, by way of further explanation.

"Dimon?" she said, puzzled. "Why would he take men to the south?"

Richard shrugged. He had no answer for that, and she realized that there was no reason why he would have. He was just a page delivering a message, after all.

"I'll come and take a look myself," she said.

He stepped aside as she swept past him, Maikeru following close behind her, his soft-shod feet making no more than a whispering noise on the flagstones. Richard, a little peeved that he couldn't answer her question, tagged along behind.

They crossed the courtyard that stood between the keep and the outer wall, quickly mounting the stairs that led to the battlements. Cassandra ran up the stone steps to a vantage point above the drawbridge. Hearing her coming, the sergeant in charge turned to greet her, then pointed an arm to the forest south of the castle.

"There, my lady," he said.

She moved to a gap in the battlements and peered downhill.

There was a relatively large body of men marching up through the park toward the castle. They were all dressed in the distinctive Araluen livery—a red surcoat over chain mail, and a polished cone-shaped helmet with a mail aventail hanging from the back to protect the wearer's neck.

They carried shields, painted red with a yellow X superimposed, and the morning sun glittered off the points of their long spears. A mounted officer led them, and although it was too far to distinguish his features, she thought she recognized Dimon. It was certainly his chestnut horse that the rider was mounted on, and his shield carried Dimon's distinctive owl's head symbol.

"They look like our men," she said. "But where did they come from?"

She looked quickly around. She could see half a dozen troops on the battlement catwalk and another three in the courtyard below. Nine men. There would be another half dozen in the barracks, having come off duty from the night watch.

All in all, she had been left with twenty-five men to hold the castle—not a lot, but sufficient, considering the strength of the walls and the castle's defenses. Now she could see nearly thirty men marching toward the drawbridge. Where had they come from? And why was Dimon leading them?

If it were, in fact, Dimon. Anyone could carry a shield with his symbol on it, and the horse, although it looked like his, could well be any chestnut. She hesitated, suspicion growing in her mind. She looked at the sergeant, but this sort of situation was above his level of competence. He was essentially a man who followed orders. Maikeru was a different matter. He had a cool, analytical mind, and he wasn't a person who saw what he expected to see.

"Maikeru, what do you think?" she asked.

The old Swordmaster had been expecting the question. "We don't have that many men," he replied. "And that may or may not be Dimon-san leading them."

The sergeant looked at the two of them, alarm evident on his face. He had simply assumed that the men approaching were bona fide troops belonging to the castle.

"My lady?" he said uncertainly. "What do you want me to do?"

Cassandra came to a decision. "Raise the drawbridge," she ordered. "If we're wrong, we can let them in later."

But it was already too late. The rider leading the group had spurred on ahead and was nearly at the bridge. The sentries there stepped out to stop him, then hesitated as they recognized him.

The hesitation was fatal. The rider drew his sword and cut left and right, killing them where they stood. Then he galloped across into the gatehouse—a massive, fortlike building that housed the drawbridge and portcullis mechanisms. Behind him, the marching body of men broke into a run, following him across the bridge. Any minute, they'd be pouring into the courtyard.

Cassandra turned to the sergeant. "Sound the alarm! Send word for the men in the barracks, and get all our men into the keep!" she ordered, and headed for the stairs at a run, shouting to the men in the courtyard to form up on her.

The sergeant hesitated, not sure what to do. Maikeru stepped close to him.

"Do as she says!" he ordered. "We're under attack."

36

CASSANDRA RAN ACROSS THE COURTYARD TO THE KEEP. Standing to one side of the door, she ushered her men inside the large building, casting anxious glances at the massive gatehouse. She could hear the sound of fighting there. Half a dozen of her troops had been inside to tend to the drawbridge and portcullis. Now they were fighting for their lives, desperately holding off the invaders who were swarming across the bridge and into the gatehouse.

There could be only one ending to that fight. The defenders were hopelessly outnumbered, and now they had been stripped of their greatest defense—the protection afforded by Castle Araluen's impregnable walls.

But their desperate delaying action might buy time for Cassandra and the rest of the depleted garrison to make it to safety. The troops in the barracks, warned by the clanging of the alarm bell, were streaming across the courtyard to join them. Seeing the last of her men go through into the keep, Cassandra followed them, slamming the door shut behind her and signaling for the locking bar to be set in place.

The sergeant and another soldier heaved the massive oak bar

into its brackets, securing the door. That would keep out the attackers for some minutes, until they could organize a battering ram and shatter the bar, then smash the door down. The keep was the castle's administration and accommodation center. It wasn't designed to be a defensive position in the event that an enemy had breached the walls. That was the south tower's purpose.

She pointed to two of the garrison soldiers, who were looking confused and alarmed at the events that were taking place.

"You two," she ordered, and they snapped to attention. "Get my father from his room and take him to the south tower. Right away!"

"Yes, my lady!" the two men responded. Now that they had been given a definite task to carry out, they lost their uncertain looks and ran for the stairs. Duncan was in a room on the fourth floor. From there, they would take him across the arched stone bridge to the south tower, and then up into the tower's higher reaches.

A few of the remaining servants had joined them, standing uncertainly, wondering what was going on. Among them, Cassandra saw Ingrid, Maddie's maidservant. She beckoned her over.

"Fetch my daughter!" she said.

But Ingrid was shaking her head, a worried look on her face. "I've just been to her room, my lady," she said. "But she isn't there. There was a bolster under her blankets to look as if she was in her bed. I think she may have been patrolling outside the castle again."

Ingrid was one of the few who knew Maddie's true identity as a Ranger, and she was aware that she had been leaving the castle at night, although she wasn't sure why. Nor did she know how Maddie left the castle and reentered. As her maid, it wasn't her place to question her mistress, and she knew that Maddie was skilled at moving from place to place without anyone seeing her do so.

Cassandra hesitated, torn with anxiety. Then she realized that if Maddie weren't in the castle, she was relatively safe, at least for the meantime. She came to a decision.

"Join the others and head for the fourth floor. We're withdrawing into the south tower," she said. Ingrid nodded and hurried away, her concern for her mistress still evident on her face.

Cassandra heard men shouting and hammering on the barred door, trying to break through. But for the moment, they had only hand weapons—battleaxes and swords—and they would be next to useless against the ironbound oak planks. She knew, however, that it wouldn't take them long to find something heavy to use as a battering ram, and then it would be a different story.

Even as she had that thought, she heard a voice shouting outside the door.

"You four men!" Dimon said. "Grab that bench and bring it here. We're going to have to knock this door down." Outside, against the wall, was a heavy oak bench, Cassandra recalled. It would serve quite well as an improvised ram. The clattering of axes and swords and fists against the door ceased. A few minutes later, she heard footsteps approaching the door at a slow run. Then something heavy slammed against the door, and it shuddered under the impact. Plaster and paint flew from the arch above the doorway. She heard Dimon again.

"Ready? One, two, three!"

SLAM! There was another massive impact against the door. More plaster and dirt fell from the lintel. This time, she was sure she saw one of the big iron hinges move a centimeter or two as the bench struck the door.

She felt a hand touch her sleeve. Maikeru.

"My lady, we should be going. That door won't last long."

She realized she had become fixated on the door as the men outside pounded on it.

Maikeru was right. It wouldn't last much longer.

SLAM!

Another thundering impact. And again, the hinge moved. She saw cracks forming in the stonework where bolts secured the hinge to the doorjamb. It was weakening fast. There were three other hinges and so far none of them had moved. But once the first one gave way, the others wouldn't be far behind.

She turned and took a quick count of the men who had made it into the keep with her. There were over a dozen of them, waiting for her next orders. She pointed to the stairs.

"Fourth floor!" she shouted. "Then across to the south tower!"

SLAM!

Again, the bench hit the door, the sound of the impact echoing through the vast entry hall of the keep. Waiting no longer, she led the rush toward the broad staircase leading to the next level. Here in the keep, the stairways weren't designed for defense. They were broad and accessible and set in the center of each floor. Once they reached the south tower, they would be ascending the spiral staircase set in the southeast corner, with removable sections designed to delay pursuers.

As they went up the successive flights, the sound of the bench hitting the door faded. But they could still hear it as they reached the fourth floor. And now there was a new quality to it—a splintering sound that told her the door was giving way.

"Keep going!" she shouted to the men following her, pointing the way toward the arched bridge that led to the south tower. She made sure they were following her order, then detoured to her own apartments, where she gathered up a few pieces of clothing, cramming them into a bag, and her *katana*. She slid the sword, in its lacquered wood scabbard, through her belt so that the long hilt stood ready to her right hand. Her sling was on her desk, coiled neatly. She slipped it under her belt, on the side opposite her sword. There was a chamois pouch of lead shot on the desk as well, and she slung it quickly over her shoulder. She took a quick final look around her apartment. There were just too many possessions in here, and not enough time to choose between them. In the end, she left them and hurried toward the door that led to the bridge. Maikeru and the sergeant from the battlements were both waiting there for her. Maikeru was as inscrutable as ever. The sergeant was nervous—worried for her welfare, she realized. She gestured for him to lead the way across the bridge, and he turned, albeit reluctantly, and headed for the south tower.

She gave Maikeru a wan little smile. "After you, *Sensei*," she said, using the Nihon-Jan word for teacher.

He shook his head. "You first, my lady. Emperor Shigeru charged me with your safety."

She was about to reply when another voice interrupted them, shouting from the top of the stairs leading from the floor below.

"Cassandra! Stop there!"

She turned and looked back, and her heart sank as she saw that it was Dimon, bloodstained sword in hand and blood staining his doublet, ascending the last few stairs to the fourth-floor level. She had clung to the hope that it had been an impostor she had seen riding across the drawbridge, that her loyal retainer and captain of the guard had not betrayed her. Now she saw that hope dashed.

Maikeru moved to interpose himself between her and the traitor now. His *katana* slid from its scabbard with a whisper of steel and wood.

She drew her own sword and stepped to one side so she could see Dimon clearly. He stopped five meters away, wary of the old Nihon-Jan Swordmaster. He glanced behind him to where two of his men were emerging from the stairway.

"Dimon," she said in a stricken voice, "what are you doing? *Why* are you doing this?"

His eyes were cold. "Because the throne is mine by right," he said angrily. "For years your family has denied me my birthright, changing the law so that a woman could inherit the crown. I've been pushed aside. And since I've been here, I've been forced to bend the knee to you, to smile and pretend everything is fine. *Yes, my lady. No, my lady. Is there anything I can do for you, my lady?* Well, everything isn't fine! I'm sick of bowing and scraping to you and your daughter. My legitimate claim to the throne has been ignored, pushed aside, trampled on."

"Your legitimate claim? You have no legitimate claim. I'm the heir and Maddie will be my heir in turn."

"I am the only *male* member of the royal family! And that means I'm the only legitimate heir!" he shouted at her, years of anger and frustration suddenly bursting loose. "I may be a distant relative, but I am a relative. And the only male one! Our ancient law says that I should be the one to inherit the crown."

She spread her hands wide in confusion. "But that law was revoked years ago. My grandfather changed it."

"And he had no right to do so!" Dimon shouted. "He did it to protect his own interests, to protect his immediate family's claim to the throne. To make sure that you succeeded Duncan."

"That's ridiculous! I wasn't even born when he changed that law. How could he know . . ."

He waved her argument aside with a furious gesture.

"He was making sure that his family would stay in power! If Duncan had a son, well and good. But if he had a daughter," he said, pointing his sword at her, "you—then his line would continue on the throne. The law of male succession had been in place for hundreds of years—perhaps thousands. He had no right to change it. It was a good law, one that had been tested by time."

"It was an unfair law and that's why he changed it," Cassandra told him, and he gave a derisive snort of laughter.

"Of course you'd say that!" he said. "It's in your interest to say that. You'd say anything to ensure that you and that brat of yours remained in power."

As he mentioned Maddie, he waved his hand vaguely toward the bridge behind her and Cassandra began to realize that he had no idea Maddie was missing from the castle. His words, and that gesture, seemed to indicate that he thought she was with her mother's party, hurrying to the south tower. And as she had that thought, a small flame of hope began to burn in her breast.

"Now lower your sword and surrender," he said. "I'll see you're well treated."

She gave a bitter laugh, seeing through the lie with no difficulty. "You won't let me live," she said. "If you want the throne, you'll have to kill me. You can't afford to leave a legitimate claimant alive."

His face worked briefly, and she saw in his eyes that she was right. He would kill her, and Madelyn, to cement his claim to the throne. Then she had a moment of revelation. Nobody would know that he had seized the throne by force. The only witnesses to that would be in the castle. And by the time he was through, they'd be dead. He could blame the entire affair on the Red Fox Clan and claim that he had driven them off—unfortunately too late to save Cassandra, Maddie and Duncan.

"My lady," Maikeru said quietly, "you must go now. I will settle with this cur."

She hesitated. Maikeru was right. She should run for the south tower now, while she had the chance. But she had a sudden flare of rage. She wanted to be the one who finished Dimon. She wanted to feel her sword cutting into him.

"Get out of my way, old man." Dimon's voice was scornful, but she noticed that he made no move toward the old Swordmaster. He was cautious of Maikeru, wary of his skill and his speed and that flashing, razor-sharp *katana*. Maikeru kept his eyes fastened on the treacherous guard commander. He spoke again, still without any sign of emotion.

"You must go now, my lady. This is the task the Emperor gave me when he sent me to you."

Sadly, she realized he was right.

She sheathed her sword, turned toward the south tower and began to make her way across the bridge, looking back over her shoulder. Maikeru had moved so that he was in the middle of the bridge, barring the way.

"Cassandra! Stop there! I warn you!" Dimon shouted, his voice cracking with rage.

"A dog like you does not speak to my lady in that fashion," Maikeru said calmly. His calmness acted as a goad to Dimon, who leapt forward, his sword swinging up and back, then coming down on a diagonal at the Swordmaster.

Only to be intercepted by the gleaming *katana*. The hardened blade rang against Dimon's sword and left a deep notch in the steel. Then Maikeru flicked his opponent's sword to one side and with astonishing speed brought the *katana* back in a short cutting stroke.

Dimon blocked it with his shield. But Maikeru followed up immediately with a bewildering series of strokes, cutting left and right at Dimon's head. One caught his helmet and sheared its owl's head crest clean off. Dimon staggered with the force of the blow, and Maikeru's next stroke caught him in the left shoulder, just above the rim of his shield, slicing through the chain mail and drawing blood.

It was only a shallow cut, but the ease with which Maikeru penetrated his defense startled Dimon. He leapt back and gestured to the men behind him.

"Kill him," he snarled.

The two men started forward, then hesitated. The narrow bridge only allowed room for one of them to attack him at a time. Then one stepped forward, his sword point low and moving in a circle, his eyes slitted. He lunged at Maikeru, hoping that he would catch the old man off guard.

His sword was deflected immediately, and as he staggered slightly, the *katana* slashed quickly across his neck and he fell, a choked scream rising to his lips. His companion watched in horror, then realized his mistake as Maikeru went on the attack. Once again the deadly *katana* found its mark and sliced through chain mail and flesh. The second man fell, lifeless, to the bridge.

Maikeru smiled grimly at Dimon. "Would you care to try again?" he invited.

Dimon looked around desperately. More of his men were pouring up the stairs, and he saw that two of them had short bows slung across their shoulders.

"You two!" he yelled. "Come here! Bring your bows!"

The two men ran to him, unslinging the bows as they did. Maikeru's eyes narrowed. This put a different complexion on things. He glanced over his shoulder, saw that Cassandra was at the end of the bridge, looking back at him.

"Go, my lady!" he shouted. "Run now!" With a sigh of relief, he saw her turn and run into the south tower, slamming the heavy door behind her. She would be safe now, he thought. He had fulfilled the task laid upon him by his Emperor.

"Shoot him!" Dimon ordered, pointing his sword at the slightly built figure who barred their way. The first of the men nocked, drew, and released. The arrow sped toward Maikeru, barely visible. But he calmly batted it aside with his sword. Dimon shook his head in surprise. He had never seen such lightning reflexes.

"Both together!" he ordered.

The two bows thrummed almost in the same instant. Maikeru caught the left-hand arrow on his sword. But the other slammed into his chest, high on the right side. He staggered under the impact and stumbled against the parapet of the bridge, his sword still in his hands, but the point now lowered.

The two men shot again and two more arrows slammed into him, both hitting vital spots.

The old Swordmaster sank to his knees, leaning against the rough stone wall and still keeping his grip on his *katana*. He saw Dimon's tall figure stepping cautiously toward him. The traitor was only a dark shape now as Maikeru's sight began to fade. But Cassandra was safe, for now. He looked up at the shadowy form above him.

"You lose," he said softly, and died.

37

Inside the south tower, Cassandra heard a howl of triumph from the men pursuing her and knew that Maikeru was dead.

Quickly, she turned the massive lock on the heavy door that led out to the bridge and ran for the spiral stairway in the southeast corner of the tower. The sergeant was waiting there for her, beckoning her urgently to join him. Behind her, she heard a rush of running feet on the bridge, then the hammering of weapons and fists on the door.

She ran. The sergeant, sword in hand, ushered her through the narrow doorway in front of him, and together they began to wind their way upward.

The stairway was narrow, barely two and a half meters across. And it spiraled upward to the right. This was intentional, and a standard piece of design in castles of the time. A right-handed spiral meant that a right-handed attacker, climbing the stairs, had to expose his entire body to bring his weapon into play, whereas a defender, above him, only needed to show his right arm and hand. It gave a distinct advantage to the defender.

Cassandra was taking the stairs two at a time, running light-footed and leaving the sergeant behind. He blundered up the stairs behind her, making a considerable noise, and then began shouting.

"The princess! Make way for the princess!"

For a few moments, she wondered why he was wasting his breath. His heavy breathing showed that he didn't have a lot to waste, after all. Then she rounded a bend in the stairway and was confronted by three of her men standing ready, weapons bared. The sergeant had been warning them that the people mounting the stairs were friendly. Otherwise, they may well have attacked the new arrivals without warning. The men smiled at her and stepped aside to let her pass. A few steps below, she heard the sergeant's heavy tread and she waited for him. He drew level with her, red faced and breathing heavily. She ushered him past her.

"Keep going!" she ordered. Then she spoke to the three waiting men. "You three come with us."

She led them up, her head spinning slightly as she spiraled round and round. Ahead of her, the sergeant was slowing down and she yelled at him, urging him to keep moving. From far below, echoing up the stairway, she heard a splintering crash as the door from the arched bridge finally gave way. Then more feet were pounding on the stairway below her.

She estimated that they had gone up another two floors, and only two more remained before they reached the sanctuary of the upper levels. The safe haven at the top of the tower occupied the eighth and ninth floors. As they came level with the seventh floor, there was a three-meter-long timber section set into the stone stairway. Two more of her men stood waiting at the top of it. She and the sergeant and three soldiers ran past the end of it, and then Cassandra turned and gestured to the waiting men.

"Pull it up," she ordered.

The timber section could be removed. Ropes ran over pulleys in the roof of the stairwell and were attached to both ends. As she passed the order, her men tailed onto the ropes and heaved. The timber bridge rose smoothly in the air until it lay flush against the ceiling of the stairwell. The men tied off the ropes and secured it in its new position. Where it had been was a three-meter gap in the stairs, with a seven-story drop below it.

"That should hold them up," she said as she heard the distant sounds of running feet and shouting men on the floors below them. Distant now, but coming closer. One of the men who had been standing by to remove the timber section was armed with a bow. She recognized his uniform. He was one of the castle archers. She pointed downstairs, to where the steps disappeared round the stone wall.

"Anyone comes round there, shoot him," she said.

"Aye, my lady." The archer nodded, stripping an arrow from the quiver at his belt and placing it on the string. He stood ready, side on, feet slightly apart, arrow nocked. As yet, he didn't bother to draw back. If anyone came round that corner, they'd be no more than six meters away and he could draw, shoot and hit his target at that distance in a matter of seconds.

Cassandra continued up the staircase, reaching the door leading to the eighth floor. She pushed through it. There were ten men in the big open space, and they turned toward the door, weapons ready, as she entered. Seeing her, they relaxed and sheathed their swords and daggers. She nodded a greeting. She looked anxiously around the small group, searching for Maddie.

But there was no sign of her. Perhaps she was on the next floor, she thought, although she didn't really believe it.

"Has anyone seen my daughter?" she asked. "Princess Madelyn?"

Blank looks and shaking heads met her inquiry. Nobody had seen the young princess. She looked around the group, seeking and finding Ingrid. The young maidservant shook her head as they made eye contact. Cassandra felt a moment of despair. What if Dimon captured her? He would use her as a bargaining chip to obtain Cassandra's surrender. And yet she knew her sense of duty would never allow her to surrender. And that would mean Maddie would be . . .

"Perhaps she's hiding somewhere, my lady," ventured the sergeant before she could finish that thought. "It's a big castle, after all."

She considered his point. He was right. There were dozens of hiding places in the castle, and Maddie had been raised here. She knew the castle well. Furthermore, even though Cassandra tended to think of Madelyn as her baby girl, the reality was that Maddie was a fourth-year Ranger apprentice, and that meant she was a formidable warrior. She was skilled with weapons and adept at concealing herself. Better yet, she had been trained to think and plan and assess a situation. She wasn't the flighty young girl that people like Dimon took her to be.

But it occurred to Cassandra that there was something she could do that might warn Maddie of the situation in the castle. She beckoned Ingrid to her.

"Go to the upper floor and hoist my standard on the flagpole," she said, then added, "Fly it upside down."

Ingrid looked puzzled. "Upside down, my lady?"

Cassandra nodded. "It's a distress symbol. If Maddie sees it, she'll know we're in the south tower. And she'll know something's wrong." As Ingrid hurried away to do her bidding, Cassandra shrugged. It was all she could do for now to warn her daughter. She just hoped Maddie would notice the flag.

Then, squaring her shoulders, she forced herself to push her worry about Maddie aside. She had to organize the defenses of the tower. She'd think about Maddie later, when things were more settled. She glanced at the sergeant. He was standing ready, waiting for orders. She indicated the small group of men watching her.

"Is this all we have?" she asked.

He glanced around the room, then answered. "We have eighteen men in all, my lady. Some of the men from the gatehouse managed to make it to the ground floor of this tower while Captain Dimon was assaulting the keep."

She nodded. Eighteen men. Not the largest force, but probably enough to hold the tower against Dimon and his men.

"How many archers?" she asked.

"Six, my lady," answered one of the other men in the room, an archer himself, wearing a corporal's rank badge. The sergeant, of course, wouldn't have had time to do a detailed head count yet. He'd arrived only a few minutes before her.

She chewed her lip thoughtfully. In this situation, there wouldn't be a lot of use for archers. She would have preferred more men-at-arms. They'd be better suited to hand-to-hand fighting on the stairs. Still, the archers could take their turn at that as well. They were trained fighting men, after all.

"Let's take a look at our supplies," she said, and the sergeant led the way to survey the stores and equipment that were maintained in the upper reaches of the south tower.

The eighth floor was a storehouse and armory. Dozens of spears and long-handled axes stood in racks along the walls—the most effective weapons for dealing with an attack from below. There were several dozen shields hanging from pegs, and an equal number of mail shirts and helmets. She counted fifteen bows and three large wooden tubs filled with arrows. There must have been close to five hundred of them in all.

Farther on, she found the food supplies: dried, salted meat; barrels of vegetables and pickles; and sacks of grain piled two meters high. She nodded thoughtfully. There was plenty of food here to sustain the defenders.

Passing the stacks of food, they came to the dormitory for the men—rows of bunks, tables and benches for those off duty, washing facilities, and several privies, built in the side of the tower to protrude over the drop. She wrinkled her nose. Not the most savory of solutions to the men's needs, but an effective one nevertheless.

Food and weapons were well supplied, she realized. But there was a more important need. Water.

"Let's check the water," she said, and headed for the steps leading to the ninth floor.

Here, there was another central staircase between the eighth and ninth levels. This staircase was wood—more like a wide, steep ladder—and could be withdrawn in the event that attackers broke through to the lower floor. They climbed to the ninth level.

This was the commander's floor—the administrative level.

Half a dozen sleeping chambers were set along the curve of the wall.

There were racks of weapons along one wall and in the middle of the floor was a large open space that served as the command center. A table with a dozen seats dominated the space. This could be used for councils of war or for eating and recreation, as the need arose. To one side was a kitchen area, well ventilated so that smoke from the large oven and open grill areas could escape.

Cassandra had studied the layout of the south tower and had visited it several times over the years, ensuring that supplies were constantly replenished and any items that were out of date or spoiled were removed. She gestured to a wooden ladder on the right-hand side.

"Water's up there," she said, and she led the way, climbing the steep ladder and shoving aside the trapdoor at the top.

The tower was surmounted by a pointed spire, covered in tiles. Inside the conical space were two large stone cisterns. There were steps at the side of these. She climbed one low flight of steps and eased open a lid in the wooden panel that covered the cistern. She peered in. Water lapped a few centimeters below the top. She cupped a handful and tasted it. It was fresh and sweet.

The other cistern was the same—nearly full with good clean water. The cisterns were fed by rainwater from the roof. They were drained regularly and allowed to refill to ensure the water didn't stagnate. It usually rained regularly in this part of the country, so continuity of supply wasn't a problem.

She climbed down and led the way down the ladder to the ninth level once more. A soldier waited there to meet them, obviously wanting to talk to her.

She raised an eyebrow. "What is it?" she asked.

"The King, my lady," he replied and she recognized him as one of the men she had detailed to bring her father to the tower. He pointed toward one of the chambers set along the wall. "We put him in that chamber, my lady. It's got a good bed and it's nice and airy for him. He's quite comfortable."

"Thank you," she said, starting toward the door he'd indicated. "I'll have a few words with him now." Then she saw the doubtful look on the man's face and stopped. "Is there a problem?"

He shook his head. "No, no, my lady. He's fine. Just, he's sleeping at the moment and maybe we shouldn't wake him."

She touched his arm gratefully. It was interesting to see the devotion and love that her father inspired in the men serving under him. Unlike Dimon, she thought bitterly.

"Thank you," she said. "Keep an eye on him and let me know when he wakes."

He knuckled his forehead in salute. "I'll do that, my lady." He stepped back and took up a position outside the chamber door. Cassandra turned back to the sergeant.

"By the way," she said, "what's your name? I can hardly go on calling you 'sergeant,' can I?"

The sergeant grinned at her. "Don't matter to me, my lady. But my mam christened me Merlon. So that's what I usually answer to."

"Merlon it is then," she said. She sat down in one of the heavy wooden chairs around the command table and gestured for him to sit as well. He did so, a little awkward at relaxing so close to the Princess Regent.

"Well, Merlon, we're in good shape here. Plenty of food and

water and weapons. We should be able to hold out indefinitely. Certainly until my husband and the Ranger Commandant get back."

"Yes, my lady. When do you think that'll be?" he asked.

She hesitated a second or two. It wouldn't be good for morale if the men knew she had no idea what was delaying Horace.

"Shouldn't be much more than a week, I'd think," she said, forcing a confident tone into her voice. She didn't want to raise any immediate expectations, and now that Merlon knew their position was secure, the prospect of a one-week wait wouldn't be too daunting. She was saved from further discussion of Horace's whereabouts when one of the archers mounted the stairs, obviously looking for her.

"Over here," she said as he glanced curiously around the open space of the ninth floor. He turned and walked toward them.

"It's Captain Dimon, my lady," he said. "He's at the gap in the stairs and he's requested a parley."

38

"Better come with me, Merlon," she said. "You should hear what he has to say."

Together, they retraced their steps down the ladder to the eighth floor, then hurried out the heavy door to the spiral staircase. The archer who had apprised her of Dimon's request for a parley followed them, and now she recognized him as the man she had left at the gap in the stairs, with orders to shoot anyone who appeared round the bend in the staircase. She smiled grimly. Presumably, Dimon had called out before he showed himself, making sure he wouldn't be an immediate target.

They reached the gap. There was nobody visible at the lower end. She glanced interrogatively at the two foot soldiers who had remained on watch.

"Where is he?" she asked.

One of them jerked a thumb downward. "He's there, my lady. Just round the curve." He grinned. "Don't think he trusted us."

She smiled in return. "He's no fool," she said. Then she raised her voice and called down the stairway, her voice echoing off the stone walls and ceiling.

"Dimon? Are you there?"

There was a pause, and then she recognized his voice. He sounded quite close, and she realized he must be just around the elbow in the stairway.

"Cassandra? I have a flag of truce here."

As she heard the words, a pole appeared round the stonework. A white cloth hung limply from it. The bearer waved it a few times, presumably to help those above see it.

"So I see," she replied.

There was another pause, and then Dimon spoke again, uncertainty in his voice. "You'll honor it?"

She was insulted by the implication that she might violate a flag of truce. But then, she realized, it was the sort of thing Dimon would do. And if he would do it, he'd assume that others would as well.

"Yes," she said, the irritation obvious in her voice. "You're safe. We won't shoot. Although God knows why not."

"I need your word," he said.

Now the irritation in her voice was even more apparent. "You've got it. Stop skulking and come out in the open."

Slowly, Dimon emerged from behind the curve in the stairway, the white flag held in his right hand. He moved out into the center of the stairs and peered upward. He shaded his eyes with his left hand. It was dim in the stairwell, and neither of them was carrying a torch.

"I can't see you too well," he said.

"I can see you perfectly," she said. "Get on with what you have to say."

"I'm offering you an accommodation," he said. "Surrender and I'll spare your life. And Madelyn's as well."

She felt a surge of relief as he said the last words. She'd been half expecting that this parley would be about Madelyn—that Dimon would tell her he'd captured her daughter and would use her to force Cassandra's surrender. Now it was obvious that he believed Maddie was in the tower with her. So she was safe—for the moment, at least.

"You'll simply let us go, will you?" she asked, the disbelief all too clear in her voice.

"I didn't say that. You'd be kept prisoner until I could send you out of the country. I'd want your sworn oath that you wouldn't try to come back and take my throne from me."

"My father's throne, I think you mean," she said, and when he didn't reply, she continued. "Why this sudden generosity, Dimon?"

"I'll have gotten what I wanted. My followers want a return to the male line of succession. Once I'm on the throne, that will have been restored. They believe having a female succeed to the throne is against reason and tradition and God's law."

"I wondered when he'd be brought into it," she said sarcastically.

"I'm offering you your life. I'll see you're well provided for. You and Madelyn could live quite well in Gallica or Toscana.

"Not Skandia, however," he added. "Erak and his Skandians might not take too kindly to having you tossed off the throne."

"Aren't you forgetting something?" she asked. "It's a wonderful plan, but I don't think my husband will stand for it once he's back from the north. Nor Gilan. I doubt you'll stay on the throne too long once they hear I've been banished."

He looked down, hesitating for a moment. Then he said regretfully, "I'm sorry to tell you, Cassandra, but Horace is dead. And Gilan."

An icy-cold hand clutched at her heart as he spoke. She couldn't conceive of a world without Horace—big, powerful, cheerful Horace. He was a tower of strength for her. He was kind and gentle and caring. And he had never been defeated in battle. He couldn't be gone. And Gilan too, with his ready smile and friendly disposition. How could they both have been killed?

"I don't believe it," she said.

Dimon shook his head again. "I'm sorry to tell you. I truly am. I really liked Horace. But that small band of rebels he went to shoo away was actually an army of a hundred and fifty men. They fought a pitched battle two days ago, and both Horace and Gilan were killed—along with most of their men."

He let her think about that. Then he continued. "So don't cling to any false hopes that they'll be back to rescue you, Cassandra. They won't. And my offer is the best one you'll get."

She paused, knowing that if she spoke immediately, the doubt in her voice would give away her uncertainty. She needed to sound strong, she realized.

"I'll need time to consider it," she said eventually.

He came back at her immediately, sensing the strength of his position. "Don't take too long. As I said, my offer is the best one you'll get, but it's only on the table for a day. After that, we'll drive you out of this tower."

"You can try," she said. She was on firmer ground now, and her voice was more confident. "But we've got food and weapons and water. We can hold out here for months. You could die of old age trying to take this tower."

"We could burn you out," he threatened.

She laughed. This time, her reaction was genuine. "You don't know a lot about the construction of this tower, do you?" she asked. "It's mostly stone. There's no wooden framework, and stone won't burn."

"The floors are timber," he pointed out. "They'll burn well enough."

She sensed the sergeant glancing at her. She met his anxious gaze and shook her head to reassure him.

"As I said, you don't know too much about the design of this tower. We've got two huge water cisterns in the roof. And one of them has pipes running down to the lower levels. The floors are hardwood, so they won't burn easily. And if you try to set them alight, we can simply drench them with water."

There was a long pause. Then Dimon replied, but without his former confidence. "And then you'll have used up your drinking water," he said.

"Rain, Dimon," she said. "The cisterns are filled by rainwater collected on the roof. And as you know, it rains quite often in this part of the country. Two or three nights of good rain will refill the cistern."

Dimon looked up at her. Anger was beginning to show on his face. He knew that the south tower was virtually impregnable—a small force could hold it indefinitely—and he didn't have time to spend on a lengthy siege.

Horace and Gilan were very much alive, even if they were contained in the old hill fort by the Wezel River. And he knew that situation wouldn't last for too much longer. His forces there were becoming restive. Messengers had told him that they'd lost a lot of men—they'd been driven back with heavy losses each time they attacked Horace's small force. Sooner or later, they would start to drift away. Mercenaries fought for profit, after all, and there was little of that to be found besieging a capable enemy in a well-defended position.

He had hoped to bluff Cassandra—to make her panic and surrender with the news that Horace was dead. Of course, he had no intention of honoring his promise to banish her. Once she and Maddie were in his hands, he would have them killed.

He faced her one more time, trying to sound more confident than he felt.

"I'll give you a day to consider my offer," he said. "One day only. After that, if you insist on defying me, you will suffer the consequences."

"I'll give you my answer this time tomorrow," she told him.

He couldn't resist one more sally. "If you're as smart as you claim to be, you'll accept," he said. Then he stepped quickly into the shelter of the curving wall and she heard his footsteps receding down the stairs.

She looked at Merlon and raised her eyebrows, puffing out her cheeks and releasing a long breath. She felt exhausted.

"Well, at least we know one thing. He doesn't have Maddie," she said.

Merlon scratched his beard thoughtfully. "That's true." He hesitated, not sure whether he should ask the next question, then decided to do so anyway.

"Do you believe him, my lady?" he asked. "About Sir Horace. Do you believe he's dead?"

She shook her head. "I just don't know, Merlon. It would explain why we've heard nothing from the north. But . . ." She hesitated.

"But what, my lady?"

"But Horace is not an easy man to kill. A lot of people have tried in the past, and it didn't work out too well for them."

"So you think he's alive?"

"Yes, I do," she said. "I think I'd feel it if he were dead."

But as she said it, she wished she could be certain.

39

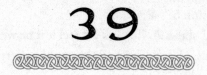

THERE WAS A BALCONY RUNNING ROUND THE TOWER AT THE ninth floor, affording a panoramic view of the land below the castle. Cassandra was pacing it now, looking out at the park-lands below and the forest in the distance while she pondered her situation. Several hours had passed since her conversation with Dimon.

Immediately below her, she had a view of the castle court-yard. She could see men there, moving from the keep to the gatehouse and occasionally to the stables. On the battlements, she could see sentries standing watch.

It all appeared normal, except that the sentries and the men in the courtyard were not part of the castle garrison. They were Dimon's men. And now they were protected from outside attack by Castle Araluen's massive fortifications. Even if Horace and Gilan did appear with their men, they would have no chance of breaking in.

She leaned on the rough stone of the balcony wall and sighed bitterly. She was in a total impasse. She and her men were safe for the moment—and for the foreseeable future. But they had no way of breaking out, of driving the invaders out of the castle.

They were outnumbered, and they continued to survive only by virtue of the well-planned defenses of the south tower.

Where was Maddie? The question kept hammering at her. Ingrid had thought she might be outside the castle. But where? And what was she doing? Cassandra racked her brains, trying to think of a way of contacting her. If Maddie was outside the castle, and if Cassandra could get a message to her, she could head north and alert Horace to the current situation. Maddie's Ranger horse, Bumper, was outside the walls, Cassandra knew, at the small farm where Gilan had arranged for him to be stabled. If Maddie could get to him, she could be at the Wezel River within three days.

If, if, if, she thought. But even if Maddie could reach the Wezel, then what?

Horace might be dead. At best, if anything Dimon had said was the truth, he was trapped in a hill fort, surrounded by a superior force. How would he break out of that trap? And if he did, he would still face the problem of breaking into Castle Araluen.

But at least he'd be *here*, close to hand. And the thought of his presence was a comforting one. Besides, once he was back, he could raise the army from the surrounding countryside. In times of war, the relatively small garrison of the castle was augmented by drafts of men-at-arms from the farms and villages of the fief. Mobilizing them would take some time—perhaps a week or two—but he would then have a sizable force for Dimon to reckon with.

The same inevitable predicament raised its head. No matter how many men he had, how could he hope to break into the castle? No attacker had managed that in living memory. Even

Morgarath, when he rebelled against her father, had bypassed the castle. She laughed bitterly. It was an ironic situation. She and her men were trapped here in the tower, but relatively safe from attack, by Dimon's men. They, in turn, would be trapped in the castle, but relatively safe from attack by Horace's forces.

And on top of that, there was still the fundamental problem facing her: *Where was Maddie?* The scenario she had just envisaged hinged on Cassandra's being able to make contact with her. And Cassandra simply couldn't see how that could be done. She heard footsteps on the balcony behind her and turned to see one of the archers hurrying round the curve of the tower toward her, saluting as he came.

"My lady, Sergeant Merlon says you should come immediately," he said, his tone urgent.

She began to make her way to the door leading back into the tower.

"What's happening?" she said. She was puzzled. Dimon had given her a day to consider his offer. She assumed that meant he would try nothing further until that deadline had expired. There was the implication of a truce in his offer. But she realized, not for the first time, that Dimon could not be trusted.

"Merlon's not sure, my lady. But there's something going on down the stairway. We can hear them moving. There's a lot of whispering going on—and it sounds like they're dragging something heavy up to the gap."

She ran down the ladder to the lower floor and headed for the stairs. Merlon and four other men, all of them archers, were standing just above the gap in the stairway, sheltering behind the bend in the stairs. The sergeant looked around as she approached, holding his finger to his lips.

"What's happening, Merlon?" she asked in a whisper.

He pointed down the stairs to the edge of the gap. "Listen, my lady," he told her.

She moved out from the shelter of the wall and craned her head to listen. The sound of low-pitched voices floated up the stairway to her, echoing off the curving stone walls. She couldn't make out what they were saying, but there was a definite sense of urgency about them. Occasionally, a voice would be raised, resulting in urgent hisses for silence. She stepped back into cover, peering round the rough stone to look down the stairwell.

"Something's going on, my lady. They're planning something," Merlon said, his voice close to her ear.

She nodded, frowning. That much was obvious. But what, exactly, did they have in mind? She held up a hand to forestall any further comment from the sergeant. There was another noise apparent now.

It sounded like something heavy and wooden being dragged up the stone stairs. She could hear slow, deliberate footsteps on the stairs now, and the occasional grunt of effort from the men below. She turned to her archers.

"Get ready."

They nodded. They all had arrows nocked.

She stepped out again for a clearer look, ignoring Merlon's warning murmur. The stairs below were empty. She could see the gap, with the yawning dark drop below it. Then the first three or four stairs below that. Then nothing.

But the dragging sound continued, getting louder with each minute. Then it stopped and she heard more whispering. She caught the eye of one of the archers and gestured to the door that opened into the eighth floor.

"Get more men," she said. "And bring half a dozen pikes." The man saluted and ran to do her bidding, and she turned her attention to the stairway again. The dragging, scraping noise had started again, much closer this time. Then she saw what was causing it.

A rectangular wooden barrier, like a moveable wall, appeared in the stairway below the gap, being shoved forward by men behind it. It was made of boards nailed to a timber framework and it filled the space between the walls of the staircase. The men pushing and lifting it moved it at an angle so that it could advance up the stairs. It stood about a meter and a half high and there was an open space twenty centimeters high at the base. The men behind it were mostly hidden from sight, although from time to time a head would appear above the top of the barrier for a second or two.

Cassandra addressed the three remaining archers. "The minute you see someone, shoot him," she said.

They all nodded. A head appeared above the barrier as its owner looked up to see what was happening above them. Instantly, an archer drew, aimed and released. But the head had disappeared again, and the arrow whizzed through empty space, then ricocheted off the stone wall below with a screech of metal on stone. She heard a curse from the man who had come so close to death.

She frowned. The wall would protect Dimon's men from the arrows and spears of her troops. But it wouldn't bridge the gap in the stairs. It was too short for that. She looked more closely, straining her eyes, and made out a pair of hinges in the barrier. Then she could see that there was a gate in the center, perhaps a meter wide. Obviously, once the barrier was in position, those behind it could open the gate—and what?

The barrier stopped a meter from the edge of the gap. On the right-hand side, one of the men pushing and shoving had grown careless. The top of his helmeted head was visible above the roughly constructed shield. The helmet made a poor target for her archers' arrows. They would skid off harmlessly.

But her sling was a different matter. She loaded a shot into the pouch and began whirling the sling around her head. Stepping out in the open, she released. There was a resounding CLANG! as the lead shot hit the helmet and the man went down, staggering back and falling down the stairs with a mighty clatter. She heard a voice shouting urgently.

"Stay down, for pity's sake! She's got a sling!"

Nobody else showed themselves above the barrier. Then they heard more scraping and slithering, and a timber bridge about a meter wide began to slide forward from under the barrier, reaching out across the gap in the stairway.

"Push it back!" she ordered and her men moved forward, pikes in hand, to obey. But they were too late. The makeshift bridge reached the upper side of the gap and fell into place. She could see that there was a transverse beam nailed to the lower end. It was set against the edge of the stairs and held the bridge in position, no matter how hard they tried to push it back.

Merlon touched her arm. "Smoke, my lady!" he said. "I smell smoke!"

She sniffed the air. He was right. There was an oily smell of smoke drifting up from the lower stairs. She frowned. The steps were stone. They wouldn't burn. So what was . . . ?

In answer, an object appeared, hurled over the top of the barrier, trailing a thin line of smoke and sailing across the gap to shatter on the steps above where she stood. Then another, and another.

They were round clay pots, she realized, and each one held a mixture of oil and pitch—and a lighted wick. As they shattered against the stone, the flame from their wicks ignited the flammable mixture inside and a cloud of noxious, dark smoke began to fill the stairway. Her men began coughing and she felt her own eyes tearing up.

"They'll try to cross in the smoke!" she warned. "Be ready!"

She turned to Merlon, standing by her with one of the ineffectual pikes. Ineffectual against the replacement bridge, perhaps, but not against the men who might try to cross it.

"Get the door open!" she ordered. "We have to let the smoke out!"

Dimly, through her streaming, itching eyes, she saw the central gate in the barrier begin to open outward, the gap between the edges growing larger. She loaded another shot and began whirling the sling. Through a veil of tears, she saw a figure step into the gap and out onto the bridge. His upper body was covered by a shield, and he held a spear in his right hand.

4O

CASSANDRA CHANGED HER AIM POINT AS THE ATTACKER advanced across the bridge. She whirled the sling one more time as he moved tentatively above the yawning gap, then released.

The shot slammed into his left knee with a sickening crack, smashing bone and tendons. The knee gave way beneath him and he slumped to one side, releasing his grip on the spear as he hung over the edge of the seven-story drop, scrabbling frantically at the rough wood to recover.

And failing.

With a horrible scream, he fell into the gap beside the make-shift bridge, plummeting down into the darkness, screaming all the way until they could hear a distant, ugly thump.

The scream was cut off.

The door in the barrier slammed shut once more. The next man in line had seen his comrade's fate and wasn't prepared to risk the crossing. Cassandra heard a raised voice shouting orders. Dimon, she realized.

"More smoke pots! Get more of the pots up here! If they can't see us, they can't shoot us!"

The smoke was clearing in the upper part of the stairway

now, although the defenders' eyes still smarted and ran with tears. The open door had created a draft to let the dense, choking clouds out.

There was a brief lull, and she heard feet running on the stairs below her. Presumably men were fetching more of the smoke pots.

Merlon pointed to the replacement bridge. "Could we maybe burn it, my lady?"

She considered the idea but shook her head. It was solid timber. "It would take too long to get it burning," she said. "And I doubt they'd leave us in peace while we did it." Some of Dimon's men had bows, she knew. They might not be as skilled as her archers, but at close quarters like this, they could hardly miss.

There was a flash of flint on steel in the dimness on the other side of the barrier.

"They're lighting the fuses," she said. "Everyone get ready." She removed her scarf and wrapped it round her nose and mouth. Turning to the youngest of the troopers standing ready, she pointed up the stairs.

"Fetch scarves and kerchiefs for everyone. And a bucket of water to soak them." Wet scarves around their noses and mouths might help against the choking smoke, she thought.

He nodded and turned, running lightly up the stairs.

She heard Dimon issuing orders once more. "Don't throw them so far! Try to lob them close to the end of the bridge."

That would concentrate the smoke where they stood waiting, she realized, and create better cover for the men crossing the bridge. She loaded her sling again and let it dangle down beside her, swinging back and forth like a snake's head as it prepared to strike.

The first of the clay pots sailed over the gap, hitting the stairway four steps above the bridge. Before it could ignite the oil and pitch inside, however, Merlon reached out with his pike and scooped it down the stairs, sending it tumbling into the gap. But his action came at a cost. Even as she began to congratulate him, he gave a gasp of pain and dropped the pike, clutching at his upper arm where a crossbow bolt had struck him. He sank awkwardly to the stairs. She reached out, grabbing his jerkin, and with the strength of desperation heaved him back into cover as another bolt ricocheted off the step behind him. He screamed in pain as she dragged him in, but managed to gasp his thanks, realizing she had saved his life.

"Think nothing of it," she said. "We need you."

Another smoke pot flew over the gap. This one went too high and smashed on the stairs above them. The resultant cloud of smoke billowed up, but someone had had the intelligence to open the doorway on the floor above them, and most of the smoke was sucked upward by the draft.

The young soldier had returned now with scarves and kerchiefs and a large bucket full of water. He began to distribute the wet cloths to the defenders, who wrapped them round their noses and mouths. He was just in time, as another two smoke pots crashed onto the steps. These were better aimed, and they hit the stonework level with Cassandra's position. She hastily dipped her scarf into the bucket and retied it. The wet cloth filtered the smoke to a certain extent, but her eyes were still smarting and weeping, and she found it hard to see. One of the pots had deposited its load of oil and pitch only a few meters from her. The young trooper seized the bucket, still half full, and dumped the water onto the burning pitch, smothering the flames.

"Good thinking!" she croaked. Then she gestured upward to the doorway. "Get more water. Get a bucket chain going!"

He nodded, his own eyes red and weeping, and darted away to do her bidding.

The flames close by her had only been temporarily doused—more by the sheer impact of the water cutting off the air to them than by the extinguishing properties of the water itself. They flickered to life once more, feeding off the pitch, and began to generate more smoke.

Through streaming, reddened eyes, she saw the gate in the barrier opening again, and another enemy soldier advanced through it. At least, she thought, the bridge was so narrow it would permit only one man at a time to cross. But if any of them gained a foothold on this side of the gap, she and her men would be in trouble.

She whirled her sling and launched a shot at the man. But he was crouched low behind his shield and didn't offer her a convenient target. The shot hit his shield with a vicious thud. He was stopped by the impact for a second. Then he continued to advance.

Two more smoke pots soared across the gap, shattering and adding their billowing fumes to the hellish scene in the stairwell.

Three arrows slammed into the man's shield, and he stopped uncertainly. The narrow bridge didn't provide the most stable footing, and crossing it in the current conditions, while being targeted by archers and with visibility uncertain, required enormous concentration.

"Step aside, my lady," said a hoarse voice behind her. She turned and saw one of her men—a tall, broad-shouldered corporal, standing ready with a heavy spear. His eyes were fixed on the enemy soldier, now two-thirds of the way across the bridge, advancing slowly. Cassandra moved to one side to give him room. He took the spear back over his right shoulder, eyes still fixed on his target, and, stepping forward, made his cast.

The spear flashed through the dark smoke and bit deeply into the man's lower leg. He let out a scream of pain and stopped, dropping to a crouch. He released his hold on his battleax and clutched at the wound in his leg. The heavy spear shaft dangled over the drop, unbalancing him and trying to drag him after it. He tried to pull the spear loose but couldn't manage it. He was stuck, unable to stand again, swaying fearfully over the gap while arrows hissed round his ears and slammed into the timber bridge beneath him.

Holding his shield in front of him, he began to back clumsily away on the bridge, propelling himself with his free hand and his uninjured leg. His shield was now festooned with arrow shafts as the archers maintained a constant barrage on him. Crossbow bolts whirred across the gap in return, and Cassandra heard a shout of pain from the stairs above her as at least one found its mark.

A lucky shot, she thought. Visibility was as poor for the attackers as the defenders. The air over the bridge was relatively clear, kept so by the draft coming up the gap in the stairwell. But everywhere else, the fumes and smoke made it almost impossible to find a target.

The wounded man made it back to the safety of the lower edge of the gap and slumped back against the barrier's closed gate. He still kept his shield in front of him, protecting himself from the steady rain of arrows that continued to thud into the wood-and-hide shield. Blood poured from the spear wound in his leg. An arrow hit him on his right arm, and he flinched and cried out. But his voice was weak, and Cassandra realized that loss of blood was weakening him.

Abruptly, the gate slammed open and several pairs of hands grabbed at him, dragging him back into safety, accompanied by another hail of arrows flashing through the open gate.

Cassandra studied the temporary bridge for several minutes, then flicked her gaze to the pike that Merlon had dropped. For the time being, both sides had stopped shooting, with no targets visible for either her archers or Dimon's crossbow men.

Earlier, Cassandra and her men had tried to push the bridge back across the gap. But the transverse beam nailed in place a meter from its end locked against the lip of the stairs and kept it from moving.

But there was no similar beam at the upper end of the bridge, she realized. So there was nothing to stop them from pulling the timber structure up the stairs.

She turned to look behind her, coughing as an eddy of smoke whirled around her. The heavyset, tall soldier who had thrown the spear was still close by. He'd do admirably for what she had in mind, she thought. She beckoned him forward and, as he knelt beside her, gestured to the fallen pike on the steps.

The pike was a combination of different weapons. Mounted on a stout ash shaft two and a half meters long, it had an ax head on one side, a spear point at the top and a vicious spike opposite the ax head.

"See the pike?" she said. The man nodded, and she pointed to the bridge. "When I give the word, drive the spike into the timbers and drag the bridge up toward us. Understand?"

The man nodded, smiling, as he caught on to her idea. If he could haul the bridge up far enough, the bottom end of its two main beams would slip off the edge of the steps and the entire structure would plunge into the gap. He started to move forward, but she gripped his arm to stop him.

"Wait till we get some cover for you," she said. Then, calling to the archers a few steps higher than she was, she gave her orders.

"Archers! Rapid shooting! Keep their heads down!"

Arrows started to fly across the gap once more in a steady stream. There were no visible targets, but the iron warheads screeched off the curved stone walls of the stairwell, striking sparks in the gloom as they did. Several arrows slammed into the wood of the barrier, but most skimmed over the top, ricocheting off the walls beyond, sometimes shattering the shafts and sending the razor-sharp broadheads spinning wildly through the air. They heard at least one hoarse yell of pain, which indicated that a broadhead had found a target. But the sudden arrow storm had the desired result. The attackers on the lower part of the stairway dropped to their bellies, hands over their heads, while the arrows hissed and spun and screeched among them.

She released her grip on the soldier's muscular arm.

"Now!" she told him, and he lunged forward, gathering in the pike as he went. Then, from a kneeling position, he raised it over his head in a two-handed grip and brought it down with all his strength, driving the long spike into the timber planking of the bridge.

Once it was set, he gathered his feet under him and began to heave the bridge forward, slowly, a few centimeters at a time. As the attackers realized what was happening, she saw hands scrabbling desperately under the barrier, trying to seize hold of the bridge and stop it. She darted out into the open, grabbing hold of the soldier's belt and adding her strength to his. Behind her, she felt someone else doing the same to her. She glanced over her shoulder and saw the young lad who had fetched the water.

"Heave!" she shouted. "Keep it moving!"

Under their combined strength, the long structure slid upward until its lower end slid off the step below them. Then it pitched up vertically and disappeared into the gap, taking the pike with it. The three of them released their grip and staggered backward on the stairs. For a moment, they listened to the clatter of the bridge falling into the darkness below, bouncing off walls, the noise gradually dying away.

The archers on the stairs gave a ragged cheer as Cassandra and her two companions dragged themselves back into cover.

Breathless, she sprawled on the stone steps with them, grinning triumphantly.

She shook her head angrily. So much for Dimon's word. She had let him lull her into a feeling of false security, assuming he would hold off until the twenty-four-hour period—and the implied truce that went with it—were over. He had caught her napping, and his attempt had come close to succeeding. She realized that she couldn't let her guard down again.

41

It was half an hour before sunup.

As was his custom, Horace leaned on the palisade above the gate, staring moodily down at the enemy camp below. The campfires that had burned through the night had died down now to glowing ashes. They twinkled in the predawn darkness, marking the lines of tents where the enemy slept. He knew there would be sentries awake, stationed around the perimeter of the camp, keeping an eye out for a possible attack.

As he was doing.

He felt a movement beside him and, glancing around, saw that Gilan had joined him in his study of the enemy.

"Morning," said Horace.

Gilan grunted a reply, then said, "Thought I'd find you here."

Horace smiled quietly. "Am I so predictable?"

"Well, you're here most mornings. If that makes you predictable, then you are."

"Just keeping an eye on things down there," Horace said.

Gilan said nothing for a minute or so. He studied the lines of campfires, the silent, darkened tents.

"I don't think they'll try anything," he said at length. "We gave them a bloody nose last time they did."

"We gave them one at the river as well—at least, you and your archers did," Horace said.

Gilan scratched his chin thoughtfully. "Yes. It's two for none, isn't it? D'you think they'll change tactics next time? Frontal assaults don't seem to be working too well for them."

"I'm not sure what else they can do—not if they want a quick ending to this."

Gilan frowned. "Maybe they plan to starve us out. We don't have enough provisions for a lengthy siege."

"We've got plenty of water," Horace said.

Gilan shrugged. "But not food. A couple of weeks would see us starving. Even worse, the horses won't last without proper fodder. So we're stuck here. We can't go anywhere. We can't break out. They still have us well and truly outnumbered, and if we try to attack them, they'll see us coming and they'll be ready for us. We'll be out in the open. They'll be behind their shield wall, and we'll be fighting at a disadvantage."

Horace nodded. "Exactly. They may send a few skirmishers up the hill from time to time to keep us on our toes. But I think they'll be perfectly happy to sit back and watch us watching them."

For a minute or so, the two friends were silent. Then Horace asked, "Do you think you could sneak out through their lines?"

Gilan nodded emphatically. "Of course I could. But then what? I can't sneak Blaze out with me. Traveling on foot, it'd take me a week or so to reach Castle Araluen, and then what? Dimon only has twenty or thirty men there. That's hardly enough to help us break out. And I couldn't bring them all back. We can't leave the castle undefended."

"That's true," Horace replied gloomily. "So I guess all we can do is wait and see what they have in mind. Unless," he said with a rueful grin, "you can come up with a brilliant strategy. I hear Rangers are good at that."

Gilan rolled his eyes. "I've heard that too," he said. "I'll let you know if anything occurs to me."

"I wish you would," said Horace.

Maddie reached the clear ground below the castle around mid-morning. Bumper was already there, back in his hidden glade, and he greeted her enthusiastically.

I was worried about you.

"I was fine," she told him. "I was just a little lost in the forest."

Fine Ranger you are.

"That's what I told myself." She unsaddled him and rubbed him down, then filled his water bucket and poured more grain into his feed bag. He munched gratefully, grinding the food noisily with his big teeth the way horses do. Once she was assured that his needs were taken care of, she started toward the edge of the trees to survey the castle.

Everything seemed normal. The drawbridge was down. There were two sentries keeping guard at the outside end, and she could see more moving on the battlements. There was no sign or sound of any fighting, which she might have expected if Dimon was attempting to take the castle. Perhaps he's already done it, she thought dismally. After all, if his plan had worked, he and his men would have simply walked in across the drawbridge. Any fighting would have been over in a matter of minutes, with the castle's defenders, and her mother, taken by surprise.

Perhaps, she thought, her mother was already dead, and she felt tears pricking her eyelids at the thought.

She leaned against the trunk of a tree while she considered what she was seeing. Everything seemed normal. But something was different. She sensed that there was one slight detail that had changed since she had last looked at the castle. But for the life of her, she couldn't work out what it was.

She scanned the castle, eyes slitted in concentration as she studied the walls, the towers, the battlements, trying to realize what it was that had pricked her attention.

Not the keep. Not the battlements along the outer wall. Not the massive gatehouse. Was it one of the towers? She studied the north tower, then the south. Completely normal, with a flag fluttering over it.

A flag? There had been no flag on the south tower last time she looked. She strained her eyes and could see a trace of red on white—a red stooping hawk.

Her mother's banner!

Looking more closely, she realized that the banner was flying upside down—the universal distress signal.

And in that moment, she knew what had happened. Dimon's coup had been successful—at least partly so. But her mother had obviously had time to retreat to the south tower—the point of last defense. With the realization that her mother was safe, at least temporarily, Maddie's spirits lifted. She looked up the slope to the small clump of bushes that concealed the entrance to the tunnel. They were undisturbed. She started forward, ready to move out of the trees, then hesitated.

It was full daylight and the battlements were manned with sentries—enemy sentries. Skilled as she was at moving without being seen, it wasn't worth the risk. The parkland was kept open and well mowed for precisely that reason—to prevent attackers from approaching unseen. If her mother was safely ensconced in the south tower, another few hours wouldn't make any difference. Maddie would wait until dusk, then make her move. In the meantime, she thought, she might as well get some rest. She'd had a long, sleepless night and an exhausting day.

The hours dragged by. Tired as she was, sleep came fitfully. She dozed, waking frequently, with her mind racing as she considered the situation. She was reminded once more of Will's dictum: *Most of our time is spent waiting. A Ranger's best asset is patience.*

At last, the sun sank below the horizon and shadows crept over the parkland. This was probably the best time for her to move, while the light was fluky and uncertain. She went back into the trees to say farewell to Bumper, and then, wrapped in her cloak, stole out onto the short grass of the park, moving in a crouch, matching her rhythm to that of the wind and cloud shadows flitting across the grass. She held the cloak tightly to keep it from flapping in the rising breeze. Movement like that could attract the eye of one of the sentries.

She ghosted up the slope as the evening grew darker. When she finally slipped into the shelter of the bushes concealing the tunnel entrance, there had been no outcry from the battlements, no sound of alarm.

She found her lantern still at the tunnel entrance where she had left it. She shook it experimentally and heard the splash of oil inside its reservoir. There was still plenty there, she thought. Enough for two passages through the tunnel. Mindful of the watching eyes on the battlements, she moved several meters into the tunnel before she struck her flint and lit the lantern wick. The yellow light flared out, wavering over the rough clay walls. She checked that she had her sling and her saxe, then set off.

She was familiar with the tunnel now, and she made good time, passing under the moat, then feeling the tunnel climbing upward. Stumbling from time to time on the uneven footing, she made it into the hidden room in the bottom cellar and moved toward the secret door.

Then stopped.

As her hand stretched out to trip the lock, she heard a murmur of voices from the other side. She put her ear to the stone and listened. She still couldn't make out what was being said. The voices started again, then one of them, raised higher than the others, came through more clearly.

". . . how you like a night in the cells. You might . . . more friendly tomorrow. Good night!"

A door clanged shut. One of the cell doors, she thought. Then she heard the *clack* of boot heels on stone. Someone was crossing the cellar and mounting the steps. She waited, her ear pressed against the stone. Her pulse was racing. That had been a near thing. Accustomed now to the fact that there was never anyone in the lower cellar, she had nearly blundered out to be discovered by one of Dimon's men. Yet it stood to reason that he might have put some of the castle staff in the cells. Mentally, she rebuked herself. She should have thought of that.

Her mother and the remaining members of the garrison might well have made it to the safety of the south tower. But even with the skeleton staff in the castle at this time of year, that would have left behind a handful of servants, cooks, messengers and other members of the castle staff—the noncombatants. Some of them may well have been cowed by Dimon and his armed men. Others would have refused to serve them. It was probable that these people had been confined to the cellars below the keep. She pondered the situation for a moment or two. She could release them, of course, and lead them to safety through the tunnel. But that would only reveal her presence to the usurper. They would be safe enough for the time being, she decided, if a little uncomfortable.

She realized she had been crouching with her head against the door for several minutes, with no further sound from the other side. But from this hidden room, she had access to two other tunnels. One led to the gatehouse. The other would take her to the hidden staircase leading up to the top of the south tower.

And that was where she wanted to go now.

42

TURNING AWAY FROM THE DOOR TO THE CELLAR, MADDIE moved to the left-hand entrance, which, from her previous reconnaissance, she knew opened into the tunnel that would take her to the south tower.

She was accustomed now to moving through the tunnels, with their uneven footing, low headroom and dim light, and she made good time, following the pool of light thrown by her lantern. She shook it again, checking the level of oil left in the reservoir. Satisfied that there was still plenty remaining, she continued on through the tunnel.

"Wouldn't want to be in here if the light went out," she muttered. Just to be sure, she lowered the wick a little, so that it would burn less fuel.

The tunnel was relatively straight and undeviating, and she soon felt it sloping upward and knew she was close to the base of the south tower—and the wooden ladders that led up to the top floors. Eventually, they loomed out of the dimness ahead of her. She paused at the base of the first flight, studying the rungs to make sure they were solid, and then she began to climb.

The flights weren't vertical, but they were steep, angling up at about seventy degrees. Each one consisted of fifteen rungs—steps, actually, as they were constructed from stout boards some twelve centimeters across. At the top of each flight, she could step across to the next fifteen steps, angling back in the opposite direction. Two flights took her up one story in the tower, so she calculated she would have eighteen flights to climb before she reached the top. She grimaced at the thought. She was fit and young and she'd manage the climb easily. But eighteen flights of steps? Luckily, her hip was only a problem if she sat still for a long period.

"That's something to be grateful for," she muttered to herself.

At first, she moved steadily, not rushing, checking each step before she trusted her weight to it. One or two creaked and moved slightly, but for the most part they were solidly set and in good condition. As she continued without finding a problem, her confidence grew and she began to climb faster.

Which, inevitably, nearly brought her to disaster. One tread on the fifth flight had rotted at the point where it was set into the upright section of the ladder. As she put her weight on it and began to step upward, it crumbled and splintered and gave way. She grabbed at the side rail desperately as her foot dropped into empty space. For a moment she hung, nearly losing her grip on the lantern. Then she recovered and, setting her teeth, hauled herself up past that broken step to the next above it. This time, she tested it carefully before committing her full weight to it.

And this time, it held.

But the near accident made her more careful, and she slowed down again, testing each step.

Ten flights. Eleven. Twelve. She was counting each stage as

she went, saying the words in a whisper. Six flights to go, she thought, stopping at the small platform between flights to stretch her leg and work her knees. She looked up, seeing a few faint rays of light above her where ventilation or observation holes were let into the outer walls of the tower. She looked down. Below her was only a black void, and for a moment her head swam.

Halfway up the thirteenth flight, she paused, sniffing the still air inside the stairway. She could smell smoke.

Not wood smoke, she realized. It had an oily smell to it—like pitch. She felt a moment of panic. Had Dimon managed to set fire to the tower? Had her mother and her troops been driven out and captured? Or worse?

There was only one way to find out. That was to continue upward. She started climbing again. On the next flight, she became conscious of a banging sound echoing down the stairway. The regular rhythm sounded like hammers hitting wood.

Someone's building something, she thought. The sound comforted her. If there was activity above, then it indicated that her mother was still secure in the tower and that her fears when she smelled the smoke were unfounded.

The hammering grew louder the farther up she went. The smoky smell was still evident, but she could see no flicker of light above her that might indicate that something was still burning. And there was no physical evidence of smoke itself—no fumes or choking clouds. Whatever it was that had been burning, it was no longer alight.

Fifteen. Sixteen. The hammering was louder now. Halfway up the seventeenth flight, she stopped and pressed her ear to the stone wall. The hammering was coming from the other side, almost level with her current position. She continued until she was at the top of the eighteenth flight, facing the stone wall.

Holding the lantern high, she stopped to catch her breath and study the wall. She could see the rectangular outline of the door, and the simple handle halfway down. There was no need for concealment or secrecy inside the hidden staircase. Just above her eye level, there was a small hole, made obvious by the gleam of light showing from the other side. She raised herself on tiptoe and peered through.

Her heart leapt as she saw Cassandra sitting not five meters away, her back to the secret door where Maddie stood. Her mother was talking to a gray-bearded sergeant in the uniform of the palace guard. His arm was in a sling, and they were seated at a wooden table in the big, well-lit room that took up most of the ninth floor.

She reached out for the door handle.

Cassandra was sitting at the large table on the ninth floor, drinking a cup of coffee, when Merlon entered.

"The barrier is almost ready, my lady," he said, indicating the hammering that came from below with a jerk of his head.

Cassandra nodded. "Good. That'll stop any further attempt to burn us out. Sit down, Merlon. Pour yourself a cup of coffee."

Taking a leaf out of Dimon's book, she had set her men to constructing a wooden wall at the edge of the gap in the stairway. That would prevent their attackers from hurling more of the clay pots filled with burning pitch up at the defenders. The pots would hit the wall and fall harmlessly into the stairwell below. The timber wall itself would be doused regularly with water to forestall any attempt to burn it.

She leaned back and stretched. She was tired, and her shoulders and neck ached with tension.

"Well, I suppose there's not much—"

She stopped as she heard a loud click from behind her. As she was turning to see what had caused it, a familiar voice spoke.

"Hello, Mum."

Cassandra gave a cry of shock, rapidly turning to delight. Maddie, dressed in her Ranger cloak and uniform, stood by the wall, in front of an open doorway. Merlon grunted in surprise, and Cassandra, recovering quickly, rose to her feet and dashed to her daughter, folding her in a bear hug.

"Maddie! Oh, Maddie! You're safe, thank goodness!"

Maddie laughed with a combination of relief and joy, half smothered in her mother's embrace. Finally, she managed to break free, just a little. No too much, just a little.

Cassandra held her back at arm's length, satisfying herself that her daughter was unharmed, tears of happiness coursing down her cheeks.

"Where on earth did you spring from? Where have you been? Are you all right?"

"Yes, yes, I'm fine, Mother. I discovered a whole network of tunnels and secret stairways inside the walls and under the castle itself." She stepped aside and indicated the dark opening behind her. "This leads down to the cellars."

"The cellars? What were you doing in the cellars?" her mother wanted to know.

"The tunnels all start from down there," Maddie explained. But the explanation left a lot unanswered.

"Tunnels? Stairways? Secret passages? What have you been doing?"

Maddie took both her mother's hands in her own to calm her. The sudden shock of seeing her daughter, of realizing she was safe, after wondering where she was, was too much for Cassandra. She began to sob. Merlon, horrified at the sight of his calm, self-assured princess losing control of her emotions, stood awkwardly, wanting to help but not knowing how.

Maddie reassured him with a glance. "Maybe you could make us some more coffee, Sergeant?" she suggested. And, as he hurried away to do so, she led Cassandra back to her chair. "Now, Mother, sit down. Calm down. And I'll tell you everything."

It took fifteen minutes, with constant interruptions and questions from Cassandra, for Maddie to describe the events of the previous few days. When she heard that Horace was safe—although besieged in the hill fort north of the Wezel River—Cassandra felt a huge weight lift from her shoulders.

"Dimon tried to tell me he was dead," she said, her voice full of venom.

Maddie shook her head. "He's safe. But he'll find it hard to break out. He's outnumbered, and the enemy can see everything he does. He can't surprise them. I thought if I could get some men and stage a surprise attack on the enemy from the rear, that would give him a chance to break out."

Cassandra considered the idea. "It would work," she said. "But where would you find the men?"

Maddie shrugged. "I thought maybe I could mobilize the army," she said. The castle only maintained a small regular garrison. The army was made up of men-at-arms, knights and foot soldiers from the surrounding farms and villages, who could be called up in the event of war or other danger.

Cassandra shook her head. "It'd take too long to gather them," she said. "And Dimon would quickly get wind of what you were doing." She stood up and began pacing the room, her brow furrowed in concentration.

"We can hold out here indefinitely," she said. "But what we need to do is find a way to break your father and Gilan out of this hill fort. Then, if they march south and hit Dimon from behind, we can break out of here at the same time and attack him from both sides. You say there's a tunnel into the gatehouse?" she asked, and Maddie nodded. "Then you could lower the drawbridge and let Horace's and Gilan's men in."

She turned, pacing again, her mind working overtime.

"But if you're going to have to launch a surprise attack on the force holding Horace and Gilan, you'll need men. Good fighting men. The kind who will put the fear of the devil into those Red Fox scum . . ."

Her voice trailed off as she racked her brains for an idea. Then, her brow cleared, and she looked at her daughter with a wide smile on her face.

"And I think I know just the men you need," she said.

TO BE CONTINUED

TURN THE PAGE FOR
A FIRST LOOK AT THE NEXT
R☉YAL RANGER
ADVENTURE

PROLOGUE

DIMON, FORMER COMMANDER OF THE PALACE GUARD AND now the leader of the rebellious Red Fox Clan, leaned on a windowsill, looked upward, and scowled. He was in a room on the top floor of the Castle Araluen keep. The south tower loomed above him, several floors higher.

He came here regularly, to stare up at the ninth floor of the south tower, where Princess Cassandra, King Duncan and their men had taken refuge. Occasionally, Dimon would see movement on the balcony that surrounded the ninth floor and once he had recognized Cassandra herself peering over into the courtyard below.

He cursed bitterly when he saw her, but she was unaware of his presence. The people on the balcony rarely seemed to look in his direction. They were more interested in the courtyard, and Cassandra's archers had already taken a savage toll on anyone who moved incautiously down there, straying too far from the shelter of the keep walls.

Under Dimon's leadership, the castle had been taken by soldiers of the Red Fox Clan. He had chanced upon the Red Fox Clan some years before. They were a disorganized, poorly motivated group of malcontents who protested against the law that allowed a woman to succeed to the throne. The law had been put in place by Cassandra's grandfather, and it meant that Cassandra would eventually become Queen of Araluen in her own right. The Red Fox Clan clung stubbornly to the old tradition that only a male heir could succeed to the throne—a position Dimon heartily endorsed, as he was distantly related to Cassandra and, so far as he knew, the only possible male heir.

Under a false name, he had joined the Clan and quietly worked his way to the top echelons of power within it. The Clan was big on angry talk and short on action. Dimon, on the other hand, was an expert orator, capable of rousing the passions of an audience and swaying them to his point of view. He had a powerful and charismatic personality and an inborn ability to make people like and respect him. He rose rapidly in the Clan, until he was appointed as their overall leader. He organized them and motivated them until they had become a potent and efficient secret army. He pandered to their beliefs and, most important, he gave them an agenda and a goal—rebellion against the Crown. His cause was aided by the fact that King Duncan had been an invalid for some time and Cassandra, his daughter, was acting as Regent in his place, providing an obvious example of the result of the law change.

Dimon used the Red Fox Clan as a tool to further his own ends. He planned to usurp the throne and have himself crowned king. He saw the Red Fox Clan as the vehicle by which he would achieve this ambition.

His chief obstacle, he believed, was Cassandra's husband, Sir Horace—the paramount knight of Araluen and the commander of the army. Horace was a highly skilled warrior and an expert strategist and tactician. He was assisted in his leadership role by the Ranger Gilan, Commandant of the redoubtable Ranger Corps and Horace's longtime friend. For Dimon to succeed, these two had to be lured away from Castle Araluen and, preferably, killed. Accordingly, he had devised a plan whereby Horace and Gilan set out to the north to quell a rebellion raised by a small force of the Red Fox Clan, taking most of the castle's garrison with them. They were intercepted along the way by a much larger force of Sonderland mercenaries and Red Fox Clan members. Outnumbered three or four to one, Horace's men had staged a fighting retreat to an ancient hill fort. Although they were currently besieged there by their ambushers, Dimon knew that a leader of Horace's ability wouldn't stay contained for long. It was vital that Dimon should act quickly to seize the throne.

Initially, all had gone well. Dimon had tricked his way past Castle Araluen's impregnable walls and massive drawbridge with a force of Red Fox Clan troops and came within an inch of capturing Cassandra and her father.

But then Maikeru, Cassandra's Nihon-Jan master swordsman, had interfered, holding Dimon and his men at bay long enough for Cassandra and Duncan to retreat to the upper levels of the south tower with a small force of loyal palace guards and archers.

The eighth and ninth floors of the south tower had been built as a last refuge in the event that the castle was captured. A section of the spiral stairway, just below the eighth floor, could be removed, leaving attackers with no access to the upper two floors—while the defenders could move between the eighth and ninth floors via an internal flight of timber stairs. The refuge was stocked with food and weapons, and large rainwater cisterns in the roof above the ninth floor provided water for the defenders.

So far, Cassandra had resisted his attempts to force his way into the eighth floor of the tower. But now, he had an idea that might just prove to be her undoing.

He turned as he heard a tentative knock at the door.

"Lord Dimon? Are you there?"

He recognized the voice. It was Ronald, the leader of his small force of engineers and siege specialists. "Come in," Dimon called.

The door opened to admit the engineer. Like many of his kind, he was an older man, his gray hair denoting years of experience in his craft. He hesitated, deferentially. All of Dimon's men knew that their leader was in a foul mood since the Nihon-Jan swordsman had foiled his plan for a quick result.

"What is it?" Dimon said testily, unreasonably annoyed by the man's nervousness.

"The materials have arrived for your device, my lord," the engineer told him. "We can begin building it immediately."

For the first time in several days, a smile crossed Dimon's face. He rubbed his hands together in anticipation.

"Excellent," he said. "Now we can make things extremely unpleasant for my cousin Cassandra. Extremely unpleasant."

1

"Dad's outnumbered and the enemy can see everything he does," Maddie said. "He can't surprise them. I thought if I could get some men and stage a surprise attack on the enemy from the rear, that would give him a chance to break out."

While the traitor Dimon assumed that Maddie was confined in the south tower with her mother, the apprentice Ranger had discovered a series of secret tunnels and stairways that allowed her to move freely in and out of the castle. Maddie had infiltrated a Red Fox Clan assembly and overheard Dimon's plan to attack Castle Araluen and trap her father and his men in the north.

Now she had returned to the castle and made her way to the ninth floor, where she and Cassandra were formulating a plan to aid her father.

Cassandra considered the idea. "It would work," she said. "But where would you find the men?"

Maddie shrugged. "I thought maybe I could mobilize the army," she said. The castle maintained only a small regular garrison. The army was made up of men-at-arms, knights and foot soldiers from the surrounding farms and villages who could be called up in the event of war or other danger.

Cassandra shook her head. "It'd take too long to gather them," she said. "And Dimon would quickly get wind of what you were doing." She stood up and began pacing the room, her brow furrowed in concentration.

"We can hold out here indefinitely," she said. "But what we need to do is find a way to break your father and Gilan out of that hill fort. Then, if they march south and hit Dimon from behind, we can break out here at the same time and attack him from both sides. You say there's a tunnel into the gatehouse?" she asked and Maddie nodded. "Then you could lower the draw-bridge and let Horace and Gilan's men in."

She turned, pacing again, her mind working overtime.

"But if you're going to have to launch a surprise attack on the force holding Horace and Gilan, you'll need men. Good fighting men. The kind who will put the fear of the devil into those Red Fox scum . . ."

Her voice trailed off as she racked her brains for an idea. Then, her brow cleared, and she looked at her daughter with a wide smile on her face.

"And I think I know just the men you need," she said.

Cassandra moved to the window, looking out over the green parkland below. There was a positive note in her voice that hadn't been there previously, and Maddie looked up curiously.

"So tell me," Maddie said.

"The Skandians," her mother replied.

For a moment, Maddie was confused. "What Skandians?"

"Hal and his men—the Heron brotherband." Cassandra's manner was becoming more positive by the minute. "They're due back from the coast any day now."

"But why should they help us?" Maddie asked.

"Because they're old friends and allies. We helped them when the Temujai tried to invade their country years ago. And we organized the ransom when the Arridans captured their Oberjarl. They owe us. And they're not the kind of people to forget a debt."

"If you say so." Maddie didn't share her mother's confidence that the Skandians would immediately come to their aid, but Cassandra knew the sea wolves better than she did. There was another point, however. "Aren't there only twelve of them?"

Cassandra smiled. "Twelve Skandians. Your father says they're the best troops in the world. If a dozen of them hit the Sonderlanders from the rear in a surprise attack, they'll cause the sort of panic and confusion you'll be looking for. Take my word for it."

"I suppose you're right," Maddie conceded. "But how will I get in touch with them?"

Cassandra walked over to a large-scale map of Araluen Fief on the wall. Maddie followed her and waited as her mother studied the map, running a finger along the River Semath as she talked to herself.

"Let's see. They headed down the Semath to the sea. The wrecked wolfship was here . . ." She stabbed her finger on the coast at a point south of the mouth of the Semath. "Hal said they'd be back in around ten days, so you've got a few days left."

She traced the path of the winding river back inland, stopping at a point where it took a sharp bend to the south. She tapped the southern headland formed by the apex of the curve.

"Here, I'd say. This would be the best point for you to intercept them. You should see them coming for some time. That'll give you time to attract their attention."

Maddie studied the point on the map for a few seconds. The promontory did seem like the best choice—close enough for her to reach in good time to intercept the *Heron* and with a good clear view downriver. And it was sufficiently distant that Dimon would have no inkling about what she was doing.

"I'd better get going then," she said.

Her mother raised her eyebrows. "What? Right away?"

"Yes. I'll go while it's still dark. That way there's less chance that Dimon's sentries will see me. I'll pack some provisions for the trip and be on my way," she said.

Cassandra nodded. "And assuming Horace and Gilan manage to break out of the fort, what's your plan then?"

"We come back here and I bring a small party through the tunnel under the moat. Once we're inside the walls of the castle, there's a hidden stairway to the gatehouse. We'll lower the drawbridge. After that, it'll be up to Dad and his men."

"And once they're inside the castle walls," Cassandra said, "I'll bring my men down the stairway and hit the Red Foxes from behind." She touched the hilt of the *katana* that was thrust through her belt in its scabbard. "I rather fancy the idea of having Dimon at the end of my sword."

Half an hour later, with a sack of food slung over her shoulder, Maddie stood by the door into the secret stairway. Cassandra stood beside her. She was loath to let her daughter go, having only just discovered that she was safe. She gestured toward the door.

"Maybe I could come down to the tunnel entrance with you," she said.

"Mum, it's eighteen vertical ladders. Do you really want to

climb down all those steps, then climb back up again?" Maddie asked her.

Cassandra shook her head ruefully. "Not really. Just . . . oh, I don't know . . . just take care of yourself."

Maddie nodded several times, not trusting herself to speak. Then she quickly embraced her mother, opened the door and disappeared into the dark stairwell.